Chapter One

I0648945

The headlights dim as the front tires begin to grind the limestone gravel. Hoping to have the element of surprise, the driver stops the car several meters from his destination and gets out. A hulking figure supporting two hundred and eighty pounds on a six foot five inch frame emerges from the vehicle in what is unmistakably the uniform of a law enforcement official. Small insignias on both shoulders indicate high rank, but their meaning is generally unknown to the public. He is well armed with two weapons attached to his forearms, two more on his thighs, and a fifth on his right wrist. These five firearms act as visible deterrents to ward off unnecessary conflict, yet he was more than willing to use them. When it comes to battle, The man is more than well prepared.

In the distance a flashing arrow can be seen pointing to his destination. He folds a piece of cherry flavored gum into his mouth and starts walking. The building in the distance is a bar and grill that often is frequented by unsociable types that make even the local law enforcement cringe in fear. That is one of the reasons the locals asked him to look into the matter of the report of a disturbance there this night. However it was the nature of the disturbance that prodded him to drive over one hundred miles at four in the morning. It was a personal problem and he wanted to handle it alone although he did request that fellow agents be on stand-by and wait further down the highway.

He reaches the parking lot of the Lucky Goose Cafe and stops. Slowly he removes his night visors and places them in his left chest pocket. Then he flips a small switch on his belt and takes a look around. The tarnished doorknob turns easily in his hand and the door offers no resistance as he pulls. No one notices him make his entrance at the back of the room.

Through the smoky haze he counts seventeen men plus a bartender. Chairs and tables are scattered throughout the room in disarray as many had been knocked over or turned upside-down. The men are all dressed in denim, leather, and tee shirts. One portly fellow jabs something on the ground with a pool cue and the entire congregation laughs. As he enters the room he sees the source of their amusement.

Two youths lay on the floor face down in puddles of their own blood. Judging by the head wounds and the amount of blood on the hardwood floor, he knew they were dead. Rage and grief fill him at once for he knew both youths and knew that they had bright futures ahead of them. Instead they were dead on a barroom floor because they chose the wrong place to get a drink.

"Fatal mistake gentlemen. Fortunately, You will not live to regret it."

As the lawman makes his statement the whole group turns at once, startled that someone had joined their party without their knowledge. All eyes go to the huge lawman with sandy brown hair, brown eyes, and firm jaw. Anger can be seen in his eyes, which causes a few of the worried brutes to focus their attention on his firearms. He takes a step back to size up the room and to judge what his actions should be.

The heavyset man grumbles to a small, lean fellow next to him.

"Thought you said the law never comes out this way!"

"Never have before," retorts his companion as he looks at the imposing figure across the room.

"A bit out of your way officer. You get lost or something?" blurts the fat man as he instantly regrets what he just said.

"No I'm not lost. In fact I found exactly what I was looking for. Did you boys forget that murder is a capital offense?"

"We didn't forget," answers the fat man with a grin on his face, "in fact, we're willing to do it again!"

"Fool! Don't say that!" whispers his friend with a high level of concern in his voice. "That there is one of then high powered world cops. And them guns of his. Those guns are capable of cutting us all down before we could even take a couple steps toward him."

The fat man shakes his head in light of this startling revelation. He tries to think of his next move. If this lawman got them to jail, they would be executed for certain. Then he starts to get an uneasy feeling as he sees a smile form on the face of the lawman.

"Your moment of indecision shows me that you are a very insecure man, Langley. Oh yes, I know who you are. Before now you had limited your activities to extortion, smuggling, and drug peddling. It's a wonder you don't already have your mail addressed to the federal prison. Since you took it upon yourself to advance on to murder, I will personally see to it that each of you soon shall take up residence in the nearest cemetery. But I wouldn't want to cause you any undue stress by worrying about these firearms, so I will discard them."

The lawman removes the clips from each weapon and places them in a black bag attached to his belt. Then he tosses each of the weapons one by one toward the far corner of the room. He secures the pouch with a couple of snaps so it is immobile and turns his full attention to his captive audience.

The group looks on in amazement and begins to find their courage again. Each man looks at their leader for instructions. But Langley is unsure as what to think. He wonders if it could be a trick. There was the possibility that there were other lawmen ready to rush the place as soon as they made a move toward this isolated law enforcement agent. It had to be a trick.

"Marley, Turk, Smith, check the windows and see if there are any cops lurking around outside. Monroe, you go look out the front door," shouts a nervous Langley.

"You're a cautious fellow, Langley. Normally I like that in a person. I assure you I came alone. For what needs to be done I can handle myself. You need not worry about going through the rigors of a trial, because I do not plan on letting the judicial system to waste expenses on you."

Langley is curious and wary of his current foe. It certainly seemed foolish for this man to discard his weapons in the presence of a large pack like this one. The possibility of an ambush is negated as each of the men shakes their respective heads to indicate no one was in sight. Langley smiles as he nods to signal his men that it was all right for them to attack their prey. Each man arms himself with whatever is handy, whether it is beer bottle, pool cue, or a piece of wood from a broken table or chair. Two men happen to have knives, which they pull out in hopes of doing some non-holiday carving. With the numbers on his side, Langley steps back in order to have the best view of his men in action.

To their demise, this officer would not be easy prey. As the first man steps forward with a beer bottle in hand, the lawman disarms him by kicking the bottle with his left foot and fells the man with a blow to the temple. A second man charges while swinging a pool cue only to have the lawman use his momentum against him as the ruffian is tossed over a table and lands on his back. Before the man can maneuver to get off the ground the lawman is upon him and steps on his throat which he crushes as he balances himself to kick under another opponent's chin as the man came forward with a raised chair leg. Another man swings a chair leg only to have the lawman deflect the blow with his left arm as he shatters the man's nose with his right fist. He ducks a swinging pool cue and crushes the left side of the batsman's rib cage. Dodging to the left to avoid a swinging beer bottle, he delivers a deathblow above the man's right ear with an elbow.

Only seconds had passed and Langley began to realize that this lawman was not going to be stopped by anyone in the room at the present time. He began to edge his way toward the doorway but the lawman sees him out of the corner of his eye. Without taking his eyes off his attackers the lawman speaks.

"Might as well stick around Langley because you will never make the highway."

Fear runs through Langley as he looks wishfully at the exit. With great reluctance his turns around and walks back to the counter. His mind raced as he tried to think of some way he might be able to stop the lawman. Then something clicks in his mind as a wide grin pushes back his fat cheeks. What he needed was in the travel gear stacked on the far side of the room near the music player. His only hope of getting out of the wasteland alive depended on his finding his equalizer. As his men kept the lawman occupied he slowly makes his way toward the bedrolls.

The lawman was unbelievably quick and wickedly powerful. He showed no fear and was extremely confidant of his fighting skills. His attackers were dismayed at his ability and started to panic. Six companions were down and this man stood there goading them to continue their attack. Upon noticing their hesitation the lawman barrels into the four crowded nearest him and knocks them to the floor.

As he drives them backwards and downward the lawman himself looses his footing and also ends up on the floor. Thinking he is vulnerable a few of the men rush in to capitalize on the situation. As he moves to get up, the lawman shatters the jaw of a man on the ground next to him with his right fist. One man scrambles to his feet and raises a chair leg to strike the lawman while he is still on his knees. Instead the man falls to the ground in pain as the lawman lands a wicked kick to the side of the man's right knee. An assailant takes advantage of the lawman's attention diverted elsewhere and breaks an oak chair across his back. The chair splinters as the lawman turns around seemingly unfazed and rewards the man for getting his attention by crushing his throat with the heel of his right foot. Another man attempted to connect against the lawman's head with a table leg, only to have his efforts thwarted as the lawman catches the weapon with his left hand and pulls the man forward breaking his neck by snapping his head back violently with his free forearm. As he drops the man he sees the fellow whose leg he had broken attempting to rise on the good leg. Taking a step forward, the lawman connects with a kick under the chin that sends the man arching backward.

In just over two minutes the lawman had eliminated nearly two thirds of his opponents as he smiles and thinks of him self as a cat in a world of mice. The floor creaks as he turns to face a man holding a knife with a retractable blade in his hand. Almost effortlessly the lawman slaps the knife hand away as he smashes the man's nose and leaves him to choke on blood and bone fragments. Across the room two men slap the palms with wood as the contemplate attacking in unison. Yet before they could advance the lawman hurtles through the air and catches each man between the eyes with the heels of his boots. His momentum carries the lawman towards his next opponent who wields a knife and wanted to practice his surgical skills. However, when the big lawman rolls into his left leg, the adversary falls forward and looses his grip on the knife. Screams of pure agony come from the man as the lawman elbows him in the back, dislodging several vertebrae. Then the lawman rolls to his left as the man tries to stab at him with a pool cue. Rising to his feet, the lawman grabs the cue and lands a crushing blow to the man's throat with his right foot. The final lackey realizes he has no chance and makes a dash for the door. He hopes to catch the lawman off guard by throwing his beer bottle at him, but the lawman merely catches it as he plants his rights foot and tags the fleeing man along the side of his neck as he tries to run past. The blow snaps the man's neck and he falls lifeless to the floor as the lawman tosses his bottle back to him.

Suddenly the lawman feels two light taps on the back of his head. The distinct odor of gunpowder invades his nostrils as he touches the back of his head. Slowly he turns around to confront Langley and sees the fat man trembling with eyes wide with disbelief. Again he pulls the trigger and the bullet catches the lawman flush in the throat. Only the bullet falls away like a rock hitting a stone wall and the lawman continues to advance.

"You ain't human!" shouts Langley as he tries to retreat only to find him trapped by the counter.

With his left foot the lawman kicks the gun out of Langley's hand and puts his right hand on the fat man's chest. Then he puts his left hand around Langley's throat under the chin and lifts the entire three hundred and twenty pounds off the ground three inches. As the fat man struggles for air, the lawman rears back and strikes him in the forehead with the heel of his right hand. The skull caves in under the force of the blow as blood and brains begin to escape. Releasing the corpse, the lawman steps away from the counter and takes a towel from a table to wipe his hands with.

His eyes focus on the two dead youths. The anger is gone but the sorrow remains in his eyes. For a moment he bows his head to reflect on their memories and then turns his head to acknowledge the presence of the bar tender.

"I had nothing to do with this, Mr. Knight. Heck, I called the authorities as soon as they started to pick on the boys!"

By the expression on the elderly bar keeper's face the lawman had no doubt he was telling the truth. He nods his head to show that he understands and walks over to the corner of the room where he had tossed his firearms. After taking a moment to inspect their condition, he loads them and places each in it's proper resting-place. Then he presses a button on his right wrist and speaks into a small black grid.

"Mason, come on in and clean up. Send for a coroner's truck and an ambulance. Out!"

A double beep answers him to acknowledge the message was received and understood. He looks around and sees the death and destruction. The death toll was sixteen, counting the two boys, and there were three survivors. Two men were unconscious with broken jaws while the third moaned in pain because of a broken back. These three would have to be tokens to the justice system to be held accountable for the crime that took place earlier this evening. More than likely all three would be tried and executed within the week. It is a system that he had helped establish and he knew it very well.

Once again his attention returns to the dead youths. Both would have had promising futures in business or law enforcement. He knew this because he had employed both of them. One youth had been nineteen-year-old Raymond Vasquez. He was from Los Angeles and was studying Pre-Law at Creighton University in Omaha. The other was eighteen-year-old Paul Snyder of Chicago. He was also a Pre-Law student at Creighton and a member of the basketball team with a promising career ahead of him. The two had met when they became part-time security guards the previous summer at a business in Omaha. It was a business, which the lawman owned, but he left its supervision to others.

The sound of footfalls outside interrupts his thoughts. He can hear the hum of a motor and the voices of several people. From outside a voice yells.

"Clayton, you in there?"

"Come on in!"

As the lawman answers he climbs over the counter of the bar. Three men dressed in similar uniforms enter the room with firearms drawn. The lawman behind the bar shakes his head and smiles.

"You boys know I would never let you walk into a situation that might be dangerous."

All four break into laughter as the three men walk up to the counter surveying the room as they proceed. All three are similar in build but none is as large as their leader. The eldest of the three is Mason Rasov, who is thirty-one years old and stands at six-foot-two while weighing one hundred and ninety five pounds. Next is Russell Jackson, who is twenty-five and is also six-foot-two but he weighs two hundred and five pounds. The youngest of the trio is Randy Buck, who is twenty-one but he is the tallest of the three at six-foot-four and weighs two hundred and fifteen pounds. All three men are very good at what they do but none is as talented as the man behind the bar fixing drinks. The regular bar keeper drinks from a whiskey bottle. The name of the temporary bar tender is Clayton Knight and he is a man of extraordinary capabilities.

The four are enjoying themselves at the counter as men in white coats enter the room. There are nine of them and each has a solemn look one their respective faces. They begin to examine the bodies and start placing the deceased in yellow bags. Then Knight notices a small gentleman who is the leader of the new arrivals.

"Hey, Conrad! Three of them are still alive, so don't put them in bags yet."

The four at the counter erupt into laughter as a thin man with a pencil-thin mustache looks up and shakes his head. He starts to ignore the group and then decides to speak his mind.

"I know my job, thank you very much. But I am surprised that you animals left any survivors for the boys at Health Central to work on. In fact, I think Judge Crenshaw will be very upset with your lack of restraint. You know how he likes to pad his record with volume convictions. I think you like your job too much, Knight."

The tone in the man's voice does not sit well with the big lawman as he explodes in anger as he drops the two bottles he has in each hand and hops over the counter. He hits the ground running and stops when he is directly in the face of the coroner. He begins to shout, as the little man is afraid to retreat.

"Like this job? Let me tell you something about this job, you little toad. The idea that my job is actually necessary in this day and age repulses me and turns my stomach. Having to see two fine and promising individuals like Ray and Paul executed by a hoard of diseased maniacs, and then to confront their parents with the details of what happened to them tears at my very soul. As for Judge Crenshaw, if he has a problem he can take it up with me. But you know as well as I do that his salary is set and he does not get paid by the case or convictions. You're just lucky I kind of like you Conrad or they might be fitting you for one of these bags you hate so much. Truthfully, I believe you should consider another line of work."

The little man is visibly shaken as Knight allows him to return to his assigned duties. The other lawmen shake their heads and turn toward their drinks as Knight starts toward them. The elderly bar keeper runs to the end of the counter and takes a frosted bottle out of the icebox and hands it to the lawman.

"Nice and cold, just the way you like it Mr. Knight. I keep them that way just for you."

Knight smiles and takes the frosted mug in hand. Then he takes a bottle off a rack and twists off the top. As he proceeds to empty the contents into the mug, foam rises up and starts to flow over the side. He quickly raises the beverage to his lips and drinks down half the container.

"Now that's how root beer should taste!"

After Knight bellows he wipes his mouth with the back of his hand. The smile had returned to his face and it was as if nothing had happened. Rasov looks on puzzled by the big man's actions. At times it seemed as though the big man had mood swings like a little child even though he was twenty-eight. Moments like this make him question the big man's intelligence, but it was a documented fact that Knight was a genius. He shakes his head as he finishes his drink.

"I have to be going, Clay," states Rasov as he gets off his barstool. "Do you want me to come over tomorrow so we can go over what happened here or are you going to forward your report directly to Washington?"

"Both, actually. So why don't you come over about noon? I have some other things I want to discuss with you."

"I guess it already is tomorrow. Then noon it is. Until then."

They watch as Rasov exits. Then Knight walks over to his two remaining men and puts a hand on each man's outer shoulder as he stands between them.

"Well, Russ. Randy. Take care of yourselves. I will let you know next week what your next assignments will be. In the between time be sure to get some rest, because you're going to need it. And take it easy on the liquor. You know my feelings on that subject."

Both men nod and Knight gives each a couple of friendly pats on the back. As he walks out the door he begins to think of youths and what he might say to their parents. He shakes his head bitterly for they should have known better than to drive into the badlands in search of a good time. While the drinking age in Nebraska was twenty-five and strictly enforced, youths often crossed the border to take advantage of lower legal limits. Now he had to tell their parents what happened and that would be a much more difficult task by far than the battle he went through minutes earlier.

He reaches his car and maneuvers himself behind the steering column. The digital clock reads 4:55 a.m. and the date was June third. If he hurried he might be able to reach home before dawn or at least before his wife left for work.

Speeding down the interstate at two hundred and ten miles per hour, Knight is relieved there is no traffic so he can have the road to himself. He prefers driving to flying, although the latter would have been much faster. However, the extra time gives him more time to think while he listens to mellow tunes on the radio. Yet he gets so caught up in his thoughts that he almost doesn't notice the exit ramp and has to sharply crank the steering wheel to the right in order to make the turnoff.

Upon arriving home, he discovers that his wife had already left for work and he is disappointed. There must have been something important she had to tend to for her to leave before dawn. Instead of dwelling on it, he decides to go about the tasks he normally took care of at this time of morning.

He pours himself a glass of milk and proceeds to his office where he locks the door behind him. Turning on the computer at his desk, he sits back staring at the black screen while sipping his milk and contemplating how he would phrase the report. After setting down the glass, his fingers dance quickly across the keyboard as he gives his version of what had happened that morning. He forwards copies to his offices in Omaha and Washington DC before reclining in his chair.

After a few moments to collect his thoughts, he accesses a private sub-directory that contains his personal dairy. To enter the sub-directory he has to enter the security code and place his hand on a scanning platform so it can check his DNA pattern to that on record. Then he retrieves a file that contains an ongoing recording of the daily events in his life. He enters his thoughts on the previous and present day's events to the moment. Then he sits back and reflects on the contents of the diary. His diary contains some information that is public knowledge but much of the remaining material is top secret because it would shock the world. He finishes the last few drops of milk and turns the diary back to the beginning as he begins to read over the highlights and relives some of the memories in his mind.

Chapter two

He was born Clayton Aaron Knight on May 4, 2021 on his parents farm near Hayes Center, Nebraska. His father, Douglas Knight, worked for a national farm corporation that owned two-thirds of the farmland in the United States. The corporation had sold his father forty-two acres he could do what he wanted with and they raised livestock and had a large garden. The land was offered at a discount as part of his contract for being the supervisor of 85,000 acres in central Nebraska. Then on August 12, 2021 his father died when a compression unit for processing corn exploded and the blast dismembered his body.

The equipment was found to be aged and faulty so the corporation, Myplex Foods International, quickly settled out of court with his mother by paying sixteen million dollars to avoid negative publicity. His mother, Jean Gladrowski-Knight, had been a professor of science theory at Midlands College in Fremont, Nebraska, but resigned when Knight was born. She had intended to take a position at the high school in Hayes Center that fall so she could be near home and her baby. It was her intention to leave young Knight with her sister Ida Gladrowski-Engstrom when she worked.

Yet with the tragic windfall of new wealth, she had the liberty to structure her career any way she saw fit. An opening for a counselor for science majors at Nebraska Wesleyan was made aware to her and she obtained the position. They moved to Lincoln and her new position allowed her plenty of time to spend with her baby.

Then when young Clayton was two years old she noticed he could read. He could read not only the children's books she had bought for him, but the magazines and literature on the coffee table as well. What truly shocked his mother was when he began to quote the authors in the scientific journals word for word. It was obvious that the child was a prodigy.

She began tutoring him at home and by the time he was three he had completed all primary and secondary school work. The government allowed him to take the necessary tests and he officially had his high school degree within the next month. Since true prodigies were rare, his mother requested that everything should be kept confidential and the authorities agreed. The end to her tutoring came when the child surprised her with information that he had received a scholarship to attend Oxford University in England.

Reluctantly, his mother allowed him the opportunity and soon both were in England. Wanting to protect him like any good mother would, she closely supervised the child's learning process to make sure the youngster did not burn himself out. However, she soon found out that he had an even greater mental capability than she had anticipated. The University allowed the child to progress at an accelerated rate, yet even they were amazed at the rate the child could intake information, process it, retain it, and reuse it flawlessly. Before everyone knew it, the child had completed the necessary work to obtain degrees in mathematics and physics-theory. Only a month shy of his forth birthday he received his bachelor degrees in those to fields. Then continuing at the accelerated pace, he obtained his masters in physics on his birthday and received his Ph.D. in early September.

His doctoral thesis in physics explained a theory he had on recreating the necessary energy to duplicate atoms. The thesis impressed the scientific community and it was printed in all the scientific journals across the world. His identity was shielded by using a pseudonym.

Then the child received an offer to return to the United States and study at the Massachusetts Institute of Technology. Even at his young age, the child could guess that it was the United States government that actually wanted him back in the states. It was apparent to little Knight that there was an unhealthy competitiveness between the nations of the world. Although they might try to use him, he realized that at his young age, there was not much else he could do besides go to school. Anyhow, he liked the idea of using one of the best facilities in the world to enhance his knowledge.

By the time young Knight had reached his tenth birthday, he had amassed twenty-seven additional degrees ranging from astronomy to zoology. He had been able to achieve what he did due to the accelerated program the school had for the gifted few that could handle it. For those who desired, the students in the accelerated program had the option of viewing the lectures of all the professors, which were kept for three semesters before being replaced by the most recent semester's lecture. The majority of the degrees were science related, such as microbiology and nuclear chemistry. Yet he also tried to broaden his mental horizons by also obtaining degrees in history, literature, and philosophy. At such an early age he had become one of the world's leading authorities on atoms, molecules, and cells. But rather limit him to the smaller mysteries of existence, he also focused his efforts toward space research. He felt the two went together well because no matter how big the universe seems to be, it can be broken down to its base elements.

When he entered MIT, he was introduced to another young genius that had become his life long friend. Han Li was a native of China and the youngest child of five. His parents are both scientists, with his father specializing in thermodynamics and his mother is the director of China's atomic research although she actually held her degree in micro engineering. Young Han Li was three years Knight's elder when they met, but neither was the standard four or seven year old child. In Knight's second year at MIT, the two began working on personal projects together not related to their schoolwork.

It was Han who introduced Knight to the world of martial arts. Han had attained his black belt in the Chinese style of Kung Fu at the age of five. While he was still receiving lessons from his Uncle Chan who lived in Baltimore on the weekends, young Han was still qualified to begin teaching. With this ancient art form, Knight was able to learn better self-discipline and improved his already superb concentration. His workouts with Han helped him develop a healthy body to go with his superior mind.

In his six years at MIT, Knight worked on many projects. Han participated in some, but most were individual pursuits. His first project required that he develop a more powerful electron microscope than the M-series commonly used. He wanted to prove that there were smaller universal fragments that built up the protons, neutrons, and electrons. These building blocks were to be called unitrons and were the base for everything in the universe. With this discovery to his credit, Knight was able to lay the foundation for what was to be the first of many great achievements.

His next research dealt with the human cell structure and DNA. During his research he was able to solve many of the mysteries that plagued scientists and doctors for years. With this research, he provided a base that would make it easier to conquer diseases and other genetic problems. Due to the fact that he wanted other researchers to understand the techniques he was using in the DNA study, he delayed advancing the project until that objective was met.

The reasoning behind the delay was two fold. First, he wanted others to master the techniques he used in DNA experimentation so that more than one person could work on the project while he pursued other ventures. Secondly, he wanted the scientific community to realize the capabilities of his mind because it took a team of forty-two scientists five months to duplicate the research he had devised in three weeks by himself. This lesson was to show the scientific community who the master truly was while catering to his ego. Yet he had weighed the advantages and disadvantages of halting the project and the advantages justified his action. The main advantage was that there would now be a team of scientists that were qualified to advance his work. On the down side, there was the disadvantage of diseases not being conquered in the time he could have been working on the project. In the long run, Knight concluded that the world would benefit by having dozens of people knowledgeable on the subject, rather than just one.

In the meantime, young Knight had focused his attention towards outer space. It had long been surmised that there was intelligent life elsewhere in the universe. Knight was determined to find out if there was and where it was because he felt that it was beyond vanity to presume that Earth was the only world to sustain intelligent life. The first thing he did was build a probe that could travel beyond the limited vision of the most advanced telescopes.

He scoffed at the primitive explorer vessels that had been launched into deep space dozens of times within the past decades. Their inefficiency in gathering data was grossly negligent and the vessels were practically useless once they lest the solar system because they were to slow in reaching the next system. Only one vessel was as close as two-thirds to it's destination and only six others had reached their halfway point. AN additional four vessels had been destroyed when they collided with space debris because they lacked adequate guidance systems and sensors to avoid such problems. Their designers believed they had created vessels capable of handling nearly any situation presented but Knight knew they had overlooked many factors. He felt that he could build a superior probe and he did.

Even with the limited money from his research grants, young Knight was able to design and construct a probe that was far more advanced than anything previously launched into space. While many other probes were huge and bulky, the Knight probe was compactly efficient at only 2.4 cubic meters. It took young Knight seven months to design the probe and four to build it. The rear of the probe had five booster jets that could propel the probe at speeds that would make some comets seem like they were standing still. The power source was an experimental energy pack that Knight designed and had high hopes for in this and future projects. The estimated life span of the energy pack was only 4.9 years, but Knight felt that was more than enough time for it to accomplish his goals.

A computer that would gather information from sensors on the probe's exterior occupied three-fourths of the interior. The information would be formulated into coded bits and then hyper-beamed to his receiver at MIT. The code was a numeric sequence he designed and was used because he didn't want to chance anyone else using his research if they happened to intercept the beam.

Knight's goal was to send the probe to an unexplored region of the universe in minimal time. To accomplish this, Knight hoped to prove another of his theories to be true. Several months earlier Knight was scanning the sky with the giant telescope at the MIT observatory. Being the scientist he is, he began playing around by observing the darkness of space through a series of different colored lenses, When he was using a dark purple lens, he noticed an oddity. In an area he estimated to be around eight hundred square meters, the empty space was noticeably distorted and was obviously different than the surrounding space.

After a little research he found that none of the previously launched space vessels had taken a path anywhere near this distortion. The space distortion was hypothesized by Knight to be a variation on the standard black hole. Yet it was obvious that it did not have the violent gravitational pull of a normal black hole. If his theory was correct, sending the probe into the distortion might send the probe to another star system, possibly in another galaxy.

On July 27, 2028 the world entered a new era in space exploration. The probe was launched at 6:21 a.m. eastern time from the Kennedy Space Center Annex in Kennedy, Massachusetts. Traveling at speeds that made it difficult to track with conventional radar, the probe reached the edge of the solar system and slowed down to take an orbit around Pluto at 1:53 p.m.

The data received while the probe orbited Pluto entertained the scientists as Knight reconfirmed the location of the distortion. It was only 451,800 miles away from Pluto at its current position of orbit around the sun.

Again the probe advanced toward the distortion after the momentary detour and at 2:02 p.m. the probe beamed back it's first measurable readings of the distortion. There seemed to be an occasional flux in light patterns and the ions near the distortion were unstable. After a slight hesitation Knight instructed the probe to proceed into the distortion. At 2:07 p.m. the probe made contact with the distortion and disappeared.

Many hours passed with the world waiting for the results. A few scientists offered the suggestion that the probe had been destroyed although the discovery of the distortion still made it a worthwhile venture. Knight ignored such notions and waited in confidence. He knew that it may take hours, days, or weeks, but he knew the probe would send a signal. It took hours. At 11:44 p.m., the receiver picked up a signal coming from the distortion. Knight decoded the message and let out a yell. The young seven-year-old genius then told the world that the probe was safe and in perfect working order.

The location the probe sent it's signal from was charted as a B-class star system with twenty-two planets orbiting the star astronomers simply called A-14 in the Alpha Capri galaxy system millions of light years away. The probe was instructed to spend the next several days studying each of the planets, starting with the one furthest from the star. Now it was the world and not just the scientific community in awe of the young genius.

To be able to pursue his space exploration the way he wanted, without constant supervision and limited government funding, young Knight figured it was time to develop some of his projects for self profit. That way he could gain independence from the government parasites and progress his research at any pace he wished. On his eighth birthday he founded Knight Enterprises, a company that would shape the world in years to come. He recruited his friend Han Li to help in developing the products.

Han was a whiz at computer programming and had mastered the art of creating holographic images. Knight helped Han in using these skills in developing a series of games. Games with the KE logo became the rage of the world and the company was a success. Knight allows Han to receive a direct percentage of the profits from the games and allowed him to do whatever he wished with the money. Han surprised many when he used a large portion of his profits to as a donation to China's nuclear research. Although his mother begged him not to, Han insisted because he wanted the money to be used to build better facilities for research. After much hesitation the Chinese government consented.

Knight used his profits to put back into the company for research on bettering the products and developing new ones. While minimal profits were reaped from the games, Knight knew they could be maximized if the principles behind the games were applied toward ventures other than entertainment. Working on his own, he revised some of the games so that military forces to train for combat could use them. Another application he came up with was a program that had many medical uses, such as taking a surgeon through a surgeon step by step through an operation before it was actually done by using the three dimensional images. While his games division turned a profit of forty-four million the first year, the practical use divisions gave him an additional ninety-three million. With the business doing so well, he decided to return to his scientific research while backing the projects himself.

Knight built fifty-five new probes to be used in his own personal venture in space exploration. The first probe had completed its survey of the entire planetary system of all twenty-two planets, their moons, and it's sun. All were deemed to be in a state unable to support life although two of the middle planets seemed to be in premature stages of evolution and might be able to sustain life in a few million years. Upon receiving the final report, he instructed the probe to self-destruct.

The first reason for destroying the probe was its appearance. In the form it and previously launched vessels took, they were obviously not a natural part of the stellar environment and that would inhibit the chance of observing possible intelligent life forms that would other wise go into hiding. Secondly, he wanted to break all ties with the government because he was tired of them using him. He reported to the scientific community that the probe had been caught in the gravitational pull of the star and was destroyed.

He had all the probes developed by his tenth birthday, which was when he launched them. That was also the same day that he thanked MIT for giving him such a wonderful education and then he broke ties with them and his government sponsors. One small way to ease the break was that he agreed to release his findings to the scientific community. Even with this concession, the government never really got over losing one of it's most prized researchers and often took advantage of opportunities to hinder him when they presented themselves.

The main difference between the first probe and those later released was appearance. While the first probe was obviously a space vessel, the others were camouflaged to appear to be asteroids and meteors. Their exteriors were covered with a synthetic layer of stone that Knight developed and it was not penetrable by known scanning devices. As he realized there might be advanced forms of life with the technology to see past his deception, he had to go with what he had. In fact, he was in the process of developing a new generation of sensors that could do just that.

Within the next three years his probes had plotted the locations of five hundred and seven space portals that led to star system all over the universe. A total of two thousand one hundred and sixty-eight planets had been surveyed along with several moons and asteroids with no signs of life. The portals transported the probes to systems within the same galaxy and others at great distances between, but Knight saw no apparent pattern as to how the portals worked. In all, his probes had been in thirty-six different galaxies and had sent back vast quantities of information, star maps, and pictures of the planets themselves. Many of the star systems seen on the maps charted by the probes consisted of virgin territory to astronomers. A total of six thousand two hundred and twenty-one new stars had to be assigned labels and every day a couple more were added to the list.

Then on October 2, 2034 he started receiving data from a probe in the distant Delta Harri galaxy. The probe had just entered the planetary system labeled as TM-3 and was going through the routine scanning procedure. The system had a class A star that was similar to Earth's sun. There were six planets in orbit around the sun with the third, fourth, and fifth giving preliminary readings of having atmospheres capable of sustaining life. The probe did a cursory survey of the sixth planet before moving on to the fifth.

At 4:05 p.m. Knight received a picture that was extremely disturbing to him. On the far side of one of the fifth planet's two moons, there was something in the shadow that was of considerable size. For a moment he thought it may have been a smaller satellite that was caught in the large moon's gravitational field and was traveling along the path of it's own orbit. He signaled the probe to investigate the moon and to leave the scanning of the planet for later. Then at 4:43 p.m. he received another picture which both shocked him and made his heart leap with joy.

Behind the moon there was what was unmistakably a spaceship and the thermal readings taken by the probe indicated there was definitely life on board the vessel. The size of the craft amazed Knight for it was basically a floating city at its eighty cubic kilometers. A ship that size could possibly hold thousands of living beings.

At 5:48 p.m. the ship moved from behind the moon and toward the planet and three minutes later began firing at the planet's surface. The probe measured a high amount of atomic activity in each blast but there was no change in radiation levels on the planet's surface where they hit their targets. Knight was very interested in the fact that this alien race had mastered the use of atomic energy with negligible levels of excess radiation. Even he was several years from accomplishing a feat so grand.

Then at 6:45 p.m. the probe took a low orbit around the planet and began registering life signs. With thermal readings and motion sensors the probe was able to detect 616,768 forms of life on the planet's surface. As he realized that the life forms on this planet were under siege by possibly another alien race, he instructed the probe to investigate the area that had first been under attack. The picture Knight received was of a city 4.5 square kilometers that had been razed to the ground. Upon studying the picture under magnification he noticed that there were actually burnt corpses among the rubble. In the picture there were a total of thirty-five which he could make out and then he instructed the probe to make an accurate count of the area. After distinguishing between organic and inorganic materials, the total count by the probe was eight hundred and seventy-two deceased.

Knight wondered why the ship had limited its attack to this part of the planet and then discontinued the assault. Using the assumption that the attackers were invaders who wanted the planet and it's inhabitants intact for future purposes, then he surmised that the attack area must have been where the main body of the planet's leadership lived. Depending on the spirit of the people, the attackers must have counted on the inhabitants submitting to their rule without much of a struggle once the leadership was gone. Nearly one decade later, Knight found out that his theory was basically correct for the inhabitants were a docile race, which willingly followed whatever faction was in power.

Then at 8:02 p.m. the probe stopped sending a signal and Knight knew that it had been destroyed. Panic entered his mind as he wondered if the attacking aliens had discovered what the probe actually was and destroyed it. Or could it have been accidentally destroyed if the aliens had begun to fire upon the planet again? The worst case scenario played in Knight's mind over and over as he supposed if the aliens were advanced enough to discover the probe then they were probably advanced enough to track it's signal back to the point of it's origination. It would be easy enough for them to follow the signal through the portals and within hours Earth would be under siege by hostile aliens.

Knowing that there was nothing the Earth could do against such technology, he decided not to tell anyone of his discovery as not to incite panic. Instead he signaled the two closest probes to that star system to investigate. Many sleepless hours passed as young Knight waited for the probes to reach their destination and at 4:33 a.m. the next morning both were in the TM-3 system. He sat on the edge of his seat as both proceeded toward the fifth planet. Everything seemed calm and the probes spotted the battleship but were not fired upon. It turned out that the first probe was indeed destroyed accidentally, although Knight knew that there was still a distinct possibility of an attack in the future.

That day young Clayton Knight made the most difficult decision of his life. He decided to keep the knowledge of the hostile aliens a secret and only reveal it to those people closest to him and who would be able comprehend the gravity of the situation. Although his mother was a very intelligent person, he decided not to tell her for he truthfully did not know where her loyalties were and thought it was best that he didn't tell her. The only person he trusted with the information that first year was Han Li. Han understood the significance of the situation and the importance of secrecy so they made a pact on their friendship that neither would tell a soul without consulting the other first.

He also knew that it was best that he did not inform the government for there would either be a cover up or the information would somehow be leaked to the press. By keeping it a secret he would keep many years of panic and stress from the public. By confining the knowledge of the issue to a limited few, Knight would be able to control the course of his actions with minimal interference from outside forces.

From that point he and Han began making plans for the future and how they should proceed with their research. Knight decided it would be up to them to come up with a means to ward off the attack. He also realized that it would be necessary to covertly manipulate the citizens of Earth to ready the planet for the invasion. What their actions involved would be the greatest conspiracy to take place in the history of the human race. In order to make the conspiracy work he also realized he would have to recruit more people.

Their business Knight Enterprises would serve as the tool with which they would infiltrate society and make their actions seem part of the natural activities of the business. To accomplish this they had to build Knight Enterprises into a powerful organization with deep financial resources that could operate on an international scale. In order to accomplish that, Knight knew the company had to diversify and increase the flow of capital. He had two projects in mind that would give the growth process a big boost.

The first project involved developing an advanced sensory system. All the current methods at that time of retrieving information were incorporated into the unit with further advancements being added to heighten the performance. When the product was finished, it was able to analyze anything and give an accurate readout on what the size, depth, density, composition, and numerous other factors. The applications for the new sensory technology were almost limitless and Knight set out exploiting many of them.

One example of how the sensors could be used was as part of a security system. The system could be set to automatically scan any person or vehicle that came within a specified distance. An image of the scanned person would appear on the screen and a readout would separate all items that were not a physical part of the person on a list next to the image. If anything could not be identified by it's shape then the system would determine if it was harmful by examining what chemical elements were present. Due to the meticulousness of the system it would be impossible for anyone to sneak a gun, bomb, or any other weapon into a bank, airport, or any other security conscious institution without the proper personnel being aware of the situation.

Another application was to install a scanning system in a satellite and to have it search the entire span of the globe for undiscovered natural resources. Then they could go about purchasing the land for the purpose of removing the riches. The satellite also was able to detect sunken ship and what their cargo were, whether lost gold or other valuable materials that could be salvaged. There were also the numerous ancient artifacts left behind by civilizations from the distant past that were buried waiting to be discovered. The financial and historical wealth they were to find made Knight dizzy but he always regained his composure when he remembered his mission and he also didn't want to fall prey to one of the seven deadly sins.

Although the riches would be easy to find, extracting them with the technology available would take several years. While Knight worked on improving mining methods he estimated that the Earth would be depleted of all it's natural resources within forty years using contemporary methods or within twenty-five if he could get his new technology into application. Yet that did not worry Knight for he was not limited to Earth for mining because he had access to the entire universe. When the time came he would set out exploring that avenue. In fact, he planned on working on that scenario long before the Earth no longer has any more to offer.

The second project required Knight to do intense research on how the human brain operates. Starting with the knowledge that the brain operates like a bio-chemical binary computer, he set out determined to crack the code on the programming system which the brain used to retrieve and store information. At the start of the project Han Li was unsure of what Knight wanted to accomplish and often called Knight "Dr. Frankenstein." While Knight took the comment as humor he did realize that what he was trying to accomplish did involve some of the theories developed by German scientists centuries earlier.

The ultimate goal of the project was to develop a series of freethinking robots which people often refer to as androids. The androids could be programmed to fulfill any task that might normally be considered either dangerous or menial. Another benefit would be that he could surround himself with help that would be totally loyal to him and he would not have to reveal his secret mission to a great many people. At the present Knight and Han had seventeen assistants helping them on other projects but they were not involved in anything that dealt with the conspiracy.

The day Knight solved the puzzle of the mystery of the brain was May 16, 2036. He pondered the possibilities of his newfound discovery. It occurred to him that it might be possible to actually inject information into humans to make them smarter. That notion was dismissed after further study showed that the human brain at its current stage of evolution is too primitive and premature to withstand such a procedure. However, he did find that the procedure could be modified so that a person of far below average intelligence could be treated and helped to a level close to average intelligence. The procedure was also successful in treating patients that began to lose their memory as a result of disease. As a result many people were able to begin leading much more productive lives and people were able to become or remain independent from others.

The first series of androids he built were faceless, with black shields covering the area where the face would be. They were programmed with a working intelligence that would enable them to handle the tasks assigned to them and so they could follow any spontaneous verbal instructions. His purpose for creating a series with very limited capabilities was so that he could study a "plain" model as to how it operated and makes the necessary improvements. One definite advantage Knight saw in even the first android models was that they were tireless workers, which could perform their assigned duties for fifty straight hours before their energy packs needed to be recharged. To make vast improvements in the capabilities of the androids he knew that he had to design a better power pack.

The second series of androids were given public exposure. That series was also faceless as to make the public feel less threatened and the sported the black face shields. This series was programmed to do specific tasks that might otherwise have been done by human workers and were able to work for two hundred and twenty continuous hours due to a redesigned energy pack. Nearly ten thousand androids were programmed for working in the mines that Knight Enterprises had just purchased. While the androids saved Knight in labor costs and they were more productive because they could work for long periods of time continuously at a faster pace than humans could, he knew there was some resentment due to the fact he was not improving the employment climate. Yet he was not worried because he knew that Knight Enterprises would eventually be the largest employer on the planet.

Another task assigned to the androids was sanitation duty. Through shrewd planning and manipulation, he was able to secure the sanitation contracts of two hundred of the largest cities in the United States, fifteen cities in Canada, twelve in Mexico, and another thirty-three scattered throughout Europe. Although he was beginning to be seen as a sanitation kingpin in the eyes of the public, resentment began to rise as he once again deprived people of jobs. Since it was part of his master plan, young Knight did not dwell on his popularity for he knew eventually things would swing in his favor.

The issue that mattered to Knight was the fact that through his obtaining the sanitation contracts for many of the world's major cities, he was able to deal with a problem that was a major concern with him. The inefficiency and waste of the refuse industry had long bothered him and now he was doing something about it. Instead of taking the collected garbage to a spot to be burned, buried or tossed into the sea, he had his collection vehicles take their loads to recycling plants. Although there had been some recycling efforts by several cities over the years, nothing previous was done on such a grand scale.

At the plant androids sorted through the refuse and removed all materials that could be recycled. A majority of the material could be salvaged, such as paper, plastics, metal, and glass. All the like materials were placed together and sent to a near-by processing center that converted the former garbage into raw products ready to be used to make new products. Anything that could not be reused was placed into special chambers where they were atomized and broken down into the base elements. The elements were separated and put into storage canisters. The canisters were sent to Knight Enterprise's laboratories for use in experiments and to be used as raw materials for constructing more androids.

All the buildings that Knight Enterprises owned were constructed by another series of androids. The androids completed their projects in much less time than humans and the quality of the workmanship was much higher. Due to the fact that these buildings were the property of Knight Enterprises, the public did not react to negatively to the fact even more jobs were being deprived from society. Knight knew that his company would have to start hiring more humans before he could start having the androids working in the public sector. The time for increased hiring seemed to be fast approaching and Knight readied himself to be in position to capitalize on any situations that might advance his purpose while turning public opinion his way.

On September 18, 2037 Knight received an invitation from the governor of Massachusetts to accompany him as his guest for a dinner at the White House. Knight knew the main reason the governor wanted to meet him was he wanted to see the person responsible for spending millions of dollars in taxes toward the state in addition to the nearly one billion dollars in taxes paid yearly to the federal government. He hadn't been seen in public for nearly six years so his mother told him it would be nice for him to get out and meet some people. Just to please his mother he accepted the invitation.

The governor's limousine picked him up in front of the Knight Enterprises building in Boston after Knight had a busy day of meetings. The driver took him to the airport where he boarded the governor's private jet which would take them to Washington DC. Since he had personally been out of the public eye for so long people actually forgot who he was and often did not associate Knight Enterprises with a single individual. As he entered the cabin the governor was obviously shocked when he saw the boy of sixteen for he had expected someone much older. Knight immediately took a dislike to the man and wondered how the public had been so naive as to elect a man like Anthony Trudeau to a position that had any power. He knew that the man had inherited a sizable fortune and had actually done little with his life, which made him a natural for the world of politics.

There were additional dinner guests in the cabin and Knight wondered what their motives for accepting the governor's invitation were. Among the guests was Emanual Ramos, the Brazilian ambassador to the United States, and his daughter Ana. Knight fell in love with her the moment he laid eyes on her. The governor introduced them and they began getting acquainted as the other guests went about socializing before the jet took off.

Miss Ramos was a student at Harvard with a dual major of business management and finance. When she mentioned that, it caught Knight's attention because she didn't seem to be any older than he was. He asked her how old she was and she answered fifteen. Then he asked her when she was to graduate and the answer was that December. When he asked her if she had received any job offers yet, her father stepped in and wanted to know what this boy was doing asking such questions.

The governor came over and apologized for not introducing Knight earlier. The shock and embarrassment on the face of Ambassador Ramos was almost comical as he learned that the boy was Clayton Knight, the scientific genius and founder of Knight Enterprises. Young Knight quickly forgave him and returned his attention to the man's daughter.

Continuing their conversation, she said that she had received a few offers, but nothing to that point had interested her. The cabin went silent after he next asked her if she would come and work for Knight Enterprises and take over as president. When she said she would have to think about it, her father almost turned white and sat down in his seat with his had over his heart. Knight felt sorry for the man yet he knew that inside the father was overflowing with pride for his daughter.

The news of the events on the plane had reached Washington DC before the jet landed. A crowd of reporters met its passengers as they departed and Knight was immediately mobbed. He took a moment to make a brief statement before pushing his way through the crowd to rejoin the party as they reached the limousine. The statement that he gave was carried on the front page of every paper across the world the next morning.

"The actions that I have taken tonight is for the best of motives. That motive is the desire to improve the world and the tool with which I do that is my business. For the business to operate at it's full potential it will need the best people and I intend to only take the very best. Thank you."

Knight smiled the entire time the limousine was in route to the White House. The shadows covered his face and he was looking out the window so no one could see his expression. He was happy that his mother talked him into taking the trip. It also pleased him that he handled the vultures at the airport so well. He meant every word he said but the true motive behind the statement was to serve as a warning to the business world.

The city of Washington DC appealed to him. He liked the intellectual atmosphere and the history behind it. Although he was growing increasingly weary of politicians, it was the life style that he was drawn to. A time would come soon when he knew that he would tire of Boston and would want to move his operations elsewhere. Washington DC seemed to be an attractive choice.

More reporters met him as he arrived at the White House, but he just ignores them and allows the secret service men to act as a curtain between himself and the pack of mangy wolves. A middle-aged man that Knight recognizes as the President greets them in the front hallway. His name was George Snow, a Democrat from Ohio who had been the mayor of Cincinnati before being elected into the Oval Office.

The political process had been so much more organized since 2012 when the people pushed for an amendment that had a committee for each major party select three people that would be best for the job. The drafting process sometimes resulted in non-politicians being picked, yet the public knew that whichever candidate won, that person was right for the job. The runner-up in the primary was also drafted as the running mate of the winner of the primary. Knight thought it was a decent process and it worked. However, he knew there would come a time for a major political change worldwide and that he would eventually be behind the manipulation that would bring about that change.

Had he not been seated to Miss Ramos for the entire evening, he knew he would have been bored out of his skull. She gave him insights on her family life by talking about her father, mother six sisters, three brothers, and the town they were from. She was the eldest and certainly had a promising future.

Knight asked her if she was accepting his offer and she said that she was. He took he had in his and kissed it and told her that she would not regret her decision. He spent the rest of the evening asking her questions, getting her opinions on various topics, and finding out where she stood in comparison to himself. He knew she was very smart and found her to be extremely beautiful. The way she smiled made goose pimples on the back of his neck. He thought that her long black hair acted as the perfect background for her tanned skin and soft brown eyes. One day this cute girl would grow into a beautiful woman he said to himself and at that moment he knew that some day he would marry her.

His mother was shocked when he told her of all that happened that evening. She knew she was in no position to control him, for it was a fact that she had not had a hold over him for over ten years. That was one of those moments that the wished she had a normal son. All she could do was smile and wish the best for him.

Knight and Ana saw each other once a week for the next few months and they talked on the phone briefly each day. The bulk of their correspondence was done by letter, which they exchanged by the dozens. They knew the majority of their time should be spent attending to the immediate tasks at hand. For Ana that involved keeping up with her school work and preparing for graduation. The time was used by Knight to work in the lab on another project with Han.

The next several days were spent by Knight and Han designing and building a shuttle craft that he hoped to possibly send to one of the conquered worlds and to have it bring some of the oppressed beings to Earth. The problem was that even if he could get the shuttle to the aliens, there still remained the invading force to contend with. Every day Knight checked the transmissions from the probes hoping an opportunity would present itself.

One sign of hope was that the inhabitants of the fourth planet had the capability of space travel. That fact came to Knight's attention one day when the aggressor aliens were attacking the third planet while one probe watched, the other probe in the system observed a small spaceship in flight. It cleared the gravity belt of the fourth planet and raced past the fifth and sixth planets. But before it could get more than 453,000 miles from the sixth planet, a battle vessel was upon it and blasted it into space dust. That episode did leave open the possibility that another ship might escape and could make it to freedom before anyone notices. That was the type of opportunity Knight was waiting for.

From data received from the probes, all three of the planets in the TM-3 system capable of sustaining life did have inhabitants living on them. However, all three planets were also under the close supervision of the aggressor race. One day a ship of one of the hostile ships was leaving the system and Knight ordered the probe to follow it. Both went through a portal and emerged in the S-2 star system in the same galaxy where there were two planets that had inhabitants. The ship encountered five more battle vessels of similar design and they proceeded to attack and conquer the two worlds.

While Knight was unable to help those under attack, he felt that he was learning a great deal by observing how the invaders conducted their attack maneuvers. In all he had observed a total of five alien races submit to the hostile force. As long as his probes were undiscovered, he would take advantage of his education on how the hostile operated and it might help him prepare for when the Earth was eventually attacked. He only hoped he had enough time to prepare some type of defense.

That December Ana Ramos graduated from Harvard with her two degrees on the eighth of the month. On December 16 she turned sixteen and as a birthday present Knight took her to the Knight Enterprises building in Boston where he presented her with a key. When they reached the twenty-fourth and top floor he walked her to the end of the hallway where the was an office that had the name plate "Ana Ramos" on the door with the word "president" below it. After giving Knight a grateful embrace, she used her key to open the door.

Once inside she surveyed every inch of the office, which measured twenty feet by forty-five feet. It was ordained with many luxuries that included a mahogany desk with 18-karat gold handles. She was still breathless with excitement when Knight called her over to show her how to access the computer. He did it once and let her have a turn at attempting it. The fact that she was able to quickly memorize the eighteen-digit security code made him happy for he knew her mental capabilities would be a great asset to the company.

After she spent a few more minutes enjoying the comforts of the office he asked her when she would be able to start work. She said that the earliest date would be January 8 because she was going back to Manaus to visit her family and was going to stay through the holidays. He said that was fine and when she did return they would go over the operations of the company in full detail. Once she had spent enough time enjoying her future executive suite, he accompanied her to the front door where a limousine took her home and he returned to the office building and went down to the laboratory in the basement.

He was all alone except for a dozen android assistants. The day before he had sent Han Li to China on business and he was going to take a vacation once his task was finished. It had become obvious to Knight that Han was becoming stressed out and knew it would do him some good to return to his roots. The task he wanted Han to do was to start the negotiation process with the governments of the Asian nations for sanitation contracts.

Another issue he wanted Han to look into was the feasibility of opening an office in Beijing. If things went according to plan, Han could spend a lot more time in China as the Asian operations director. Although the idea of Han being so far away distressed Knight, he knew the Chinese culture was much easier on Han's nerves than the American life style he was leading. The health of his friend was very important to him and he knew eventually Han would mature to a stage where he did not become so easily overwrought and could adjust to any life style.

Knight decided to use the idle time to work on new projects. His first venture dealt with developing and new type of material that was a cross between plastic and metal. It was created by microscopically weaving strands of the two materials together and tempering them at extremely high temperatures. The result was a light and durable material that was practically indestructible. He named the material knightronium. Its applications were almost endless and his first use for his newest advancement was to construct the shuttle out of it.

His next product involved his once again improving the energy packs. The problem he had to overcome was how to store the most possible energy in the least amount of space. How he solved the problem involved constructing microscopic storage units that could be linked together in a chain and then coiled tightly into a ball. The chain making and coiling was a very delicate process that had to be done by machine and required very close supervision by either Knight or an android. The ball was placed in a protective casing of knightronium that had connecting circuits for each end of the chain. Charging the pack involved flooding energy through the intake circuit and the storage units filled up in a domino effect. There was a high level of energy in a pack when it was fully charged due to the fact there were so many little storage units in the pack that if the chain were unwound and placed flat it would be several kilometers long.

When completed a power pack was the size of a deck of cards and could power an android for eight hundred continuous days. Due to the size and precision of the new pack, the inefficiency level was almost nonexistent at 0.062 percent. The energy pack was one of his favorite devices for it had so many applications and he felt that there was always room for improvement. While many projects had a definite beginning and end, his obsession with the energy packs seemed never ending.

While he was still at the helm of his company, he decided to strike a bitter blow to the business world by making a bold move and utilizing his two latest advancements in one product. That product was to be a new line of automobiles that would carry his name. It was a risky venture he was undertaking for he knew he was moving fast and there would be staunch opposition. Yet once Knight made up his mind about something, nothing could stop him until he reached his goal. By using the technology at his disposal he could shape the economies of the world which to a certain extent he already had.

He began working on the designs for his vehicles, which he would show Ana when she returned. Each model instilled his visionary view of using the most advanced technology while still seeming to be domestic. A total of six vehicles would be introduced in the beginning as he tried to start out by getting a foothold in each of the markets. To appeal to those interested in a large luxury vehicle he offered the Knight Emperor. For those on the fast track he had a high-powered sports car called the Knight Thoroughbred. He had an all-terrain vehicle called the Knight Gladiator. As some people liked small cars he offered a compact called the Knight Shamrock. His quarter ton pickup went by the name of Knight P-500. Finally he designed a twelve-seat passenger van which he named the Knight Express.

Over the years there had been numerous attempts to produce electric or battery powered vehicles and all basically failed. Those that make have worked had been publicly sabotaged by the oil industry and the automobile manufacturers of the world. Numerous hindering lawsuits had been waged against the makers of many of the electric cars and many were forced into bankruptcy as they tried to fend off the attacks. Others just took themselves out of the market to end the constant harassment they were under. There were a couple of instances where the car maker held on to make a respectable showing only to have special interest groups persuade law makers to pressure them out of business by making special Congressional committees which harassed the car manufacturers with endless investigations and special hearings. That was one aspect of the challenge that especially appealed to Knight for he wanted to take on those who used such corrupt tactics and he wanted to expose the politicians for the self serving cretins that they were.

This was one battle that Knight was prepared to wage to the bitter end for his industry had the financial resources to fight on for many years no matter what the opposition threw at him. Yet somehow he knew it would not take years for he intending to strike back at his future enemies just as quickly and viciously and planned to have the issue resolved in his favor in a reasonable amount of time. AS he planned his marketing strategy he also planned his options for attacks and counterattacks. His immediate goal was to sway Ana as to the merits of his venture.

Although Ana was surprised when she heard of Knight's venture, she thought it would be a test to see if she had what it took to see a major project through to the end. She also liked the idea because it would ultimately be for the betterment of the people. Working together they set out to make their new dream a reality.

His construction teams built manufacturing plants in Portland, Oregon, Milwaukee, Wisconsin, Atlanta, Georgia, and Santa Fe, New Mexico by the end of February. Those four cities were chosen because they had the highest unemployment rates among the nation's larger cities and he wanted to hire people in areas it would help the most. Then he also had plants built in Mexico in the cities of Juarez, Tampico, Merida, and Guadalajara. While he chose that nation because it had an economy that needed a boost, his real reason for opening plants outside of the United States was to guarantee production would continue after the inevitable injunctions came to close down the plants.

Production started in March and over twenty thousand automobiles were produced before the government closed the plants in mid June. Knight quickly mounted a publicity campaign that pointed out the government had forced 9600 American workers off the job while the Mexican government allowed the four plants there to remain in operation. One point that Knight liked to continually stress was the fact that it was a travesty that the government could be corrupted by special interest groups that wanted to enhance their own positions and did not care that society was being denied advancements that would improve living.

His media campaign cost millions but he got his message across and people started to express their displeasure with the government action. The issue came to a head when a special congressional hearing was called to address the subject and it was televised nationally every day. This addition media exposure worked to Knight's advantage as the nation began to cheer for the two intellectual teens, he and Ana, who clearly outclassed the Congressmen and Senators on the panel. The politicians found that they were clearly overmatched intellectually as Knight and Ana time and again testified with confidence and often belittled those posing the questions.

The hearings ended in the favor of Knight Enterprises and left the politicians in a quandary. Every single one of the politicians on the panel lost their next election due to the negative images the hearings left in the minds of the public. With their attacks on the two youths who appeared very wholesome and model teenagers, the political career of each individual came to a halt. As a result of the hearings, Knight had soaring popularity and was obviously someone not to cross as his power was just beginning to surge.

After the hearings, Knight Enterprises filed counter suits against those industries that had attacked him. While feeling in a particularly vicious mood, he launched a successful media campaign for the public to boycott all products offered by his adversaries. The financial wounds cut so deep that all were forced to drop their lawsuits. As Knight was not one to back down, he decided he would go for the jugular while the industries were in weakened states and were easy prey. Under Knight's instruction Ana led Knight Enterprises in takeover battles but left the oil producing industries alone because he had different plans for them in the future. They were able to avoid monopoly anti-trust laws due to the fact that there was legislation pending in the Senate that would modify regulation of monopolies. When the legislation finally did pass, all investigations into Knight's activities were stopped as officials saw there was nothing to gain by continuing. By September all eight major auto manufactures were under the control of Knight Enterprises and the executive levels of each company was promptly cut to the bone. All were publicly reprimanded before joining the ranks of the unemployed. Revenge was savored like a delicacy as young Knight cautiously built his power base.

Those who were not blinded by his charismatic, boyish charm could see that Knight was gaining power and was using Knight Enterprises as his steamroller to clear the path. From the shadows his enemies watched him with envy and anger hoping for a chance to bring him down. Their only problem was how to stop him without being crushed them in the process of trying.

By that December Knight Enterprises had become the world's leading automobile manufacturer. Using it's newfound power the company was able to persuade every nation on the planet to pass anti-pollution laws that greatly restricted the use of gas burning vehicles. That left Knight in a position that forced all the other car manufacturers to come begging for help. Since he did believe in the philosophy of free enterprise, he agreed to sell energy packs to the other manufacturers at a reasonable price and even allowed them to borrow some of his plant technicians to instruct them on the proper installation procedures.

With millions of used cars that would be rendered basically useless, Knight decided to open specialty shops across the globe that would convert the cars to pack powered vehicles. The shops also made modifications on all two and three wheel vehicles that formally had gasoline engines. His technicians were also contracted to modify the engines of all flying modes of transport. Although it would be a temporary enterprise, it did stimulate the economy by providing people with several hundred jobs.

That December was also when he had asked Ana to marry him. The date was the twenty-first and she said yes. They decided on a January wedding for they did not see any purpose in waiting a great length of time. It was to be a small ceremony and a judge would marry them. Although both were from Catholic families, Knight was having thoughts on the hypocrisy of religion and felt a plain legal ceremony served his needs at the time. Although he did believe in God and it would greatly disappoint his mother whose family tradition with the Catholic church went back centuries through her ancestors in Poland, he could not take part in a ritual if his heart was not in it.

On January 25, 2039 the two young people united their love and were wed. According to the papers, Ana Marie Ramos and Clayton Aaron Knight were married in a small ceremony in the executive offices of Knight Enterprises. The guests included all of Ana's family and friends while Knight only had his mother present with Han Li also there to be his best man. He had considered inviting his relatives from Nebraska but since he hadn't seen any of them since he was two although his mother had always returned twice a month.

The wedding was the first time Knight had met the members of Ana's family, with the exception of her father. He noticed that Ana received her beauty from her mother Teresa, who still appeared youthful at the age of forty-three. Since he had no siblings of his own he took a special liking to those of Ana. Ana introduced them to him in the order of their ages: Roselita, 16, Miguel, 14, Maria, 12, Pablo, 11, the triplets Angelina, Isabela, and Patricia, 10, Andre, 9 and Carmen, 8.

The two decided on a month tour of Europe for their honeymoon. The trip did Knight much good for it was the longest stretch of time that him mind was not preoccupied with either his work or school studies. On the trip the two got to know each other very well both physically and intellectually. He told her of everything he had discovered through his scientific endeavors, including the alien race that may one-day make it's way to Earth.

Although she was shocked by the revelation, the importance of the situation was readily understood and she took an oath of secrecy without hesitation. Then she made a suggestion to Knight that reaffirmed his belief and trust in her. Since he was already playing manipulation games with the people of the planet, then why not transplant androids with human appearances among the population to help influence them. For the longest time he sat there with a broad grin on his face and then told her that it was already in the works.

Despite the fact that it conflicted with some of his views on how man should be allowed to confront the fates without external interference, the circumstances that he had knowledge of made him conclude that man and Earth could not survive without his interference. He knew that the invading aliens would not annihilate the entire population of Earth. Rather the survivors would be forced to their authority while making the concept of freedom nonexistent. At it's current stage, the society of Earth could not tolerate such a catastrophe for it had been over three decades since any nation had endured such oppression.

The last of the tyrannical strongholds was eliminated in 2013 when a dictator in Chad was overthrown and executed. It was only two years previous that the last nation to use martial law to govern its people collapsed because of revolution and democracy was installed in Turkey. Because they had grown to cherish their freedom, Knight knew that the people of Earth would not survive an attack without heavy losses. That was one of the reasons that Knight had made a pledge to himself that he would save the people of the planet, even if it compromised his standards and those of society.

By May 1, 2039 Knight had constructed 11,000 human-like androids. He called them infiltrators. Their features reflected the many races and cultures he planned to infiltrate. In a way, he knew that what he was conducting was an invasion of his own. The fact that he was about to begin practicing espionage against each of the two hundred and eight nations of the world made him feel as if his methods and motives were turning him toward the way of the criminal. Yet he quickly dismissed such a notion because his motives dealt with protecting society and not destroying it.

Each android possessed all human characteristics as best Knight could program them. They could express the entire range of emotions, use rational thought, and when necessary operate on instinct rather than thought. That final feature was a survival mode that only went into effect when the android was in extreme danger. Even then, the android was equipped with the necessary technology to overcome any possible situation.

The exteriors of the infiltrators had all the features that made them appear human. They were covered with a non-organic synthetic flesh, synthetic hair, a muscular, toned body, the appearance of respiration, and a network of veins that actually pulsated at the proper points when the android exerted itself. Each infiltrator also had fully operational sex organs because Knight knew there would be times the situation would necessitate their use in order to keep their cover or to obtain information. Although all the first series of infiltrators were male in appearance, Knight had a female model in the works that he was programming with the help of contributions from Ana.

The interior of each android consisted of such advancements in technology that the scientific community would have been beyond ecstatic if he wasn't keeping them a secret. Just below the skin was a network of extremely sensitive and delicate sensors that took a broad range of readings, which were relayed, to a storage bank in the brain. Besides picking up information, some of the sensors also simultaneously sent out signals that thwarted any attempt to scan, x-ray, or observe the infiltrator with any type of mechanical device. Instead of the actual readings, the device would pick up readings that made the infiltrator seem human. That was one of the many special security measures to ensure the anonymity of his infiltrators.

In the area normally occupied by the heart and lungs, a power unit pulsated and gave the android enough energy to operate for 4,600 days continuously without the need of a recharge. This allowed the infiltrator to stay under cover for over twelve years if necessary. The energy pack also enabled the infiltrators to summons up great strength, but only when there was no other alternative. Tension meters in the laboratory indicated that the androids could lift up to 12,622 pounds and leap either eighty-three feet vertically or forty feet horizontally. The units were also capable of reaching speeds of eighty-six miles per hour. The use of those talents would be left up to the judgment of the individual unit.

To keep track of each android, a microscopic chip was placed behind each eye and reserve chips were stored in hidden compartments under each fingernail. The chips emitted a signal that could only be picked up by special receivers that he designed. The signals were relayed from the android to the nearest of the satellites in orbit that Knight had launched just for this purpose. The signals were then redirected to his headquarters in Boston where he had the signal converted into data that could be stored on computer.

The signals operated as both a homing beacon, that allowed Knight to track the every movement of each infiltrator, and a transport for coded messages that included the information picked up on the sensors plus an ongoing report by the infiltrator as it evaluated it's activities. All the information was stored in a super computer that was one thousand cubic meters in size and capable of retrieving information from 365,000 android units simultaneously. While Knight did not know if he would actually transplant that many infiltrators among the human population, he knew the number might be close and wanted the capability if the need arose.

The first series of androids dispatched were sent only to locations of power or of manipulation relevance. Although units were sent to every nation, the proportion of their dispersal was based on where the nation ranked in the mainstream as a world power. Thus the top twenty power nations of the world received sixty-one percent of the units. Once there, the infiltrators concentrated on gaining positions in government, law enforcement, and teaching. Each unit was to enter its assigned profession at the beginning access level and advance upward in their field naturally.

He did not want an infiltrator to call attention to it by entering at a high level, because he also wanted the units to get to know their respective areas of employment. And to include in their evaluations how efficiently they operated and what changes for the better could be made. Then the unit could advance itself naturally by helping instigate the changes, which would create a better work environment for the other people. The idea had occurred to Knight that he could replace the leaders of the world with his androids, but that would not benefit his plans significantly. He also had no desire to rob the planet of those who were natural born leaders for that would make him no better than the invader aliens.

The final purpose of the infiltrators was to make evaluations of the people they made contact with and were closely tied to. Using these evaluations, Knight would compile a list of people to recruit to work for Knight Enterprises. He wanted the best people available and refused to settle for anything less and by filling the positions with people rather than assigning androids to them would further stimulate the economy. One of the first men recruited by Knight became a close friend and was invited into his secret world. That man was Dr. William Avery.

William Avery was a man who had used his physical and mental talents to overcome the social and economical barriers of his childhood. As a child he grew up in a poor, black community in the Mississippi delta. His father worked as a deliveryman for one of the many mail services and his mother was a seamstress. Avery was the eldest of eighteen children and grew to despise his life style at an early age. He found that his avenues for escape would involve schoolwork, at which he was exceptional, and sports.

The two sports at which he excelled were football and track although he was an above average basketball player. Because he reached his full height by the age of fifteen, he had developed into a well-coordinated physical specimen by his junior year of high school. His height was seven-foot-one, but since the world had gone metric at the turn of the century, he was just another person over two meters tall. With his large frame he was able to comfortably carry three hundred and sixty pounds, most of which was muscle. By the end of his junior year he was receiving recruiting letters from all over the country to play football, track, and even basketball.

He was an outstanding offensive lineman in football, an excellent shot putter in track, and a decent center in basketball. The summer before his senior year he gained international attention by winning the gold medal for the United States in the shot put at the 2028 Olympic games in Marseilles, France. That winter he decided to attend college at Washington University where he eventually was an All-American offensive guard each of his four years. He also competed on the school track team in both the shot put and discus and was the national champion in the shot put all four years and was the national champion in the discus his senior year after he had finally mastered the form.

In 2032 he had successfully defended his gold medal at the Olympic games in Tripoli, Lebanon. After graduating from Washington University with a 3.94 G.P.A. in Pre-Med he chose to go to medical school instead of pursuing a professional career in football. Before graduating in 2036, he entered his final Olympic competition in Dacca, Bangladesh. He won his final gold medal with a heave of 30.2 meters to become the first person to crack the thirty-meter mark.

In his four years of medical school at the Columbia School of Medicine, Avery had spent his time religiously in both the weight room and the library. The many hours of study paid off as he finished second in his class out of seven hundred and forty-four students. He immediately accepted a position at the Medical Research Institute in Houston, Texas. That is where he stayed for seven years before Clayton Knight approached him with an offer to join his research team.

Knight was interested in Avery because of his record for accomplishing the goals that he set. The reports also said he was an excellent medical scientist and was likely to eventually make a significant breakthrough in science medicine. Knight also observed that William Avery was possibly the only person capable of continuing the type of medical research that Knight had begun. In addition to the lab work, Avery became Knight's personal physician.

Although Knight was a healthy young man, Avery said that his body was under developed because he spent so much time at work and not enough exercising. What exercise he did get consisted of teaching and practicing martial arts with Ana. As of August 2039 he was near his full height when he stood six-foot-four, but his body was a slender one hundred and thirty-five pounds. Then Avery introduced Knight to the worlds of weight lifting and bodybuilding. By November Knight weighed one hundred and seventy-five pounds and was beginning to develop an athletic appearance.

Actually, Knight found that he was becoming addicted to the feeling he had when he exerted himself in a strenuous exercise session. Avery cautioned him not to progress too quickly, but the natural metabolic rate of Knight's body allowed him to recover faster from his workouts and he spent a lot of time delving into his new hobby. He had progressed to the point by the end of November where his endurance allowed him to workout for two and one half-hours continuously. The doctor was amazed at his progress, but monitored the sessions cautiously to be safe.

Chapter three

Then came 2040, the year of terror. Although the official time span ranged from December 30, 2039 to December 5, 2040, historians just pointed toward the entire year for simplicity. What happened was a combination of two things. First, the terrorist organizations of the world united and began a reign of destruction. Second, the poverty stricken people of the world became swayed by the terrorist leaders and turned on the establishment in revolt.

The terrorists were sponsors by a wealthy international crime organization based in Ireland called the Four Powers. One of their main goals was world domination that they planned on achieving when they filled void they would create. Their main tools for creating the void were assassination and sabotage. Using those two tools they hoped to create a vacuum by eliminating the wealthy.

On December 30, 2039 their plan went into effect when they assassinated American billionaire James La Sale along with his wife and ten security guards in Yonkers, New York. That same morning they blew up a thirty-nine-story building containing Japanese tycoon Hanso Tarao and killed him and nine hundred and fifty-two office workers. A group calling itself People Against World Oppression claimed responsibility. Their goal was to convince people that the only way to truly achieve freedom in the world was to do away with the wealthy. The message met receptive ears and they were able to convince many that it was a just cause.

On January 4, 2040 people began rioting in many over the larger poverty stricken nations of the world. The poor turned to murder because they saw it as a way to possibly change life so that it would be better for them. Many were the type to be easy influenced by mob mentality and went with the flow. At the same time the terrorists continued on down the list it had for people to be assassinated.

Besides the murder of La Salle, activity in the United States remained relatively calm because the mobs were often quickly dispersed without much commotion by law enforcement and military forces. That is until January 16. On that day Clayton Knight experienced one of the major set backs in his life.

It was 7:30 p.m. and he and his mother were walking out of The Royal Cuisine restaurant in Washington DC. He had considered taking some security precautions, but his mother requested that they have a quiet dinner alone without a large escort. Ana had been feeling ill and wanted to catch up on some reading rather than accompany them that cool, winter evening.

As soon as the two reached the sidewalk and waved to summon their limousine, a hail of bullets fell upon them. His mother was immediately thrust backward and crashed through the large glass window that showcased a seafood display. When the first bullets hit Knight, he was spun around and fell face first to the concrete. Bullets still rained from above as his body shuddered as the last few billets made impact. There was a brief silence that was broken by the distant shrill of sirens as authorities made their way to the scene.

The paramedics pulled the lifeless body of what had been an energetic woman from the window. The corpse had only seven bullet wounds but two were to the head. Three others had struck the chest area with one passing through the heart and the other two became lodged in the right lung. One bullet had just grazed the right shoulder and the final one had torn through her right biceps. Many diners could not keep down their meals after seeing her bloody form among the glass and blood. Reports would show that she had died instantly.

Other medical technicians were working on the body of Knight. Blood was sprayed all over the sidewalk and the front of the white, stoned building. There was torn flesh and shattered bones protruding from Knight's still body. At the sight of his condition everyone assumed he was dead. After his body had been loaded into an ambulance and the vehicle had started moving, a paramedic noticed his eye twitch. After attaching a scanner he noted that there was brain wave activity along with a very slow, yet constant heartbeat. The information was relayed to the hospital as the ambulance was immediately rerouted to the Washington Trauma Center. Dr. Avery was also notified and he rushed to take a jet from Boston to Washington DC along with Ana.

Before Dr. Avery arrived the doctors had done little besides attempting to refurnish the body with blood to make up for what it had lost. The medical staff was amazed at how the body maintained an unbelievably low blood pressure without faltering. Their instruments had picked up an unusually high amount of brain wave activity and the patterns had them worried and confused.

DR, Avery arrived at the center at 8:40 p.m. with a team of five android assistants. The doctors explained the situation and gave him all the data they had collected. He then excused the entire staff and had security seal off the corridor. After the corridor had been cleared he entered the operating room and took his first look at Knight. At first the shock overwhelmed him, but he quickly regained his composure.

An oxygen machine was assisting Knight in breathing and blood was flowing into and out of his body through a network of transparent tubing. The report indicated there had been twenty-two points of entry and nine exit wounds. One bullet had struck the left frontal lobe above the eye with it still being lodged in the brain. Another bullet had entered through his right cheek below the eye and exited below the lobe of his right ear. Eight bullets had struck the upper torso area from shoulder to shoulder and all luckily had missed vital organs. Three bullets had entered the left side of the rib cage with one tearing the pancreas and the others lodging in the large intestine. Those three bullets had hit him while he had been spinning around.

The final nine bullets had entered while he was face down on the ground. Two had struck the back of his right shoulder, with one bullet passing through the body as it shattered the collarbone. Another bullet broke a bone on his left fore arm as it passed through. Two additional bullets entered the left side of his back and tore muscle before becoming lodged in the intestines. Another bullet was buried in his right buttock. The final three bullets had torn into his right leg and broke it in two places. AS he looked at his friend, the doctor knew that the man should actually already have been dead.

Dr. Avery and his team worked for sixteen hours and removed all the bullets except the one in the brain. He waited on removing that one until he had studied the situation carefully and was better rested so he could handle the delicate procedure. All the other wounds were taken care of as he performed minor reconstructive surgery and stopped all the external and internal bleeding.

He noticed that the blood pressure stayed at the same low level through out the entire operation and finally rose slightly when they completed that first marathon session. It occurred to him that Knight may have possibly been in control of his physical functions due to his many years of discipline gained by practicing the martial arts. He thought that Knight may have been aware of all that was going on while he struggled to maintain control as his life teetered on the brink of death. After pondering the situation for a few moments, the doctor left the room to sleep before starting the next series of surgeries.

Over the next fourteen days Dr. Avery repaired the damage to the brain, reconstructed the broken bones, and mended the damaged vital organs and muscles. It was all necessary surgery and since Knight never actually got any weaker, the doctor kept pressing on with one operation after another. After the final operation, Knight stayed in a self-induced comatose state for the next two months as his body healed. In that time, Dr. Avery did several tests on Knight and also got to know Ana much better.

During those two months, the doctor made some startling discoveries about Knight. Even in his comatose state, his brain was still wild with activity. The charts were such a jumbled mess that the doctor almost thought the test results of about twenty people were laid one on top of the other. Avery knew the man was a genius, but wondered what went on in his head, as he remained unconscious. What could he possibly have been thinking? That question entered Dr. Avery's mind many times and it prompted him to perform more tests.

After an extensive battery of tests he came to the conclusion that Knight was not human. It was true that he had the form of his fellow man and had the same anatomy. Yet there were many things about him that were different and would have got unnoticed to the untrained eye. All indications that Knight was either an advanced being or a mutant.

The only reason the term 'mutant' came to Dr. Avery's mind was because there was an unusual strain in the DNA of Knight and all of the doctor's training instructed him that such a deviation from the norm had to be a mutation. On the other hand, there were also slight differences in his cell structure, adrenaline, metabolism, and several other physical attributes that pointed to the argument that he may have been an advanced being. When he could progress no further, he confronted Ana with his findings and she was as shocked with the discovery as the doctor was.

It was sixty-nine days after the assassination attempt that Knight emerged from his comatose state. He was sore and very weak, but when his eyes opened to the sight of Avery and Ana standing over him. He managed a smile. He knew that he would have to endure extensive rehabilitation in order to approach his previous physical condition. When he awoke he was an unsightly one hundred and fourteen pounds and it was a struggle to do the simplest task. Then he realized that he had total recall of every moment of the entire sixty-nine day period as if he had been awake the entire time. He thought that may have been a contributing factor as to why he was so drained.

Then he was prompted to ask the doctor why he took the liberty to conduct so many unnecessary, extensive tests.

The doctor told him of his findings and Knight was surprised himself although he did realize he was a little different than his fellow man. The news of their discovery was to be kept secret in the same regard of the alien invasion for both would cause undue panic and speculation.

That night the three of them returned to Boston where Knight could rehabilitate in more familiar surroundings. Ana told him that she had the public relations department release the news that he assassination attempt had been successful. She also had Knight Enterprises buy the trauma center and closed it in his memory as memorials were erected at the entrances. Another trauma center was constructed a few blocks away and went under the name Knight Memorial Trauma Center. It had been dedicated in the memory of Knight himself and his mother. He smiled in appreciation of her cunning and made a mental note to rededicate the center personally to honor his mother.

She then told him that four days after he had been shot, the American President Montgomery Black was assassinated as he stood on the front steps of the White House. The assassin was apprehended but committed suicide in route to the jail by swallowing a poisonous capsule. Knight thought that was a pity because Black had been a decent man and had represented the Republican party well. Many must have mourned the loss of the former U.S. Senator from New Jersey.

Then Knight winced at the thought of the Vice-President actually coming into power. Knight never cared for Franklin Moore when he was governor of California and knew the man would be even more contemptible in a position of real power. Ana put Knight's mind at ease when she told him that Moore was killed just the previous week while examining damage done by terrorists in his hometown of Sacramento. It had been a suicide mission as a plane full of explosives crashed near where the President had been giving a speech.

His relief was quickly replaced by anger as he thought of the way the terrorists were ruining the planet he had been working so hard to save. He was momentarily relieved when Ana told her that the current President was Grant Esser, the former U.S. Senator from Nevada who had finished third in the primaries. Because Esser had been from a low-income working class family he had instilled that background into his political philosophy, as he was truly a man of the people. Knight knew that Esser was just the man that could help the United States rebuild when the turmoil was over and would offer a helping hand to the rest of the world. Yet it was important that Knight saw to it that Esser did not die.

It wasn't until June 3 that Knight had fully recovered from surgery although his metabolism allowed him to rehabilitate much faster than normal. Dr. Avery asked him if he wanted the scars removed and after thinking it over Knight decided to keep them as a reminder of his vulnerability and his time of weakness. He did, however, have the scars on his face removed because Ana pleaded with him to. During those months of recovery Ana had been of great comfort and support and her feelings toward him did not change even though she now was aware of the fact he was not an average man.

He was grateful that she was so understanding and began to cherish her all the more now that his mother was gone. He had been angered and devastated by the death of his mother, but grew to accept it after a couple of weeks. He realized that she was gone and it was impossible to bring her back. Yet he could extract revenge in her memory and vowed to avenge her death.

Over the next few days, he worked on and completed a project he wished he had finished years earlier. The project involved developing a force field that could be used by an individual. Years previous the Soviet government had developed a larger, primitive version of the force field that relied on tremendous amounts of energy to remain operational. It was proven to be too costly and they abandoned the project in 2019.

Knight knew that he had solved the power problem when he first developed the energy packs, but adapting a force field for individual use involved many obstacles he had to overcome. He cleared a major hurdle when he was able to make a force field that would be attracted to the person's DNA and it would bond with the person. When the person first activates the force field there is a slight tingling sensation that rushes through the entire body. After a few seconds the sensation disappears and the person can hardly notice that they are encased in a nearly impenetrable field that stands only five millimeters from the body. All manners of projectiles are useless, as are lasers, and most electric charges. Although Knight knew that the field could be shorted, the means to do so was beyond the technology of anyone else on Earth and he did not see it as a major problem.

The force field apparatus was attached to a belt for convenience and could be activated or deactivated by simply adjusting a switch. Due to the fact that each apparatus was very difficult to make and the procedure was extremely expensive, he only made four. One each for himself, Ana, Dr. Avery, and Han Li.

With that behind him, he set out on making a fabric that would be as indestructible as the metal he had developed. He wanted the fabric to have similar characteristics with the exception of conductivity so the wearer would not be vulnerable to electrocution. The task was finally accomplished due to the minimizing of the use of metallic thread and the major portion of the fabric was made of non-conductive elements such as carbon.   The weaving of the material was constructed in a geometric pattern that helped disperse the force of an impact against the clothing so the wearer could still function after being shot or hit and they would not endure deep bruising or fractured bones. A hood was also made that went with the suit so the head would also remain protected. A transparent shield attached to the front of the hood acted as protection, while allowing the wearer a unobstructed field of vision. The shield also acted as a filter so the wearer could breath clearly in any environment, no matter how polluted. Gloves were also made to go with the suit, although it was up to the individual as to when they wore the gloves as well as the hood.

The next step was to develop a line of superior weaponry. First, he developed two versions of a rapid-fire handgun. The first was larger and was intended for long range combat. It had a range of nine hundred meters and fired thirty-five shots per second. A holder for two of these weapons was attached to each thigh of the uniform. While there were many weapons that could fire at a faster rate, not many were more enduring for this weapon held 16,500 shots in the clip. The projectiles that came out of the weapon were very small but traveled at such a great velocity that each shot could penetrate one and one half meters of concrete. So for every shot that found it's target, there were two wounds guaranteed, even if the person was wearing body armor.

The second weapon was smaller and was designed for closer combat, as the range was two hundred meters. This weapon also fired thirty-five shots per second at the same velocity, but only held 6,700 shots in the clip. These weapons attached to holders on each fore arm.

He named the more powerful weapon the CK-900 and the other the CK-200. The names were derived by using his initials along with the maximum firing range of each weapon. Although he had originally had a computer select names for them at random, he felt it would be more appropriate to actually pick a name that had some relevance.

Another weapon he developed was a wrist laser. The unit is attached to either wrist and is activated by holding down three buttons simultaneously with the opposite hand. The tree button system was installed to prevent accidental firings; although once the mechanism was firing it could be set on automatic so the off hand could be freed up. The weapon was as accurate as the person could point and had a range of one hundred and fifty meters. It was basically a close range weapon and was useful in cutting through nearly any material. When it came to cutting the unit was capable of slicing through up to nine meters of the densest rock or titanium steel, whatever the situation called for. The settings could be altered to adjust the firing or cutting distance. The weapon was effective for up to fifty-five hours of use and had a gauge that showed exactly how much time was left on the charge.

The final product he made was a modification on a martial arts weapon, but he ended up being the only one who used it. He named them kacs, which were his initials backwards. Each one was a small round disk with a razor sharp edge and they could be tossed a maximum of seventy meters. What he liked most about these weapons was the fact that they reached their target silently so the victim had no warning.

With the weaponry developed and the uniforms made, Knight set out to form his own personal army. On July 2, Knight founded the Global Law Enforcement and Security Agency, which became known by its acronym: GLESA. That was also the same day that he announced to the world that he was still alive and released a statement that he would do everything in his power to stop the chaos caused by the terrorists.

In GLESA he planned on employing a combination of human and android personnel. Immediately he started recruiting the best four hundred individuals for the world over who were skilled in various levels of combat. Fifty-seven percent came from the United States, Great Britain, and the Soviet Union. The rest were from one hundred and eight of the remaining two hundred and five nations of the world.

In the meantime, Knight modified the design on some of his androids so they would be more efficient in combat. He installed a new sensory system that could scan five hundred meters in all directions simultaneously. The system could lock on four targets at the same time and the android was capable of firing at two of the targets at the same time and then instantly concentrate on the other two targets and fire. The tracking system would constantly be searching to fulfill the capacity of four targets. While the scanning system was limited to two hundred meters for a simultaneous scan, the unit was capable of being modified so the android could search in one direction at a time to find a target up to fifteen hundred meters away. The type of attack the android was under would be the determinant as to which scanning system the android used.

He made only three hundred and eight of the units for he only wanted to make the minimum needed in the least amount of time. One hundred of the units were to team up with his human recruits as the team leader. The other two hundred and eight were assigned to protect each of the world's leaders. While these units did possess human features, people were told they were androids so they would not under estimate their capabilities and so they would not be shocked when they functioned in combat.

The uniforms were black with a jagged red line that started at both shoulders and ran down each side to the bottom of the pant legs. Each man and android were assigned two CK-900 which attached to the side of each thigh, two CK-200's which clipped to the holders on each fore arm, and a laser unit which attached to the wrist of their writing hand. If the person was ambidextrous, such as Knight and the androids, then they had the option of wearing a laser unit on each wrist.

A communicator was on a band that interlinked with the laser unit on the wrist. The communicators had a range of sixteen miles to enable freedom of movement between agents and they also allowed Knight to track their movements as a satellite orbiting the planet picked up their signals. Another method of tracking the agents were several tiny chips that were within the fabric of the uniform that allowed Knight to monitor the movements of each agent no matter where they went on the planet.

They were divided into one hundred teams that consisted of one android and four humans. The androids served as the team leaders, but Knight was the supreme leader. He did allow each team to investigate using their judgments and could proceed without authorization from him. He believed in freethinking and this idea was instilled within the androids, so they were open to suggestions from the other team member. By July 20, he had teams investigating within each of the world's continents with the exception of Antarctica.

All had been quiet since July 9, when the terrorists assassinated a group of Saudi oil ministers holding a meeting on a yacht in the Persian Gulf. Sixteen bodies were recovered from the remains of the burning vessel. It was the first official site of investigation by his GLESA agents, only no major leads were found. With the terrorists becoming increasingly inactive, Knight felt that they might either be losing power or were being cautious because they did not know what to think about his organization.

Then on July 30, the terrorists struck again by detonating an explosive near a gas main in Cain, France. Several houses and a shopping mall were destroyed in the wealthy eighth district and over three hundred people lost their lives. Among the dead were sixty-two children of which twenty-four had been in a day car center in the mall. Two teams were on the scene within the hour because they had been investigating leads in nearby towns. They examined they scene of the explosion and discovered a partially destroyed detonator that had been used in the bomb. It was a piece of hardware of unique design and was known to be manufactured in only two countries: Italy and El Salvador.

That piece of evidence led to the eventual downfall of the Four Powers and their followers. Using computer records and detective, the detonator in question was purchased by a company in Italy as part of a larger shipment. The company in question was Valerian Construction and Excavation that had a legitimate use for the explosives. The owner was Paolo Valerian and he was known to have connections in organized crime yet he often seemed immune to prosecution due to the fact that his family had many members in high positions in the government. After interrogating Valerian, Knight came to the conclusion that the Italian businessman was also one of the mysterious Four Powers. Knight thought it was rather careless and sloppy planning by Valerian to become so closely involved in the terrorist acts by using explosives his company had purchased. Then again, no one had ever praised the man for being brilliant.

After further interrogations and investigation, Knight felt he had enough evidence to bring Valerian into custody and charged him with conspiracy. In an attempt to ease tensions between him and Italian authorities, he allowed Valerian to remain in the custody of the Rome police. The world was shocked and other law enforcement agencies were angry with GLESA for succeeding where they had failed. The fact that Valerian had staged an assassination attempt on his own life had diverted all suspicion from him previously. Valerian was a known paranoid and always traveled with a large entourage of security. While Valerian was wounded in the attack and many of his security force were killed, they were successful in eliminating the assassins. For a while, Knight felt a special bond with Valerian because they had been the only two to survive an assassination attempt by the terrorists. Yet he never did like the man and through further investigation he came to the conclusion that the attempt on Valerian's life had been carefully choreographed.

Over the next several days Knight encountered interference and lack of cooperation from the other law enforcement agencies of the world and several governments. There were several motives for their actions, but it basically came down to the fact that a new, upstart organization was better than they were and they did not want to appear to be incompetent in the eye's of the public. To overcome the problem, Knight arranged a special teleconference with the leaders that were against him. During the meeting he expressed his disappointment in their mature behavior, as they should have been taking the considerations of the public before their own. He said that he saw no reason why all of the agencies and authorities involved could not work together. He assured them that he had no intention of making any of their organizations obsolete, yet thought it would be for the better if he pushed them to improve their efficiency. In the end a compromise was reached although Knight knew that there was still much resentment against him and his agency.

Before the meeting Valerian had been held in the custody of the Italian authorities and they had been unsuccessful at obtaining any information from him after several interrogation sessions. With their new agreement of cooperation, the Italians allowed Knight to do what was needed to break Valerian's will. The factor that prodded the Italians to letting Knight have his way was the fact that the international media received a message that stated that the Big Four would rock the world on October 2 if Valerian was not released.

After two hours alone with Valerian Knight had what he needed. He had performed a brain scan on Valerian in which he copied what was basically the man's collective knowledge. Yet it would take another eight days to decode the information and to organize it in a chronological report. Since he had the information, he went against his better judgment and decided to allow them to release Valerian with surveillance.

As Valerian left the headquarters of the Rome police on September 23, a sniper killed him when he reached the bottom of the stairway. In a surprising turn of events, the Rome police were actually able to capture the fleeing sniper. The man had the appearance of a vagrant and neither his fingerprints nor DNA composite were on record in the international crime network computer. The man refused to take and was subsequently placed under heavy guard by the Rome police and an android GLESA agent. In the meantime Knight assigned a team to help investigate the identity of the assassin.

On September 30 Knight was able to find the information he desired from the brain programming of Valerian. The information he obtained would quicken the downfall of the terrorists for he had names, dates, and detailed descriptions of how the organization operated. He found the names and dates of all past and future assassination victims and the name of the person responsible for carrying out each task. He found his name and found that he had been rescheduled to be killed on October 2. It seemed to be a popular date for the terrorists and he tried to figure out why. He wondered if it was his death that was to shake the world or possibly there was something else planned. For some reason Valerian had not been made aware of anything special about October 2, so some decision must have been made in his absence.

All of the dates of attack followed a specific sequence that was familiar to Knight, but he had trouble recalling it. He decided not to worry about it until he had finished the decoding. Then he found another important piece of information that would aid him toward victory. Buried deep within the subconscious was the names of the other members of the Four Powers. The names of the other three were much more impressive than that of Valerian. The remaining three of the Powers: Bret Hardy, the English ambassador to the United States, Dmitri Baradin, a high ranking general in the Soviet army, and Sebastian Ruthvan, the director of recruiting for the Central Intelligence Agency.

He also found the names of several lesser people in the organization. Among the names was the name of the assassin assigned to Rome for the last two weeks. As he looked at the name, Knight wondered if the man in the cell was indeed John Alcott, the infamous Irish radical. Alcott had never been arrested but had never been shy about writing and phoning the press to claim responsibility for terrorist acts in the past. Knight was happy that he was able to get this information from Valerian, for the list in front of him would enable him to neutralize the organization and to have all of it's members on trial within two months.

Then a chill ran down his spine as he remembered the significance of the dates. Every single date was either a holiday on the unholy, satanic calendar or the birth dates and death dates of the thirty-two disciples of the devil that had been executed in Montreal, London, Paris, and New Orleans between 2006 and 2014. In his extensive reading over the years, that had been a topic that had interested him for some unknown reason and he cringed as he matched every date of terrorist action within the past year to those in his memory. He had read that each of those executed had been an admitted Satan worshipper and had freely killed for several years before their international cult was exposed and stopped by two clergymen: Fr. Jerry Da Ville of New Orleans and Rev. Jacob Bass of London. The two had banded together and vowed to stop the cult and each testified at all thirty-two trials with the information they had accumulated. Mysteriously, both men had died in their sleep in April of 2021. Now Knight wondered if they really had died of natural causes.

Could the guiding force behind the Four Powers have been the Satanic church? In a frantic effort to collaborate or dismiss such a notion, Knight searched the programming to find evidence that Valerian did worship the devil. When he found it the chills once again ran through him and he became momentarily paralyzed as he pondered the relevance of his discovery. Valerian had began following the way of the dark side in his late teens and Knight found references and descriptions of horrendously barbaric acts that the twisted fiend had done in his twenty years as a follower of the devil. To be dealing with an organization of minds as sick as this worried him. He could handle the possibility of an alien invasion, but the thought of an organization spurred on by the teachings of Satan disturbed him.

The day of October 2 arrived and Knight decided to be exceedingly cautious. Security was on alert at his home and the sensors scanning around his home and the Knight Enterprises building failed to pick up anything unusual. He told Ana to wear her force field at all times that day and he assigned an android to guard her to ease his mind.

That day he was scheduled to address a panel of world leaders from several of the more powerful nations. At that point he had not yet revealed his discovery of the satanic factor and had decided that the meeting would not be the appropriate place to bring it up without further evidence. The meeting was in the Capital Building in Washington DC and since he was in charge of security, he did not want to be late.

For the sake of the meeting and out of respect for the world leaders, he discarded his GLESA uniform and wore a tuxedo. His force field belt was concealed by the cummerbund and he had a CK-200 gun secured to each of his ankles. He would have liked to have worn a wrist laser, but it would not fir under the sleeve of his jacket. He made a note that he would have to modify the laser for future occasions.

He arrived at the Capital Building at 1:15 p.m. for the meeting scheduled at two. At the top of the stairs he saw two men in GLESA uniforms and even he could not tell if they were human or android. Several secret service agents were also visible in the immediate area. As he reached the door, the agents told him that there was a vehicle coming up the street at a high rate of speed. It was a van and the side door slid open as gunfire echoed off the stone walls. He saw a few of the secret service agents fall to the ground as he felt a slight tapping on his face, chest, and stomach. He was greatly relieved that the force field had not faltered. Dropping to one knee, he takes a firearm in each hand as both his agents return fire. He joins in their deadly session of target practice. One of the agents was using his laser and had removed the front passenger wheel and disabled the engine. Two men emerged from the back of the van with machineguns in hand and were promptly cut to ribbons by the superior firepower. A bullet hit the gas tank and the van went up in flames. It was one time that Knight was glad that some one had not rendered his services to convert a car from gas powered to electric.

From the interior of the building he could hear a man shouting, and another of his agents emerged through the door. He said that there were reports of bombings in London, Montreal, New Orleans, and Paris within the last hour. Hundreds were dead and the damage was tremendous. For Knight, that news solidified his theory that the terrorists were sponsored by the Satanic church. He told the agent that had just spoken to him to go in and apologize to the world leaders for him that he would be unable to attend the meeting and to give the excuse that he was shaken about being shot at. The members of the panel should also be informed that he would relay all necessary information to each of them later in the day.

It puzzled Knight as to why they wanted him dead so badly. There was the fact that he was now the richest man in the world, due to the fact that the terrorists had eliminated the five on the list ahead of him. It seemed to be one of their priorities to eliminate all the rich elite. There was also the fact that he had founded GLESA and he was sure that was something that did not sit too well with them. Yet deep down he felt that there was another motive that he may never know.

He returned to his home to think. If the terrorists had indeed been motivated by wealth, then the fall of their leaders would stop the movement. But anytime a movement has the support of a religious organization, no matter how legitimate, then the roots of the movement would run deep and would not be easily stopped. He decided that he would go to Rome the following day to see John Alcott. There was the possibility he could get additional information as to the motives of the organization out of him. To his disappointment, when Knight contacted Rome to notify them of his arrival, they informed him that Alcott had taken his own life earlier that day by crushing his throat on the edge of the toilet. Knight came to the conclusion that even his superior mind could not comprehend the capabilities of someone who saw the world through a warped perception.

On October 3, the hunt began for the animals responsible for putting the world in upheaval. All were apprehended by December 1 with the exception of Sebastian Ruthvan. He had eluded authorities and then disappeared. Rumor has it that he had escaped to South Africa, but Knight knew he could be anywhere in the world. He would be difficult to find because Ruthvan was a survival expert and could live in seclusion for years. His only hope for catching Ruthvan was if he made a mistake or if one of his infiltrators happened across him. Both were unlikely to happen although Knight hoped for the best.

Then on December 5 a bomb leveled a convent in the Andes Mountains of Argentina and sixteen nuns were killed. The incident might have never been called to Knight's attention had an envelope not been nailed to a near by tree which was addressed to Clayton Knight. When he opened it, a deep fear touched his soul and he dropped the letter and envelope immediately upon reading it. The contents of the letter consisted of a single sentence and a signature.

"I'll be back! Sebastian."

The letter was written in blood and tests determined that it was indeed the blood of Sebastian Ruthvan. Knight wonders how long he would be looking over his shoulder in fear of the madman. It would be best, he decided if he could purge the entire episode from his conscience as quickly as possible and to move on with his life.

Chapter four

That Christmas Knight and Ana decided they wanted to start a family. He made the decision that he did not want to raise a family in the frantic paced life of the east coast, so he decided to move operations west. Nebraska was where he decided to locate, for it would allow him to return to his roots and would be a serene atmosphere to raise a family.

The move also involved relocating the main headquarters for both Knight Enterprises and GLESA. A logical choice seemed to be to place both in Omaha; an average sized city of 920,000. Through the opportunities brought by Knight's relocating in Omaha, the city eventually doubled in size to 1.78 million people. Knight made arrangements to purchase two large tracts of land, which were both in the interior of the city. Both locations held old shopping malls that would be razed. The same company owned both centers so negotiations were brief once he offered them an exaggerated price that they willingly agreed to. Once the negotiating was complete, he immediately had a construction team survey each location to begin plans for the new buildings.

Then he went to a real estate broker to search for a location that would suit his specifications for a new house. Since it was the middle of winter, he had no desire to rush all over the state to inspect each tract of land, but rather settled on the comprehensive brochures on each property. When he saw a particular deal that involved 10,000 acres of land that were being offered by Blem Farms, a corporate farming organization. The land was originally going to be offered to a Japanese company, but he was determined to have it and offered a purchase price quadruple what had been previously offered.

The land was expansive enough to hold a small town. In a way, that was what Knight had in mind. The land was in Saunders County between the towns of Wahoo and Mead. He liked the fact that it would not be a great distance from Omaha. He felt that life in the Midwest would be better for raising a family and the pace would be less of a strain on him.

When Knight returned to Boston after his purchasing excursion, the estimates on the cost and time to build the office building and law enforcement building were ready. The office building could be finished within ninety-five to one hundred and fifteen days at a cost of 160.3 million dollars. It was to be forty-five stories tall with four sub-basements. To build the GLESA building it would only take seventy-five to eighty-five days at a cost of 112.7 million dollars. It was to be only twelve stories tall with only two sub-basements.

He later received the estimates for completing his residence as to his specifications. The time frame to complete the residence and other additions was two hundred and five to two hundred and twenty-eight days. That was longer than he would have liked, but since he had lived in Boston for so many years, the wait would be tolerable. The cost of construction at the estate would total

2.7 billion dollars and he thought it would be worth every penny.

Both decided that they wanted a large family. She wanted one because she came from a large family and he felt it was something he always wanted due to the fact he was an only child. To get the family off to a quick start they consented in using a fertility drug called sisozinval. The drug had been in use since 2028 and had been highly successful in producing multiple births. Couples that wished to get a large family in the shortest time possible commonly used it. Although fourteen percent of the users had single births, seventy-eight percent had twins and the remaining eight- percent had from three to six babies. Knight also liked the fact that in ninety-three percent of the multiple births the children were fraternal, not identical. The idea of having children with different physical characteristics was more appealing to him from the standpoint of lack of confusion. Yet he was also receptive to the possibility of having children that were identical. On February 8, 2041, tests showed that Ana was pregnant with five young ones in the womb.

It was decided that they would continue to lead their normal lives up until the babies were born. After that, they would see what the circumstances were before they made any further decisions. In the meantime, Ana remained at the helm of Knight Enterprises.

That February Ana began to act on one of Knight's childhood wishes by using Knight Enterprises as the instrument to fulfill the task. On February 15 she put in bids to takeover both Myplex Foods International and Blem Farms. Those two organizations were the two largest corporate farm operators in the world and owned eighty-eight percent of the farm land in the United States and thirty-two percent of the farmland in the rest of the world. By March 10 the board at Myplex agreed to sell for the price of two hundred and forty-nine billion dollars. The following day Blem Farms consented to an offer of two hundred and thirty-one billion dollars. The sum of four hundred and eighty billion was paid in full, leaving Knight Enterprises with only forty-eight billion in liquid assets.

That still left Knight Enterprises at number nine in the world, down from their previous mark of number one. Yet Knight felt that if he was to accomplish his goals, the level of liquidity of the company would have to surpass the trillion-dollar mark. It was a point that had never been achieved by an individual person or company and only by two nations for a brief period of time. The challenge of reaching that goal appealed to him and he planned to strive for it within the foreseeable future.

He then instructed Ana to make an attempt to secure DEG Systems of Tokyo, Japan. That company owned eight percent of the farmland in America, but they also had sixty-eight percent of the fertile land of the planet in their control. He knew that a total payment for such a venture was not realistic, but instead had Ana push for a payment schedule with Knight Enterprises offering twenty-five billion in good faith as the down payment. By May 17, an agreement was reached where DEG Systems would come under Knight Enterprise's control for the sum of 663 billion dollars. A total of twenty-five years was given to pay in full, but until that time a few chosen individuals from DEG Systems would sit on the board of directors at Knight Enterprises. Knight planned on having the debt paid off in a year.

If Clayton Knight had been a tyrant, owning over ninety-nine percent of the world's farmland would have put him in a position to manipulate the governments and people of the world. That possibility led to many days of panic in the private chambers of the world leaders. However, he had no intention of employing such cruel tactics. The fact was he was already manipulating the world just fine without resorting to such methods. His goal was to finally get DEG Systems paid off and to then disband the farm corporations so he could return the farms to the people. Although Sharp Ventures of Houston, Texas owned the remaining farmland in the United States, it was in his plans to force that company out of business within the year so they could not present a problem. With the revised anti-trust laws put in place a few years earlier, Knight Enterprises was free to grow as long as they stayed within the lax new guidelines.

To eliminate his debt and to reach his financial goal, Knight felt he would have to expand his mining operations. Although there were still plenty of hidden treasures on Earth, he felt it would best suit his purpose if he searched for new riches elsewhere. TO accomplish that, he placed mining camps on the moon, mars, and in the asteroid belt.

By July 22 he was beginning operations on the moon and within a week a deposit of tin was found below the surface that had an estimated value of sixty-five million dollars. It was just the beginning and Knight was happy that all the previous survey teams that ever landed on the moon had equipment too primitive to pick up the hidden riches below the surface. The rest of the solar system was open domain and he was now willing to exploit the fact that he was the only one capable of capitalizing on it.

A ship reached Mars on August 5 and the android crew had camp set up by August 26. Knight was only using androids in his mining operations as not to subject humans to unforeseen dangers. There was also the factor that androids had greater abilities that would enable everything to progress much faster. Another factor was that it would cost him a fortune just to keep the human workers supplied with food, water, and oxygen. The first mine to strike it rich found a bromine deposit on September 6 that was worth only 4.51 million dollars. He figured that every little bit would help and in the long run, enough small deposits would enable him to pay off the debt.

Six mining teams were sent to different sectors of the asteroid belt. He decided he would start with only six and if they were successful, he would send more. That date approached sooner than Knight dreamed because teams one and four found deposits of tungsten and mercury on their first day, September 23. The tungsten deposit found by team one had an estimated value of three hundred and eighty million dollars. The mercury deposit found by team four was worth about seventy-five million dollars. On September 25 team six found a deposit of zinc valued at two hundred and eighty-five million dollars. The jackpot was hit on September 28 when team two found a huge deposit of gold and silver worth in the neighborhood of five hundred and seventy-five billion dollars.

Knight was ecstatic for everything was happening at even a quicker pace than he had imagined. On October 3, he sent a ship full of more androids that stopped at various locations with materials to building mining and processing centers. He thought it would be better to process it in space so they could transport more riches in a pure state than make more trips with bulky ore. At some point he figured that his net worth would grow so large that even he would have trouble calculating it. The amount did not matter to him, as long as he had the necessary funds to continue with his plans.

On October 21, 2041, Clayton Knight's life changed for the better when he became a father. All five of the babies were boys and they were born at 4:05, 4:06, 4:16, 4:18, and 4:27 in the early morning hours. Ana did not feel any pain because the Herit method was used in which the patient is given a low-voltage shock to the pain center of the brain and the patient is devoid of most feeling for nearly forty minutes. The practice had been a tradition in childbirth since 2025, although it had been developed by Dr. Amerigo Herit in 2018, and was used in ninety-seven percent of all hospital births.

All five boys were healthy and had different physical characteristics. Both factors pleased Knight tremendously. The boys were named in order of their birth: Franklin William, Jacob Alexander, Vincent Daniel, Henry Thomas, and Christopher Martin. Although those were their proper names, to Knight they would be Frank, Jake, Vince, Hank, and Chris. He had always preferred informality and hoped such an ideology would help to build a close bond with his children.

On November 10, it was discovered that Ana was expecting again, that time with four children. By that time they were living on their estate in Nebraska and she had taken a leave of absence for an indefinite period of time from Knight Enterprises. Knight had given her the option of running the company from home, but she decided she wanted to rest and to take time to be with the children. He told her she could stay away from the business for as long as she wanted because he and Han Li could keep things under control.

She used much of the time getting accustomed to the new surroundings and all the estate had to offer. The size of their home took her by surprise because Knight had kept everything a secret. The design of the Knight estate was actually the fulfillment of another of Knight's childhood dreams.

The house stood in the center of the estate and was made of white stone and red brick. It was five stories high with two basement levels. On the top story there were two offices that were connected by a bathroom, a large library, and several storage rooms. There were a total of twelve bedrooms and six bathrooms on the fourth floor and twelve bedrooms and twelve bathrooms on the third floor. Because the master bedroom was so large, there were only eight bedrooms and eight bathrooms on the second floor. There were also several closets and storage rooms on each of the middle three floors. The main floor was larger than the upper floors because three of the rooms extended past the main body of the house. Those three were the ballroom, the banquet hall, and the exercise facility.

The main hallway, the ballroom, and the banquet hall were all designed in similar fashion. All had classic marble floors, oak woodwork, and crystal chandeliers for lighting. The main hallway had three sets of double oak doors which lead to the ball room, the living room, and another hall way which has an elevator. As one enters the hall way through the front door, the doors to the ball room are on the left, the doors to the living room are to the right, and the doors to the elevator are straight ahead under the balcony connecting the duel staircases.

The ballroom has a capacity to hold a standing crowd of one thousand people and there was plenty of room to dance if there was a smaller crowd. As a person enters the ballroom there is a stage to the left, two pairs of French doors to the far right, and a descending staircase and an escalator straight ahead on the far side of the room. The stairs and escalator descend down to an underground parking garage that had six levels and could accommodate a total of 1200 vehicles. The French doors lead to the banquet hall that has eight long, oak table capable of sitting thirty each. Knight and Ana hoped that it would be used quite often in the future when they played hosts to parties and other gatherings.

In the banquet hall there were two more oak doors. One leads to a kitchen and the other leads to a hallway with twenty bathrooms. The kitchen was only one of three in the residence with another on the other side of the house and another being in the basement. The one by the banquet hall was the largest because it had to accommodate more cooking.

In the main hallway the right hand doors lead to the living room which has two fireplaces on the left and two large picture windows on the right, as one enters the room. In between the windows sits a large monitor which can be used to watch television, close circuit programming, or for a videoconference. On the far side of the room are pair of sliding glass doors that lead to a bar. Although Knight and Ana do not drink they do like to be good hosts to those who do. At several positions scattered through out the room are seven davenports, eighteen padded chairs, two reclining chairs, four coffee tables, and fourteen end tables. A decorator had arranged the room because Knight knew he had little talent in that particular field.

To the right of the second fireplace there was a door which leads to the dining room. The doors to the left of the bar leads to a game room and the door to the right of the bar led to another hallway. The hallway held three doors, two on the right and one on the left. The first door on the right led to a bathroom, the second to a small library, and the door on the left went into the game room. At the end of the hall way there was another elevator

The game room consisted of six billiards tables, one snooker table, three bumper pool tables, three table tennis tables, two dart boards, a skee ball alley, six pin ball machines, three dozen arcade games, and every board game ever invented stacked alphabetically on a wall shelf. The game room was in a way an attempt by Knight to make up for his abnormal childhood and he wanted to make sure his children did not go without anything he may have missed out on. A sliding glass door on the far side of the room leads outside where there was a patio and an Olympic sized swimming pool.

The remaining two thirds of the main floor consisted of another dining area by which the family kitchen was several hallways, closets, bathrooms, and the exercise facility. The exercise facility was very large and contained nearly every piece of exercise equipment invented. There were weight machines, free weights, exercise bikes, rowing machines, stair climbers, gymnastic equipment, a wading pool, hot tub, and dozens of electronic monitoring devices. Around the perimeter of the facility a three-lane track was laid. Another feature was a state of the art stereo system which had most of the speakers located near the weight lifting equipment. Since Knight enjoyed working out so much, he wanted to create an atmosphere that would enable him to work out for two or three hours a day without becoming bored or stressed.

The first level of the basement continued on the sports theme. There was a regulation sized basketball court; an indoor Olympic sized pool, a four-lane bowling alley, a court for racquetball or handball, a tennis court, and two locker rooms. A large target range that could accommodate either firearms or archery was also present and Knight encouraged Ana to use this as often as she had time. That level also contained two gigantic climate control units that maintained the house at the comfortable seventy-degree level year round.

The first basement level could be accessed by the two elevators or by one of four stairways. The four stairways only extended from the main level to the first basement level while the two elevators reached the first basement level one all of the upper levels of the house. There were also four stairways, which only led from the main floor up to the second floor. A single stairwell located near the central elevator could access all five of the above ground levels. Knight liked the design of the elaborate staircase system, yet often used the elevator for the sake of time.

The lowest basement level could only be accessed by the central elevator and by a secret tunnel system. The bottom level contained a laboratory that enabled Knight to work on his projects without having to always travels to Omaha to use the lab in Knight Enterprises. In was an exact duplicate of the lab in Knight Enterprises and had a team of androids on duty around the clock watching after the computers and his projects.

The laboratory and the top level of the house were security restricted. While the central stairwell and elevator did lead to the top level, access could not be obtained without the proper security code. Only those within his inner circle were given the codes for reasons of security and secrecy. Both of the two security levels also housed monitors that showed the views of more than one thousand-surveillance camera within the house and on the estate grounds.

The monitors in the basement were constantly being watched by four androids while those in his office remained concealed behind a retractable wooden panel until he wished to view them. The monitors in his office took up an entire wall as the entire wall slides up into the ceiling. He was very security conscience for the purpose of protecting his important research and his family.

The rest of the estate was as impressive as the main residence. In the remainder of the estate there was an apartment complex for security personnel and other employees, a gymnasium, four ball diamonds, a football field, a fishing pond, a water tower, a power center, another parking garage, a museum, a private zoo, eight tennis courts, an air strip, three airplane hangers, a heliport, an eighteen hole golf course, and several interior roads. The landscape was cluttered with various types of trees, shrubbery, rocks, and flowers. During the winter the appearance of the landscape is greatly diminished, but during the other seasons it is a wondrous sight. Even the network of roads that connects the estate, while extensive, it is not enough to take away from the lands natural beauty.

A four-meter high stone wall ran along the entire perimeter of the estate. The wall was one meter thick and on top of it was capped by an electrified platform and a dome of electrified wire mesh that reached an additional one-meter high. Motion sensors and surveillance cameras were positions all along the exterior and interior of the wall.

While the main bulk of the estate security force consisted of androids, about twenty percent were human. The entire security staff wore the GLESA uniform and the leader was a former CIA man named Jason Wolf. The security personnel carried the standard GLESA weaponry and were aided by a laser system that popped out of the ground like underground sprinklers. The four estate gates are patrolled by one android and three humans, one of which was in charge of a German Shepherd attack dog. The dog was mainly for visual effect, although Knight saw some advantages to their presence. In all there was a force of four hundred androids on patrol around the clock and eighty humans that split the time in shifts of six hours.

The tenants of the apartment complex included the eighty security guards, sixteen maintenance personnel, twelve landscape specialists, eight cooks, fourteen maids, two chauffeurs, a butler, three nurses, and a doctor. The doctor was basically employed to take care of the employees because Dr. Avery was the Knight family physician. There was also the fact that Dr. Avery chose to live in Omaha, so it was comforting to Knight that Dr. Kenneth Smith was on the estate in case the was an extreme emergency and neither Knight nor Dr. Avery could be reached in time. Since Knight had greater medical knowledge than either Dr. Avery or Dr. Smith, although he did not have a medical license nor did he attend medical school, he felt he could handle any emergencies within his own family if he were present. In the future Knight also planned to hire a governess for the children when Ana decided she would return to work.

The gymnasium was for the employees and they could use any of the other estate fitness features when they were not on duty. Within the gymnasium were three levels. The top level had a regulation basketball court, two locker rooms, two saunas, and an indoor tennis court. The second level contained a swimming pool that was larger than Olympic sized and a small weight room. A much larger weight room was on the bottom level, as well as eight courts for either racquetball or handball. Knight wanted his employees to stay fit and to be occupied with something self enhancing when they in their free hours. Since they were also given access to use the golf course that was where Dr. Smith spent most of his time.

The golf course started with the first tee only fifteen meters from the back of the main residence and the remaining seventeen holes crisscrossing the middle of the estate. The eighteenth hole was twenty meters from the first tee and only thirty-five meters from the main residence. To the east of the house was the outdoor pool and east of that were the tennis courts. On the left or west side of the house was an open field of grass and flowers that concealed the underground parking garage which had it's entrance twenty meters down along the main driveway. In front of the house was a circular driveway that was showcased by a granite fountain inside it's crescent.

The fountain was five meters high and had a Christmas tree appearance. It could shoot water two meters into the air from a spout at the top and the water then cascaded down each of the sixteen levels. In the winter the fountain could remain operational by using heated water, although Knight thought it was best to turn it off during snowstorms and other severe weather. At night the fountain was enhanced by a lighting system that could either be normal or multi-colored.

Within the estate roads were grids that kept the temperature regulated so the snow would melt in the winter and they would not be heat collectors in the summer. To compliment the roads, there was also an elaborate underground tunnel system. One tunnel led from the basement of the apartment complex to the underground-parking garage of the main residence. That enabled the workers to travel to the house even during poor weather.

The remaining tunnels required security clearance to use as they were concealed behind locked panels. One tunnel led from the lab to a network of tunnels that led to the residence parking garage, the hangers, the museum, the zoo and the power plant. Another tunnel led from the parking garage to a secluded part of the estate near the perimeter wall. The purpose of this tunnel was so he could go to that pre-chosen isolated location quickly if he wanted to be alone and think.

On the north side of the estate was the hangers and airstrip. Within one hanger was a six seat, two-engine passenger plane. Another held two twelve seat luxury jets.

The third held a space shuttle capable of holding one hundred people if necessary. To the east of the hangers is a heliport that serves as the resting-place for A-1000 surveillance copter that sits under a transparent, retractable dome. The airstrip extends west from the hangers and is four hundred meters long. Tall evergreens run along the edge of the strip to conceal it from the sky, unless someone is directly overhead.

The private museum that Knight cherished was only smaller than the Smithsonian in regard to the volume of its contents. The building itself was an architectural masterpiece because each floor of the seven-story building covered ten square acres. The mining scanning equipment he had crisscrossed the globe with discovered much of the historical contents. The result was many exhibits on cultures through out the world over a span of the years. There were also biological exhibits on animal and plant life.

In the lowest of three basement levels was the exhibit, which he was most proud of: a visual display on the evolution of all three modes of transportation. Three modes were classified by whether they traveled by land, air or water. Although many of the exhibits were models, he had several actual examples of cars, planes, boats, two trains, a small submarine, and a space capsule he had recovered from the bottom of the Atlantic Ocean. Two of the boats he was most proud of were a Spanish galleon from the year 1595 and a Chinese junk from 1720. The contents of the museum were constantly increasing and he often lent exhibits to museums around the world for the public to view. Yet when he did lend out an exhibit, he provided the security for he had no wish to lose any of his priceless collection. The contents of the museum alone put the financial net worth of Knight in the hundreds of billions.

Another feature of the estate was the one thousand-acre complex that housed a private zoo that housed examples of every animal known to man outside of the insect world. He also did have an extensive collection of insects but did not hope to collect every species for that would be a venture that would be too time consuming to attempt. While there were laws against his having many of the animals, he knew they were much safer under his supervision, than in the wild, or in a lesser facility. While the exhibits were mainly for pleasure, he did some work with the animals and had been successful in getting some of the rarer animals to breed.

To accommodate the number of animals he had in a limited amount of space, he again used a combination of above ground and subterranean levels. He wished each animal to have spacious quarters as natural to his or her original habitat as possible. The pens were climate controlled to simulate the weather of each animal's home region and plant life native to the animals past
Were also placed within the landscaped environments. During the months of good weather the larger animals were allowed to roam in the outdoors.

The zoo was another testament of the skill of Knight's construction crew because he had become more daring in the number of levels in each complex. The structures ranged from ten to fifteen levels high and from ten to twenty deep. Below the subterranean levels, he had enormous tanks constructed, which held millions of gallons of water. He had tanks that held both fresh and salt water. Within these hundreds of tanks, he placed thousands of varieties of fish, ranging from guppies to the great white shark. He also placed water-loving mammals such as dolphins and porpoises in their own special tanks. Within the largest of the tanks he created special environments in which he placed the five species of whales, including the monstrous blue whales.

The tanks were one thousand meters deep to enable the whales to dive to comfortable depths and there were ten meters of oxygen rich air at the top of the tanks for the whales to breathe. The extra space was also to allow the whales to jump out of the water if they desired. The whales had some freedom of movement as the tanks were five hundred meters long and two hundred meters wide and even the blue whale rarely exceeded forty meters in length. He knew that the radical environmentalist groups would go into a frenzy if they found out about his captives, yet he did not care for the animals were safer in his zoo than to fend against the poachers and the pollution.

Near the zoo was another underground parking garage that contained an automobile collection that Knight had assembled. The two types of vehicles in the collection were sports cars and luxury models. He had every make and model ever made which fell into those two categories. The collection consisted of thousands of cars and Knight was considering adding additional levels so he could expand the storage level to make certain that he always had space to keep the collection up to date.

When it came to collecting Knight had a driving obsession that pushed him until the collection was complete. That was the case whether it was cars, coins, stamps, or the animals. His coin and stamp collections were on display in the museum, where they were arranged chronologically by nation.

Knight was proud of his estate because it was not only his home, but it also served as a monument to him and was a symbol of his successes. Although he was extremely intelligent, he still had an ego that had to be satisfied. His residence and the rest of the estate were constructed to his precise specifications. It was with that same meticulousness that he hoped to change the world into the image he thought was best.

That did not mean that Knight wanted to rule the world. Far from it. All he wanted to accomplish was to change things for the better and to establish a foundation from which civilizations could build for years to come. He also wanted to prepare the planet for the alien invasion while allowing people to continue with their normal lives. In all of his years of research everything followed the premise that the end result of whatever he was working on should benefit the world as a whole.

He realized that a few individuals would not benefit by his work, but they were often out of the mainstream in the fringe that included the fanatics and radicals. Through out history he noticed that governments and businesses were started by individuals with the intentions of helping the community as a whole, yet in the long run they strayed from their original goals and became primarily concerned with the welfare of the organization. Entities created by people, such as democratic governments and business corporations, often moved away from a focus on the people and toward the advancement of the interests of the entity. It did not take long for things to get out of control and the original objectives are forgotten. The people that come into power in later generations, whether it was in business or government, often had little perspective as to how the entity interacted with society and before long they are making decisions that are hurting the people that originally had been helped.

That was the scenario that Knight wanted to be careful to avoid. He knew that power corrupted, yet he always tried to keep focused on his objectives and not to stray from the imaginary path that would enable him to reach his goals. While he knew many people saw him as a power hungry fiend, he did not let those judgments interfere with his decision making process. If he did begin to falter in that regard, he hoped that Ana and Han would feel they were in a position to tell him so.

In the December of 2041, Knight started an extensive research program that involved himself, Dr. Avery, and Han Li. Since everything was running smoothly in the Asian sector, Knight felt it was more important to have Han's scientific expertise with him rather than behind a desk-performing mind numbing paper shuffling tasks. The project dealt with genetic research in both the fields of animal and plant life. Dr. Avery was in charge of the animal research phase and Han directed the progress of the plant research. Knight offered his input to both projects as his busy schedule allowed. While Knight had many secondary, long-range goals, the immediate purpose of the project was to gain insights on cell structure so that they could be stimulated to grow and multiply upon request.

The team led by Han was the first to make a breakthrough and it enabled them to take a major step toward their goal. What they discovered was a process where the plant could be chemically stimulated to accelerate the growth rate. Once the procedure was perfected, it was used to enable food crops to mature much quicker. The reagent they invented was called hanliobital in honor of Han and it could be applied in the form of a liquid spray or in a solidified granule that was mixed with fertilizer. The liquid form had a greater effect on the plants due to immediate contact with higher dosage intake. The drug that had the most similar reaction in humans was a steroid, although haniobital actually increased the growth maturity process while steroids only enabled the human user to gain bulk faster.

Through experimentation, they found that they could make a plant grow at any rate they wanted, within certain limitations, depending on the dosage and the frequency of applications. Depending on the plant, maturity could be reached up to five times quicker than the normal growth rate of a plant without stimulants. The result was that it was possible to produce three to five food crops in the time it had previously been limited to one a season. A drawback was soil erosion, but Knight helped them develop a fertilizer that was actually a manufactured version of topsoil. The fertilizer was applied to the field before each new crop was planted and it ultimately counteracted the effects of erosion by allowing the environment to keep many of its natural nutrients.

The product was on the market by the spring of 2043. That was also the time period in which Knight Enterprises had relinquished control of the farms over to individual farming families. While Knight offered any help the farmers needed they were free to operate however each independent owner saw fit.

Knight saw both the positive and negative sides of his plant research and their impacts on the world. The most obvious benefit was that it would finally eliminate world hunger, for increased crop production would enable the farmers to produce enough to easily feed the 9.3 billion citizens of the planet. With a farmer producing three to five crops a year rather than one, they would be insured against one or two bad crops due to bad weather or other factors. Another benefit was the production of clothing could increase because the crops that were used to make the materials could be increased. A third benefit would be an increase in lumber supply, for even trees could be stimulated to grow three to five times faster.

Another positive benefit dealing with the trees was that planting trees in areas that had been damaged by floods or fire could restore the ecology system. The additional trees would also help counter the pollution and other influences that had decreased the levels of oxygen in the atmosphere. The environment could be restored to the shape of years previous in a short period of time and areas that become damaged due to natural or human causes would not have to remain so for extended periods of time.

In the short run, Knight predicted there would be an unique situation where the world would be overcome by drastic deflation where prices would fall at an incredible rate. The period would not last longer than three or four months and when the fall was complete the economic base of the planet would be much stronger. During that period of falling prices, several businesses would consider folding, but Knight Enterprises would guarantee financial backing to any entity that needed help during the troubled period. When it was over, inflation would again return, although the rate and impact would not be nearly so great as in the years previous.

On the flip side of the plant growth issue was the negative impact from the drug world. Knight was fully aware of the fact that the stimulate would make it's way into the hands of drug growers despite precautions against such. The results would be the growers would be able to produce more crops that would allow more drugs to be available, the prices would drop, and the poison would be much more accessible. That meant that there might be an epidemic of drug use like the one in the 1980's and 1990's. Yet this epidemic would likely be worse because the world was still recovering from the chaos that took place in 2040 and would be more vulnerable to such diversions.

Since Knight thought the positive aspects far out weighed the negative, he went ahead in marketing and producing the product. The prospect of feeding those who had long known hunger was far more important to him than the possibility of someone being stupid enough to be lured into using something so addictive and dangerous. Yet he knew there were many people in that category and his only chance in protecting them from their weaknesses was to expand the GLESA organization and attempt to combat the situation.

After the turmoil of 2040 was resolved, Knight managed to link GLESA with the United Nations as their trouble shooting force. If there was a crime-taking place against humanity by either terrorists or anti-government forces, teams of GLESA agents were deployed to resolve the situation. That was also the case if one nation unjustly attacked another in an act of aggression. Under that scenario the GLESA agents were called upon to capture the leadership of attacking nation to be tried before the World Court. Until the leadership was captured, the forces of GLESA were deployed to protect the victim nation and were free to wreck havoc with the invading force. It was a good method to keep the peace and the imposing stature of Knight's organization was often enough to act as a deterrent.

When Knight decided to expand the organization, he increased the force to ten thousand field agents, with only one thousand being androids. He also increased the number of non-combat personnel to fifteen thousand for positions such as researchers, investigators, maintenance personnel, and clerical workers. While his was still not the largest organization of its type in the world, it was by far the best.

He also began infiltrating hundreds of androids into the crime world. They were to protect their cover at all costs, but were not allowed to kill innocent people. He did, however, allow them to kill other members of the crime element. Also if there were a situation that would involve the killing of an innocent person or persons, the infiltrator had orders to kill the criminal or criminals. That was the only time they would blow their cover and would subsequently return for reassignment with a new identity and appearance.

Knight saw life as a precious commodity, and while he realized that humans stood high on the later, he felt that the lesser life forms also had rights to live. He viewed the creatures of the Earth as all being equal under God. Yet if one of them had harmful tendencies toward the rest, such as a rabid dog or termite, then that creature had to be eliminated for the good of the whole. Following that ideology, he saw a person that was willing to cause deadly harm toward others as no better than a diseased rodent that needed to be exterminated. He held on to his beliefs and did not care if anyone agreed with him because he knew that his way would ultimately lead to the improvement of the entire social system.

Knight did use influence to push his views on the nation's lawmakers and was able to bring about several changes inspired by the events of 2040. First was the implementation of lie detectors as a verification of the truthfulness and validity of all testimony in a trial. The idea had been first introduced in 1996, but public opinion led to the abandonment of the experiment. With the advancements in sensory technology, it was difficult to dispute the accuracy rating of one hundred percent when it was used to obtain truthful testimony. The results of the readings went a long way in determining whether a person was guilty or innocent and it also cut back on court time.

If a person was found guilty, they would serve out their sentence in a penal institution. The policy of probation was abolished and the standards by which individuals obtained parole were changed. Under the new guidelines, an individual could only gain parole after ninety percent of their sentence had been served and they had taken place in a self-improvement program. The process of appeals also changed. It was stated that an individual was limited to one appeal and the proceedings had to take place within one month of the original sentence.

The punishments decreed at the trial may range from serving one day to life. If the individual was sentenced to life then there was no chance of parole. There were also no more multiple life sentences because they were guaranteed to spend their life in prison and it was redundant to say he would remain after he finished his first sentence. Time served in jail no longer counted toward the time they would serve in the sentence, so if they were sentenced to only one day, they would have to remain one more day.

The penalty of death was also considered for crimes committed against others. The determining factors in considering the death penalty were the brutality involved, the number of victims, the extent of remorse by the criminal, past criminal history, and the evidence against the accused. The use of lie detectors was most useful in these types of trials. The crimes punishable by death were murder, rape, second offense child molestation, and second offense contributor to child pornography.   Murder was condensed to a single category, with the terms manslaughter, first degree, and second degree being eliminated. Even if it was accidental, the circumstances brought out in court would be the determinant as to what the sentence would be. Rape, whether against a woman or a man, is viewed as a tremendous violation of an individual and would be considered an offense punishable by death if there were brutality involved or if the offender violated more than one victim. Yet no matter what the circumstances involved, the minimum sentence for rape was twenty-five years. Child molestation and child pornography were viewed as horrendous affronts to the development of the young individuals because the young ones involved were often too young to defend themselves and were often scarred emotionally and psychologically for life. The minimum sentence for either of these crimes was twenty years. The appeal process for any of the capital offenses was the standard one-month. Yet if there were no grounds for appeal, the guilty party would be executed within one week of sentencing.

Besides the addition of lie detectors, there were other changes in the judicial process. Each court had five judges to hear testimony, unless it was a jury trial and then there was only one. If it were a non-jury trial, a decision up to the accused, then the five judges would make a decision among themselves with a majority ruling the deciding factor. Whether it was a jury or non-jury trial, the judges had the option of asking questions during the course of the trial in they were in the interest of justice. The judges were also not restricted to their bench, for when they were asking questions they could move about the courtroom while they were addressing the individual.

If the accused requested a trial of his peers, the case would be held before twelve jurors. Yet the jurors would not be ordinary citizens, but rather professionals of the court that were more qualified to make the appropriate decisions. The jurors were often chosen from a pool of lawyers, judges, and law enforcement officials. The finding of the jury would be accepted as long as there were a ten to two majority.

In the event of an appeal the trial would be closed and held only in front of the panel of five judges. The basic premise behind the new justice system had returned to the idea of justice being served by the guilty being punished. The days of pampering criminals were long gone and if an individual committed a crime he would have to accept the punishment.

To deal with the problem of the prison systems becoming grossly overcrowded, Knight instructed his construction teams to build one hundred maximum security prisons through out the United States. An additional prisons were constructed at various sites in the other countries of the world. While he did not expect reimbursement, he did receive partial support from the world's governments and other corporate organizations. That helped to reaffirm his belief that the people of the world preferred freedom and that freedom included the protection of the proper citizenry by incarcerating those that violate the social norms.

The prison themselves were all identical as the structure showed that there was an emphasis on the term 'maximum security'. The structure was twenty stories high and twenty levels deep. Along the perimeter of the complex was an electric wire mesh fence ten meters high. Along the fence were several guards, security cameras, motion sensors, and an automatic laser system that fired at anything in an unauthorized area. A single blast from the laser was not fatal, yet it would leave an individual incapacitated for several days. The feat of escape could nor be accomplished as the individual would either be severely injured or killed.

Within the interior of the prison were several impressive facilities, but their use had to be earned. Along the lines of self-improvement were an impressive exercise facility and a well-stocked library. There was also a large cafeteria that Knight allowed to be stocked with a large variety of food because the slop that was normally found in other penal institutions would often be enough to make a starving goat turn it's nose up in disgust. He also did not see why they should not eat well even though they were being punished and a well-fed person was easier to get along with.

Prisoners had their own cell that was twelve feet by fifteen feet and the ceiling was twelve feet high. There was also a separate room that was three feet by six feet that contained a shower, sink, and combination toilet and bidet. Surveillance cameras, which were hidden from view and unknown to the prisoner, were in the main quarters and in the bathroom. In the hallway there were other cameras that were visible to the prisoners. The room consisted of a single bed, chair, and bookcase. The door to the cell was solid metal, not enabling the prisoner to see into the hallway or the other prisoners. The door stayed secure by magnetic locks and closed airtight. Within the room was a transparent opening that was five inches by ten inches that allowed the prisoner to see outside and let daylight into the room. Two vents the same size as the windows were in the ceiling with one pumping in oxygen and the other pumping air out. Another use of the vents was to flood the room with knock out gas if it became necessary. Between the vents was a flat panel that produced all the light necessary to adequately read in any corner of the room.

Each prisoner was placed in a cell by themselves as a measure of privacy, but also as a method of breaking their will and way of thinking. In their first week in the complex, the prisoner is isolated from all human contact as their meals are placed into the room by a rotating panel on trays that are shipped directly from the cafeteria. The prisoner only hears a voice over an intercom, which asks them to choose what they want for the meal.

At the beginning of the second week the individual is introduced to a counselor that will spend from one to four hours a day with the prisoner in their cell as the sessions are monitored and recorded by the cameras. At the end of the second week the prisoner would be given the opportunity to leave the cell for the first time, but only to walk the abandoned hallways as a form of exercise as the counselor accompanies him. Depending on the progress of the individual, the counselor may be the only person the prisoner has any contact with for a month up to a year.

When the counselor deems the prisoner ready, they would be allowed to meet another prisoner who was also under the counselor's supervision. The two would have duel sessions with the counselor in alternate cells for a month before they would be allowed to be alone for increments of time starting with ten minutes building up to an hour. If they acted correctly and not improperly, the two would be allowed to continue meeting in private sessions along with the dual sessions with the counselor. However, if at any time they talked or behaved improperly, they would be immediately separated and placed in total isolation for a week before the counselor would confront them individually with what they did wrong.

At a certain point deemed appropriate by the counselor, the prisoners would be allowed to choose a pet for their own. The pet would be in their custody for a trial period to see if they could handle the responsibility. If they succeeded during the trial period the pet was theirs for good. Their choices for a pet were fish, bird, hamster, cat or dog. The pets would already have been house broken as not to cause the prisoner any undue stress. In the category of dogs the prisoner could pick any species that did not normally exceed the size of twenty-five pounds. If the prisoner happened to choose a cat or dog, the age of the animal was normally eight weeks to six months to ensure a bonding from the animal to the owner. With the other animals the age did not matter.

After the prisoner had shown they could responsibly care for the pet for a period of one month, the counselor then allowed the two prisoners from the dual group to meet a larger group of ten to twenty prisoners. From that moment, the prisoner would begin to blend into the prison community. They were given access to the prison library, athletic facilities, and given an opportunity to work in a garden on the outside. They were also given the opportunity to have a radio, television, and videotape machine placed in their room. From the library they could check out court approved movies.

Before they had free access to the library the individual had been limited to one book at a time which they chose from a severely limited list. The individual also had the option of having the main book of their particular religion for theirs to keep if they so desired. If the individual could not read, that was one of the things the counselor worked on in their sessions. An illiterate would also be given the option of having a pad of paper and crayons so they could pass the time.

When the prisoner had reached the point of free access, to get out of their room they only had to make a request over the intercom and the door would unlock. The prisoners were required to remain in their cells from midnight to 6 a.m., but could roam the complex the rest of the day. However, their pets were restricted to the location of their individual cells. The activities of all the prisoners were monitored at all times and if a rule were broken, they would be placed in isolation for a period of one day to one month, depending on the offense. /the only companion of the prisoner during isolation would be their pet.

Knight found that his system worked better than any other did. The prisoners that had been released back into society after a stay in one of his facilities were better at dealing with others and could better handle responsibilities. While the program was extremely expensive, the benefits it had toward making society more of a livable atmosphere made it worth it.

It was not until January of 2044 that the research team of Dr. Avery finally made their breakthrough in animal cell research. Had Knight helped more in the process they may have progressed much faster, but he had many other responsibilities to attend to. The major task accomplished by Dr. Avery and his team dealt with the cloning of cells. Although it had been attempted since the mid twentieth century to clone cells there had always been a moral cloud that seemed to inhibit the research in depth. Since Knight felt that those views were unfounded, he assigned Dr. Avery and his team to accomplish all they could in the fields of genetics and cloning.

While Knight had no desire to clone a person, he did see certain advantages to being able to clone a select group of cells. Using the processes of reconstructive surgery and cosmetic remodeling, Knight felt the applications could greatly benefit the medical world. For years doctors had been performing many types of organ transplants with the main problem being the ability to find a donor that was compatible to the patient. There was also the problem of the patient rejecting the alien tissue, which could lead to many other complications. Then the doctors would have to resume the search process to find another donor.

What Dr. Avery accomplished involved collecting a sampling of cells from an organ, cloning the cells, and then constructing a suitable organ for transplant. The original problem involved the difficulty of finding healthy cells on a damaged organ. After much experimentation, they were able to perfect the process so they could manipulate the cells; little by little so that a generation of cells far removed from the original would be healthy. They were able to accomplish that due to the fact that the genetic makeup of each cell held the blue print of what a healthy cell actually was, so they tampered with the DNA until they reached the desired results. The process was effective ninety-two percent of the time.

Once a group of healthy cells had been created, the cloning process would be continually repeated until there were enough cells to construct an organ. Depending on the damage and the type of organ involved, the process normally took from seventy to three hundred and ten hours. Absolute knowledge of the makeup of each organ was necessary to correctly construct it, but that information was already available due to research Knight had done years previous. Once an actual organ was ready for transplant, the operation took from seventy to ninety minutes if there were no complications.

By 2046 the number of transplant patients that submitted to the procedure was 12,945 and the number of rejections was only eight. The near perfect success rate was phenomenal and the procedure was lauded by the medical world. Dr. Avery was called a medical genius and received several awards because of the discovery. Knight allowed the doctor to enjoy the time in the spotlight because he needed a rest after the tedious months of research necessary to find the answer. He also let the comments about the doctor being a greater mind than he did slide because Avery was his friend and it was indeed brilliant work.

While the doctor had been busy with the cell research, Knight had been working on perfecting the process of purifying water. Once the process had been refined it was possible to remove any substance from the liquid and all that would remain would be a pure, fresh collection of oxygen and hydrogen molecules and nothing else. It was the cleanest water ever produced outside of the laboratory and he could use the process to clean up all of the polluted rivers and lakes around the world. It also meant that there would be an endless supply of drinking water, since he could even draw the source water from the oceans. The fact that the oceans consisted of more than half of the surface area of the planet, they could be considered giant reservoirs.

By August of 2045, he had pumping stations constructed at various positions on all seven continents near the major bodies of water. The water was pumped from the source and transferred to a nearby conversion plant that could convert the source water to pure water at a rate of two hundred thousand gallons a minute at the cost of only one penny for every twenty thousand gallons. The water was then pumped to a station that was the starting point of an extensive pipe system that spanned the nations of the world. With his pipes he was able to transport the water to all corners of the world, even to those in the desert environments.

He sold the water to the people at the most minimal of profits and it appeared he was giving it away at cost. Yet due to the volume of water that people consumed, he actually made billions of dollars. It even surprised him for he had not taken the time to calculate the fractions of a penny he made on each gallon and to multiply that by the average consumption by the people of the planet. Very few made any comments about the fact since he was still charging them a lower rate than all of the previous water distributors. As a result. Knight had a monopoly on the water sales and distribution markets.

By January 1, 2046, Knight Enterprises was an international conglomerate that had a power base that could not be compared to anything past or present. Ana was back at the helm and she had led the company into so many diversification ventures that it was mind numbing. The fact was, in one way or another; Knight Enterprises actually employed nearly one tenth of the world's population of 9.4 billion. For a time Ana was considering taking the company public by allowing shares to be sold on the open market. But Knight talked her out of it because it would have weakened their power base and it would allow the people to see just how far the long arm of Knight Enterprises actually reached.

They owned restaurants, department stores, apartment complexes, hotels, motels, mines, airports, television stations, radio stations, newspapers, magazines, book publishers, automobile dealerships, transport companies, construction companies, shipping lines, financial institutions, and a movie studio. The company was also interlinked with several thousand small businesses worldwide. While Knight did not favor the situation of allowing the company to reach such grand proportions, Ana enjoyed the power and fun she was having by being in charge of a trillion-dollar corporation. Since there was no real harm being done, he allowed her to run the business any way she thought was appropriate. While he kept a cursory tab on how Knight Enterprise ran so she did not jeopardize his long range goals, he concentrated the majority of his time to his two favorite entities: GLESA and the Blackhole.

Gradually Knight started to take an active role in the crime fighting aspect of GLESA. His role was not only administrative, but also that of a field operative. He had personally chosen those that comprised the team that were his allies in combat. The first on the list was Mason Rasov, a weapons specialist that had been a captain in the Soviet army. Rasov had an American mother that kept close ties to her relatives in the United States, so the adjustment was not terribly taxing on him. The next man chosen was Russell Jackson, a major from the United States army who was a computer genius and had excellent investigative skills. Jackson was also honed in several areas of combat. The final member of the team was Randy Buck, a young man who had joined the Texas rangers immediately after graduating from high school at the age of sixteen. The boy had made a name for himself with his shooting prowess and his fighting skills. Individually they were formidable warriors, but when teamed with Knight they became an invincible, deadly force.

Over the years the organization of GLESA had changed little except gaining in size. The uniform appeared the same yet changes had been made in it's construction that enabled the wearer to tolerate temperatures in the range of seventy-five below to two hundred and thirty. The previous range had only been thirty-five below to one hundred and twenty degrees. A night visor had also been improved upon. While the visor had once been optional, it was now mandatory. One improvement in the visor was the addition of a visual enhancement mode that allowed the wearer to see up to five miles away with the distance seeming to be a few feet from them. Through much prodding, Knight had also convinced a few agents the merits of carrying a few dozen kacs with them in a pouch attached to their waist.

When Knight was not involved in the activities of GLESA, he was occupied by the operation of the Blackhole, which was a name that had been given to his sports empire. The Blackhole was also the name of the sports complex that he erected in the on the out skirts of Omaha. Within that complex all of the teams which he owned played their games. He founded most of the teams, while he purchased the franchises of a few sports and moved them to Omaha and subsequently changed the team logos. There were a total of five male sport franchises and four female. The male sports were football, baseball, hockey, basketball, and soccer. The female franchises were softball, volleyball, basketball, and soccer.

Knight had personally selected then names and team logo of each club and had fun doing so. Part of the fun was that none of the names ended in the letter 's'. The football team was the Omaha Earthquake and the logo was the word 'earthquake' written twice one on top of the other in a double vision or shaking effect. The baseball team was the Omaha Thunder and their mascot was a Norseman who carried a large drum to beat on. The men's basketball team was the Omaha Gold and the uniforms actually had gold treads sewn into them. The hockey team was the Omaha Icemen and their mascot was a snowman. The men's soccer team was the Omaha Tide with a male surfer as their mascot.

The softball team was the Omaha Starburst and their uniforms had colorful shooting stars on them. The ladies basketball team was the Omaha Fire with their uniforms home bright red and orange and they had a person twirling a flaming baton as their mascot. The volleyball team was called Omaha Pride and their mascot was a gentleman in a tuxedo with a banner with the team name on it running across his chest. The ladies soccer team was the Omaha Wave with their mascot being a female surfer.

The Blackhole complex was just north of Omaha and it consisted of twelve structures and a massive array of parking lots. There was a football stadium, baseball stadium, an auditorium, softball stadium, and hockey rink, and seven parking garages. The seating capacity of the football stadium was eighty-five thousand, the baseball stadium held sixty thousand, the softball complex held thirty thousand, and the hockey rink could accommodate twenty thousand spectators. The auditorium where the basketball teams and volleyball team played their games had a capacity of twenty thousand spectators. While it was excessive to have all of the stadiums he felt it was necessary to avoid scheduling conflicts. While none of the stadiums were the largest of their types in America, it was obvious that the Blackhole was a class operation that kept the welfare of the spectator in mind.

Knight saw to it that the complex maintained a superior level of cleanliness as one of his tasks as owner. He also personally scheduled all of the games of each team and always tried to offer attractive packages for the home events. He often scheduled double headers where the men and women's basketball teams would play back-to-back. The same applied for the men and women's soccer teams when they played their games on the football field in the spring. He also allowed people to use the ticket stubs from the baseball games to gain entrance to the softball games. The amount of money Knight spent on this endeavor did not matter to him for he was in it for the enjoyment of the sport. Yet he also knew that when he built his sports empire into a winning organization, then the money would naturally start flowing in.

To fill the rosters of his teams, Knight searched the world for the best athletes available. It was not necessary that they played the particular sport previously because Knight felt a superior athlete could be trained to play any sport. He spent a great deal of effort in recruiting Olympians because they were often the best athletes. To ensure the proper development of the players, he hired coaches that held the philosophy that the athletes were people and not commodities. It was a philosophy that Knight stressed and it helped in creating an atmosphere of friendship among the players and coaches.

Knight hired coaches that had the ability to start with an athlete from scratch and teach them all the fundamentals. It did not matter how long they had played the particular sport because Knight felt even an experienced player would improve after a renewed interest in stressing the fundamentals. He required all his players to put forth a maximum effort at all times, both physically and mentally. All of his athletes were required to obey strict guideline prohibiting the use of alcohol, drugs, and tobacco products. He warned them that if any were found with an illegal substance, he would personally see them to their prison cell. As to drinking and use of tobacco he told them it was for the betterment of their own physical well being and he was paying them handsomely so they could find their diversions elsewhere.

Any player that violated the teams substance abuse policy would be suspended and required to perform community service before being allowed to rejoin the team. He reminded them that he had the technology at his disposal to scan their bodies for illegal substances without their being aware of it. It was not too difficult to convince them that it was easier to live a healthy life style than to try and sneak around doing something that was against policy.

In the four years from the start of his sports empire in 2045, Omaha had evolved into the Mecca of championship sports. While it was natural that each of his teams struggled for the first year or two, they all had achieved a level of excellence with each winning at least one championship. The trophy case in Knight's home office was filled with the championship trophies and rings he had received for actually participating as a member of a few of those teams.

Unlike many other owners Knight had the ability to make an excellent showing for himself on the playing field and took advantage of that natural ability and actually played in home games when he had time. He did not limit himself to playing a single sport, for he participated with the football, baseball, basketball, and hockey teams. Due to the fact that he was an avid body builder his physical condition was superior and he played positions that suited his size.

Knight found that many of his Sundays were clear so he was able to participate in twenty-five football games over the first four years. He had a policy of only playing if a starter had been injured and football provided many opportunities to play. Of the twenty-five games he played six at offensive tackle, one at center, fourteen at defensive tackle, three at nose guard and one at outside linebacker. His statistics were comparable to any other starter and the players and coaches were never reluctant about allowing their owner to play. In the eighteen games he played on defense he totaled two hundred and sixty-six tackles, seventeen quarterback sacks, eight interceptions, two fumble recoveries, one hundred and twenty-four quarterback hurries, and eighteen fumbles caused. Another statistic that stood out was the fact that the Earthquake held their opponents scoreless in seventeen of the eighteen games he played on the defense. When Knight played his intensity was extremely high and few could hinder his six-foot-five and two hundred and eighty-pound body once he gained his momentum.

In baseball Knight had participated in forty-seven games over the first four years. At different times he played at the three positions in the outfield for forty-one of the games. The remaining six games were divided between first base and catcher, with him playing each position three times. As a batter he was consistent no matter what position he played. Through his first forty-seven games his average was .519 with one hundred and thirty-four hits that included twenty-nine doubles, two triples, and twenty-three home runs. While his home run ratio was phenomenal, the fact that they all came at his home stadium made the feat all the more amazing because the fences were so far from home plate. The fences were three hundred and eighty feet down the lines and four hundred and ninety feet to dead center. With his tremendous speed he had also amassed twenty-two stolen bases and one hundred and four putouts in the outfield while going errorless in all his games. He also exhibited tremendous eye and hand coordination by striking out only eight times in his two hundred and fifty-eight official at bats.

While football and baseball were his two favorite sports, he also took the time to play on the basketball and hockey teams when the opportunity presented itself. As a basketball player he only played the position of forward. In twenty- eight games he had seven hundred and thirty-four points, two hundred and forty-four rebounds, twenty blocked shots, seven steals, and one assist. That left him with a respectable showing as his averages were 26.2 points and 8.7 rebounds a game. In hockey he played only nine games and all were at the position of goalie. All nine games were victories as Knight came away with seven shut outs and two single goal games to his credit.

The original name for the sports complex had been Knight Athletics, but Knight changed it after the second year after he read an article published in a sports magazine. The article appeared in an obscure sports journal called Sport Heritage, yet Knight liked to read anything that was about his teams. The author noted that there was something strange that had been occurring in Omaha: athletes went in but none came out. He stated that it was like Omaha was a sports version of the blackhole. Knight liked the phrase because it did accurately describe how he was handling his sports organizations.

Knight took the approach as to compare a sports team to a business. While this was how all the other owners saw it as anyhow, Knight took a different approach. In a business all the best personnel are desired to enhance the company and they are often kept around for the duration of their careers. It was not a desirable situation to have a bright; young executive leave the business and go over to the competition so their productivity would improve. That was the same philosophy Knight had about his athletes. In that regard it made sense that if he did not allow his better players to go to other teams, they could not make an impact on how those teams played against his.

To accomplish that feat Knight basically signed all of his athletes to lifetime contracts. He never traded a single player and when they retired he would find positions for them within the vast Knight Enterprises business empire. It seemed to be a logical maneuver since dedicated athletes also often made dedicated businesspersons. When the need arose to actually trade for a player, Knight made it a practice to compensate the other team with money and draft choices and they also had the option of choosing a player or players from his farm systems.

For each of his sports, he had a developmental teams that served as the farm system to prepare athletes for Omaha. The players on these teams were signed to standard year-to-year contracts. Knight owned each of the farm teams to guarantee he would have complete control on how the players would be developed.

As would be expected, baseball had the most extensive farm system. The AAA team played in the California league while it was based in Reno, Nevada. His AA team played in the Southern league and was based in Valdosta, Georgia. He owned a total of six A teams and they comprised their own league, which was where they were all based.

The softball team had a similar structure to the baseball system. The AAA team was in Grand Rapids, Michigan and the AA team was in Peoria, Illinois and both were independents. A six team A league played in the state of Iowa.

The other sports had less extensive farm systems. The hockey team had a semi-pro team in Duluth, Minnesota and junior level teams around the world in the cities of Brooks, Alberta in Canada, Kherson in the Soviet Union, and Stockholm, Sweden. The soccer teams had a pool of players developing in four team indoor leagues in Rhode Island for the men and in Oregon for the women. For football he had a semi-pro football team based in Arvada, Colorado and he also owned a team in the Canadian Football League called the Fredericton Fame from Fredericton, New Brunswick. His farm teams for men and women's basketball consisted of four team leagues in North Dakota and Delaware respectively. Finally, for volleyball he had a junior team based in Las Cruces, New Mexico that competed in the international junior circuit.

Over the years the number of games each of the sports played in a season often increased. During the regular season they played a total of two hundred games in baseball, twenty in football, one hundred in basketball and hockey, sixty in soccer, seventy-five in volleyball, and one hundred and fifty in softball. Post season games varied per sport as it ranged from a maximum of four for football to a maximum of thirty-five for hockey.

By the end of the fourth year all of his teams were operating on an advanced level. Knight was extremely proud of al of his athletes for they worked extremely hard in achieving that level of excellence. While each team had managed to capture at least one championship, others had quickly reached the plateau of superiority by capturing as many as three championships in the short period the franchises were in existence.

The men's sports made a respectable showing against fierce competition. The football team had a dismal showing it's first two seasons with records of 8-12 and 10-10, yet managed to pull everything together in 2048 to go undefeated and win the Super Bowl with a 24-0 record. That feat was repeated the following year as the team was on a fifty-one game winning streak. The baseball team gained respect their first year by finishing second in the National League West with a record of 115-85. Then they started to dominate and won the World Series in 2046, 2047, and 2048 while posting records of 131-79, 142-66, and 170-44.

The basketball team started out like the football team by starting with two less than perfect years and then made it to the championship in back-to-back years. In the first two years of the franchise they went a mediocre 39-61 and 36-64. Then they had a Cinderella season in 2047 by winning the championship with a 84-44 record and followed that up with a year of 87-41. Yet in 2048 they lost the seventh game of the championship series to the Detroit Pistons on a heart breaking buzzer beater.

The hockey team progressed in similar fashion. They started out with a horrendous 15-85 and rebounded to post records of 51-61. In 2049 they achieved success by capturing the Stanley Cup with a 83-44 record.

The men's soccer team made the most gradual progress of any of the teams and finally became one of the dominant teams of the sport. They started out with a 27-33 record and gradually improved to 33-27 and 41-22. In 2048 they won the World Championships and posted a record of 60-8.

The women's soccer team soccer team managed to operate with a level of consistency from the beginning yet lost many close games in going 26-34 in their first season. Everything went their way the next season as they captured the 2046 World Championship with a 65-7 record. They proved they would be yearly contenders by being the runners-up in 2047 with a 57-14 record and winning the championship again in 2048 when they were 58-10.

The women's basketball team followed a course similar to the men's. Their fist two seasons they were sub par as they posted records of 33-67 and 32-68. Then they had a Cinderella season to accompany that of the men as they won the championship with a record of 65-55. Their record improved the following year as they were 77-45, but Austin swept them in four straight in the championship series.

His other two women's teams had combined to win a total of six championships in softball and volleyball. Both teams had reached a level of excellence that was comparable to that of his baseball and football teams. The softball team was a horrendous 21-129 their first year, but bounced back to take three consecutive Softball World Series with records of 99-59, 110-48, and 118-40. The volleyball team was a respectable 38-37 their first season and built on that to go 65-15, 69-10, and 71-8 as they captured three consecutive World Cup championships.

All of Knight's teams had very impressive home records as they helped give the Blackhole another reputation. Many teams went into the complex with confidence that they could defeat one of his teams on their home turf, yet when they left the confidence was gone as they more than likely left in defeat. One result of their winning ways was that they were either hailed as America's team or despised for trouncing the underdogs. No matter what the public saw in his teams, Knight knew that he was providing the highest level of sports entertainment and in the long run the rest of the teams would eventually improve their games to become more competitive. Until that time, Knight was content to revel in the quick success of his champions.

Besides the number of games being increased, Knight noted that there had been several changes in sports since the turn of the century. Some of the changes were due to improvements in technology and others were the results of rule changes. No matter what the original reasons were, Knight felt the results were vast improvements for the games.

One change, that Knight was happy to help continue, was the drastic increase in the popularity of professional female sports. There had been superficial interest in female athletics in the twentieth century in the sports of softball, basketball, and volleyball. However, it wasn't until after 2010 that the interest started to rise and it became a big money enterprise.

A major change that came after the turn of the century was the transfer from the standard to the metric measurement system. While it was not a major change to the rest of the world, those in the United States felt the greatest impact. Due to the change the regulation football field was one hundred meters long instead of one hundred yards long. A result of that was all the statistics for athletes before the year 2000 had to be converted so there could be accurate comparisons. In baseball the fields no longer were measured in feet, but had the distance in meters on the fences. The basketball hoop remained at the height of three meters, which was the same as ten feet in pre-2000 terms.

In the sport of hockey there had been two major changes since 2015. One change was the elimination of ties by implementing a sudden death rule that forced the teams to play five-minute periods until one of them scored. The other change involved stricter penalties for fighting and vicious conduct. Any player that became involved in a fight or performed an unnecessarily violent act upon another player would be suspended for three games or could receive expulsion from the league if they were repeat offenders. Knight liked the fighting rule because it added extra protection for the better players and it had allowed the sport to become a game of skill rather than a brawl on ice.

The level of officiating drastically improved due to the implementation of technology. In football a radar monitored the field and touch sensitive lasers that helped determine first downs and our-of-bounds situations. The football itself had tiny electronic devices implanted into it that determined when someone was holding it, how high it was off the ground, and it's exact location on the field at all times. That helped eliminate a lot of the controversy around fumbles, interceptions, and touchdowns.

In baseball and softball the strike zone was monitored by radar which was modified for each player. The umpire had an electronic receiver which told him if it were a ball or strike. Yet the discretion as to whether a certain play was safe or one was still up to the official. The human element remained but a considerable amount of the inconsistency remained.

Careers were lengthened in several sports because of the improvements to equipment. In those sports in which contact was common, Knight allowed the use of his improved plastics in the making of padding of the helmets. Knee braces were also improved so that they absorbed the majority of an impact, as the joint remained stabilized. All of the equipment allowed the players to enjoy a full range of motion while they were secure with the fact that they were better protected.

Within the first six years of their marriage, Knight accompanied Ana to the hospital six times to witness the births of his eighteen children. After the first group of five, the following visits produced children in the increments of four, five, two, one, and one. The group of four was born on June 10, 2042, and consisted of four girls and a boy: Amanda Lynn, Richard Andrew, Deborah Anne, and Theresa Katherine. On July 1, 2043 a second group of five boys were born: Alexander Gustav, Douglas Wilber, Emanual Randolph, Kenneth Solomon, and Curtis Owen. After that point they decided to discontinue the use of the fertility drug, but on June 21, 2044 they still had twin girls: Melissa Christine and Constance Yvette. The first single birth produced a girl on May 29, 2045, which they named Elizabeth Bernadette. Their final child was a boy named Ian Hamilton that was born on September 29, 2046.

Their rundown of their informal names by which Knight would call them were: Frank, Jake, Vince, Hank, Chris, Amy, Rich, Debbie, Terry, Alex, Doug, Manny, Kenny,

Curt, Lisa, Connie, Liz, and Ian. The final child seemed special to them because they planned on him being the last and they thought it would be appropriate if they gave him a formal name that also seemed informal. Twelve boys and six girls gave the Knights a large household, but they knew they had the means to care for them.

Although their parents regarded Ian and Liz as a little special, they loved all the children the same. Knight was pleased with the fact that each of the children possessed distinguishable characteristics and non-of them were identical. He had a family that made him feel complete and he vowed to love, cherish and protect them for a lifetime. Having a family also helped Knight move a bit closer to the rest of the human race in the respect of his increased capacity to care for other people.

By November of 2046 Knight was in the need to release his creative talents and he began to devote much of his time in the labs in Knight Enterprises and at his home. While he still spent much time following the operations of GLESA and his sport franchises, he felt it was necessary that he channel his pent up mental energies into new projects. The life that Knight lived was always at a frantic pace for Knight felt that he had to be accomplishing something and that idle time was a sign of complacency.

To start his first project he called in the management team of his construction company and instructed them to begin making plans for a large-scale venture. The project involved an attempt to deal with the problem of over crowding in many of the larger cities in the world. That was accomplished by going underground.

With the technology available to them, it was possible to go four hundred and twenty-five levels down without any safety problems. Beyond that mark would cause the structure to collapse within six months due to stress factors. To ensure additional safety, Knight instructed the builders not to go past the four hundred level mark.

Each complex was basically the equivalent of a small city due to the fact at full capacity it could accommodate up to twenty-four thousand comfortably. In Asia the complexes were especially popular because of the large rooms on each apartment. Because Knight Enterprises remained in control of the complexes after construction was complete, the rent pricing for each apartment was set at very reasonable rates. There were also levels that were set aside for those who could not afford to pay, in small gesture to help the poor and homeless.

Each complex had a security system of cameras and sensor equipment. The sensors monitored for sound, heat, smoke, and motion. If the sensors picked up anything out of the ordinary, there were GLESA security personnel on duty to investigate. The sensors also monitored the flow of the water and electricity and alerted the maintenance personnel if there was a problem or a potential problem developing. The sensors were on the alert for heat and smoke for possible fires or hot spots that could cause fires. In the event of a fire, the complex had it's own system to deal with the situation.

The sensors monitored all of the life signs of the residents for energy saving and medical reasons. If an individual left a room any objects consuming electricity would be turned off. If there were no individuals in the entire apartment, the electricity and water would automatically be turned off. The systems would reactivate when a person entered the apartment. It was also within the capabilities of the sensors to distinguish when a person was ill or their body was not functioning properly, such as the event of a heart attack or stroke. The system also knew the difference of whether a person had left the apartment or they had died. When the system picked up on any abnormalities in the individuals, the proper authorities where immediately contacted.

Knight had designed a fire fighting system that was used in the complexes and he also made a system that was adaptable to any building. He also modified the system so that it could be used manually by fire fighters to battle the flames at structures without the system. In those buildings with the system, when a fire starts in a location the area is immediately sealed off by the nearest doors shutting airtight. If it is a building with windows, then there would be a panel that would drop down in front of the glass to seal off the room and to protect the glass. If there are people in the room, an alarm will sound and they will be notified they have ten seconds to evacuate the area. Once the room is sealed, the air is drawn out of the room through the vents by a pump system that creates near vacuum conditions. Once the pumping starts, the fire is out within five seconds. As the sensors determine there is no longer a danger, oxygen rich air is then pumped back into the room within ten seconds.

If a person had the misfortune of being trapped in the room they only had to be able to hold their breath for fifteen seconds to survive. Any person unable to survive would be classified as a fatality to the fire. To guard against such tragedies, Knight offered special packages that contained oxygen masks to be placed at strategic locations throughout their residence or building.

By May 14, 2047 all buildings ten stories or taller were required to have the system. It was another instance where Knight used his influence to push something into law. Yet it was a situation that was for the safety of those that worked or lived in the taller structures, so Knight had no regrets about forcing the legislators to see things his way.

For those structures shorter than ten stories and did not have the system, a portable system could be used. A large plastic cover is placed over the structure by either dropping it by helicopter or by shooting it from a special gun similar to a bazooka. While the cover was being secured the structure would be scanned for life signs and any individuals would be retrieved before the cover was airtight. The edges are secured to the ground with weighted coils that are put in place by the fire fighters. A pump is attached to a special fastener on the cover and the air is drawn from the house or building. A meter tells the firefighters when conditions inside the structure had reached the level where flames could no longer exist. They immediately begin to remove the cover to allow air to return to the structure. Or if the community could afford it, air would be pumped back into the house or building.

When everything is done properly, the entire operation took only two to five minutes, depending on the size of the structure. One of the positive aspects of the operation was that there was much less damage to the structure because the fire was under control so quickly and there would not be water damage. Once the fire fighters became familiar with the system, their efficiency increased greatly and many more lives were saved and less property was lost.

It was on July 7, 2047 that one of Knight's probes observed a shuttle escape from the fourth planet of the TM-3 system and proceed unmolested to the space portal. After some elusive galaxy hopping, the craft finally stopped in the CN-10 system of the College Alpha galaxy. The system had thirteen planets and the craft made it's way toward the largest moon of three moons orbiting the fifth planet.

The probe kept its distance as not to attract attention as it maintained surveillance on the shuttle. There were life reading on the shuttle, but the probe was at a distance too great to obtain an accurate analysis. The prospect of retrieving the fugitives elated Knight, for it may give him valuable insights about the alien invaders. All other projects were put on hold as he devoted all his resources to dealing with the situation.

On July 22 he sent a shuttle with an android crew to meet with the alien craft and he hoped it would not be too difficult to get them to come back. In order to maintain the level of secrecy necessary, he instructed the androids to return to his moon colony mining operation with any fugitive aliens they recover. To justify his actions to the rest of the world, he released a statement that the shuttle was going to test the portals for the possibility of space exploration within a couple of years by human crews.

Another benefit Knight reaped by having the original probe follow the fugitive craft was that it was exposed to sixteen new space portals. Their positions were mapped and he signaled all available probes to begin exploring the virgin territory. The more he knew about the accessible reaches of space before the invasion, the better he could devise an escape plan if it became necessary.

The idea of accompanying the android crew to meet the alien shuttle was tempting, but he had too much to tend to on Earth and there was also a danger factor involved by approaching the aliens. As Knight closely watched all transmissions, he learned that his shuttle touched down on the alien moon at 8:48 a.m. on July 24. He knew that there would likely be a language barrier, so he prepared the androids with several alternatives including using all known Earth languages and dialects, sending pictogram video messages, and trying an assortment of mathematics patterns.

For security reasons, the shuttle transmitted a minimal amount of information with the remainder relayed to the probe. The first communication attempts involving the math patterns drew no response. The as they started to send the pictogram messages, they also bombarded all communication channels with all the languages at their disposal. TO the surprise of Knight, one of the aliens actually responded in English. The situation was quickly explained to the aliens and they agreed to board Knight's shuttle. Knight felt it was best if they came on his shuttle rather than their own because many nations on the planet had the capability to effectively monitor within the solar system as for as Neptune, so they alien craft could not approach without being noticed. Or so he thought. In the meantime, Knight began preparing for a trip of his own to the moon to meet the shuttle as it arrived.

He watched the shuttle land at 6:24 a.m. on July 26 inside a special hanger adjoining the mining complex. The crew chief had instructed Knight that there were twenty-six passengers and alerted him of any necessary minor preparations that would need to be made to accommodate them. After a few minutes the passengers began to make their descent. To Knight's surprise, four distinct alien races were represented among his new guests.

One of the aliens was a fur-covered male that stood six-foot-four and weighed around six hundred and seventy pounds. He had large, brown eyes, a human-like nose, and a smiling mouth that showed several razor sharp teeth and fangs. The alien had white fur except for a patch of brown on the chest. There were five digits on each hand and four on each foot. At the end of each digit there were short, but sharp claws. Despite the formidable appearance of the alien, Knight saw something in it's eyes which told him that the individual possessed great intelligence and was most likely the leader of the group.

Two aliens appeared to be made out of clay as their features and bodies seemed to be molded by a craftsman. Their heads looked like a cascading mud hill as their eyes peered out from sunken sockets with a red glow. While they did not appear to have necks their heads seemed to be able to swivel on the axis. It was only when they talked to the fur-covered alien that their mouths became visible because the rest of the time the seam was not noticeable. When they spoke, their language was guttural in nature and at times sounded like someone trying to talk while under water. He did not understand what they said, but the fur covered alien answered in the same tongue. Knight estimated that they were about five-foot-eight and weighed two hundred and forty-five pounds.

Another pair of aliens had very human-like features. Aside from the fact that their skin was dark red and they had snow white hair, they could almost pass for human. It was surmised by Knight and later confirmed that these two were from the inhabited planet closest to the sun. While the first three aliens did not appear to be wearing clothing these two seemed quite comfortable in their apparel. Each wore light blue pants, a sleeveless white shirt, and black boots that went up to their knees. Both seemed to be in excellent physical condition as he estimated they were both five-foot-ten and one hundred and forty pounds.

The final two adults of the visiting party also had tremendous physical appearances as they were about six-foot-one and weighed two hundred and sixty-five pounds. These two and the children that accompanied them could easily pass for human. Among the children there were fourteen boys and five girls and they all appeared very healthy. The males wore white pants that went down to the middle of the calf and lightweight shoes that looked like moccasins. The only clothing covering their upper bodies was a width of cloth that tucked into their pants and extended upward to under the throat where a thin collar went around the neck to hold it in place. The cloth covered the abdominal region and the middle torso area, but allowed the proud wearers to show off their muscular features if they had them. The girls were all dressed in long white robes with hoods resting on the backs and a pouch in the front to conceal their hands. They wore sandals that were brown in color instead of the moccasins. All of the males were bald, with the adults sporting heavy beards, and the girls had long, flowing black hair.

Knight was wondering how a collection of such contrasting individuals happened to get together when he noticed one of the red-tinted aliens using sign language to give a message to the white furry alien. The leader of the group then spoke to Knight in English and began to explain the circumstances that had brought them to their present location. He introduced himself as Mochar, a member of the hostile invading alien race before he switched alliances. The individual who had flashed the hand signals was Droz Vatsali, an ambassador from Yalur, known to Knight as the third planet in the TM-3 system. The other fellow was his brother Wir; one of the generals of their planet's conquered army. The two clay men were Corpca Neafgry and Amer Darlish, mercenaries from the fifth planets of the TM-3 system known to them as Augh. The two large adults were Ridge Kets and Pak Orak, two members of the royal army to the planet of Ballar. The children were the sons and daughters of King Phram V who was executed by the invaders when they were establishing control. The eldest boy of the fourteen was Phram VI, the heir to the crown. Their meeting was arranged by Mochar, because it was his shuttle and he was in danger of being assassinated himself for his vocal objections to the actions of his own race.

Mochar explained to Knight that it was his race that comprised the leadership of the invading force. It had started two centuries earlier when he was in just his fifth decade of life. The inhabitants from his planet often lived for eight or none hundred years. Their planet was in the Terus Lat galaxy in the system known to Knight as OE-2. The inhabitants called their planet Kornerd.

Kornerd was very advanced in technology and had long ago mastered the ways of space exploration. The former leaders of the Kornerd had been very interested in the mysteries of space so it was a very important industry to the people of the planet. Before the invasions, the explorers of Kornerd had plotted over three million star systems and had found over 18,900 planets that supported various types of life. The information compiled by the Kornerdites took a span of 35,000 years.

There had been two social factions on Kornerd: the intellectuals and the laborers. Mochar was of the intellectual sect, but had close ties to many of the laborers. One day a laborer named Zhar Rahk turned rebel and managed to rally a force large enough to overthrow the establishment. After he declared himself the new leader of the planet, he ordered the execution of thousands of the intellectuals. He stopped the killing when he realized he would need the services of the intellectuals to achieve his goals. When the social climate returned to a level of normalcy, Rahk told the people that they were observing the beginning of the Rahk dynasty and his power would continue to grow as he intended to start conquering other planets.

Then about one hundred and ninety years ago they began conquering planets one at a time sector by sector. To date they had one thousand and seventeen planets under the influence of the Rahk dynasty. The territory that was under Rahk's rule became known as the domain. With the pattern that Rahk was following, Mochar told Knight that the Earth was scheduled to be added to the domain within six or seven years.

Knight learned that scout ships were routinely sent to the planets within the two-year timetable every few weeks. Until that time, reconnaissance missions were only carried out once or twice a year. As another method of collecting information, spies would be implanted among the general population of the more advanced planets to better observe their capabilities. Earth was one of those planets and Mochar said spies had been on Earth since about 1890. Those spies had often submitted to extensive cosmetic and dental surgery and were required to study hours of tapes of how the inhabitants of a particular planets typically behaved. To the best of Mochar's knowledge, there were one hundred and eighty-eight spies on Earth as of 2035.

As a matter of trivia, he also told Knight that over the years two scout ships had crashed on Earth. The survivors were ordered to stay on Earth and continue surveillance as a punishment of their crashing. These particular scouts had not undergone the surgery and training so they had to observe the population from afar. They were forced to live off the land and on occasion they would encounter some of the inhabitants of the planet. Mochar smiled as he stated the basis of these sightings had helped create the legend of Big Foot.

The position Mochar held before his escape was that of the overseer for certain planets in a sector. It was a position of importance and he was able to use his influence to contact the inhabitants of the other worlds. Because he despised everything Rahk stood for, he decided he would help as many people to freedom as possible. However, the twenty-five who came with him were the only one willing to risk escape.

They had hoped to reach a planet advanced enough to defend against any forces that would be in pursuit. It was also an objective to gain support from the advanced civilization and return to fight the minions of Rahk. Their destination was a solar system on the far side of the galaxy that had three such civilizations. But due to a malfunction in the ship's fuel system, they had to land before even reaching the one-quarter point of the journey. It was while they were making repairs that Knight's ship appeared and it caused much confusion because it was unlike anything in Rahk's armada. When the android spoke in English, Mochar recognized it as one of the languages of Earth and the tension was lessened. Mochar said that although he had once studied the languages of all the planets, he was embarrassed to say that lack of use had erased most of them from his mind over time. Yet he still remained fluent in the primary languages of twenty-two planets, he was proud to report.

Their original destination had been for one of the planets in the Stolis Random solar system by the name of Pir. It was the most advanced of the three inhabited planets and was not scheduled to be invaded for more than sixty years. He was disappointed about being side tracked to Earth because the last time he saw the file on the technology level of Earth it was only a fifty-two one a scale of one hundred. Yet when the androids were helping transfer the individuals between shuttles, he made a check on Earth and found that as of 2045 their technology status had been upgraded to an unbelievable level seventy-three within the last twenty years. Since Pir was only a level seventy planet, he thought going might actually best help them to Earth.

Knight told him that he was responsible for that upgrade in technology and that the people of Earth knew nothing of Mochar and his companions. Upon further review of the technology scale system, Knight and Mochar revised Earth's actual rating to eighty-three, since there were many advancements Knight had made that were not in public view. He told Mochar the extent of his research and the knowledge he had of their situation. It was obvious by the look in his eyes that he was in utter amazement as Knight talked. He wondered how one individual could accomplish so much, when there were entire civilizations that made little progress within the span of their existence's. This man was certainly a unique individual and Mochar freely stated that he was glad Knight was on their side. Hope for the future of free planets remained alive as long as this man remained committed to the cause.

Knight arranged for the royal family and their protectors to stay at his estate. The remaining five stayed on the moon in quarters that Knight had constructed to their personal preferences. Those five, especially Mochar, would be his private consultants on the issue of the invasion for he would turn to them for input and their theories about resisting Rahk's forces.
Mochar was their spokesman and he and Knight often communicated on a secure channel by video telephone. Together they worked to prepare the Earth and maybe someday to free their own worlds. Although the situation was enough to drive a normal man insane, Knight thrived on the challenge and embraced the possibility of going into combat against the mighty Zhar Rahk.

With a more detailed understanding of how Rahk worked and the type of technology he was up against, because Mochar said Kornerd had been at the technology level eighty-five, Knight knew what pace he needed to push himself and what changes needed to be made. He knew that it would not be long before he had taken Earth to a level of technology equal or greater to that which Kornerd had. But there was no way of gauging if Kornerd was also making advancements. Another problem was the limited time schedule involved and he didn't know if it could be done before the invasion. To raise the level of technology as high as he did in such a short time was a tremendous accomplishment, but as the levels get higher, the standards and methods of grading are stricter and it becomes harder to push from one level to the next. He was able to grasp the rating system used by the people of Kornerd and knew the more a planet advanced, the more difficult it would be to continue to advance as it gets closer to the maximum. So he knew to be able to counter the technology of Rahk, he would also have to use what he had to their maximum levels of efficiency.

One of the first tasks was to prepare the battlefield for combat. He wanted to spread the Rahk armada out and possibly catch it by surprise. Yet the element of surprise may not accomplish much since it would only be one or two ships initially sent to handle the conquest. Once those are dispatched, then the greater part of the armada would most likely be sent. The goal was to use the entire solar system as the battlefield and attempt to keep the brunt of the attack from even reaching Earth.

It would be necessary to place satellites at strategic positions through out the asteroid belt as the first line of defense. The bulk of the second line of defense would consist of more satellites armed with weaponry Knight had yet to construct. The third line of defense would consist of fighter ships that he would design. The fourth line of defense would be an elaborate system of force fields that would encircle the entire planet. That was yet another project Knight had to complete. The final line of defense would consist of the fighting force that will consist of the militaries of the world. That final line of defense will only be made possible after Knight actually alerts the world of the danger and helps coordinate their most efficient use.

Since there were too many variables to guarantee the eventual outcome would be in Earth's favor, Knight had a private ship available to take his family and friends in the event escape became the only option. That was a situation he wanted to avoid at all costs. Therefore he was making every possible preparation to ensure victory.

At the same time he was also interested in searching for and eliminating the alien spies that had infiltrated the planet's population. With the help of Mochar, he put all android units on continual alert as they were to scan all persons and search for any that had an internal anatomical makeup similar to Mochar. He also began to review all past and present sensor reports from security units positioned worldwide.

The fact that Rahk had placed spies among the population in order to learn how to conquer them struck Knight as ironic, since he placed his infiltrators among the public in order to learn how to save them. The fate of the Earth relied on which individual could best accomplish their objectives while working from opposite ends of the spectrum. Deep down, Knight felt that victory in the fight for Earth might come down to whether Zhar Rahk or himself dies. If that turns out to be the case, then Knight knew that each day would have to serve as preparation for the ultimate one on one confrontation of all time.

Chapter five

Clayton Knight sits at his desk while looking at the trophy case across the room. He clears the diary program from the computer screen as he continues to gaze at the nearly two dozen trophies and other artifacts which he knew would be joined by others. They were symbols of his life accomplishments, yet there was no collection of items that could accurately represent the contributions Knight had given the world in his twenty-eight years. He takes a sip of milk as he reflects on the events that morning. It made him realize that life was limited to a few short years and what each person accomplished within that time was often that by which they would be measured in comparison to others once they were gone. He knew that his measuring stick was tall, but he was still only a mortal man no matter what his capabilities were. He hoped that history would portray him in a favorable light even if all his actions do not appease the morals of the whole.

The clock on the wall reads 11:36 a.m. and the digital calendar below it flashes "June 3, 2049" in red characters on a black background. In just a week was the birthday party for four of his children who would be seven. He makes a note to consult with Ana about the party.

The elevator hums softly as it descends to the main floor. Knight enters the dining room and summons the cook to whom he relates his breakfast menu. He sits at the long table and begins to survey the newspapers stacked on a tray near his chair. Turning to the sports page he looks over the statistics of his teams. He was pleased that the baseball team had won the first game in a five game series in Pittsburgh 4-0 with the pitcher throwing a one-hitter. It also made him smile to see that the softball team had swept a three game series in nearby Des Moines by destroying the opponent 12-0 behind a no-hitter. Then he proceeded to scan through seventy-two newspapers in five languages to get an idea how the average person viewed the events of the world.

His breakfast is served as he returns the last paper to the tray. To satisfy his tremendous appetite Knight proceeds to eat a bowl of oatmeal, twelve sausage patties, a plate of hash browns, two poached eggs, twenty pieces of buttered toast, eight pancakes, two waffles, and two blueberry muffins. His thirst is quenched with two pitchers of milk and a pitcher of orange juice. The big man enjoys the flavoring of every mouthful with a passion. When he finishes he compliments the cook and leaves the dining area.

He proceeds to the library where his children are receiving their daily tutoring. Their governess, Dr. Jacqueline Davies, monitors their progress and lets each advance at their own pace. Knight encouraged a full load of courses although they were still at an early age. Yet he did not want to pressure the children so he allowed the governess to instruct them with whatever methods necessary to keep the stress at a minimum.

The eldest children were seven years old and would be turning eight in October. Each was on a program consisting of studies in English, science, social studies, mathematics, and a foreign language of each individual's choosing. Frank and Vince chose Spanish, Jake and Chris chose French, and were all alone in his studies of Russian.

The younger children were on programs that were less encompassing. The next youngest group of children was on a program that consists of only English and mathematics. The next age group was limited to honing their English skills. The four youngest children were allowed to use the time to express their talents in any manner they wished. There was a special area where they could paint or draw pictures, use coloring books, mold items from clay, or one of hundreds of other creative possibilities.

While all the children were extremely bright due to the fact their parents were geniuses, the two youngest children seemed to have the greatest capabilities. Although Ian and Liz were only two and four respectively, both were already reading with a ten- year-old reading proficiency and showed extreme creativity in their paintings, drawings, and clay figures. Knight wondered if the fact that each was from a single birth had any bearing on the matter or if it was coincidence. In the future he would have Dr. Avery run some tests on them to see if they had any unique characteristics. Until that time, he would allow each to progress as normally as possible.

The governess was well liked by all the children and was seen by both Knight and his wife as a very special individual. She always showed a positive outlook on life and insisted everyone call her Jackie. Originally she lived in Sydney, Australia, but moved to the United States with her family at the age of fifteen when her father was transferred to Fresno, California by his manufacturing business. She obtained her bachelor degree in education from Stanford University, where she also played for the tennis team. In the following years she received her masters and a Ph.D. in child psychology. She enjoyed children very much but had trouble finding a position she liked. Then she answered an ad in a San Diego newspaper for a governess and soon thereafter was working for the Knights. Besides being paid very well, she had full access to most of the house and had a bedroom on the fourth floor. Due to her easiness in handling the children, the Knights are very relieved to know that the children are in very capable hands when they are away.

As Knight walks into the library little Ian shouts "Papa!" runs across the room, and hugs the right knee of the big man. Knight smiles as he reaches down to pick up the child. The boy's beaming smile touches his heart as he proceeds to hug his son and then rubs the dark hair of the child leaving it disheveled. As he starts to carry the boy into the hallway he looks over his shoulder to see Dr. Davies smiling.

" So, how are your studies, Ian? "

" Very well, papa. "

" Is Dr. Davies challenging you enough? "

" In some ways. "

" Can you be more specific? "

The boy suddenly becomes uncomfortable and is unable to keep eye contact with his father.

" Well, you see, about all she has me do is that art stuff. That may be fine for Lizzie, but I want to be doing what Frank and Jake are doing. "

Knight looks upon the child with tremendous pride. To see young Ian wanting to press himself and use his natural abilities almost overwhelmed him. While young Elizabeth was obviously a great artistic prodigy, for she was already a master at oil painting and sculpting while only four, Ian on the other hand was more adept to conceptual learning. In the past few weeks he had noticed Ian taking an interest in his eldest brothers' studies. He knew that it was in part due to admiration for his older siblings, but there was much more involved. There was a hunger for knowledge that the boy wanted to satisfy. It was his eyes that told his father the hunger was there and Knight felt that it was time he helped the boy along.

Until that moment Knight had kept his promise to himself that he would not push any of his children, but would allow them to progress at a fairly normal rate for their ability levels. For the other children that was fine because they were content with the pace they were at, Ian, however, would have his intellectual growth retarded if he were to continue under the current regimen.
Deep within himself, Knight knew there was the possibility the child possessed an intelligence as great or greater than his own.

He sets the boy on the floor and kneels on his left knee while resting his large right hand on the boy's left shoulder. Looking directly into his son's eyes he asks, " Do you think you can handle the increase in your studies? "

The boy corrects his stance and stands as tall as he can. A grin breaks across his face, as he can not contain his happiness.

" Most certainly, papa! I will be happy to welcome it. "

" Then I will have a talk with Dr. Davies and we will start you on a new program tomorrow. Now return to your brothers and sisters and complete today's lesson. "

With his pulse racing due to the exciting news, the child scampers down the hall toward his classroom. These were the moments that brought the most pleasure to Knight. While his entire family was very dear to him, Ian was his little gem. When the boy was gone from sight, Knight decided that it was a good time to check on the Ballarian party. At this time of the day he knew he would most likely find them in the exercise center.

When he entered the exercise center he noticed the larger of the two guardians, Pak Orak, using the free weights doing squats lifts. The other guardian was in the swimming pool watching over the smaller children as they swam laps. The rest of the children were scattered throughout the complex working with weight machines, gymnastic apparatus, and running around the track. The Ballarians were a fitness oriented society and Knight was more than willing to allow them full access to his facilities so they could fulfill their dedication to physical maintenance.

He stood in the doorway for a few minutes and waved at Orak when he looked in his direction. When he was turning to leave the eldest boy, Gles, Spotted him. Quickly the boy dropped from the gymnastics rings and ran across the complex. Knight was half way down the corridor when the young man reached the doorway. Only slightly raising his voice Gles said, "Wait!"

Slightly surprised Knight turned around and saw the heir to the Ballarian crown rushing toward him. Although not yet sixteen, the boy had a maturity that was beyond his years. It may have been due to the fact that he was the eldest and was aware of his responsibilities now that his parents were dead which left him with many burdens. Being a monarch in exile there was something burning in his heart that made him realize that he would never be truly happy until he was back among his people to live out his family legacy. Whatever the reasons, Knight liked how the prince conducted himself and always enjoyed talking with him.

Knight extended his right hand and the prince grasped it with both of his. His smile was broad which showed off his white teeth and contrasted his bronze features. Although all the Ballarian males were bald due to genetics, they were capable of growing facial hair and the prince had recently started a dark beard which he hoped one day would be as full as the beard his father had. At six feet he was at his full height and he sported a well toned one hundred and seventy-pound body.

" May I speak with you, Clayton? "

" Certainly, Gles. What's on your mind? "

" I've been thinking. I have had many things on my mind but one thing in particular. From what I know and have seen and from what you have told me, you are capable of many things. What I don't understand is how you can sit by and wait with apparent contentment while that terrible hoard makes it's way toward your planet. You know about them. Why don't you attack them first? "

" I wish I could, Gles. I really do! But the truth is that at the present time I am not ready to take a viable defensive stance, let alone taking an offensive approach to this. As you well know it is a very difficult position that I am in. Our main opponent right now is time. Given enough time any thing is possible, but we have to contend with the opposition's timetable, which we are not totally certain about. Given the time to make changes necessary to withstand an attack and the time to develop the weapons necessary to force them back, we might be able to stage a good fight. If all goes well, some day I will personally see you back to your home and will watch your coronation with the great pride. "

" I would like that very much. Let us hope that the day does come. For now it is only a dream. "

" Hope and faith may be two of the greatest allies which we have personal control over. It is best not to lose track of either one. Keep the faith in that dream and together we'll see it come true. This I promise you. "

A soft buzzer sounds on the communication band around Knight's wrist and upon checking it he sees that there is someone calling on the security line. This piqued his curiosity since he was not expecting anyone to call for several hours. Upon excusing himself from the presence of the prince he proceeds to his office to receive the call.

As he sits behind his desk, he types in the appropriate security code and hears a dial tone coming from the monitor. As he pushes another button a face appears on the screen. It was Mason Rasov and from the look on his face Knight knew that he was not calling with good news.

" Speak freely Mason. It is a secure line. "

" I'm afraid I have much bad news to tell you Clay. "

" What is it? "

" It's about this morning. Judge Crenshaw stuck it to you Clay and he didn't waste any time doing it! "

Knight shakes his head and shields his eyes with his right hand. He leans back and puts his feet on the desk and places his hands behind his head. He figures he may as well be comfortable as he receives the message that he knew might be coming.

" Proceed. "

" Well, to begin with another of the bar room brawlers died an hour ago. The one that you broke his back. The preliminary is that a bone fragment ruptured a lung and it filled with blood. They will send you the official report later. But that's not where the trouble lies.

" Shortly after the other two were taken in for processing the Judge was there and took them aside and met with them behind closed doors for several minutes. Although it's very unusual he had the right. When he came out he had written testimony from the two and then he arranged to have the lie detector tests waived on both. That's when I knew something was up. About an hour later both men were released by the authority of the Judge without even appearing before a tribunal.

" Then the Judge started a witch hunt with you as the target. With the testimony he obtained he submitted to the law enforcement committee that the two survivors were victims caught in the middle of a major scandal in which a vigilante law enforcement official went beyond the parameters set by the system. Your name won't be mentioned publicly, but he is coming at you through the back door.

" A few minutes ago I received word that he gained permission from a World court tribunal to launch an investigation into the affairs and operations of GLESA. They also ruled that you have to pay restitution to the families of those you killed and wounded this morning. That is all except for Burt Wilfred Langley. Langley was named as the murderer of the boys at the bar. The way the Judge tells it, the others were just innocent bystanders. He claims that you attacked them unprovoked. Since we weren't there we couldn't dispute this claim. We immediately tried to get the bar tender to back you up but he has disappeared. It seems the Judge is covering all the bases.

" And finally our friend the judge sought and was able to convince the United Nations to order you not to associate with GLESA until the investigation is completed. He pointed out an old charter that states that the United Nations security council has the ultimate authority over any organization that operates under its name and it could deal with personnel in any manner that was appropriate. Obviously the Judge has had a very busy morning. "

" It would seem so. My options are obviously very limited due to the extreme that Crenshaw has carried his crusade against me. Although the bastard is correct in some of his observations, his blatant attempt to railroad me is beyond contempt. He has made the situation political and you know how I despise politics. Yet there is also the public point of view to be considered and one has to wonder what Crenshaw would leak to the public whether it be truthful or not. Yes, it would indeed seem that Crenshaw has been very busy within the past few hours. However, that would be more of a compliment to the speed and efficiency of the justice system of today rather than the abilities of Crenshaw. Yet this also points out that there are still flaws in the system when it allows the likes of Crenshaw to circumvent and manipulate the system the way he has.

" One option would be to pull out of the United Nations. We allowed ourselves to be aligned with the UN in order to let them take advantage of our services to better protect and maintain world peace. That is something we could continue to do without being associated with the UN. It would be less glamorous not being associated with such a prestigious organization. On the other hand we could get the same results as a free lance operation. Then there is the issue of public perception again. The immediate response would more than likely be negative, but that could be overcome over time. Yet when it comes down to the truth, leaving the United Nations is not something that I want to do because I believe we can do more good as long as we are associated with them and they are an organization I respect. I also have a suspicion that Crenshaw would like us to pull out for reasons other than his hatred for me. This first option we shall dismiss.

" The second option is that we exterminate Crenshaw. Let me finish my analysis before you comment Mason.

Killing Crenshaw would likely bring immediate satisfaction for he has been an opposing factor of GLESA since the beginning. Yet while his death would bring personal gratification it would go against the basic principle on which I formed GLESA and try to live my life. Truthfully he does not really meet the qualifications to warrant death although he is a major pain in the butt. If this were justification to kill someone the population of the planet would drop drastically. There is also the fact that killing Crenshaw would not benefit our situation since he has already set things in motion and his absence would not stop it. There are other ways to deal with Crenshaw without getting blood on our hands and troubling the conscience. "

" The option of choice is that which is proposed by the opposing factions. I will step down as commander of GLESA until this so called investigation is completed. In the meantime, I leave you in charge Mason, since you are second in command. Continue to operate as if nothing has happened and give those doing the investigating complete cooperation. But do not let them interfere with the operations of GLESA   as some political entities try to do in situations such as this. "

" Is that how you want it? "

" Yes. "

" But will you come back to GLESA when things blow over? "

" You know I will. I gave this organization life and view it as one of my children. And who could stay away from such a wonderful child? Anyhow, if I don't come back, no one will be able to keep you and your partners in line. "

" Yes, that might be true. "

" Do me one favor, will you? "

" Cancel the security on Judge Crenshaw. If he wants security, he can pay for it out of his own pocket rather than expect us to continue it as a courtesy. "

" Consider it done. By the way, what will you do with so much time on your hands? "

" Probably spend some more time in the laboratory. I may even try to get in a few more ball games to take my mind off things. And most important, I will have more time to spend with the children. You know it has been weeks since I have seen your lovely Katrina and the boys. I want you and your family over sometime soon. "

" Yes that would be good. Let's try and do it a week from this Saturday. That will give me time to get things running smoothly in your absence. "

" Sounds good. Think maybe I'll see you at the ballpark? "

" Why? "

" Well, GLESA does provide security even when I'm not in charge. "

" You know I can't stand baseball. "

" Okay. Then it's a week from Saturday. "

" See you then. "

The screen goes blank and Knight is alone with his thoughts. Much of what had happened he had seen as a possibility from the time when he founded GLESA. It was only natural for Judge Crenshaw to hate him because his father had been one of the Senators he forced out of office years earlier. Although Knight knew that revenge that revenge was one of the factors controlling the Judge's actions, instinct told him there were others. He would allow Crenshaw his moments of glory, but as soon as he uncovered what the other factors were, Knight wanted to personally bring the Judge down.

Taking a personal interest in a case put Knight in the situation he was currently enduring. Although he knew the risks, he did not let emotions cloud his judgment. All the lines had been drawn, some by him, and he still willingly crossed over them. When he was notified of the circumstances those two boys were in, it immediately raised his ire. He used his influence to have the case handled by his team. That was his first judgment flaw, for he should have let another law enforcement agency handle it so he could distance himself. His second mistake was leaving the rest of the team on the highway while he went in like a maverick. Third, he had the opportunity to apprehend the criminals without incident, but his anger made fighting seem like a better choice. The final point was a judgment call that he would continue to make again and again. If he had not activated his force field, the effect of his blows would not have been so destructive.

The field makes him nearly invulnerable and he may as well have been beating his victims with a metal club. While the field did stop him from harm by stopping the bullets, Knight knew that he should have used more self-control. He realized it was not the force field that was the issue, but the method of attack. Although the field made it seem as if he had hands made of steel. It was the placement of the blows that was the crucial factor. Even without the protective field, he would have killed ten and maimed seven instead of killing fifteen and maiming two. He could have easily taken them out without killing them or causing permanent damage.

This realization stunned Knight and it was very disturbing. How could someone as intelligent as himself let his emotions blind him so much that he would willingly destroy? He did believe that there were situations where his actions would have been warranted. This, however, was not one of them. No matter how much more advanced he was than other people were, he was still only human. While being human he would have flaws and he knew that this flaw was psychological. Maybe it could be corrected. Yet that would mean therapy and his ego could not withstand that. Either he solved the problem himself or it wouldn't be taken care of at all. Although he admitted to himself that he had a problem, he viewed it as not being very serious and could be dealt with in time.

The next order of business was where to progress from where he was. He would basically go on with his other endeavors as if they were more urgent than GLESA. The problem lied in where to divide the time. First he decided the majority of his time would be spent with his family. However, the time schedule of the alien invasion was another important factor to consider. The time with his family would be beneficial because he did feel that he was becoming drained. Taking a rest and then returning to his research with a fresh outlook would probably be the best scenario.

Thus he began rearranging his schedule to accommodate the gained time from his leave from GLESA. It would be two weeks at the earliest and six months on the outside. Due to the unknown time factor. He would schedule only a month at a time and keep to that schedule even if the inquiry concludes before that time.

After completing his tentative schedule he decided it would be relaxing if he played a round of golf. He changed cloths to a white short sleeve shirt with one green and one red stripe each running from his right shoulder down diagonally to his left hip. He wore a pair of gray slacks and black golf shoes. On his head he donned the team cap he wore when he played for the Omaha Thunder.

Out the back door he walked and set the bag down by the first tee. From the top pouch he pulls out a tee and a ball and places them between the two red markers. He returns to the bag and opens a second pouch and removes a plastic bottle. The bottle contains a cream that is a sun block that also helps keep the body cool. He applies cream liberally to his face, neck, and arms. Although the cream is grease less, he wipes his hand on a towel after returning the bottle to its pouch. He knows he will be free from sunburn because the sun block will remain active for eight hours, more than enough time to complete his game. He also knows that although the air temperature was now in the upper eighties, he would remain cool because the water base formula slowly evaporates on the skin aiding the cooling process. Although the product had first been developed in the late twentieth century, current advances allowed for the cream to be suited to each person's genetic makeup. While that made the product more expensive, it was also much more efficient and effective.

With his pre-game preparation completed, he proceeds to choose a club. The ball screams off the tee and dives for cover three hundred eighty feet away in the middle of the fairway. Knight proceeds to birdie the first three holes before his concentration is distracted as he begins thinking of the day's events. He alternates pars and bogeys on the next twelve holes before he can regain his composure. Although he was able to salvage a one under par score of seventy-one with a birdie, eagle, and birdie on each of the last three respective holes; he is upset with his breakdown. Due to the fact that each of the course's eighteen holes were duplication of eighteen of the most difficult holes in the world, the score would seem very respectable. However, the fact that Knight normally shot in the sixty to sixty-three range made the day disheartening for him. It bothered him that his game of rest was disrupted by the very reason he was forced to vacation. He decided he would talk to Dr. Avery about his condition.

Walking back to the house he notices Ana on the patio, sitting in a chair that is facing away from him. She is busy going over business data and is too engrossed to notice her husband approaching. Her long black hair is draped over the back of the chair, covering most of the tan, bamboo material. The white sun hat she wears is a perfect contrast to her hair and bronze body. She is wearing a navy blue, one-piece bathing suit beneath a peach blouse which has all but the bottom two buttons unfastened. Her bare feet are propped up on an identical tan, bamboo chair. On her lap is a portable computer unit that is basically an electronic notebook.

The unit itself is a self-contained portable computer that requires only a small power pack. It was another product of the late twentieth century, motivated by the increased paper conservation movement. By the year 2000, nearly every classroom in America and soon the world were using them. While the product itself was similar in size and weight to a good-sized hardbound textbook, it was very practical because it eliminated the need for multiple notebooks and could store several years of input by a student. The body of the product consisted of a screen the size of a standard sheet of paper; a keyboard built into the lower portion, and an electronic pen.

A user had the option of typing in the information or adding lines on the screen and writing it out by hand using the electronic pen which had a soft tip which would not scratch the screen. The keyboard was touch sensitive and silent as not to disturb the teacher and other students. There was full cursor control and when the user utilized the electronic pen, they had total creative control as whether to write with or without lines, to print or write in cursive, or to use the pen to draw pictures or diagrams. Each screen is saved with the touch of a button or saved automatically when they scroll to a new screen. Each subject is saved on a separate file and it is feasible for a student to store his or her entire academic career from grade school to college on the same unit.

Another option is to get the unit to print what is on the screen onto paper. The unit had a built-in printer, but due to the size of the unit, it could only hold twenty sheets of paper at a time. It was also possible to transfer information from the unit to a larger master unit similar to the ones utilized by the teachers. A student would attach a jack from the teacher's unit to theirs and copy the screen or file. It was a practical way of collecting homework and since each student had their own identification number integrated into the file, it made cheating much more difficult for a student could not simply copy the homework of another. These units revolutionized education and had applications in numerous other fields.

The unit Ana used was solely for business purposes, although she still had the one from her school days. She was busy entering business data into the unit, which would do the computations she needed. Knight quietly placed his golf bag on the grass and slipped off his golf shoes. Slowly he crosses the flat, stone patio until he was directly behind her. Leaning over the chair he proceeds to kiss her behind her right ear and on the neck.

" Better hurry, for my husband might be home soon. "

" Uh huh," was his only response as he continued.

She puts her feet on the ground and tosses the computer onto the opposite chair. She slowly rises to her feet as Knight continues to kiss and caress her neck and shoulders. As she turns around she does her best to look surprised with eyebrows raised and mouth wide open. Her left hand held her blouse held tight while the right proceeds to twirl a lock of hair as if she was nervous.

" Clay! It's you! "

He lets out a laugh for he knew the game she is playing and would let her continue. Standing in front of him was the woman he has loved and will love for years to come. Yet she had the need to play these psychological mind games to keep the relationship fresh. Because it made her happy he always went along.

" Disappointed? "

" No, no. I just wasn't expecting you back so soon. "

" Were you expecting someone else? "

" Me? No. Why would you think that? "

He couldn't help but laugh. Although it was her game, he was never very good at playing along. She had to put her hand over her mouth, but he could tell by her eyes that she was smiling. The game was over.

" Didn't the children tell you I was home? "

She returned to her chair as he circled to take the opposite one. He placed the unit on the table to his left and gazes into her dark eyes as he settles into a comfortable position.

" They mentioned it. I also heard what happened to those two boys. Terrible thing. I sent our condolences to the families and arranged to pay for the burials. That's the way you would have wanted it. Right? "

He nodded. They were so compatible that sometimes he believed they were extensions of the same person.

" Heard I was suspended? "

She looked puzzled. " Suspended? From what? "

" From GLESA It's more of a leave of absence but they will call it a suspension. It's for the best anyhow. It will allow me more time to spend with you and the family."

" You're around here too much as it is. "

Their eyes interlock and they both laugh. He takes her hands in his and leans over and kisses her left cheek. Her presence had an extremely calming effect on him and he knew he would never make it through what was to come without her. They stand up together and walk through the double doors that access the patio into the house. Hand in hand they walk for each has passion on their mind.

Four days had passed and Knight felt well rested. He had done nothing strenuous or mind taxing. Six hours of sleep each night had replaced his normal two. His days were filled with some light reading, light workouts in the gym, time with the children, and a daily round of golf. It was golf that was a loose gauge of his improvement as his scores improved to 69, 66, and 62 for the three days. In another few days he would resume his research. Until then it would be games and relaxation.

On this day knight would skip the round of golf for he was going to play baseball. Early that morning he received a call from the General Manager of the Omaha Thunder, Grady Page. He said that the previous night the right fielder, Juan Ortega, had broken his collarbone when he dived for a ball and collided with the fence near the visiting team's bullpen. Although he did make the catch, the injury would keep him out of the line up for at least two weeks. Knight knew that the bone would have been fused immediately by the team doctor, but Ortega would need extensive rehabilitation to return to his old form. The team had a double header that day against St. Louis and Knight would play both games. The first game started at 2:15 p.m. so he wanted to be there by noon.

It was a quarter to nine and Ana had already left for the office. The children were occupied with their studies and the Ballarian party were holding a ceremony in the chapel for this would have been a festive religious holiday back on their planet. Knight had enjoyed a delicious and plentiful breakfast and was heading toward the back patio to do some light reading by the pool.

Before opening the first magazine removed two pills from a bottle on the patio table and swallowed them with a glass of apple juice. The pills were a combination vitamin supplement and internal cleanser. The digestive enzymes of the stomach active the pills to release chemicals which act like missiles by homing in on excess material the body doesn't need such as cholesterol. Although he does exercise regularly, the pills allow him to eat foods he normally should not. With his diet taken care of, he proceeds to read.

At 11:30 an aide comes onto the patio and informs him of the time. Leaving the aide to tidy up the patio area, he rushes to the garage area and selects a 2045 Knight KM-9 to the stadium. It was the most advanced of his sports car line. Since he was on vacation he decided not to change out of the gray sweat suit he was wearing.

Once he cleared the estate gates he put the pedal to the floor and began checking the GLESA security monitor on his portable system. He wanted to check the traffic conditions and the positions of all law enforcement vehicles along the highway, for it would be somewhat embarrassing if he got a speeding ticket on the way to the stadium.

Chapter six

When he reached the Blackhole at 11:50, he knew it was going to be a great day. Once the car passed the first security checkpoint his mind was more at ease, for he never wore his force field to their games. Although the car he drove was modified to withstand an extensive assault, there was always cause for concern. Inside the perimeter of the Blackhole, the finest security in the world was present because an elite branch of GLESA guarded it. These were not the normal security assigned to other companies, but the most advanced surveillance and scanning equipment designed and two-thirds of the personnel were androids with full sensor capabilities. This place held a special interest in his heart, so Knight was not going to take any chances with his or his ball players' safety. The surroundings may appear relaxed, yet Knight knew the complex was very security tight.

He reached his locker and the uniform with double zeroes hung on a bar. Removing his sweat suit, he stood there in his under pants as he sorted out the different articles of clothing that comprised the uniform. Around the corner came a rookie outfielder from Canada, Nigel Welland. Since he had only been called up from AAA two weeks prior, he had never met the club's owner. All he could do is stare in disbelief at the size and build of the man next to his locker. It was the scars that really caught his attention, for they gave the hulking person an ominous foreboding and Welland felt he didn't want anything to do with the man.

From behind Welland came the team's starting catcher, Anthony Vega, a Cuban who spoke seven languages and that came in handy on this team. The Cuban chewed on a cigar as he saw Knight and then saw the young rookie staring at him. He saw the look on the boy's face and couldn't help but smile. He whispers into the boy's ear.

" Don't worry, kid. He's not as scary as he looks. "

Vega put his left hand on the boy's right shoulder and shakes him slightly. This seems to break the trance he was in and he looks around to see the smiling face of the Cuban. The reassurance of this team leader helped steady the boy and Vega could see that.

" Heard you were going to play today. Think you're up to it, Clay? "

Knight turned around as he snapped the fasteners of the uniform jersey in place. He saw his friend Vega and the young ball player whose eyes widened as he stepped toward them. It was humorous to him that he could instill such a reaction in another person. Then again, he did realize that he was a rather large and imposing figure.

" Decided to give it a try. With you behind the plate calling the pitches, I may not get much of a workout. Eh, Tony? "

Vega laughs and stretches out his hand and the two shake and then slap each other on the back. Good friends were what the players of the Omaha Thunder had become, especially those who were the regular starters. Very few new faces joined the team each year, due to their unique contracts and the conditioning of the athletes also cut down on injuries which limited the need to call players up from the farm system. But some players do retire and there are occasional injuries in a 200 game season. The regulars were more like family and they readily accepted Knight into the fold. It was not the fact that he was the team's owner, for many other clubs actually hated their owners. The main reason was that Knight is a likable person who fit in well with his players. This was aided by the fact that they admired his abilities, which equaled or surpassed all the regulars and they liked that he could step in and do the job.

Vega motions to Welland.

" Come 'ere, Nigel. This is the fella that signs your checks. He's also going to start for Juan today, so you watch him closely and maybe you will learn something today."

The boy timidly steps forward and extends his hand.

" Nice to meet you, sir. "

" Sir? What's this sir, nonsense? Did you and the boys put him up to that?"

The boy gets a worried look on his face and looks to Vega for guidance as he prepares to apologize. Before he can say a word, a smile breaks across Knight's face and he lightly slaps the boy on the back.

" Lighten up, son! The name's Clay. Clayton Knight. But I want those on my teams to call me Clay. None of that sir stuff. Okay?"

" Okay."

" Nigel Welland, isn't it?"

" Yes."

" I thought so. You see I keep a close eye on my prospects. Last year you batted .314 in Reno at only seventeen years of age. Fairly impressive, son. Broke into single A ball at sixteen after graduating high school and hit .413 at Flagstaff. I like it that you attained your degree early. Shows you are more than average upstairs. Have you been advised how things operate around here?"

" Yes, Mr. Knight."

"Its Clay, son. We're all informal here. Anyhow after you're done with baseball, and with your talent that might not be for a long time, you can be assured you will always be secure thanks to Knight Enterprises."

" You're that Knight?"

" Bright boy, Eh Tony? Yes son, but it's my lovely spouse who runs the show there now. But be assured your future will always be secure. For as of this moment, you will be a permanent member of the team."

" Thank you, Clay. Thank you!"

" Now go and take some batting practice."

" Yes, sir! I mean, Clay."

" You're catching on. Now scram!"

The boy scrambles down the aisle and disappears around the corner. Vega looks Knight in the eyes and smiles, which raises his eyebrows.

" You were planning on keeping the kid anyhow, weren't you? This wasn't any sudden outburst of generosity."

" Tony, you wound me. Sure I was planning on keeping him. The kid has major talent. Wasn't he already hitting .371 in Reno before he was called up last week? Howard has used him sparingly, but he's gone six for eight so far. I'm a nice guy, Tony, but I'm no fool."

" Never said you were."

" I'm going to do some simulator time. See you later."

" Concentrate on Nelson and Valute."

" Thanks, I will. "

Knight finishes putting on his uniform and then walks down the hall past the rehabilitation center. After punching in a security code, he enters a large chamber that is completely dark except for a dim light that shines over a computer terminal. What the room actually consists of is a holographic chamber, a pitching machine, and the computer.

The hologram machine and the pitching machine would coincide with the image's release of the ball could duplicate every pitcher who had ever been taped in history. There had been attempts to construct a similar batting aide using projectors and pitching machines together, but it was very inferior. An identical chamber was in the women's softball complex. All players were ordered to silence, although there were rumors that the chambers existed. To make things more competitive, Knight actually considered leasing chambers to the other clubs at a minimal price. He realized there would be some negative drawbacks regarding his teams' dominance, but he thought that more competition would be the best situation for the advancement of the game. Yet he wasn't going to make any definite decision on the subject for at least another year which would extend his team's dominance for that much longer.

By using the chamber a player could practice against a pitcher's best pitches without having to face them on the field. That was one of the reasons the Thunder were so good and had three players achieve batting averages superior to .400 for the first time in history. They had been seeing a pitcher's best stuff even before they stepped up to the plate. Due to the fact that everything is duplicated, speed, location, and movement, the batter can have an assortment of balls and strikes to make it seem more realistic. Or they can work repeatedly on one troublesome pitch if they desired. When they finished their session they would receive a computer analysis as to how they hit each pitch: how far it traveled and location on the field.

Knight walked onto the playing field confident he could handle that day's pitchers. The rest of the team was running sprints, stretching, and playing catch. The other team had already arrived but had yet to emerge from their locker room. It was understandable that they were reluctant to come out because the Thunder were having another banner year with a 56-17 record which was inflated due the fact they were riding a twenty-two game winning streak. Since this was a different brand of baseball being played there was no basis for comparison to the teams of the twentieth century. Some would say that baseball is baseball, but it is unrealistic to compare a team from one century to that from another. No matter what anyone said, Knight knew that he had assembled the most talented team in the game for its era.

The starters for the Thunder had a good combination of average hitters and power hitters. This was slightly confusing because all the players had respectable batting averages and were all capable of putting the ball out of the park. Some just excelled in one phase more than the other. With the batting order virtually unchanged for three years, except for the occasional injured player, each team member got in a groove and knew what to expect from those in the line-up around them. The combination of these being tremendous athletes, having a strenuous off-season workout schedule, and the hologram chamber allowed the Omaha Thunder to compile some phenomenal statistics.

In the lead off position was the second baseman, Kim Hamako, from Takada, Japan. He was one of the three starters to achieve a batting average over .400 the previous year. His average was .421 in 2048 and he supplemented that with eighteen home runs. So far this year he was batting only .370 but had already matched his previous years total of home runs. Once on base he was a base stealing threat while amassing an even hundred in 2048 and already had sixty-one this year. Hamako throws and bats left-handed.

Batting second was third baseman William Brand of Washington DC Brandt was a power treat as he totaled fifty-eight home runs in 2048 and had twenty-seven so far this year. His batting average was a respectable .305 last year and .309 this year. Another accomplishment was the string of 301 games without an error he was currently on. Brandt throws right handed but bats left-handed.

Following Brandt is another American, the left fielder John Lewis from Chicago, Illinois. Lewis was the second player to bat over .400 the previous year with a .413 average. This year he cooled off considerably to amass a .331 average. Like Hamako, he had a decent home run total in 2048 with twenty-seven and had almost reached it this year with twenty-one through seventy-three games. The previous year he had a respectable eighty-five stolen bases and already had fifty-seven this year. Lewis throws right-handed and is a switch hitter.

The most feared power hitter in the league batted cleanup and he is first baseman Mikhal Royou from Kursk, Ukraine. In 2048 he had an incredible eighty-four home runs and was on pace to surpass that because he already had thirty-seven entering the game. Royou was able to do so well because other teams had trouble pitching around him. There are almost always players on base and another power hitter who also hits for average follows him. As might be expected, Royou had the drawback of having the worst average of the starting lineup. In 2048 his average was only at .280, but was improving his pitch selection and was batting .290 this year. He throws and bats left-handed.

The man who allowed Royou to do what he does is the catcher, Anthony Vega of Palmer, Cuba. While in 2048 he had the lowest average of the .400 hitters with .401, this year he was the most likely to repeat with a .399 average entering the game. To go with his eye for the ball was the ability to put it over the fence with regular consistency. Last year he had forty-one round trippers and this year he was challenging Royou with thirty-one. Since he was a young catcher at twenty-six, he could run the bases better than most. The previous year he had ninety-two stolen bases and had twenty-five entering the game. He throws right-handed and is a switch hitter.

Normally lending support to Vega is right fielder Juan Ortega of Ponce, Puerto Rico. In the previous season he hit

.359, had sixteen home runs, and seventy-nine stolen bases. Before his injury he was batting .320 with ten home runs and twenty-two stolen bases. The team had confidence that Knight could do an adequate job in Ortega's slot and on this night their rhythm might not be disrupted much.

Batting seventh was centerfielder Sean O'Casey of Castletown, Ireland. He was the speediest man on the team and had a cannon for an arm. In 2048 he batted .305 to go with twenty-seven home runs and 122 stolen bases. So far this year he was batting only .294 with eleven home runs but had fifty-three stolen bases entering the game. He was on pace to challenge his own record of 154 set two years previous. O'Casey throws and bats right-handed.

In the eighth slot was Victor Wise, a talented shortstop from Torrence, California. It would be appropriate to say that Wise was truly batting second clean up in an order as potent as this one was. In 2048 he batted .320 with thirty-two home runs but was limited to twelve stolen bases. So far this year he had a .307 average and twenty home runs to go with that an improved thirteen stolen bases.

The ninth spot in the order was always held by the pitchers. Traditionally this was a weak spot in the batting order, but with the facilities at their disposal they were able to greatly improve their hitting ability. As a group the pitchers had an average of .268 the previous year. Two of the starting pitchers had averages over .300. Quinn Brewer, a left hander from Huntsville, Alabama had a .317 average and had five home runs. Yoshida Shusaki from Osaka, Japan had a .307 average and one home run. Lawrence St. John of Glendale, California was the pitcher with the most home runs at seven to go with a .257 average. The accomplishments of these three top hitting pitchers entering the game: Brewer batting .327 with three home runs, Shusaki batting .303 with one home run, and St. John batting .289 with six home runs.

In regard to pitching ability the staff was quite excellent. Although the team played so many games, they only used a five-man rotation. The ace of the staff was Pablo Cortex, a right hander with a powerful arm from Veracruz, Mexico. He possesses an ominous 100-mile per hour fastball which he mixes with a curveball, changeup, and slider. In 2048 he had a 37-4 record with 419 strikeouts and only seventy-two walks. Because he puts so much into his pitching he batted only .131 the previous year. Cortez was off to a blistering start the current season with an unblemished 10-0 record with 151 strikeouts, but already has forty walks. His earned run average was also down to 2.05 compared to 2.55 the previous season. He was also batting an improved .168.

Following Cortez in the rotation is lest hander Shusaki, who is a finesse pitcher. Although he possessed only an eighty-four mile per hour fastball, he mixed it well with an odd combination of curves, sinkers, and knuckleballs. His previous years stats were a 26-2 record with 135 strikeouts, only thirty-five walks, and a 2.49 ERA This year he was struggling with a 3-7 record and had a dismal ratio of fourteen strikeouts to twenty-nine walks. His ERA had also skyrocketed to 5.87. Since the coaching staff found a mechanical flaw, which they corrected, it seemed only a matter of time until he broke the slump.

Third in the rotation was another fire balling right hander in St. John. While he had only three pitches in a fastball, curve, and change-up, his uncanny control makes him almost more unbearable to face than Cortez. That control and a ninety-eight mile per hour fastball has helped him to claim the league's strikeout title for three years consecutive. In 2048 he was 28-10 with 538 strikeouts and 124 base on balls to go with an 1.84 ERA Only a rare lack of run support kept him from having a better win-loss record. So far this year he was 10-4 with 173 strikeouts, forty-two walks, and an 1.91 ERA In some respects, St. John was the ace of the staff, the team just played better behind Cortez.

Fourth in the order was Brewer, another finesse pitcher with a wide assortment of pitches. While have a better than average eighty-eight mile per hour fastball, he could also mix in a change-up, fork ball, screw ball, or slider to confuse a hitter. Like everyone else he did well the previous year. He was 29-4 with 254 strikeouts, 117 base on balls, and a 3.39 ERA This year he was struggling like Shusaki, but not as bad. He was 6-2 with 137 strikeouts and 138 walks and his ERA was up to 4.71.

The final starter of the rotation also was the workhorse of the staff because he sometimes would come out of the bullpen to be short relief if one of the starters got in trouble. He was right hander Tomas Villa of Panama City, Panama. In 2048 he was 30-19 with 336 strikeouts and 138 walks and a 3.91 ERA He did all that with only an eighty-six mile per hour fast ball and a curve ball. In the off season he perfected a slider that has helped improve his stats greatly. Being the workhorse he picks up the garbage the others couldn't handle. In the previous year he picked up more losses than he probably should have, but this year he was getting a lot more wins than normal. Entering the game he had a phenomenal 17-2 record with 184 strikeouts and forty-four walks to go with an 1.68 ERA If he doesn't burn out, he could end St. John's strikeout reign at the end of the season.

The king of the bullpen is Jose Verde of Caracus, Venezuela. He has a ninety-nine mile per hour fastball and a wicked screwball that make him a feared stopper. Although he does have a decent curve and change-up, he rarely uses them. In 2048 he had a record 105 saves to go with an 8-3 record. Entering the game he already had thirty-two saves and a 2-1 record. It doesn't matter if Verde is facing a right-handed batter or a left handed one for both hit extremely poor against him. In his four-year career right handers hit only .109 against him while left handers fared only slightly better at .114.

The rest of the players were an assortment of players recruited from around the world and it was up to the manager to utilize them in the best possible fashion. Those players included three left handed pitchers: Juan Cruz of Reynosa, Mexico, Jose Rivas of San Juan, Puerto Rico, and Mike Beard of Enid, Minnesota. Julio Lopez was a right-handed pitcher from Cuzco, Peru. The remaining twelve players were catcher Tyson Dundee of Stockton, California, Infielders Cleveland Wilkes of Burlington, Vermont, Joe Twilley of Fort Mitchell, Kentucky, Fred Russell of Houlton, Maine, Cliff Cummings of San Antonio, Texas, Bill Dent of Dublin, Ohio, Yasui Okamoto of Toyama, Japan and outfielders Jack Player of South Hadley, Massachusetts, Tim Bosco of Norfolk, Virginia, Miguel

Alcala of Guadalajara, Mexico,   Vladislav Ekimov of Murmansk, Ukraine, and the newly acquired Nigel Welland of Lethbridge, ALberta.

The manager of the Omaha Thunder was forty-eight year old Howard Cook of Syracuse, New York. Before being hired to take the helm of the Thunder, Cook was a very successful college coach at the University of Texas where he guided the school to six national championships in an eleven-year period. Knight gave Cook complete control over the team and makes no attempt to interfere. The only time they ever argued was when trying to decide which players to go after. The thing knight liked about Cook was his coaching style, which stressed both power and speed. He worked closely with the players and helped transform them into the most prolific home run hitting and base stealing team in the history of the game. Cook did not mind that Knight was willing to play on the team for he was willing to take an athlete of that caliber anytime.

The fact that Cook had led the team to three straight World Series Championships made him well respected. However, there was a difference between respecting someone and liking them. Although Howard Cook was a very nice person, the fact that his team dominated the game so made many people despise him. This was the curse of many great coaches, for the better they did, the more people hated them and wanted to root for the underdog. Cook accepted that as the way things were meant to be and continued to direct his team to pummel the opposition mercilessly without regret. This was a common trait held by all of the coaches of the Knight owned teams.

Knight saw that batting practice was about to get under way and he picks up his favorite bat. It is made out of a synthetic wood-like material called woodyn, which became necessary due to a combination of a shortage of trees and a desire by baseball enthusiasts to stay with wooden bats. He steps into the batting cage after the pitching coach had warmed up his arm. Tiley Keyes was destined to be inducted into the Hall of Fame since he was the first pitcher of the post-2000 era to record 400 victories. Only two others had done it since and none of the current players were anywhere close to accomplishing that feat. Knight felt it was feasible that a few of the Thunder's pitchers had the ability to reach that mark. At 53, Keyes was no longer in his prime, but he was a competent batting practice pitcher. As coach, there were few equals for he communicated his ideas easily with his pitchers and helped them overcome their weaknesses under his watchful eye.

Knight took only ten pitches and sent nine of them over the fence. Four went over the left field wall, two over center, and three over right. The tenth ball hit the top of the center field wall at the four hundred-eighty foot sign. There was a buzz in the press box as those there to cover the game frantically checked their programs to find out who the batter was. To those who were new to the park, there was profound disbelief when they learned that it was the owner. However, those who were regulars quickly accepted it as fact and went about their pre-game preparations.

He walks over to the dugout and encounters the left fielder. John Lewis ties his shoes. Knight picks up his glove and proceeds to bend the leather to limber it up.

" Impressive showing, Clay. Thinking of duplicating it in the game?"

" If given the opportunity."

" Well, don't look too good. Ortega has his pride and wouldn't want to have to wear shoes bigger than his when he gets back."

" He's a big boy and plays his game and I play mine. It's something to think over, but to be honest I won't give it much thought."

Lewis nods as if he understands. Then he smiles and picks up a ball that he tosses to Knight.

" If that's the way you're going to approach it, we better get your arm limbered up so you don't embarrass yourself in right."

" Thanks for the concern. "

They both walk onto the field and toss the ball back and forth. By this time the Cardinals had finally emerged from their locker room and were going through their warm-up routines. The general attitude of the team was one of complacency. They were the cellar dweller of the National League East and had been there since early in the season. Entering the game they seemed to be the Thunder's mirror opposites. They had a record of 18-55 and were currently enduring a fourteen game losing streak. The leagues coldest team was taking on the hottest. It was a mismatch on paper and everyone expected it to be that way on the field.

Knight knew the type of team they were facing and felt a little remorse for the under dogs. It was this type of mismatch that influenced Knight to consider offering the holographic batting chamber to the rest of the teams. Yet he did not want to make a decision on the matter until the situation concerning the alien threat was concluded. If there was the chance he could not contain the threat, he wanted the history of baseball to conclude with his team at the top.

After the national anthem concludes, the umpire shouts, " Play ball!"

It is the time in the rotation for Cortes to take the mound. That also meant that Shusaki would be pitching the second game of the double header. The Cardinals saw a dim ray of hope with Shusaki pitching for they thought they might escape the Blackhole with at least one victory.

Even before Knight could get comfortable in right field the top of the first inning was over because Cortez had struck out the side on ten pitches. This indicated to Knight that he would not be getting much work defensively in the first game. St. Louis knew they were in for a long day.

Hamako leads of the bottom of the inning with a single. He steals second on the first pitch to the plate, which Brandt lets pass for a strike. The Cardinal's manager decides to intentionally walk Brandt, but the pitcher then loses touch with the strike zone and walks Lewis too. Bases are loaded as the feared Royov steps to the plate. After taking the first pitch for a ball, he lifts a ball that is caught at the warning track, which allows Hamako to score. Runners are on first and third as Vega approaches the plate. He slaps the first pitch between first and second which allows Brandt to score.

Two men are on base as Knight eyes the pitcher with disdain. Chuck Nelson is a good pitcher but today was not going to be a good day. Knight takes a pitch for a strike. The runners lead off as Nelson delivers another pitch that Knight swings at but misses. He looks at the pitcher in disbelief but his glares are ignored. The third pitch is low and outside which allows Knight to collect himself. He watches Nelson windup and deliver a curve ball which he greets with a mighty swing. The ball flies on a line over the left field fence and lands seven rows up.

Home runs were actually rare in the Blackhole because of the distance of the fences. The fans cheer in appreciation. Of his team's many home runs over the years, only thirty-six percent came in their home stadium. That is one reason the team is feared more on the road than at home, because they were able to hit home runs almost at will due to the fact that they were hungry for home runs and the other teams' parks obliged them.

At the end of the first inning the score was seven to nothing. Cortez almost duplicated his first inning performance by striking out the side in fourteen pitches. Fans in the upper center field deck had six signs hanging over the railing which each had a "K" on it. Everyone knew that he was in a groove and many more signs would be hanging from the railing by the end of the game.

Vega led off the second and slaps a 1-1 pitch over the first baseman's head for a single. Knight steps to the plate and can see anger in Nelson's eyes. Few pitchers gave up home runs in the Blackhole and it was certainly humiliating to be one of them. The first pitch is outside by nearly a foot and Knight readies himself for the second pitch. Nelson releases a ninety-six mile per hour fastball, which heads right for Knight's head. Instead of diving out of the way, Knight just reaches up with his left hand and catches the ball a few inches from his face. He tosses the ball to the catcher and looks at the umpire.

" Ball two?"

For a second the umpire is bewildered. He had never seen anything like that before. Yet the rules did state that the batter did have to make an attempt to get out of the way of the ball for it to be considered hit-by-pitch. The umpire regains his wits and shouts his verdict.

" Ball two!"

The catcher throws the ball back to Nelson who is visibly shaken for having his attempt for revenge thwarted in such a manner. He was still shaking when he delivers the 2-0 pitch. It was a sinker that didn't sink and Knight took advantage of the error by smashing the ball over the center field fence. At the end of the inning it was ten to nothing and Nelson was too disturbed to continue.

The top of the third was identical to the first with Cortez striking out the side on ten pitches. He proceeds to strike out the next ten batters before someone actually made contact and grounded out to the second baseman in the seventh inning. In the eighth inning the Cardinal's clean-up hitter, shortstop Bill Gloss, got a piece of a 2-1 pitch that went screaming over Royov's head at first base. Knight took off running and dived with his body outstretched to catch the ball just inches before it would have touched the ground. Cortez walked the first two batters of the ninth to lose his perfect game, but struck out the next three on twelve pitches to get a no-hitter. It was rare for Cortez to finish a game but it was the second no-hitter of his career. Twenty-two strikeouts countered the two walks as he raised his record to 11-0 for the season. Knight was happy to have preserved the feat by making his only catch of the game, which was the only ball to make it out of the infield. Even though Cortez was nearly flawless, the team would allowed him to be much less than perfect because the final score was 23-0.

In regard to his offensive performance, Knight was very pleased with himself. He went four for seven with three home runs and nine runs batted in. Young Welland took over his final at-bat in the first game and made good with a single that was barely out of the reach of the jumping second baseman. Being on a winning team was a very enjoyable experience and Knight was appreciative that he was in a position to take advantage of such a team that produced that feeling so often.

The second game was much closer, although the outcome was never in doubt. Twelve to five was the final and the Cardinals felt that they were starting to build some momentum. It was an optimistic outlook for they had another double header with the Thunder tomorrow and then a five game series in New York against the East leader. Offensively Knight went three for five in the second game with another home run and three runs batted in. That made the total for the day four home runs which was a remarkable feat in any ballpark. The only other home run that day was a grand slam by Royov in the fifth inning of the second game.

The day's performance was a drastic improvement over the second game of the season in which Knight had replaced Royov at first base. In that game he was one for six with a solo home run and had an error at first base. With three games under his belt for the season, he was eight for eighteen, a .444 average with five home runs and thirteen runs batted in. He was disappointed that he had yet to get a stolen base this year but he would concentrate on that when he played next later in the year. It did please him that he did raise his career statistics. In his limited career he now had 142 hits, twenty-eight home runs, sixty runs batted in, while maintaining a .514 average in fifty games.

Chapter seven

Knight opened his eyes as a bright light shines on his face. He is lying flat on an examining table as Dr. Avery proceeds to scan his body and make routine checks of the body's operations. This was the third battery of tests within an hour and Knight was becoming restless. At the moment the doctor was concentrating on his head area and was implementing all the technology at his disposal to conduct a thorough examination.

There were three dozen wires running from Knight's head and face with each attaches to a sensor. The doctor also had two automatic scanning machines probing Knight from the back and to the left. In his hand, the doctor held a manual scanning device, which he moved slowly around Knight's head repeatedly. Then he suddenly puts the scanner on the counter, turns off the other machines, and begins plucking the wires off of Knight. Then he goes over to the main computer and has the scanners transfer their information into it. The data scrolls down the screen as the doctor sits there trying to make sense of the information just collected.

Knight rolls off the table and walks over to the counter where his clothes lay. He pulls a light blue shirt over his head and then puts on a pair of off-white dress pants. Then he pulls on white sock and then slips his feet into his running shoes. He adjusts the shoe fasteners before looking across the room at his friend.

Walking across the room he questions himself as to why he talked himself into participating in these tests. He hopes that it was not a waste of time for that was something he could little afford to misuse. Then he asks the doctor his opinion that he hopes will put his mind at ease.

" What's the diagnosis, Doc?"

" Hard to tell. I mean that physically, both externally and internally, everything is sound and operating at what could be considered perfection. However, it's your brain I'm worried about. In all honesty, both you and I know you are not normal. I mean the way your brain operates and is able to use more of the capacity and use it so efficiently. I only partially understand it, but it scares the hell out of me. You know what a normal brain scan chart looks like. See how it's ordered and calm and systematic. Now let me bring up what we just took from you and take a look."

When it comes up on the screen, Knight's eyes widen and his knees start to buckle. He grabs the back of the doctor's chair to balance himself and squeezes the cushion to release some of the tension and anxiety he was feeling. He full well understood what was on the screen much better than the doctor did. His friend continued to speak.

" Just look at this jumbled mess. There is no order and the chart is criss-crossing the screen over and over. It's as though multiple charts had been laid on top of one another."

He turns around and sees the look on Knight's face. The doctor looks back at the screen and then at Knight again. Then he knew he was on to something.

" That's it, isn't it. I mean when you were comatose years earlier I had results similar to this, but not as bad. You've got more going on in your head than anyone could have dreamed of. "

Knight averts his eyes from the screen and then turns around completely so his back is to the doctor. He crosses his arms and turns his head to talk over his shoulder.

" It's more than that. Years ago when I was doing research into how the brain operates, I took scan readings from a wide array of the population. There was one group that had readings that were remotely similar to these. They were of those people that were proven to have more than one distinct personality."

The doctor rises from his chair and pats Knight on his right shoulder.

" This would explain so much. I mean my diverse interests and ability to think and comprehend about so many varied subjects. It would also help to explain how I lost control the other night."

He pulls himself away from Dr. Avery and turns around to face him.

" Dammit, Bill! Why me? Maybe it makes me who I am. But who the hell am I? It's not as though another completely different personality took control without me knowing it for I don't have any episodes of blackouts. The changes are subtle and almost within the sub-conscience itself. I knew what I was doing, but it wasn't until I later reflected on it that I realized that I actually had no control in the situation. Is there any hope, Bill? I need your input. Don't leave me hanging!"

" You know as well as I do that there has been very little progress made within the last two hundred years in dealing with the mind. You're the worlds fore most expert on the subject, Clay. You've cracked many of the mysteries behind how the brain operates. You've done extensive research on how the neurotransmitters work and how different sequences have different consequences and countless other things. I'm afraid all I could tell you is what you have published from your research. In reality, if there is anyone that can treat the problem and deal with the subject, it's you."

" Oh, sure! That's like asking a madman to cure his own insanity. "

" You're not that far along and you know it. At the present, it would seem that all the personalities are pretty well integrated. All you have to do is keep your wits about you. You should be able to deal with the problem."

" Easy for you to say. You're not the one who has to find a cure for your own disease."

" Stop right there, Clay. Is it really a disease you have or something else? I don't think you should approach this from the standpoint that you are dealing with a disease. While I concede mental disease is a serious problem, I think it's more a mending process, like setting and fusing a broken bone. There's no virus or foreign influence. I think time will be your most important asset. You will also be able to get in tune with yourself."

Knight couldn't help but laugh. Although it was a traumatic situation for himself, the doctor was keeping his cool and thinking so rationally. He knew that his friend was right in how to approach it and he started to calm down.

" What do you suggest? Put a splint on my brain?"

With this wisecrack the doctor knew that the conversation was returning to a more normal mode. He smiles and reaches out and grabs Knight by both shoulders and holds him at arm's length.

" I'll help you through it. This is more important than any of my other research and certainly more challenging. And I know it will be more educational to see how you approach this and how you will set out to solve it. I'm sure that your old buddy, Han Li can add some creative insights on how to approach this situation. But remember there is no need to panic. This situation has never been considered fatal and you have obviously been handling it fairly well although you didn't know what you had."

" True, but the trick will be seeing how I handle it now that I know what I have. In all frankness, it scares the hell out of me!"

" That's to be expected, but I'm certain you will get over that. I'm sure Ana can help you through it."

" I don't want Ana to know."

" Why? It's not as though you're going through something that's terminal."

" I just don't, okay! At least not for now. I don't want this to go beyond myself, you, and Han."

" Whatever you say. Hey, I have an idea. You said you will be getting back into your other research full tilt next week. Before you do that, why don't we do a little fishing trip for a few days to let you relax some more before you get involved in that hectic world of high tech."

" You just want to keep an eye on me."

" Maybe. but it's a good offer. Want to join me. I was going down home anyway and fishing is more fun when there's someone with you. "

" Okay. You talked me into it. I'll tell you what, Tomorrow Ana is throwing a birthday party for some of the children at noon. She's taking the day off and everything. Why don't you come over and we'll leave from my house after the party."

" Sounds good. Now tell me which kids they are again. I may have delivered them, but I don't keep a close eye on birthdays, especially my own. I want to know what type of presents to bring."

" It's Amy, Rich, Debbie, and Terry. But don't burden your checkbook too much. That's Ana and my responsibility. Why don't you come over at eight and we can get in a round of golf before. Isn't that what doctors like? A leisurely round of golf."

" That's stereotyping, but yes I do like to play. But your game is much more polished than that and mine course of yours is a killer. I'll be there at a quarter to eight. And tell your blasted security not to hassle me this time. I don't like a damn security check run on me every time I come over to visit. It's not good for my game."

" Will do. See you tomorrow."

There is an overcast sky and a cool breeze blows from the northeast as Knight and Avery approach the house. Knight looks up and smiles as he approves of the gray colored heavens. It is days like this one that he liked best. He really didn't know why, but it left him feeling serene and he was thankful for it. Then he hears his friend comment on their concluded game.

" I'm never going to play with you again. It's so humiliating getting beat by such a margin by someone who has no interest in the game."

" No interest? Would I have built such an elaborate course for something I had no interest in? You're just mad because you play five days a week, every week it's in season and I play maybe thirty, thirty-five times a year. Sure I'm getting a lot of playing time in now and that's because of this unscheduled vacation. You also don't appreciate my laid back approach to the game and maybe you interpret that as disinterest. Anyhow, you're much too big to be hitting that little ball. You should have stuck to football where you can hit people. They might be moving, but you would have a better chance of making contact."

" Are you knocking my game? Let me tell you something! It requires skill for someone my size to play as well as I do. And I do play well. In fact, I have won my home course's annual charity tournament three of the last five years. So don't tell me I can't play this game. It's just this blasted course! You have all the angles figured out but it's new to a stranger."

" Stranger? How many times have you played here? Fifteen times a year? No, I think it's more than that because I've been told you sometimes play here when I'm out of state. So it's probably twenty times a year. You know the lay out of the course about as well as I do. The reason you're sore is because I beat you sixty-one strokes to seventy-nine. You don't like to lose any more than I do. But you may be better off not playing me any more because you know you can't beat me."

" You know, you have an inflated head! Anyone is beatable! You may beat me nine times out of ten, but I've caught you on days when you weren't so hot."

" Did you beat me?"

" Well, no dammit! You know what I mean. You can be had and one of these days I'm gong to do it."

" That's the spirit. Keep plugging away and maybe you'll do the improbable."

" You didn't say impossible."

" No, I didn't."

" Then there is hope!"

" But not for you. Let's go inside and see how things are progressing. It should be getting near time for the party to start."

" Don't you own a watch?"

" You know I do. There's no time limit in golf so I don't wear one. If you don't have anymore questions let's go inside. "

" Eleven thirty-two."

" What?"

" That's the time. Oh, now it's eleven thirty-three. See. I've one of those gadgets that tell time."

" Wise ass. Well, let's go inside anyway. Maybe you can make yourself useful for once."

" And I invited you to go fishing with me? It's gonna be a long trip."

The two men proceed down the marble-floored hallway and their shoes give advance notice of their arrival. They stop in the doorway of the recreational room and see the streamers, balloons, and banners covering the ceiling and walls. Ana approaches them with a stern look on her face.

" Would it be too much to ask that you change out of those shoes. If I wanted to hear a tap dance routine I would have hired a professional."

Knight looks at Avery.

" She must be a real fun person to be around at the office."

" Yea! She seems to be a real moral booster to me."

Ana cracks a smile and pushes both of them out of the doorway.

" Just do it, okay? I want everything to be perfect. So why don't you clowns stay out of my hair for fifteen minutes and maybe we can finish."

Knight cranes his neck around the corner for another look.

" Looks fine to me."

" Out!"

" Okay, okay. I didn't know artists were so touchy. By the way, where are the birthday troopers?"

" They're in the library studying. And they don't know about any of this so don't spoil it."

She turns around and starts barking orders at the aides that are helping her. Knight and Avery laugh and stroll down the hall while trying not to make as much noise so they don't receive another tongue-lashing. Then Knight realizes it would be easier to take the shoes off and does. The doctor follows suit.

" She's a lot sweeter than I remember."

" She's just a bit edgy because she was starting another diversification project and things weren't running too smooth when she e left the office last night. I think she's under too much stress. Today will do her a lot of good, but I think that its time to cut loose some of the holding companies that Knight Enterprises oversees. It would lighten some of the burden and would allow the expansion to fill that gap. I'll talk to her about it when she calms down."

" What's the expansion? Or should I ask? "

" We have no secrets from you, Bill. You know that. She wants to get into cosmetics and fashion. It's something she's always wanted to do since college and what the heck, I see nothing wrong with it. When things get rolling she'll be a happier person to be around."

" She has total control of the company , right? Aren't you still chairman of the board. Don't you take much interest in how the company operates?"

" I find it tiresome and tedious dealing with politicians and business sharks day in and day out. I am grateful to stay out of the picture. Ana is fully capable of handling whatever comes up and she thrives on confronting the vultures that comprise the essence of her world. I basically refuse to have anything to do with it. It was a drain on me when I was a kid and I've had my fill.

" As you know, Knight Enterprises is a private corporation which is extremely unusual for an organization of its size. I basically own the entire organization outright and have delegated the responsibility of running it to Ana. I have never considered for a second allowing us to go public. Then there would be unnecessary meddling and we want to stay private. We have our little secrets and it wouldn't be prudent if any part of the public were to have access to that information. Ana tells me what's going on and I have the computer to check on operations if I want to. But basically, she runs the show how she wants to and I let her."

Doctor Avery nods his head as he soaks in what Knight is saying and is intrigued by this new insight. He knew the basic history of the life of Clayton Knight. He also shared in some very dangerous secrets. In all the years he had known him Knight never failed to surprise him. It seemed that every time they were together he learned something new, which was not that surprising since Knight had so much to offer. Many times Avery felt like a student in the presence of a great educator. That was somewhat unusual considering that Knight was aver a decade younger than he was and that Avery had an extensive educational background.

Yet age has nothing to do with the intelligence and insights people have. Experience may allow a person to express their thoughts in more ways. However, when a person gives birth to a new idea, it is up to that person how they raise that idea into it's own life. Then after a person gives an idea shape and essence others can study it, learn from it, and even criticize it. Avery knew that Knight was responsible for more original thought and ideas than possibly any other person in the history of the planet. The day that he understood that was the day Dr. Avery realized just how truly special Clayton Knight was.

The two men changed their clothes and returned to the rec. room where the party was about to begin. Four women enter, each carrying a sheet cake with seven burning candles. Each cake was a different flavor, which was suited to the favorite of each child. Amy's cake is chocolate marble with white icing. Rich's cake is German chocolate with coconut icing. Debbie's is Vanilla with white icing. Terry's is chocolate with chocolate icing. The traditional song that marks such an occasion begins and flows normally until the point where people are to insert the name. There is mutual confusion and everyone looks around and laughs. Then Ana tells the children to make a wish and blow out their candles. Then another woman enters with a vat of vanilla ice cream, which happens to be the favorite of all four children. Each person had the choice of what cake they wanted to sample. So not to make any of the children feel left out, both Knight and Ana take a piece from each cake. Dr. Avery is happy to do the same although his motives are not the same.

When everyone is finished eating they gather around the billiard table draped with a protective plastic covering. On the table several presents are stacked. Paper and ribbon fly everywhere as the children remove them to reveal toys, games, and even new clothes. When everything on the table is unwrapped two ladies enter the room each carrying a box.

One box holds a seven-week-old male German Shepherd puppy that is presented to young Richard. He picks it up with glee and shows it off to his brothers. The girls had gathered around the other box, which contained three white, female Himalayan-Persian kittens. Each girl squeals with joy and selects a kitten that would be her very own.

The doctor looks over at Knight and smiles at the tears of happiness forming in the proud man's eyes. Ana comes over and rests her head on the left shoulder of her husband as he puts his arm around her. Although they were different from many other people when it came to parenting, it was a common link that they held with the rest of the world.

Rich comes over to thank his parents for the puppy and Knight messes up his hair affectionately which draws a stern look from his wife. He then strokes the puppy a couple times before he sends the boy back to his brothers. The puppy had come from their kennel on the estate and was decided on by both Knight and Ana.

The doctor approaches the proud parents.

" You know, it's times like this that I really envy you two."

Knight looks at his friend and answers.

" Well, it's a situation that's easily remedied. You have to find yourself a woman and settle down."

" I'm afraid it's too late for an old wolf like me."

" What kind of talk is that. You're still in the prime of your life. I'm sure there are thousands of women out there who would kill to marry a man in your position. Tell him, Ana."

She pushes away from her spouse and gives him an incredulous look. She shakes her head in disbelief.

" Tell him what? That there's a bride out there that's right for the choosing? It just doesn't work that way, Clay. If you think every marriage is like ours then you have lost touch with reality. Our situation is unique. Sure we hit it off and everything has been sunshine and roses for us, but there are people who go for years and never find someone compatible. Others try to force it and things don't work out. Maybe Bill is better off the way he is and you should stop trying to be the savior of everyone you come in contact with."

Knight looks around the room and is relieved that all the children are too occupied with their toys and pets to notice their mother make such a scene. He grabs her by the arm and leads her out into the hallway. Dr. Avery lets them pass and walks over to examine the puppy the boys have. Once in the hallway, Ana pulls her arm free and looses her balance. She takes a few awkward steps, staggers before stopping, and returns to an upright position. She then turns to confront her husband.

" Who do you think you are manhandling me like that! Why if I were a man I'd.."

" What the hell were you doing carrying on in there like that. It's bad enough that you were tearing Bill down, but you were doing it in front of the children. Luckily, they were too busy to notice their mother the raving lunatic."

" Don't call me a lunatic. I'm not the one with the superiority complex! You want to be thought of as if you are God the all-mighty!"

" Is that how you think of me. You think I do what I do just so I can get some perverse sense of pleasure out of saving people's lives. What's wrong with you? You've been edgy and uptight the last couple of days. It's not that time of the month, is it?"

" No!"

" Is there another man? It's Rodney, that pencil-necked desk jockey you promoted to vice-president last month. Is that it?"

" Rodney? If I wanted an affair, I'm certain I could do much, much better than him."

" You're not having an affair?"

" No!"

" Is it the stress from work? "

" Of course not."

" Then what is it?"

" I'm pregnant, dammit! Okay? We said Ian was going to be the last. I'm in the middle of operating a new project and you're so busy doing God knows what!"

" You're sure about this?"

" Yes!"

" And Bill knows?"

" No, I went to another doctor."

" Why?"

" Because you and Bill are so close and I didn't want him to tell you."

" If it's because of the strain I was under, I'm past that. And.."

" It wasn't that. It's that I don't know if I want to carry it."

Knight could not believe his ears. The loving mother of eighteen children was unwilling to spread her love to one more. He sits down on the floor with his back against the wall. She averts her eyes when he looks up at her.

" Not keep it? Darling, do you know what you're saying? You would be going against everything I believe in, you believe in, and remember your entire family. Are you under so much stress that you would be willing to do something so drastic? Your mother would die if she heard you talking of such a thing."

" You leave my mother out of this. This is me, not her. She isn't in the position I'm in."

" What position are you in? You're president of my company. I love you dearly, but if that's the basis for your argument, just remember that I appointed you to that position and as much as it would pain me, I can remove you. That would not be in either of our best interests. This is something that has come about by the two of us working together and we will get through it together. There is no need for you to concern yourself about work. You know there is no need for you to take a leave of absence. If you choose, you can have the baby and be running the company the next day."

" What kind of mother would I be then?"

" Hopefully the kind you are now. Ana, you are the most loving and caring person I know and each of our children knows this. Neither one of us is the ideal parent, but we give our children all we can and that includes healthy doses of love. If you wanted to cut back on your ten or twelve hour work days in town, you could most of your work from the office upstairs. That is something for you to decide. But no matter what, I'm here for you and love you and I know we can get through this together. Okay?"

" Okay."

She kneels down in front of him and he takes her face in his hands. With his thumbs he wipes away tears rolling down her cheeks. She smiles and then collapses into his arms. He hugs her and holds her close.

Bringing one more life into the world would not be much of a burden on them. He did think, however, that if she reacted this way on this occasion, they would have to alter their sexual routine to ensure there is not a next time.

" When is it due?"

" First week of March."

" Don't you think Bill should examine you? He is the family doctor, you know."

" I know I'm pregnant."

" You know what I mean. It might crush him to learn you went to another doctor and then don't let him know. I'll tell him on the way down, so you don't have to."

" I appreciate that. And tell him no hard feelings. Although he is a professional and all, he is still a close friend of yours.."

" Yes, yes. We already went over that. Think you're capable of rejoining the party?"

" I'll be in after I freshen up."

She stands up and walks down the hall as Knight rises to his feet. He touches the inside of his left eye and winces. He had a headache developing and he fully understood why. He goes over to the doorway and motions for one of the aides to come over. After whispering his instructions the aide leaves to get a glass of water and two pain pills. Then he notices Dr. Avery coming across the room.

" It wasn't anything too serious, I hope."

" No. Everything is just fine. I'll let you in on it a little later."

He brushes past the doctor and goes over to see his children. He tells them he is going on a little trip and wants them to be good while he was gone. One of the boys asks if he could go. Knight laughs and responds.

" You know, Doug, that is a good idea. Someday before the end of the summer, I'll take you boys to do some fishing at one of the lakes here in Nebraska. but Dr. Avery and I have made plans for just the two of us and I'm afraid we're going to have to stick with that. Anyhow, you are going to have your hands full getting acquainted with the new puppy and keeping up with your studies. Come her and say good-bye to your papa."

Each child comes over and gives him a hug and kiss and they wave at Dr. Avery and himself as they exited the room.

Chapter eight

Fear is what enters the man's eyes. He surveys his surroundings with uncertainty and pulls wildly at the restraints, which keep him immobile. Sweat stings his eyes as his effort brings no results. He winces as his eyes burn and all he can do is wait for it to stop. After a few minutes his vision is restored and he looks over the area again. It was a ceremonial chamber that he was very familiar with. He had participated in and directed many of the ceremonies that had taken place here. Within a few hours this would be his place of death.

He knew what would happen to him for he had done it to many others. It wasn't death that he feared because he actually embraced it. Torture. That was what he feared. Minutes and then hours of agonizing torture and death would be his only escape.

A sharp pain shoots through his head and he stifles a scream. The pain was a reminder of why he was in this most undesirable position. Even if he didn't die today, he would be dead within a couple of weeks because he had a terminal case of a rare disease.

Maybe if he had stayed in civilization things would be different, but his past actions had forced him to flee. If the disease had been caught in it's early stages, it could have been treated and he would have been cured. But that would have required that he return to civilization and again he would have faced death. Of his three options, his current appealed to him most although he was having second thoughts.

Two dozen lights go on and the man has to squint in order to see. Processions of people in black robes come toward him out of the darkness. Behind them he sees the person that would be his executioner. The person also wore the traditional black robe, but they also had on the ceremonial mask of the high priest. The fear was replaced by anger, for that had been his mask and he did not like to see anyone else wear it.

He notices the master of ceremonies is wearing thick, rubber gloves. They intended to spill his blood, but they did not want to chance getting it on themselves because it was believed the disease was highly contagious. Walking around the altar he was on, the robed individuals form a circle that shields him from most of the light except for that directly above him. In the background he hears the sound of a gong which signals the start of the ritual. His executioner approaches him and stands next to him fingering a table with several instruments of pain on it.

" I'll be waiting for you in hell!"

The figure nods and picks up the first instrument. The purpose of the ceremony was to progressively raise the level of pain the person would endure. At first it was more a combination of irritation and pain rather than just pure pain. As the ritual progressed there would be mutilation and much loss of blood. To insure that the victim did not die before the appropriate time there was a blood transfusion machine that would be attached to him as he started to lose more blood. To ensure that he remained conscious to feel the entire extent of the torture, the table also contained several drug filled syringes that would be administered at certain intervals to keep him aware,

The masked figure begins by plucking the man's chest hairs one by one. He shakes slightly at the discomfort as each is removed. After the chest hairs, he his progressively deprived of his knuckle hairs, eye brows, nostril hairs, and eye lashes. Each is removed one at a time and once that portion of the ritual was over it had already taken a toll on the man. Sensing this, the masked figure gives him the first shot to ensure that he be ready for the next steps. The hair pulling was the most time consuming portion of the ritual, yet it was in comparison the least painful. The man tried to steady himself for what was to come.

Screams filled the chamber as he tried to find a release for the pain. His fingernails and toenails had been removed and the ghoulish fiend was extracting the last of his teeth. All had been done without pain deadeners. Next his fingers and toes are cut off, knuckle by knuckle, alternating left hand, right hand, left foot, and right foot. By this time he had seven vials of their drugs pumped into him and was going to remain conscious and alive until they deemed it was not to be so.

Although he had trouble focusing through the pain and the drugs, the man knew that it was almost over and hoped they would not delay. Again the masked figure picks up another knife and cuts off the man's ears, nose, and lips. His cries are muffled as the knife enters his mouth and comes out with his tongue. There is a high pitched, whining sound coming from the man as the figure picks up a narrow, sharp instrument and with two, quick jabs leave the man sightless and almost entering into unconsciousness.

One last needle enters his skin and he is aware of his pain again. Finally, the master of the ceremony takes another knife and lifts it overhead before plunging it into the chest of the man. After some cutting the blade is removed and a gloved hand reaches into the cavity to remove the heart. It is held proudly above the now dead victim as a show of power and then placed back on the chest of the corpse. Normally the heart would have been eaten, but since it was diseased that part of the ceremony was skipped. The masked figure steps back and the gong sounds. One by one they leave the altar and then the chamber until the executioner is there alone.

Then two men wearing military fatigues enter the chamber and approach the motionless figure. They stop as the figure turns around and hands them a sheet of paper and an envelope. Then it gestures toward the corpse.

" Burn it! It is useless now. Follow the instructions on the sheet or you will find a similar fate. The money is as we agreed."

The voice is muffled by the mask and the men have difficulty making out what is said, but they do. As the fiend leaves the chamber the men work to put the body on a burlap bag. They dare not carry out the orders for they knew that the threat was valid and the executioner very much enjoyed such ceremonies. They also had extreme fear of that person for they just inherited an empire of terror. They knew this person was much more ambitious than the corpse was and would work to expand the empire.

They take the corpse to a clearing in the jungle that is behind the fortress where the ceremony took place. After soaking the bag with a flammable liquid, one of the men tosses a match to start the fire. The other man looks up and can see someone on an upper balcony shielded in the darkness. A chill goes through him as he quickly turns away for he knew it was the person they just spoke with in the chamber. Both men just stood silent looking into the flames. In the bag was their former high priest and they feared what was to come. For with the death of Sebastian Ruthvan, a new age of terror would be born.

Knight looks over at his friend as he reads a medical journal. The man is engrossed in an article and seems oblivious to the rest of the world. They were traveling down the interstate in one of Knight's multi-purpose vans or MPV. It was the newest model on the market by knight motors and Knight was proud of the luxury features. Although they were going into the wilds of Mississippi, there was no need for two men as cultured as they were to rough it in the traditional sense.

After running through a selection of stations and not finding anything satisfactory, Knight selects a disk from his collection and puts it in the player. The speaker unleashes the voice of Whitman Dade, the newest star from Knight Records. The young star had a range of songs that could be classified as country, pop, and rhythm and blues. His voice was smooth and melodious and it had a soothing effect on a person. Knight tapped his fingers on the steering wheel to the beat as the doctor finished reading.

" You actually listen to this stuff?"

" What's wrong with it? He's good."

" Man, this stuff corrupts the minds of minors."

" What century are you from? There's nothing in the lyrics that can be considered dangerous or inappropriate for a minor. Dade is actually ultra-conservative compared to a lot of the performers out there. Not everyone can limit their tastes to such a small field as classical music."

" What's wrong with classical music?"

"Nothing. I listen to it myself and I like some of it very much. I'm just saying don't write off the new stuff. You never give anything a chance once you get set in your ways about something."

" Forget I brought it up."

" Gladly."

The doctor begins to thumb through his journal and then sets it beside his seat. Knight figures it would be a good time to talk about Ana.

" Remember back at the house how Ana was so uptight, Bill?"

" How could I forget? Her tongue was sharper than one of my scalpels."

" Whatever. Well, the reason was because she's with child. She's kind of upset about it, being with the business going as it is and all."

" Wait a minute. She's pregnant and didn't come to me? Hell, I've delivered eighteen of your children and she didn't come to me!"

" You know how she can be. She said that she didn't want to go to you because we're friends and she didn't want me to know just yet."

" What? She doesn't think I'm professional? If she didn't want me to tell you she was pregnant, I wouldn't have."

" You wouldn't?"

" It works both ways, pal. You want me to keep your secret about what's going on in your head. That has a lot to do with we're friends, but it also has to do with our oath of confidentiality. You wouldn't want me to tell Ana about it would you?"

" Of course not. But it's not the same thing."

" It's not? How are they different? Just because one applies to you and another to her."

"In this situation, yes. Having a baby takes two people and both should be privy to that information. What's wrong with me doesn't affect both of us."

" It doesn't?"

" No, it doesn't! Anyway, how did I get on the defensive when you were the one who was crushed?"

" Don't ask me, you're the genius. But if you believe that these two situations are that much different, then you're not as smart as I thought you were."

Knight looks over at his friend and then focuses on the road again. He turns up the volume and the speakers are shouting the voice of Dade's ballad "Unusual Eagle". It plays for a minute and then Knight turns the volume back down.

" Okay, I'll tell her when I get back. I don't think it will do her any good, but I can see where you're coming from."

Avery nods his head and begins to slap his knee to the beat of the music.

" Hey, you were right. This music isn't that bad."

" That's two of us going one-eighty on an issue. This is going to be an interesting trip."

It is ten till five in the afternoon when their MPV crosses the Mississippi state line. Both men are feeling hungry yet aren't exactly thrilled at the prospect of eating at one of the roadside cafes that dot the countryside. They have the on-board computer search the map for the nearest town with a restaurant. The answer is Brer, Mississippi, a small town of two hundred. It just happened to be their next exit five miles down the road. Dr. Avery says he never heard of it, but admitted that he didn't frequent this part of the state much.

They see the off ramp and leave the interstate. There is a rest stop for campers near the exit, but they do not see a sign indicating which direction the town was. Hoping that the map was reliable, Knight turns the MPV down a gravel road. Dr. Avery has a worried look on his face as the vehicle starts to kick up dust as it speeds down the road. As they pass a grove of evergreens Knight notices a paved road to the right that goes over a hill. Knight makes the turn and slows the speed as he starts over the hill. A couple hundred yards ahead of them is a line of buildings that seemed to be stores. There was also an occasional house along the roadside.

The town seemed to be deserted because there was not a single person or animal in sight. At the far edge of the town they notice a building that has a sign on the tree out front. The sign reads "Zekes Place: Food and Drinks". After stopping the vehicle they get out to take a look around Knight notices that the doctor seems edgy.

" Looks like a class place in a rural sense. Maybe it's not four star, but.."

" Clay, I've got a bad feeling about this place."

" What's to worry about? I made you bring your force field belt, although I was surprised to see you almost leave it at my house where the children could get at it."

He reaches behind the driver's seat and picks up the belt. Avery gladly takes it and puts it around his waist. Once it felt secure, he flips the switch to activate the field.

" Didn't you bring yours"

" Are you kidding? I rarely go anywhere without it. There are people who don't like me, you know."

" He lifts up his jacket to let the doctor see that he had it on. The doctor nods and gestures for Knight to lead the way. Knight smiles and walks toward the tavern while his friend stayed four feet behind him. Reaching the door he finds it unlocked and he opens it. Both he and the doctor step into the entryway.

"Hello! Anyone here?"

A voice answers them from what they assume is the kitchen.

" Yo! What can I do for ya?"

A man in his early twenties walks through a swinging door. The light is dim, but Knight can tell he is smiling. He was about five-foot-ten and had a slim build. He wore a light blue shirt and dark pants with a towel folded over his belt. He wipes his hands on the towel as he walks toward them.

" We were wondering if you are open for business?"

" Sure! Sure am. Just never get nobody this time of day. Folks eat at home for supper normally. Then the men folk come around later in the evening to talk and drink. Nope. Never get nobody in here this time of day."

" Do you have a menu?"

" Sure do! Let me get one for you. Isn't your friend going to join you."

" That's why we came. His appetite is bigger than mine."

Knight gestures for his friend to enter the dining area. From the darkness emerges the giant figure of the doctor. The man seems shocked and puts his back against the bar. While Knight that it was due to his friend's size, the doctor recognized the look in the man's eyes. His reaction was because of the color of his skin. Knight spies a corner booth and walks to it and his friend follows. They sit on opposite sides of the table and the wood of the benches lets out a complaint at their weight. The little man comes over and hands a menu to Knight while his eyes are on Dr. Avery the entire time.

" I don't know if I can serve you."

knight is looking at the menu as he speaks.

" Low on supplies? I bet that can be a problem, being hidden off the main road like you are."

" No, that's not it."

Knight looks up and sees the man's eyes locked on his friend. He finally understood what was going on and it infuriated him. It was the middle of the twenty-first century and he didn't know how people could still have racial prejudices. He realized that there were some people that would never overcome prejudice and pass it on to their children. But he wasn't going to stand by and let his friend be insulted. He didn't want to cause a scene, however, and didn't want to spend his vacation trying to shape someone else's views. he reaches into his jacket pocket and pulls out his wallet. From the wallet he removes two hundred dollars and places it on the table near the man. The man looks at Knight with confused features.

" All we want is to eat and then will leave your little town The money is to ensure good service and the hope that you can keep your prejudices in check while we're here."

The man looks at the money, picks it up, and nods his acknowledgment. He takes a note pad and pen from his pocket and nods again. Knight decides to place his order first.

"I'll have two steaks, well done. Three baked potatoes, three ears of corn, and a pitcher of milk to wash it down. And give me a side order of green beans while you're at it."

The man looks at Dr. Avery and awaits his response.

"I'll have the same."

After scribbling on the note pad, he turns and exits the room through the swinging door into the kitchen. Knight stands the menu on edge at the far end of the table against the wall. He returns his attention to the doctor and is assaulted with a menacing glare."

"What?"

" You shouldn't have done that, Clay. I'd rather eat somewhere else than eat somewhere I'm not welcome."

" Yes, I understand that. But since we're here and he's willing to serve us, we might as well stay and eat. And if he wouldn't serve us I'd just get on the car phone and have the federal authorities here within minutes. People can be bigoted, but the law won't let that interfere with how they conduct their business or who they do business with."

" If you think so."

The doctor looks in the direction of the kitchen. He leans over the table so that his whisper can be heard. Knight leans forward so he can hear the words.

" What if he tries to poison us?"

" Ah! The cautious one you are, dear doctor. You must remember that your traveling companion is one who very much wants to avoid being assassinated by his enemies, both known and unknown. I take no chances when I am in public, yet I can't watch everyone every second. As to your question, we can check out what he brings us with this."

He pulls out a device that fits in the palm of his right hand from another jacket pocket. the doctor smile for he recognizes it to be a portable sensory unit capable of giving an instantaneous read out on it's small screen the contents of any object. Knight returns the device to his jacket pocket as the doctor nods with approval.

After a few minutes the man emerges from the kitchen carrying a large tray. He places the plates of food in front of them first. Then he sets down their glasses and two pitchers of milk. He picks up one of the pitchers intent on pouring the contents into Knight's glass, but Knight stops him by raising his hand.

" We'll pour our own, thank you."

" Okay. Sorry that took so long, but the power unit in the stove has been shorting out and I had to fuse a coil."

" That's all right. I'll call you over if we need anything else."

The man nods and turns away. Knight takes out the scanner and passes it over the food, drinks, glasses, and silverware. He looks at the screen and smiles.

There isn't anything here that shouldn't be. Go ahead and dig in, Doc."

Both men commence to eating and are nearly finished when the doctor notices the man slip into the darkness of the entryway. There he takes the receiver off the phone and starts to dial.

"Clay."

" I see him."

" Who do you think he's calling?"

" Couldn't say for sure, but instinct tells me he's calling more narrow-minded bigots to join the party."

" Let's get out of here!"

" Relax. They can't do anything to you as long as you keep your field activated."

" Even so, I'm not in the mood for a confrontation."

" Then if it comes to that, just let me do the talking. With any luck it may come to blows."

" Clay!"

" Settle down, Do! I'll try and restrain myself since I don't want that investigating panel to delay my return to GLESA any longer than it needs to be."

" Just remember that."

" Geez. For a big guy, you're such a baby."

" Sorry, it's just the way I was raised."

" Well, if it comes down to it, imagine they're the defenders trying to get to the quarterback and you have to defend him at all costs."

" Yea, right."

" I'm serious, Bill. If it comes down to it, don't want to be taking on a bunch of local yokels by myself. Okay?"

" Then let's get out of here!"

" Man, you're no fun. What ever happened to your sense of adventure?"

" I lost it when I turned forty. Anyway, this isn't the place for playing war games. People have to live down here after we're gone."

" Don't give me any of that! If these folks do anything that's illegal, I still have a civic responsibility to stop it. Anyhow, it might be fun."

" Clay, that's the type of attitude that got your butt booted from GLESA. Now drink your milk and let's get out of here."

" Yes, mother."

Knight cleans his plate and empties his glass. Then he stretches his arms and rises to his feet. He starts for the door and the doctor is close behind him. The little man is standing in the doorway.

"Yes, that sure was good food. Wasn't it, Bill"

" I guess so."

The little man looks at the doctor with disdain. He takes a step back and it is obvious that he is trying to block the door.

" Leaving so soon?"

" Yea, well we want to get to our fishing camp before dark. What I gave you before surely covered everything, so why don't you let us pass!"

The last few words spoken by Knight had a menacing edge to them and the man stepped away from the door and pressed himself against the wall fearing harm might come to him. The doctor pushes past Knight and goes out the door. Knight takes another bill out of his wallet and stuffs it in the man's shirt pocket. Then he lightly slaps the man's face twice.

" Yes, that sure was good food."

He left the man who was trying to find a crack in the wall to slip into as he walks out the door. The doctor is standing by the passenger door waiting for Knight to unlock it. As Knight walks toward the doctor, five vehicles come speeding down the road from both directions, two from the left and three from the right. They all stop in front of the tavern and block the MPV from backing out. Then the little man comes running out and heads directly for his friends.

"Mind moving your car?" Knight shouts as he reaches the doctor.

All the other men get out of their cars and Knight counts eleven in all. Less than a minute's work if it came down to it and the doctor wouldn't have to lift a finger. Then another car pulls up from the right and a big man in a sheriff's uniform gets out. He looks at the doctor and shakes his head.

" You boys are a bit out of your way, ain't cha?"

" So nice of you folks to come down here and greet us like this."

Knight had walked up to the sheriff while he was talking and was standing toe to toe with him and they saw eye to eye.

" I don't think you understand, boy!"

Knight looks at the other men and two of them had picked up shotguns. Then he turns his attention back to the sheriff who he estimated to be about the doctor's age. Knight smiled as he speaks.

" I understand perfectly well, deputy."

The man's eyes get wide and Knight can see the anger building up within him. The sheriff takes a step back and is swaying side to side as he shouts at Knight.

" You ignorant, Yankee! Can't you read? This badge says 'sheriff'!"

" That may be what it says, but it doesn't mean you've earned the title."

" What the hell is that you say? Lucas, unload your truck. I'm gonna enjoy watching these two swing."

Knight watches as the man named Lucas removes two thick ropes from the back of his truck and throws both of them over a thick branch. Then he proceeds to make a hangman's loop in the end of each rope.

" You've done this before, haven't you?"

" Sure have! We's a private community and don't like strangers here about. And we sure as hell don't want no tar babies polluting the place! And you Ned says you got a heap of cash on you. Ain't it so, Ned?"

" Sure is."

The little man thinks he's safer with the advantage of numbers but still cowers as Knight looks at him. Then Knight looks over at the doctor who is extremely worried. He had enough to get an indictment on each of them and sees no need to carry on any longer.

" Should have taken a safer line of work, deputy."

The sheriff would not let this insult pass and rushes at the man who wronged him with vengeance in his eyes. He is upon Knight in a second and Knight stands his ground. He crashes into Knight, but could not budge him. They are touching chest to chest as Knight reaches down and grabs the two revolvers out of the sheriff's holsters. Holding the sheriff close with both his elbows digging into the sheriff's rib cage, he fires and downs the two men holding the shot guns. One man catches a bullet in the wrist above the hand he had on the trigger. He shoots the other man through each shoulder. Both men lose control of their guns and drop them to the ground. Knight drops the revolvers and then head butts the sheriff. He allows the big man to drop to his knees where he kicks his teeth out.

He sees the little man from the tavern trying to escape and before he can take three steps, Knight catches him with a blow to the back of the neck. That sends him reeling into the tavern door, which he meets head on and he falls back unconscious. The other eight men all try to rush him at the same time, then slow down so they encircle him Knight tenses as if he were a caged animal. Dr. Avery notices that they had forgotten about him, but he is afraid to move. He just looks on in amazement as Knight operates on his aggressors.

One man rushes him and Knight catches him with a knee to the mid-section and elbows the back of his head as he pulls him forward by his shirt. Another used this distraction to grab Knight from behind only to find himself quickly flipped over his shoulder. The man finds the ground hard upon his landing and has the wind forced from his lungs. Two men charge from opposite directions and Knight leaps into the air and nails each upon the jaw with a boot. The man called Lucas rushes and Knight grabs his right hand with his own and pulls the man toward the ground, momentarily interrupting the journey by smashing his knee into the man's chin. Going on the offensive, Knight runs over to confront two more attackers. He levels the one to his left with a kick to the head above the man's left ear with his right foot. Then he spins around and sends the other man flying when his right foot impacts upon the man's chest. The only man Knight had yet to touch tried to flee, but Knight jumps over one of the cars and greets the man with a kick to the back of the head with his left foot.

He drags this man back to join the others when he notices the man he had flipped struggling to get up. He helps the man to his feet by his hair and then smashes him back to the ground with a forearm to the chest. The man's head hits the ground a moment before his feet do and he flops like a fish on dry land. At that moment the man Knight had shot in the wrist was trying to steady the weapon with his opposite hand as he approached Knight. Dr. Avery sees this and rushes over and slaps the gun out of the man's hand and knocks the man to the ground with a blow to the forehead with the back of his right hand. Knight turns around in time to see the man hit the ground and lets out a laugh.

" Just had to get in the action didn't you, Bill?"

" I just didn't like the thought of someone shooting someone from behind. Not much sport in that, even if he couldn't hurt you."

" You know what, Bill? I could be mistaken, but I believe that I didn't kill any of them. Maybe things are looking up. Now maybe I can fight with a clear head without my emotions getting the best of me."

" The way I see it, Clay, you're deadly whether your mind is clouded or not. You just beat the crap out of these people for the fun of it. Sure, they deserved it..."

" That's just it, Bill. They deserved it. I'm not one of those skirt-toting pansies who stands on the sidelines when an old-fashioned butt kicking will solve the problem. I know we don't see eye to eye on this, so why don't you drop it."

" Did you call me a pansy?"

" Hey, if you think it suits you."

" Just because I don't see things from a macho view point as you do doesn't mean I'm a pansy. I'm just a pacifist."

" Just drop it, Bill. Okay? I've got nothing against the way you handle yourself and you can withhold your opinions of me. This is one topic we can obviously not talk about, so let's not."

" Fine."

" I'd better get on the phone to get someone down here to clean this up. I can't go to GLESA and don't feel like dealing with the feds, so I will call Colonel Randolph Jackson of the Mississippi State Patrol. His son's in GLESA and we seemed to get along the last time we met."

The sunlight is dancing on the water as they cast their lines. Dr. Avery remains standing as Knight settles into his folding chair. In the distance there are trout jumping in and out of the water and they hoped to entice one or two over to grab the bait on the end of their hooks. Knight thinks the surroundings are quite scenic with the tall grass following the curve of the stream and the trees in the background. He holds the pole with his knees as he shuts his eyes and leans back to let the warmth of the sun caress his face. It really didn't matter to him whether they caught anything, because he did not really feel like eating fish. He might eat it if Dr. Avery caught something, but he had never really acquired a taste for water dwellers.

They stayed on the bank waiting for the fish to come to them. Neither thought there was much fun in using high-tech equipment to wage battle with the fish and would rather just try and guess what the fish might do. If they took the bait, so be it. Knight opens one eye as the doctor finally sits down in his chair. Then he shuts the eye again.

" It's sure going to be a nice day."

" Yes, it's cooler than normal for this time of year."

" It's still morning."

" I know. Don't start with me, Clay."

Knight leans forward and opens his eyes. His friend stares into the water and holds his rod between both hands as he leans forward in his chair. Sweat was beginning to form on his brow and knight couldn't help but smile.

" You know, Bill. You've been fighting me a bit more than usual lately. Do I really rub you wrong that often?"

" I don't know what it is. Part of it might be that I resent you having a family and I'm always caught up in my work and never really gave it a second thought until recently. I've also been doing some thinking about this alien situation. Clay, I know you have the resources and technology to evacuate the entire planet if it became necessary. You've discovered hundreds of planets that could sustain life. Have you considered it?"

" Of course I have. But how willing would you be to leave and start all over in another place?"

" Wouldn't really want to."

" Right! And that would be the attitude of the majority of the people you would talk to. There are adventurous people such as myself who would be willing to, but we're a very small percentage of the population. But in truth, it wouldn't do any good to evacuate. According to our figures, there are still eight aliens still living among the population here on the planet. If we tried to evacuate, they would notify their leaders and we'd have war before the first ship could leave the solar system. And we are far from being able to hold our own in such a battle, let alone protect ourselves. When I get back, I'm going to amerce myself deep into the subject and should be able to make some advances. I only hope that Mochar's information is correct and we are able to complete what we have to in the time frame he has given me. I also hope we can eliminate the alien spies here on the planet before they somehow catch on as to what's going on."

" How are you dealing with the spies?"

" I have teams of androids trying to hunt them down. When they find one, they have orders to execute it. We have had pretty good success so far, but as their numbers decrease the androids are running across them far less frequently."

" And if they catch on?"

" We're done for. Mochar said they have no loyalty to each other , so they don't contact each other. They only report to their leaders. He also said it was common for a spy to go weeks and even months without sending a report. And they count on an occasional spy getting killed while on mission. You know, like in a car accident. With any luck, these factors, along with the fact that it is extremely rare for the alien leadership to send a transmission of their own to Earth, we might be able to pull it off."

" And if we can't?"

" I already have a spaceship hidden away for my family and friends to escape. It would be a last resort, but it would be better than living under the alien rule. I've also been working on a new model for a space ship using some of the alien ideas. With some luck and enough time, I may have a fleet of them battle ready by the time the invasion starts. It's basically a race with the clock, but no matter what we will survive."

That ended the conversation because Knight felt a tug on his line and begins to reel it his catch. Struggling on the end of the line is an eight-pound trout. The look of joy on the doctor's face was the only thing that stopped Knight from returning the fish to it's home. He knew he would regret his decision with that first bite of fried fish. Yet the peaceful surroundings more than made up for the small sacrifice he might have to make. He would enjoy what remaining time they still had on their trip.

Chapter nine

Two weeks had passed since the fishing trip and Knight was once again busy with his research. True to form, he had three projects underway at the same time. The first had nothing to do with the other two, but he felt it was time that he started it. What Knight was attempting to do was design a car that could transform itself into a vehicle capable of flight. This he knew would be the easiest of the three projects to achieve for the changes he needed to implement were somewhat basic. That was how he saw it anyhow, although the engineers at Knight Motors had their doubts.

When he had finished the design in the middle of the third week, he was anxious to see it applied. He immediately contacted his engineers and gave them the information needed to start building a proto-type. At the start of the fifth week it was finished. After several test drives and flights by an android crew, everything was working flawlessly. The shape of the vehicle was similar to a rounded wedge. The proto-type could seat five comfortably although the dimensions could be changed so it could seat only two passengers or up to thirty-five. The larger model was more like a bus, but the principle was the same.

When the driver wanted the vehicle to go airborne, they would activate three turbo thrusters beneath the vehicle that would lift it off the ground. AS the vehicle rises, the tires fold upward and rest flat against the panel. At the same moment, panels above the tires are extending from beneath the vehicle to give it wings. Although the wings run the length of the car, they start out narrow at the front and widen as it reaches the rear. As a vehicle of flight it retained the wedge shape it had on land and when seen from below it looks like a flying triangle. On the rear panel of the vehicle are four turbo jets side by side that propel the vehicle forward. These are not revealed until a cover panel is lowered and serves as a platform for the exhaust tubes as they push out. The principle was similar to retractable headlights.

Under ideal testing conditions the proto-type was able to reach speeds of 320 miles per hour as a car and 1040 miles per hour as a jet. Knight felt that with a slight modification of the power system these results could be increased, although there was really no need for it to go that fast or faster while on land. Yet there were situations it might be necessary to have such a capability would be a crucial edge, so he decided not to hinder the land capabilities. The interior of the vehicle had to be modified so that humans could reach such speeds without passing out. This called for special stabilizers and close monitoring of the internal atmosphere.

In the beginning he would only produce these vehicles for us by GLESA and himself. After extended exposure he would allow them to be sold to government agencies around the world. However, he thought it would be best if the general public never had access to such a vehicle. There were many inferior drivers behind the wheel of normal cars and given the opportunity to drive such a high powered vehicle would only magnify their deficiencies and would result in many unnecessary accidents. AS long as he was in control of manufacturing, they would never be distributed to the public.

The next project he started and completed was the creation of a new weapons system. What he accomplished was the harnessing of an energy plasma that could be encased in a modified laser beam. The beam would carry the energy plasma to its destination and unload it there. The plasma reacted with whatever it came in contact with and weakened and often destroyed the bonds between cells of the material. If the material did not disintegrate, it's weakened state still left it extremely vulnerable. Repeated bombardments with the beam would eventually atomize whatever the target was.

Knight discovered that there was not a substance on Earth strong enough nor could he construct a force field powerful enough to withstand the continued assault of his new weapon. While he had a powerful weapon, he basically had no way to defend against it if the opposition also had it. Upon consulting with Mochar, he learned that Rahk's forces did not have such technology at the time he escaped. Although all his research was based on Earth technology and elements, Knight was also assured the Rahk did not have anything to defend against it either. Yet finding a defense against it would be very crucial and that would remain one of his top priorities.

One of the few drawbacks of the system was that only small amounts of plasma could be stored in the same container because in larger quantities it began to react and destroy the containers. So storage became a problem.

Although he devised a loading system that could release several vials of the plasma in sequence into the laser beam, it did take considerable time. That meant that there would be considerable time between shots. The quickest Knight could run the system without an explosive reaction was seven minutes between shots. He knew that he had to improve that somehow for seven minutes was a considerable amount of time when in the heat of battle. Yet since he was dealing with such a deadly substance, he thought it might be best to leave things as they were and concentrate on producing multiple firing systems and also other weaponry.

The final project was the development of a new spacecraft. AS he had mentioned to Dr. Avery, he was following some of the alien design principles in the making of the new ship. The main feature he borrowed was the shape: flat and round like a cup and saucer. It was ironic because that shape which people had claimed to see for years in the sky was actually a superior style of spacecraft.

The shape had many advantages when combined with the proper technology. Unlike the conventional craft, this would be able to go in any direction in a moment's notice rather than just forward or up and down. Another advantage was the storage capacity. Since the body of the ship was shaped like a dome, the amount of storage depended on how high the dome was and how wide the base was. The engines and other operational systems were located in the base so the possibilities were many for use of the space above them. One of the advantages that Knight liked best was that he was able to use the design to enhance another superior weapons system. Although the energy plasma cannon, or E-P cannon as he labeled it, was presently unstoppable, it had extremely limited usage. Therefore, it became necessary to have another weapons system on the ship.

What Knight did was cover the surface of the ship with a mesh of fibers consisting of tiny grids that were connected to the ship's sensors also located on the skin of the ship. Each little grid was a release point for an energy beam. This made the ship capable of firing in any direction. It was also capable of firing in multiple directs. Or if necessary, it was capable of firing in all directions simultaneously with a short burst. The point of control for the firing system was a round sphere that was touch activated to fire in the direction of the point indicated on the sphere. Such a system required a tremendous energy supply but that was a minor issue for Knight.

When he finished that project he was extremely happy, for now he knew that he might have a fighting chance when the invasion came. He only hoped that he had enough time to mass-produce a fleet of these new ships. For sake of privacy, most of the production would be done at his operations center on the moon. He would count on Mochar to keep things running smoothly.

When he pondered at what he had accomplished and the possibilities it scared even him. To have created any one of these devices would be the accomplishment of a lifetime for any other scientist. But he had created these and numerous other things in his relatively short career and he wondered what his limits were. When it came down to it, he felt that his only limits might be those he placed on himself.

It was August 15 when he had completed the last of his projects. The speed at which Knight worked would be difficult for the average human mind to comprehend. Even the fact that he worked continuously with only two hours of sleep a day did little to explain this. When he was asked this question once by Dr. Avery, he would only say that it was due to his superior mind and that he had his androids to assist him. He dismissed it as a moot point since he had created the androids so they were an extension of himself.

The androids allowed Knight to accomplish projects much faster than if he were to do it by himself. Time was a precious commodity and the more he accomplished in the least amount of time the better. When he reminds himself of this point he is grateful for the androids and scolds himself for any egotistical thoughts he may have had.

It was twelve days earlier that the investigation into GLESA's affairs had concluded and the organization came through it with a reputation as clean as before. The day before the United Nations stated that Knight could return to

GLESA and offered a formal apology for the inconvenience. Knight waited until today to answer them. He informed them that he accepted their apology and would return to the helm. In truth, he was happy for the inconvenience for it had allowed him to accomplish so much.

But then he remembered why he was inconvenienced in the first place and decided it was time he paid Judge Crenshaw a visit. The visit would be more than an opportunity to gloat over his vindication. That would just be one of the added benefits. The real reason he was going to visit the man he hated with a passion was revenge. He did not care what anyone else thought. It was a fruit he would not deny himself.

It is dark when he reaches the stairs of the courthouse. There are sessions in progress but not on the floor he was going to. He is dressed in his GLESA uniform, which would serve as a sort of slap in the face of the judge. It is the folder that he holds in his hand that is the true poison that will ruin the judge's evening and eventually his life.

The stairwell is empty which he expected it to be at eleven at night. He passes each of the security cameras but makes no acknowledgment that he sees them. When he reaches the fifth floor he pauses before opening the door. After a moment of collecting his thoughts he opens the door and steps into the hallway. Two security androids are standing in front of the judge's office. Although only one was necessary, the judge always insisted on two. They only nod as he approaches and then return their attention to staring straight ahead. He opens the door and enters the office.

The judge is leaning over his desk signing some paper work that he had put off. The light of the computer terminal behind him makes his white hair look blue. Knight is able to reach the edge of the desk before he realizes he is not alone. He quickly looks up and is startled.

" How did you get in here?"

" That's one of the advantages of it being my company that contracts judicial security. Did you catch that, Judge? It's my organization again, if you didn't hear. That's why you have two of my guards at the door rather than some beer belly and his six-pack."

" They don't seem to be doing a very good job at keeping the undesirable elements out."

" You don't like me, Judge. Right?"

" Quite frankly, I loathe you!"

" It's because of your father, isn't it? He was a crooked politician and I figure all the apples from the same tree are rotten to the core, also. Isn't that so?"

" I don't have to take this."

" Take it? Old man, I haven't even begun to dish it out. You stay right there in that chair or it will be your last resting place."

" You can't threaten me. I'm a judge!"

" Were a judge. You see this folder I'm holding. It contains a report of the illegal activities you have been involved in since you have been on the bench. Sure there's minor stuff like illegal campaign contributions. Yet I don't think your judicial brethren are going to like the fact that you are on the payroll of Tito Catal. Nobody likes the stooge of a drug lord."

" How? You have no proof!"

" Sure I do. Testimony and plenty of it. I've even got pictures of you and Tito chumming it up together."

" Blackmail. That's what this is!"

" No, if this was blackmail I would be asking you for something. No, I was just being kind enough to inform you that I submitted a report to your superiors and was going to give you a copy."

He tosses the folder on the desk. The judge grabs it and tears it open. There is a fifty-two-page report on all of his illegal activity since he was appointed to the bench ten years earlier. There are also a dozen pictures of the judge with all known crime figures. The judge looks up in disbelief. There are tears actually forming in his eyes. He lays the folder to the side of the desk.

" How?"

" I have my sources deep within the crime world, Judge. You were dirty, baby, and you got caught. But don't feel bad, it just runs in the family. I just wanted to be with you on your last night as a judge. That's the kind of guy I am, you know."

" You bastard!"

" No, I know who my parents were. Maybe if you were one however, you wouldn't be in this mess."

With that he turns his back on the judge and exits the office. The androids nod and he starts walking down the hall when one of the androids speaks.

" The Judge has removed a gun from his desk."

Knight turns around and hears the shot. Poor bastard couldn't even wait until he left the building. Yet that might have been his intention. Maybe he was trying to get at him one last time. Knight knew it wouldn't work for he felt no remorse for what he did because he thought it was for the best. Although it could be viewed that the judge's blood was on his hands, he felt he could live with that.

He walks back into the office and sees the judge slumped over his desk. The weight of his body pinned his right arm against the desk so that his right hand was holding the blood-covered gun out in front of him. Blood and brains covered the white wall with a grotesque collage. Knight turns away. He was wrong. This would affect him.

Was there an inner evil that drove him to do such things? He did not know. Everyone has their own personal dark side, his just seemed more dangerous than most. He just hoped all the good he had done might make up for the bad he might do. He felt there was no way to control it and he might have to accept it as part of himself.

He returns to the hallway where the androids are staring aimlessly ahead.

" Return to headquarters and I will reassign you in the morning."

They nod and start to walk away.

" And boys."

They stop and turn around.

" Don't reveal what happened here to anyone. Don't bother submitting a report. Understand?"

They nod and remain there staring at him.

" Dismissed!"

AS they disappeared down the hall, he sits down in the hallway against the wall. He looks into the office at the dead man and his rendering on the wall. A tear falls down his cheek and he is angry at himself for feeling grief for this man. Then he thinks: which is the normal emotion, anger or grief? He didn't know. Was the revenge worth it? He once had concluded that nothing would be gained by the judge's death. Now that it was fact, he felt nothing had changed. Could he have been satisfied knowing Crenshaw would spend years in prison? He would never know the answer to that question.

After a minute he gets up and walks into the office again. He picks up the phone and calls downstairs to the local police. It is going to be a long night and he sits on the couch opposite the desk to await their arrival.

Chapter ten

It was five in the morning before he concluded his business with the local authorities. Upon seeing the time he decides he would go to Knight Enterprises and wait for Ana in her office. The streets of Omaha are deserted with the exception of the occasional early riser. He pulls his car into the parking garage and is greeted by a smiling attendant. He his in no mood for someone so cheery, so he just waves courteously and drives by without saying a word. After punching the correct code series he hears the elevator descending down the shaft and the door opens before he has time to make himself comfortable for the normal wait. Even the building was nearly deserted. He reaches the door to Ana's office and wearily punches the security code. The couch across from the desk seems inviting and he decides to rest his eyes until Ana came in.

He is more tired than he thought. In a few moments he is asleep only to be coaxed out of his slumber by Ana's voice.

" Clay. Clay!"

He opens his eyes to her smiling face. Her hair is up with a blue ribbon holding it in place. She is wearing a dark blue jacket that covers a lacy white blouse. Her bark blue skirt did little to hid her form an Knight had to raise his eyebrows. The perfume she wore seemed like the nectar of the gods.

" Is that how you normally dress at the office?"

" It's going to be a slow day and I want to be comfortable. How long have you been here?"

" What time is it?"

" Seven-thirty."

" Man, I must have been tired. I slept for a little more than two hours."

" She looks at him as if she were not impressed.

" You run yourself ragged. One of these times you're going to lie down and find that a month had passed when you come to."

" No thank you. I already went through that once. Remember? Anyhow, I don't have time to be loafing. I'm going to jump back into GLESA today and I'm going to be busy getting acquainted with the cases I missed."

" Just try and be home for dinner."

" Why? What's cooking?"

" A Chinese feast."

He looks across at he as she sits on the edge of the desk. There are no signs that she is pregnant, but she always did hold her shape well. The way she is smiling he guesses what is on her mind.

" Han is coming to town. Isn't he?"

" Yes and he's bringing a dinner companion."

" Sounds serious. Do you know who she is? As if I have to ask."

" Very funny. Her name is Suzie Ti. I understand she's a model and is from a government family."

" So she's Chinese. Han is traditional, isn't he? He couldn't get an international flavoring like I did."

" Don't be a pig!"

" Sorry. Anyhow, it will be nice to see Han settle down and give up his playboy lifestyle."

" Not if he follows your lead."

" What?"

" Marriage hasn't stopped you from roaming the planet at will living it up with your little police squad and playing games with your playground teams. I mean, let's face it, Clay. You never did grow up."

He just sits there with a slight grin on his face and smiling eyes. It would be easy enough to respond, but he could see she starting on one of her tangents and no matter what he said she would turn it around and use it against him. Silence, he has found, is the best method to eventually extinguish this type of fire.

She paces back and forth shouting and lecturing about all her pent up frustrations with him. Although his eyes follow her movements, he doesn't hear a word she says. His thoughts have gone elsewhere. In his mind he is setting his weeks itinerary and tries to balance the time between home, GLESA, and his research. He notices Ana grab the back of her neck and flip her hair as she raises her arms to stretch. This is a signal to Knight that had picked up which meant she was winding down. He then returns his thoughts and listening back to her.

" I appreciate the input. dear. I really do. Glad I could warm up your debating skills before the board meeting."

He stands up and walks over to where she is standing by the desk. His left arm goes around her left shoulder and he kisses her on the right cheek. Then he straightens himself and starts for the door.

" You've a lot to do, so I'll see you tonight. I'll be at GLESA headquarters if you need me. And remember honey, I love you."

" I love you, too."

She has a confused look on her face, which is vivid in Knight's mind, as he passes through the door and starts down the hall. A smile crosses his face as he ponders the little deceptions that are necessary to make it through relationships. Deception and compromise seemed to be the major components of his marriage. Then it suddenly dawned on him that his marriage may be in trouble.

He stops and turns to look down the long hallway from where he had just came. To the outside world, he probably seemed to have the perfect life. But it wasn't perfect. Just complicated. An intricate web on deceptions, accomplishments, wants, and needs. Honesty was an element that was lacking in Knight's life and he realized that it had carried over into his family life. It becomes easy to deceive when you have little secrets that you hide from the rest of the world.

Somewhere his priorities got crossed and he began to neglect the person closest to him. Somehow he had started to view her as a subordinate whose main function was to run his business. Maybe he had heard part of her lecture after all.

His head swivels as his eyes focus on the elevator, then to Ana's office, and back to the elevator again. The universe could wait. Down the hall he walks as his heart pounds and tears form in his eyes. When he reaches the doorway Ana is on the phone with her chair turned so she is looking out the window. Knight pulls the double door shut and locks them. Toward her desk he is drawn. The phone jack is by her desk and he disconnects it. She immediately spins around in her chair.

" Clay! Do you know who that was?"

" I don't care."

He leans over the desk and takes the receiver from her hand and returns it to its proper place. She looks at him with inquisitive eyes. He walks around the desk to be closer to he. He leans down so that his lips touch her forehead and the collapses to his knees. The tears start to flow down his cheeks.

" I love you, Ana!"

She caresses his hair as he weeps into her lap. Her eyes turn toward heaven and she silently mouths the words 'thank you'.

" Clay. Clay. Listen to me. Everything will be all right. We'll get through everything together. I promise you that things will be better from know on. Understand?"

He nods. Then he positions himself so that he is able to put one arm under her knees and the other behind her back. Her body is raised from the chair almost effortlessly. Then he carries her towards the couch.

" Clay. The meeting!"

" They can wait."

" And this can't?"

" No."

" Why not?"

" Because I love you. "

" Then they can wait."

Knight enters the lobby of the GLESA building and is immediately surrounded by a swarm of reporters. The questions are melded together and the buzz is almost incoherent. Finally a voice is heard above the rest.

" Mr. Knight, is it true that you found the body of Judge Crenshaw?"

" Yes it is."

" Is it also true that you had a meeting with Judge Crenshaw just prior to his death."

" Yes. "

" What was said at the meeting?"

" I'm not at liberty to say at this time."

Another voice comes from the back of the crowd.

" Not at liberty? Christ! The man kills himself just seconds after your meeting and you're not at liberty to say?"

The buzz of the crowd goes incoherent to Knight again as he forces his way toward the voice. Finally he sees a stocky young man in a white sweater and white dress pants grinning from ear to ear. The grin quickly disappears when he actually sees how large Knight actually is.

" You seem pretty well informed."

" I got my sources."

" What paper do you work for?"

" It's a school paper."

" What School? "

" The Greater Omaha Community College."

Knight grabs the young man by the arm.

" You're under arrest. O'Leary! Rice! Clear the corridor. I want total silence in less than a minute."

The young man tries to pull away but the grip is vice-like. Knight starts to walk and his prisoner goes limp. Looking down at him Knight just shakes his head.

" You can either walk or I can drag you. The interrogation room is three flights up and if you're not walking I'm taking the stairs."

He starts walking with a solid grasp on the young man's arm while he is dragging behind. The prisoner tries to kick himself free, which only puts more stress on the arm.

" Okay! I'll walk! I'll walk!"

" If you insist."

" Why don't you put cuffs on me?"

" What fun would there be in that?"

" Fun? Hey, you're harassing me! Well, I've got rights! Wait till my lawyer hears about this. Boy will you be in for it."

Knight reaches around to grab back of the young man's collar with his other hand. Both of the smaller man's feet leave the ground as Knight raises him and then slams him against the wall. Grimacing with pain the man looks down to see than he is pinned against the wall nearly two feet off the ground. The pressure applied to his arm increases slightly as Knight begins to talk.

" I'm in for it? Boy, you're in my domain and it's up to me whether or not the world hears from you again! So you have sources. What kind of sources could a trash artist reporter from the GOCC Gazette named Marty Nugent have? Yea, punk, I know who you are. I've read some of the trash you write. Sensationalism! Controversy! That's the kind of tripe slime like yourself thrive on. Maybe someday you can get a job working for one of the national scandal rags.

" That's your game, isn't it Marty? To possibly work for your grandfather who publishes " The Yellow Moon". You're trying to impress someone who staffs his paper with people he finds writing on bathroom walls. But at what price, Marty? What price are you willing to pay to reach such lows? Maybe sell out your sister? Maggie Nugent is a good cop and you would be willing to ruin her career to advance yours. I Know Maggie and she's a good kid. I know she must see something salvageable in the sludge called Marty Nugent to even associate with you. Even if you are her brother.

" Maggie has a promising career with the local police. Maybe someday I might even consider offering her a position here at GLESA. But you are her biggest liability. She was at the judge's office last night and I'm going to have to lecture her on confidentiality. Either that or let her superiors handle it. Trust me when I say that they will not be as forgiving as I am. You may be her family, but the best thing you can do for her is to stay out of her life until you realize what's right."

He lets the young man drop to the floor where he starts sobbing. Knight thought that maybe the kid had a chance to turn things around. In the meantime, he would lock him up and have his sister come down to get him out. He would also make it a point to scold her for revealing confidential information. From around the corner comes a GLESA agent.

" Tom. Take Mr. Nugent up to holding cell three while I make arrangements to contact his family."

" Sure."

The young man looks up from the floor.

" What about my one phone call?"

Knight smiles.

" As I said, this is my place and I made the rules. One of the first rules out the window was the phone calls. If you have someone you have to call, write it down, and maybe, just maybe, I'll have an agent make the call for you."

" You don't like me much, do you?"

" Not in the least."

The young man and the agent walk to the elevator and board it. Why did he take such a dislike to the boy? It probably had more to do with his wanting to protect his sister Maggie. He had already offered her a position with GLESA, but she declining stating she was happy with the Omaha Police Department.

Now that the sideshow was over, Knight felt it was Knight to get down and do some business. His office was on the seventh floor and he jogs up the stairs to burn off some of the excess adrenaline left over from the confrontation. When he arrives at the door of his office there is a large box with a Cuban return address in front of it. Two curious agents are walking around the box. Knight smiles as he approaches them.

" Come to any conclusions? Jerry? Rex?"

" No, sir. There are no explosives present or else that would have been detected by the building security system. If you would allow us to do some further tests, we may be able to determine what's inside before you open it up."

" It's tempting, Jerry. But I'm sure time would be much better spent just opening the box. Although I am curious, for I don't recognize the return address."

" May we carry it inside for you, sir?"

" That would be nice, Rex. But let me remind you that it is not necessary to suck up to me and you can try calling me 'Clay' if you can get comfortable with the idea. Remember you two are no longer in the FBI."

" Thank you, sir. I mean, Clay."

" You'll get used to it. Jerry, could you get the other end of the box while I unlock the door."

Both men seem to struggle as they carry the package through the doorway. Careful as not to disturb the unknown contents, they both drop to their knees and gently place the box on the floor. Hanging above the fireplace is two crossed sabers, one of which Knight takes down to open the box. The blade proves to be rigid enough to provide the leverage needed to separate the top panel boards. As the agents remove the lid a wispy vapor starts to escape and the agents jump back startled.

" Is it poisonous?"

" Would I enlist you two to do such a menial task if it were life threatening? All scans indicate there are no hazardous materials within the contents of that shipment. There is probably a large quantity of dry ice in the box."

The agent names Jerry Kliburn leans over and looks in the box.

" He's right."

" Well, what do you expect?" retorts Rex Abbott under his breath.

A bearded man in a white coat enters the room with protective goggles and gloves on. He hands extra goggles and gloves to each of the agents. Shortly after the agents have their goggles in place, a tall. dark haired woman enters carrying a plastic tarpaulin, which she drapes, over the floor near the box.

" Very good. Now Dr. Tannum, if you wouldn't mind helping these gentlemen remove the top layers of dry ice."

" The four work in tandem as Knight leans against his desk observing their progress. One of the agents looks over at Knight. They have found the primary contents of the box. Slowly he approaches the group as they remove the last of the impeding dry ice. Agent Kliburn turns to Knight.

" It's a corpse."

" A burnt corpse," agent Abbott.

" The FBI trained you two so well. Dr. Tannum, if you and Jeff would take the remains of the deceased to the laboratory, I would like a history on this person as soon as possible. Most importantly, the identity. Yes, Jerry. Rex. I must admit I knew the contents of the box before it was opened. The preliminary scans when the deliveryman entered the building showed as much. The reason I called you two here was for a much more important reason than to be manual labor. I want you two to find out who sent me a dead and admittedly too well done body to me. It was addressed to me and I want to know the answers. Understood?"

" Yes, sir!"

" Perfectly, sir!"

Knight shakes his head. Then he notices the lid of the box in the mirror by the coat rack. On the underside there seemed to be writing which he can't make out in the mirror. Quickly he circles the box to find nothing on the lid. The agents look at him quizzically. He looks up and realizes they are still there. He waves his hand to shoo them from the office.

" You have your orders. Go! Go!'

The two hurry from the office and Knight returns to his puzzle. There seems to be nothing there, but in the mirror he saw something. He picks up the lid and carries it over to the mirror. He starts to tilt it at various angles and once again the words become visible. Only they appear backwards due to the distortion caused by the mirror. Clever, he thought. The writing was imbedded in the grain of the wood so that it could only be read at a certain angle. The method was unknown to him, but he thought it was very ingenious.

Who ever sent the box must have counted on him running tests on it. They knew he would find out who the body was and this would prompt him to check out the box for further evidence. It was just a fluke that he happened to notice the writing in the mirror. He knew the identity of the body must be of importance and somehow had a link between Knight and the sender. Maybe the lid would help him identify the corpse before the lab results came back.

Knight returned to his desk and sat down in his chair. Again he turned the lid to find the correct angle. When he found it the inscription was easier to read. It read: " You may have defeated our master. But he has trained us to overcome. He promised his vengeance. Only the one has fallen. Therefore vengeance will be had by the many."

A chill goes through his body. It is the same chill he had when he had once realized that he had stumbled across a group of Satanists years earlier. It was also the same chill he had outside the torched convent in Argentina. A burned convent and now a burned corpse. The horror is almost too great to even allow him to reach for the phone.

" Ruthvan. Sebastian Ruthvan. Check the DNA samples on record against those on record... I hope I'm wrong too. Bye"

Knight sit staring as the sun glistens off the lone saber above the fireplace. Its mate was still among the dry ice on the tarpaulin and would have to wait to return to its resting-place. The day seemed to be getting longer and longer. If he could take one back, this would be it. But he knew that was impossible, so he would have to shift gears and prepare for the worst.

The worst? How would they get revenge? Kill him? Many had tried although it was their organization that came closest to succeeding. That was years ago. He was much better prepared now. Yet he was so tired and almost welcomed the chance to return to a coma for some rest.

The buzz of the phone startles him.

" Hello....I was afraid of that..Yea, literally. I'll see you in an hour for your final report..Jeff?..Could you have someone come up and remove this mess from my office...Thanks. Have them take it to the lab for analysis...Until then."

Why would they send his corpse? It was a symbol of some sort. Representing the razed convent was too obvious. This meant that there was a new power base from where they were working from. Would their leaders be as radical and deceptive as their predecessors? More than likely since that was their trademark. Could their organization be as well connected as before? It might be likely since evil and corruption often ran together and while corruption reached into many places, the evil often touched the same places as well. Knight seemed to be chosen to deal with these situations, although the strain was getting to him.

He rises from his chair and makes his way to the lab in the basement. Sterile. And white. Those are the first thoughts that enter his mind every time he enters the lab. Always a controlled and pristine environment where change and discovery were closely monitored by human and electronic eyes. Maybe it was the inhuman aspect of research that was draining him so much. Although it was his first love, the time was so demanding. Even for a prodigy like himself there was a limit on how much a person could endure. This would be the link he would cut from his schedule until his sanity returned to normal. Or until he had more time. The future would determine what choices he would make.

He sees Dr. Tannan and walks over to her.

" Yes, Clayton. This was indeed Sebastian Ruthvan. Seems to have been mutilated before his death. Besides missing his digits and teeth, his heart is gone. Tests indicate he would have died in weeks anyway due to non-treatment of a nasty little disease called Nymbitis Stomitosa."

" Really? That means he died in South America."

" Or India, Central Africa, the South Pacific. To be honest, Clay, there are dozens of places he could have picked it up."

" True enough. But I'm counting on the fact that he was last seen in South America and it would have been very difficult for him to get out unnoticed. Although it's not impossible. If not, we may never find where he died. So he was mutilated?"

" Yes."

" Good. They probably didn't do anything to him I would have liked to do."

" But Clay.."

" Yea, yea. I know, that would put me on the same level as them. In truth, Dr. Tannum, it becomes necessary to operate at their level if they are to be defeated. I know that sounds depraved, but I have dealt with them before and have seen what they are capable of. We are not dealing with people who have the same values and morals we do. In fact they may be mirror opposites. That's how backward they are. Somehow good and bad got turned around and these sick people don't know the difference."

" Then may God help you."

" I hope so. I really do."

Chapter eleven

Knight stands in front of the mirror and examines his tuxedo. He frowns at the image he sees.

" Why do we have to get all dressed up? It's just Han and his girl."

His wife emerges from the dressing room in a strapless, black evening gown. From her ear lobes hang quarter-sized diamond earrings and an emerald necklace rests on her chest. The sight of this vision of beauty makes Knight stare with gratitude. His mind must have been further gone than he thought if he forgot she looked like this.

" Because I want to do something special for Han. He's your friend, too. Don't you want what's best for him?"

" Yes, but does he know?"

" Of course."

" And he agreed? Doesn't sound like the Han I know. This girl must really be something for him to be willing to put up with this."

" We'll see at dinner, won't we? Anyhow, this will get in practice for the company ball I'm giving next month. Remember?"

" I try not to, believe me. And why are we eating Chinese? It's not like they don't have that every day back home."

" Honestly, Clay. You're worse than one of the kids. We are having Chinese cuisine because Han's fiancee has rarely traveled outside of the Orient and prefers not to try new foods."

" You said she was a model?"

" Right."

" Okay, I guess that explains why she wants to follow a strict diet."

" Very good, Clay. Maybe you should go into law enforcement."

" Cute. I'll meet you in the dining area when they arrive. I'm going to the basement."

" Clay! Can't that wait until after dinner?"

" It could. But there is no time like the present. Anyhow, you're better at welcoming guests than I am."

" You're just anti-social."

" Maybe. I'll see you in the dining room just the same."

Knight punches the security code into the elevator panel and proceeds to the sub-level. It is as good a time as any to monitor the alien progress. If he did it now his mind would not be on it during dinner. The doors open and all the androids raise their hands momentarily to acknowledge his presence. Then they all continue with their individual activities.

There are rows of computers, monitors, control panels, and circuit boards all controlled by a massive super computer on the sub-level below him. Six dozen androids are kept busy by constantly making adjustments on the control panels, recording data and replacing defective parts as soon as they begin to falter. This sterile environment was like a second home to Knight although he knew he had to take some time away from it.

An android hands Knight a computer read-out ant walks away. It states that another alien spy had been found and executed. This one was in Lithuania. To date sixty percent of the aliens were found in the United States, Great Britain, France, and the territory that once comprised the Soviet Union. The rest had been hunted down in various places scattered across the globe. According to Mochar's figures, there should only be eight spies remaining. That was eight too many and the frequency of finding them was decreasing. He hoped none of the spies were in a position to possibly guess what he was up to. Yet if they were, wouldn't the invasion have started by now? All he could do was wait and see.

He walks over to a wall that is covered with several monitors. Each monitor shows a transmission being sent by his many probes exploring the universe. Thirty-two of the probes were being used to monitor the alien activities. He often questioned Mochar about the possibility of the probes being discovered. Mochar always said it was possible, although the idea would seem outlandish to the alien leadership and they would not be guarding against such a possibility. Knight only hoped. His transmissions were so tightly focused that the only way they could be intercepted is if a ship passed between the sender and receiver. Each probe was constantly scanning to avoid such a mishap.

Nothing seemed out of the ordinary. To verify this with a more knowledgeable opinion Knight decides to contact Mochar. The alien scientist was on the moon monitoring the same transmissions. He sits down in front of a blank monitor and presses a red button. A second later a hairy face is on the screen which first smiles and then frowns."

" Knight! Good to see you! Have you seen the monitors? Specifically, number seventeen."

" Yes, I have. I'm looking at it right now. Why?"

" Bad news my friend. The planet is Terial. It has been an ally to my scientific community for centuries. They are a very advance race and would be considered a ninety-eight out of one hundred on the scale of technology. They are a peace loving people and are now extreme pacifists. That may be their downfall and ours."

" Meaning? Please get to the point, Mochar."

" Well, centuries ago they were a warring people and conquered much of the universe. Similar to what Zhar Rahk is doing. Then suddenly the leadership got what you would call religion, saw a vision or something, and claimed to see the error of their ways. Eventually order was restored and the leader, whose name was Orlok Marlen, transformed his people from a violent race into a peace loving one. However, as a reminder of the past they kept the armory and his armada of ships intact."

" Don't tell me."

" You guessed it! Zhar Rahk was probably able to take the planet without much of a struggle and now will have their technology at his disposal."

" Tell me. You said all the fighting took place centuries ago. Just how advanced was the weaponry on your scale of technology?"

" Good point. Yet I'm afraid they were still operating at a level of ninety-two. However, these battleships of yours would also be classified on the same level."

" But if they could persuade the people of Terial to modify the ships and bring them in line with their modern levels.."

" Possible, but if I'm not mistaken, and I hope I'm not, the Terialians are such pacifists that they would refuse to even assist in making the adjustments."

" I hope you are right. Does that mean that Zhar Rhak would slaughter the inhabitants?"

" There's a chance, although more than likely he will rely on them for their other advances and leave them alone. However, he will more than likely have a few token executions to show the extent of his power."

" To date I have three battleships at the same level of Rahk's. So what was the size of the Terialian armada?"

" Six hundred ships."

" Six hundred! Out gunned two hundred to one? Sounds like it would be a good time to start thinking retreat."

" Yes, that is a possibility. But they are not here yet. You should have some time to build an armada of your own."

" Just to make sure, you're on my side. Right?"

" Certainly."

" Just checking. So with this new technology, will they be able to detect the probes? Or will they continue to dismiss them?"

" Depends on the extent of the Terialian cooperation. I am certain the Terialians are aware of your probe above their planet. Yet they seem not to have informed Rahk's forces because it is still functioning. They may keep their silence, although captivity does things to the mind. but given their history they shouldn't crack."

" And how long have you been aware of the Terialian situation?"

" As your probe can tell you, Rahk's forces only entered orbit within the day. So there was no extreme emergency and it is better to wait and observe."

" True, but when were you going to notify me?"

" When the situation deemed it necessary."

" Thank you for enlightening me as to the new urgency of this situation. Please notify me if there are any drastic changes. Okay?"

" But, of course."

" Out."

The screen goes blank. How far could he trust Mochar? True enough he could have reported his position by now and he didn't have to apprise him of the Terialian situation. Did he still have loyalty to his own kind? Sure, Mochar said that he and Rahk were not the same kind, two different classes. Yet there had to be some sort of bond. It didn't matter. This new information certainly over shadowed any covert alliance. Could he overcome ?

If he tripled production of the battle ships he might have fifty ships available by the time of the scheduled invasion. That would still leave him out gunned twelve to one but it was better odds. He also knew that only a few invading ships would be sent on initial contact so he would have the advantage at that point. Yet the entire invasion fleet would eventually come. Fifty ships would about be the limit he could produce in that time frame due to the resources needed to make them and his mining operations were currently operating at peak production levels. he would have to start preparing the steps necessary to start two new production centers on the moon. Or maybe Mars. Yes, one production center on the moon would be enough. The new ones would go on Mars to avoid the prying eyes of scientists and satellites.

A buzzer sounds and a blue light by the elevator flashes. The guests have arrived. It was strange how the prospect of doom had increased his appetite. Shouldn't it be the opposite? Why argue when it's time for dinner.

Han takes Knight's hand with enthusiasm and they pat each other on the back. The smiles are contagious as the women enjoy seeing the two men reconfirm their friendship. Han waves for his companion to come over.

" Clay, this is Suzie Ti. We're to be married in October. October third."

" Congratulations."

Knight takes the woman's bronze hand and kisses it. When their eyes meet she blushes and turns toward Han. Her black hair is cut short and it off sets her dark eyes. She is dressed in a black strapless evening gown, but it is more ornamental than his wife's.

" It's a pleasure to meet you, Miss Ti."

" Thank you."

Han leans closer to Knight.

" I would like you to be my best man."

" It would be an honor. I would have been hurt if you didn't ask. October third? That's kind of soon, isn't it?"

" Well Clay, when it comes to love what difference does it make how long you wait from when you meet and when you get married?"

" It doesn't, I guess."

Suzie giggles and puts her hands on Han's left shoulder and rests her head on them as she looks at Knight. They did look good together with Han in his black tuxedo and her in a black dress. Han seemed to be wearing his hair shorter than normal. Knight wondered if it was her influence.

" So where will the ceremony be?"

Knight asks the question as he crosses the room to lead them toward the living room.

" We decided to have it at an old temple outside of Tokyo. It was where we met and we wanted to have a neutral site as not to offend either of our families. The view is excellent and weather permitting, we can have the ceremony outside."

" Sounds nice. Dinner is ready," says Ana as she motions to a servant in the doorway.

Ana takes a seat next to her husband. Across the table sits Han and his fiancee. Knight sits opposite Miss Ti and Ana is sitting opposite Han. Suzie is not shy about getting things started and takes on of the ladles and scoops some rice onto her plate. Then she takes another helping.

" I'm famished."

" As well am I, "adds Knight as he takes the ladle from Suzie when she is finished.

" Would you rather one of the servants did that ?"

Ana asks the question because she notices the tiny droplets of sauce splash onto Suzie's dress as she puts it on her plate.

" Nonsense!" says Knight. "We're all capable of serving ourselves. "

The two guests nod in agreement. Ana shrugs it off and begins to serve herself.

" So, Mister Knight.." starts Miss Ti.

" Please, call me 'Clay'."

" Okay. Clay? Han tells me you two have known each other since childhood."

" Yes. We went to MIT together and started into business together. Not your average sand box fare."

" You also have your own police department?"

" It's more than a police department. GLESA stands for Global Law Enforcement and Security Agency. We can go where you average police department can't and we provide security for many of the world's dignitaries. It keeps me busy while Ana handles the task of running the business. By the way, Han, Ana is expecting."

Han had been playing with his food when Knight made this announcement. He looks up from his plate with a smile looking first at Knight and then Ana.

" Oh really? Congratulation!"

" You must be so happy," inserts Suzie. "Is it your first?"

Ana squints her eyes at Knight to show her displeasure in the fact that he brought up the subject.

" No. This will be our nineteenth."

Suzie misses her plate with the fork and it drops from her hand to the floor.

" Nineteen?"

This is the only word from her mouth and it was obvious that she was having trouble grasping the concept.

Han notices the awkward silence that was developing and decides to shift the topic in another direction.

" So, Clay. Are you going to put on the helmet and pads on this year or do you think you're getting too old?"

The laughter between the two seems to break the tension. He points his fork at Han and shakes his head before taking another bite. Then he gives his reply.

" The day I'm too old to play sports is the day I couldn't put you on the canvas."

" A pretty brash statement coming from the student to the teacher."

" Not brash. Fact. I've advanced far beyond your teachings. In fact, maybe I should be the master and you the pupil."

Miss Ti looks around confused.

" What are you talking about?'

" Martial arts," Ana informs her. "They are just talking trying to impress us."

" Impress you? It's easy enough to see which one of us is better."

" Clay!"

" Are you up to it, Han? It'll just take a few minutes. Your old clothes are in the same locker."

" Okay."

Knight leaves the room followed by Ana who is determined to burn his ears. Miss Ti stares at her fiancee while he finishes his tea.

" Why are you doing this? Has he been drinking?"

" Clay doesn't drink."

" Then why does he act that way?"

" It's just the way he is. The man's a genius. You have to allow for a few quirks in the personality."

" You aren't going to hurt him, are you?"

" In truth, if he wanted to, he could kick my butt."

" Then why are you doing it?"

" Because he wants to."

" Men! Always with something to prove!"

Han just smiles and rises from his chair. He starts to leave the room and as Suzie realizes she doesn't know her way around this strange house, she runs to catch up. He puts his arm around her as they walk down the hall.

Both men stand on the mat wearing only the white pants to their uniforms. The gymnasium lights accentuate their finely toned, muscular bodies. Han winces momentarily as he gazes upon the scars of the larger man, but then focuses his concentration on developing a strategy.

" Well, Clay, are we going to have contact or no contact?"

" Full contact."

" The rules?"

" No rules."

" Fight to the death?"

Both men smile.

" Cute."

" Then how do we determine a winner?"

" We'll know who the winner is when there is one."

Han takes a step back and glares at his friend. This sounded like Knight didn't plan on showing any mercy. When he gets out of the hospital he would have to contact Dr. Avery to confirm his suspicions. He steps forward and they each bow while keeping an eye on each other. For the moment he would forget about friendship and concentrate on survival.

Both men advance toward the center of the mat bobbing and weaving while waiting for the other to make the first move. It was only natural that Knight would be the one to take the offensive. His kick to Han's side is deflected with a left hand while he strikes at Knight with his right. Knight swats away the incoming fist with a downward motion with his left hand. The two trade blows and kicks for what seems like hours, but Knight sees the clock and only twenty minutes has passed. Until now the receiver has been able to defy the attacker by warding off all blows. Knight decides it is time for that to change.

Knight catches Han square in the chest with a kick that lifts him upwards and backwards until he lands on the edge of the mat and rolls off. Han looks at his foe with amazement at the power of the kick. He also realizes that Knight had just been toying with him until landing the first strike. It was time to change strategy.

With a running start he leaps at Knight with his right leg extended with the intention of duplicating what had happened to him by aiming his foot at Knight's chest. Standing his ground, Knight pushes up with both hands as Han closes in on his mark. Timed perfectly, Knight pushes up on the heel of Han's right foot and flips him over backwards toward the direction he just came from. Han lands on his right hip and rolls off the mat again. He stands up shaking his head and walks toward his adversary cautiously.

He aims a chop at Knight's chin and to his surprise Knight stands there defenseless and lets it connect. The blow snaps his head back, but he does not move. Then he smiles as he raises his arms inviting his friend to strike him again. Again Han tries to kick him in the chest in hopes of making him fly off the mat. Yet before the foot reaches its target, Knight drops to the floor and with a sweeping kick knocks Han's anchor foot out from under him. As Han falls Knight taps him lightly across the throat with the side of his open right hand. Although it did not hurt, Han quickly rises to his feet holding his throat with his left hand.

" Give up? " asks Knight.

" Better believe it! Dying once is enough. You may not be so generous next time. I'll admit you have improved."

" Thanks. You know I could never actually hurt you. Although that blow you landed sure had some malice behind it."

Knight rubs his chin.

" How was I to know you were actually going to let me hit you? Anyhow, maybe it knocked some sense into you."

" With all that's going on, I wish you would have knocked me out."

" Pardon?"

" Not here. I'll tell you after we change."

" Okay. I'm curious. How do you keep in practice? I mean, your skills certainly aren't lacking."

" Androids. I program the moves into them and they also make some advances through creativity. They can alter their levels of speed and strength. So as I improve they will increase their outputs. I also work out with them set at advanced levels beyond where I currently am at for that is the only way to truly improve yourself, by practicing against someone better than yourself. I do some work against multiple attackers. Normally it's just six or eight, but if I'm feeling really good sometimes I take on from twelve to twenty. Since they don't get tired it can be quite a workout."

" Think maybe you could loan me a couple?"

" Loan? They're yours! I'll make arrangements to ship them tonight."

" Great. Well, I'm going to hit the showers. Did you want me to meet you in your office upstairs afterwards? Or somewhere else?"

" The office will be fine. We'd better hurry or the girls may get tired of waiting in the living room. It's a shame they didn't want to watch."

" Humility is better gained in private."

" Then it's best they didn't stay. I'll meet you upstairs in a few minutes."

" Sure."

The two women are preoccupied with conversation and fail to notice the men approach. Neither is wearing their dinner attire for they had changed into more comfortable clothing for the rest of the evening. Ana is sitting on the carpeted floor with he back against a furry, brown coach. Her left arm rests on one of the cushions and her right rests on her hip while her legs are hidden beneath her white night gown as they are pulled close to her. Suzie sits in a large, tan recliner with her feet resting on the extended footrest and her hands are folded on top of her stomach. She is barefoot and is wearing navy blue slacks that only reach down to the top of her calves. Her black, nylon robe is nearly transparent and is open to reveal her bare stomach because she wore a loose fitting halter-top. The men enter the room wearing matching gray sweat suits.

Suzie's eyes leave Ana and focus on the men. This prompts Ana to turn her head. Knight sits behind his wife and puts his left arm over the back of the couch. Han crosses the room and sits on the arm of the chair and takes his fiancee's left hand in his right. After Han leans over and kisses her, she smiles and squeezes his hand.

" Ana says she is having a party on September twelfth. We're going, right?"

" I've already reserved our seats for the dinner," answers Han as he winks at Knight.

" It'll be fun. You'll get to rub elbows with dignitaries and the social elite," announces Knight with an edge of sarcasm.

Ana lightly elbows his leg next to her.

" And you better show up. I've already talked to some people who are interested in meeting the founder and CEO of Knight Enterprises. None of this running off to some little country in the need of a cop!"

" Wouldn't Han be good enough? He was one of the company's founders."

She answers him with a hard elbow to the shin.

" Ouch! Guess not. Looks like I'll be seeing you at the party."

The four continue talking well into the early morning hours. As the four o'clock hour approaches they realize the time and decide to turn in. Han and his fiancee retire to separate rooms at the opposite ends of the hall while Ana retires to her bedroom. Knight is not one who sleeps much so he goes to his office to dwell on past and future events and how to deal with them. Within minutes there is total silence except for the hum of the computer terminal at Knight's desk.

Chapter twelve

Sunlight bathes his body as Knight sits next to the pool wearing only shorts as he reads his collection of newspapers. It is ten-thirty and none of his dinner companions had yet risen. Ana had juggled her schedule to make allowances for staying home to spend time with her guests and any work that needed done she could do from her office upstairs. An editorial from a Chicago columnist amuses Knight as he reaches for his glass of water. Strange. It is out of reach.

Knight leans forward to grab the glass and takes a drink. He places the glass by the edge of the table closer to him. Before his attention returns to the editorial page, his periphery vision lets him notice that the glass is slowly moving toward the center of the table. He watches it return to the position it had been before he leaned for it. Then he hears giggling coming from the patio doorway.

Trying to use the curtain as a shield is Knight's youngest child, Ian. When he sees that his father has spotted him he disappears from sight. Curious, Knight puts down his newspaper and goes to investigate and to question his son.

When he enters the recreation room the boy is seated in a chair pretending to be engrossed by a textbook on mythology. His father crosses the room and sits on the floor next to the chair. The boy continues to stare intently into the book.

" Ian, how did you do that?"

" Do what?"

" Move the glass."

" It was a trick."

" What kind of trick?"

" A mind trick."

" Can you elaborate?"

" I wanted the glass to move and it moved."

Knight sits there stunned and amazed. Did the child actually possess some sort of great power? The situation needed to be handled with extreme caution.

" What other kinds of tricks can you do?"

" All sorts."

" How long have you been able to perform these tricks?"

" Only a few days. It just happened."

" What was the first trick you did?"

The boy finally puts the book down. He turns in the chair and looks directly into his father's eyes.

" The days ago I was in the library and wanted a book that was on a high shelf. There was no one around to help me and I really wanted the book. I was staring at it trying to figure out how to get it. Then all of a sudden, it slid from its place and fell down to my feet. That was the first time I performed a trick."

A chill goes through Knight. He didn't know if the boy was blessed or cursed. Maybe it was the next stage of mutation or evolution, whatever someone might call it. One thing was for certain: Dr. Avery would have a field day running tests on little Ian trying to come up with an explanation.

" Okay, Ian. Let me try something."

From his pocket he removes a quarter and shows it to the boy. The boy smiles.

" I'm going to toss this into the air. See if you can stop it from hitting the ground. Okay?"

" Okay."

The coin leaves his hand and nearly touches the ceiling at its apex. Downward the coin falls and then suddenly stops in mid air. Knight notices that the coin is parallel on the same horizon as the eyes of the boy. Again a chill goes through his body. Then the coin starts to spin on its axis, first slowly and then faster and faster. The boy is amusing himself and there is a large smile on his face.

Knight speaks in a soft, gentle tone as not to startle the boy.

" Ian, could you put the coin back in my hand?"

The boy nods as Knight puts out his hand with the palm up parallel to his waist. The coin slowly crosses the room and comes to a rest in his father's palm. His hand closes over the coin and he looks down at the boy who is proud of his achievement.

To what extent could the boy's power grow? He would have to get Han and take Ian to Dr. Avery. What would he tell Ana? The truth obviously, but he would have to convince her to stay and play hostess to Suzie while they were away. But why go away? He had the necessary facilities in the basement. It would be easier to have the doctor come here. Knight pats his son on the head and leaves the room to make the call.

Dr. William Avery, Han Li, and Knight stand by the wall as the smiling boy stares at them and then turns his attention to the androids who are walking around. Neither Dr. Avery nor Han had ever heard of a case of an individual with such advanced capabilities as Ian. Sure there were some possessions documented, but they all dismissed that notion. All three believed the boy was an advanced version of his father. Also there were no changes in the boy's personality and he had made no threatening actions toward any one.

Dr. Avery leans closer to Knight.

" I'm certain this is just a natural progression from your genetic structure. It may be a fluke since non of the other children, particularly Liz, haven't shown similar capabilities."

Han leans forward.

" The amazing thing is how quickly his powers are taking hold. Only three days? Amazing!"

Knight nods.

" The scientist in me wants to see what he is capable of. However, being his father, I want to shield him from any unnecessary shock to his psyche."

Dr. Avery puts his hand on Knights right shoulder.

" Clay, the boy's intelligent. Maybe even at or above your level at that age. I'm sure he will understand what we're doing. Anyhow, your being here will lessen any tension there might be. It's not like Han and I are total strangers to him either. We have the well being of the boy in mind first and foremost. Maybe understanding it ourselves will enable us to help him cope with it as he progresses."

" I know what you're saying, Doc. Man, Ana would like to be by her baby's side. It's probably better she isn't here, though. She can get emotional and it would more than likely upset Ian. Okay, let's see what he is capable of at this early stage of development. Han, could you set up the first test?"

" Sure."

Knight walks over to his son and kneels next to him while putting a hand on his left shoulder. The boy is all smiles because he is enjoying the attention and likes visiting his father's laboratory for the first time.

" You understand, we're just trying to see what you are capable of. You don't have to do anything if you don't want to. I'll be here the entire time so you don't have anything to worry about. Okay?"

" Don't worry, papa. I can handle it."

The first test was to determine in terms of strength how much the boy was capable of lifting. To determine this a bar with a cable attached to it is interlinked with a tension meter. This would allow an accurate reading with a single attempt rather than relying on multiple attempts at different weights until an maximum is reached. The cable it situated so that at it's maximum length it is at the boy's eye level when he is standing. All the controls are adjusted as Knight walks the boy into the chamber when Dr. Avery is waiting.

After taking off his shirt, the boy helps the doctor and his father attaches little sensor modules to his torso and head. The sensors are wireless and each tuned to a different monitoring system. There are also several exterior sensors located at various positions throughout the chamber. As they finish positioning the sensors, Han begins taking readings in the control room to have for comparison. Dr. Avery leaves the chamber and Knight backs away to the far wall to observe.

Ian stands next to the bar, which lies flat on the ground. A moment later he has it floating at eye level. The bar pulls on the cable as the boy's face starts to show signs of strain. After twelve seconds the bar falls to the ground and the boy steps back as the bar bounces up. He looks to his father for approval and his greeted with a reassuring smile. Then he turns back to the bar and performs the feat twice more. As the bar falls the third time, Knight walks over to his son, pats him on the head, and walks him out of the chamber.

Knight and Ian enter the control room with the boy still shirtless and wearing the sensors. Dr. Avery and Han are going over the data compiled from the three lifts. The results of the lifts were relatively close with him lifting 327.25 pounds on the first attempt, 327.3 pounds on the second, and three hundred and twenty seven pounds on the final attempt. By comparison Knight weighed two hundred and eighty pounds, Han one hundred and seventy pounds and Dr. Avery tipped the scales at three hundred and forty pounds. It astonished them how a person's mental strength could far exceed their physical strength. Knight knew that Ian could not lift more than thirty pounds manually. They knew as Ian grew older both would increase, but to what extent they did not know.

Other sensor reading showed that Ian's body functions were reacting as if he were actually performing a physical activity. His heart rate increased slightly, as did his breathing. The boy was also on the verge of perspiring. If he had continues a few seconds longer he would have been drenched with sweat. Of the most interest to them were the brain wave readings. They made Knight's seem normal in comparison.

Next they wanted to test for extra sensory powers with the standard test of cards with shapes and colors on them. Han and Dr. Avery are on one side on a divider communicating by intercom while Knight and Ian are on the other side. Dr. Avery removes a card from the stack and says "okay". The boy proceeds to tell him that it is a blue star. The shapes are easy for Ian to pick up on for he is correct on all one thousand attempts. Colors, however, were slightly more difficult for he chose the correct color only eight hundred and forty-two times out of one thousand. The difficulty seemed to lie with the closeness of green, blue and purple on the color spectrum. Ian seemed to have a slight case of color blindness. They didn't know if he would overcome that and only time would tell.

They next decided to see if Ian could manipulate objects without actually seeing them. One test, thought up by Han, was to place a deck of shuffled playing cards in a wooden cabinet and to spread the cards out. The box for the cards is also placed on the shelf and the door is closed. Relying on the fact he had proven his ability to differentiate between shapes, they instructed him to arrange the cards by suits, lowest to highest, and put the cards back in the box. Ian sat down in a chair and closed his eyes. When later they asked why he closed his eyes, he said it allowed him to visualize better. After twenty-two minutes he opened his eyes and smiled. Han opened the door of the cabinet and saw only the box with not a single card in sight. He picked up the pack and it was full. Removing the contents they found the clubs on top, then the diamonds, hearts, and spades. All were arranged from deuce to ace. Beneath the ace of spades were the two jokers. Dr. Avery thought that was amusing.

Next was a test devised by Dr. Avery. He took a sack full of coins: quarters, dimes, and nickels. The contents were dumped into a large metal box. Again Ian was asked to sort by like coins and to stack them in groups of ten.

After forty-eight minutes the task was complete and all the coins were situated in the box according to specification.

The final test of this nature was Knight's and involved a chamber with concrete walls four feet thick. Ian was to sit in the center of the chamber. On the opposite end of the basement there was an identical chamber. In that chamber there is a table with two glasses on it, one containing water. Knight devised the test to see if the boy could overcome the thick barriers and to see if the boy could perform a task over such a great distance, four hundred and twenty-five feet. It would also be an interesting trick to observe because the goal was to move the water from one glass to the other without moving the glasses.

For several minutes the boy fidgeted in the chair as he tried to get a fix on the other room. Then in the fourteenth minute the boy stood absolutely still and grasped both sides of the chair seat. His eyes were closed and his head started to move slightly side to side. During the sixteenth minute, to the enjoyment of the three that watched on the monitor, the water started to leave the glass in a thin stream. The water arched over to the other glass and the rest flowed through the air along the same arch. As the last of the water left the original glass, it went along the same path leaving nothing but air behind it. Knight laughed for it was a nice artistic touch in which Ian had made the transfer. It would have been simple enough for him to have lifted the entire contents out of the one glass and float it over to the other glass. Since the event was being taped, Ian wanted to show off a little bit.

The four of them ate lunch right there in the laboratory and Ian was enjoying the experience. He may have been a genius and possessed great powers, but compared to Knight's other children he was extremely shy. He was an introvert. Being in a controlled environment like the laboratory made him feel very comfortable and it was fun for him to interact with the others in this manner. All through lunch Ian watched the movements of the androids intently while his father and friends talked about a multitude of subjects.

When the break is over, they proceed on to the next test. They want to see if Ian had any control over the elements.

First they took him back to the concrete chamber. Knight put a match in a vice and asked Ian to light it. A second later it ignited. That was simple enough, but a match was supposed to burn. Next Han put a sheet of paper in the vice and asked Ian to ignite it.

The boy stares intently at the paper for two minutes and then closes his eyes. After a minute the top edge of the paper starts to smoke and within another second the entire sheet is engulfed in flames. As the paper turned to ash, Han walked over with a log of wood from a Maple tree. Again the item is placed in the vice. This time the log was in flames after only twelve seconds for the boy knew how to do it.

Next Dr. Avery brought in a block of metal. It had a melting point of 1835 degrees centigrade. It was a special metal they had developed and they didn't figure on the boy melting it. What they hoped to accomplish was to measure the maximum level of heat the boy could generate. knowing what his task was, Ian focuses on the block as the others study the readings. After giving it his best effort, Ian collapses into the chair exhausted. Knight rushed over to his son and carries him out of the chamber to get him some water. Dr. Avery and Han go to retrieve the read-out of the test results.

When Knight returns with Ian, they have a computer generated drawing with the assigned thermal readings in different colors. They concluded that the point where Ian had focused his concentration was the hot spot. this area was the size of a pinhead and measured nine hundred and eleven degrees centigrade. The temperatures of the immediate surrounding region decreased to six hundred and twenty-eight degrees and the rest of the block was four hundred and fifteen degrees. Even the air around the block was warmed to one hundred and fifty degrees for a radius of half a foot. It was ninety-four degrees centigrade the next foot, sixty degrees the next foot, thirty degrees the next, and room temperature by the fifth foot. Although Ian was focusing his attention to one point, for some reason he could not explain, he felt some of the energy flowing out of him and missing the mark. Since the boy did not have total control over what he was doing, they concluded that the additional risk factor was significant enough to discontinue after the next experiment.

In the final experiment of the day, they wanted to see if Ian could control the temperature in the other direction. Again they returned to the concrete chamber where Ian would return his attention to the block. Sitting in the chair the boy stares wide-eyed at the block without blinking. Nothing happens. Knight goes over to his son and touches him on the shoulder. Ian pulls away.

" It's all right, Ian. We can continue this another time and you'll be successful."

" No! I want to do it now! And I will!"

" Are you certain about this?"

" Yes!"

" Okay, we'll give it one more try. Then we'll go up and see how your mother is doing. Okay?"

" Okay."

The boy positions himself in the chair with a renewed determination. knight thought it was admirable that the boy had the drive to see a project through. Han and Dr. Avery enter the chamber as Ian begins to shake uncontrollably. Suddenly there is frost on the ground and icicles start to form on the block. AS the boy exhales his breath is visible. The three rush toward the boy as the water vapor in the room is crystallized and it starts to snow. Knight grabs the boy's shoulders while his eyes are locked on the block. As Knight shakes the boy they hear a crackling sound. They all look at the block and see it is cracking in several places. Finally the boy collapses and falls forward where his father catches him. He cradles his son as the others look at the block in awe of what they had just seen. Then Knight carries the boy from the chamber followed by his friends.

" Ana is going to kill me!"

" There's no way we could have known the kind of power he could unleash," consoled Dr. Avery as he passes a scanner over the boy's body. " Fortunately he's only suffering from extreme fatigue. He should come around in a few minutes."

Knight places the boy flat on a counter top and covers him with a blanket. Then he places another folded blanket beneath the youth's head. He removed the tiny sensors from his son's head and neck, but leaves those on his torso while the blanket covers them. In anger he tosses the tiny devices across the room and falls to his knees while both hands remain in contact with the blanket covering his son. He shakes his head and then looks up at Han.

" Why didn't I stop him? I could have stopped him! I'll never forgive myself..."

" He'll be all right, Clay. You know you shouldn't beat yourself up over this. The boy's a lot like you. If you hadn't let him do it now, he might have come back later and did it without our supervision. It's that Knight inner drive to succeed. You may as well accept the fact that your baby there is going to do things as you did and it's not likely there's anything we can do to stop him."

" I don't want to stand by helplessly while my son grows out of control."

" Then don't be helpless. You have the resources to guide him and keep him out of harm. And you can count on me and Bill to help. Right, Doc?"

" Certainly. There's nothing that can't be overcome, Clay, Heck, someone in your position should see this as a minor challenge. Helping your son is a minor task compared to say, saving the universe."

" I'd gladly let the universe go to hell if it meant protecting Ian."

Han kneels down next to Knight.

" I know you don't want the universe to go to hell. You've devoted years of your life fighting so that doesn't happen. We'll get through this. Us and Ana. You have one heck of a woman up there, Clay, and I'm sure she is up to the challenge."

Under the blanket there is movement.

" Papa?"

Knight gets to his feet and tears of joy blur his vision as he looks upon his son's face. The boy's left hand comes out from beneath the blanket and Knight grasps it with both of his.

" I'm sorry, papa. Sorry I worried you."

" It's all right. You just get your strength up and we'll talk later."

" I just had to show that I could do it. I did it, didn't I? Papa?"

" Yes you did. Now lie here and rest and we'll go see your mother at dinner in a few minutes."

" Okay."

Knight leans over and kisses the boy on the cheek.

" I love you, Ian."

" I love you, too"

Knight goes off with the other two to examine the data. Maybe there would be something that could clue them to what had happened. If they were to help the boy then a thorough understanding of what happens to him when they did the experiments was necessary. The data was extensive and they knew they would not get through it all that night. They would, however, use the few minutes before dinner to organize the data so it would be easier to go through later. It was going to be a long night.

Chapter thirteen

Music filled the room as the one hundred and eighty-four-member orchestra ran through their renditions of classical songs. Red, white, and blue streamers looped down from the rafters. Laughter and conversation could be heard from the hallway where Knight was standing. Dressed in a black tuxedo with a navy blue tie and cummerbund, he peered through a tiny window at the activity in the ballroom.

He hated these formal functions and hated even more the type of people that comprised the majority of the guest list. It was one thing to tolerate meeting one of them in passing, but to spend a whole evening with a room full of them? Maybe he was anti-social. But if this was the best society had to offer he would rather be a recluse. Overcoming his hesitation, he pushes his way through the door.

On the far side of the room he spots Ana talking to a group mixed with politicians, corporate executives, and the elite of tinsel town. Seated to the left are Han and his fiancee who are talking to the vice-president of the United States and his wife. Han notices Knight and waves him over.

" Clay, I believe you know vice-president Bailey. And of course, his lovely wife, Elizabeth."

" Yes. Nice to see you again, Michael."

Knight shakes the hand of the big man and then turns to his wife.

" Is Ana being a gracious hostess? Is there anything I can get you, Elizabeth?"

The woman smiles and extends her hand, which Knight takes and kisses.

" No, Mr. Knight. There is nothing that I require at the moment. Just soaking in the atmosphere of the festivities is enough for me. And, yes, your wife is a very fine hostess. I wish there were more like her in Washington."

From the inflection it was obvious that she was implying that his family should move to Washington DC As much as that might please Ana, he was not about to reenter the chaotic lifestyle of the east coast. Seven times he had been offered various positions in presidential cabinets. Seven times he had turned them down. He just nods politely to the woman and takes a seat next to Han, across from the Vice-President.

Knight liked Bailey about as much as he could like a politician. If it was in the stars, the man would make a fine President someday. But that day may be a few years away because the current President, Peter Heathcote was doing a fine job and had the highest approval rating of any Democratic politician in decades. Bailey was a handsome older man with silver hair of sixty-three years who was six-foot-three and a solid two hundred pounds. He was a retired Air Force general and served two terms as governor of Florida. His spouse had been a nurse in the Air Force and they met and married twenty-one years ago. She was fourteen years younger and her Italian heritage was obvious in her youthful face.

A new tune starts by the orchestra and the Vice-President and his wife both look at each other and rise from their chairs simultaneously.

" Excuse us, Clay. But the wife and I have an appointment to keep on the dance floor."

" Then by all means."

Knight and Han both rise and bow slightly to dismiss their table companions. Knight sits down, but Han remains standing. He turns to his fiancee.

" Suzie, would you like to dance?"

" Of course. I was just waiting for you to ask."

" Do you mind, Clay?"

Knight waves them away with the back of his hand.

" Have fun!"

As they walk away he mutters under his breath.

" Someone has to."

A waiter brings him a glass of apple cider, which he nurses unenthusiastically while he watches the orchestra play. Out of the side of his right eye he sees a peach colored dress approach and he cringes for he knows it is Ana.

" Clay! Why are you just sitting here? There are people here that would like to meet you."

He smiles and rises to his feet.

" Just lead the way."

She starts to walk off. Knight finishes his cider and puts the glass on the table. As he follows his spouse he speaks quietly to himself.

" Let the sideshow begin."

Ana introduces him to Senators, Congressmen, actors, directors, producers, and various businessmen who envisioned themselves as giants of industry. Then she introduces him to the Archbishop of the eastern Nebraska diocese. Knight takes the man's hand and shakes it vigorously.

" Archbishop, it's nice to see a wholesome face here."

" Pardon?"

" Like a lamb among the wolves."

" Sorry, I don't follow."

" Never mind. I caught the mass you gave last Christmas. Very nice."

" Thank you. I didn't know you were there."

" I was in the back. By the door."

" Oh. Ana tells me you earmarked that donation to the diocese for the schools."

Knight looks at Ana and she turns and waves at someone.

" Yes I did. I've always felt education was very important and the parochial system has always been very strong in preparing our youth for the future. A little infusion of cash should help prevent that system from deteriorating. I've also given donations to help get the public school systems back on track. Education is a commodity that can not be neglected or mankind will find itself unprepared when the future becomes the present."

" True. Very true. It's nice to hear your views on this subject. The hour is growing late and I'm afraid I'm not used to staying up late like I once did. It was a pleasure to meet you, Mr. Knight."

" The pleasure was all mine. And please call me 'Clay'."

" Very well, Clay. I'll be watching for you at the back door of future services."

" I'll try to oblige."

" Good. Ana."

The elderly man turns and walks toward the door. A dozen aides soon join him and they escort him to the exit. Knight was sorry to see him go. When Knight turns back to his wife, she is talking to a young woman with long, black hair and a dark tan that was accentuated by the bale blue dress she was wearing.

" Clay, this is Maria Ortiz. She is the niece of Ambassador Javier of Argentina."

" Nice to meet you. Niece? That would mean your father is Dr. Antonio Ortiz, the personal physician of President Esteban Alcazar."

The girl's face lit up. The smile is radiant and she takes a step closer to the gentle giant. Ana notices some new guests arriving and walks over to greet them.

" Yes he is! Do you know him?"

" We've met on three occasions at medical conventions. He was an eloquent speaker. He must be proud to have such a beautiful daughter."

The girl laughs.

" I don't know about that. I think it's my three brothers that he is proud of. Diego and Manuel are successful doctors and my eldest brother Jorge is a high ranking official in my country's government. To my father, I'm just a school girl who is better off staying out of sight."

Knight nods trying to be sympathetic.

" So, how did you find out about the party?"

" My uncle received an invitation, but he has taken ill. I asked if I could come in his place and he made arrangements with your wife. So here I am!"

" And so you are. So where do or did you go to school?"

" I spent a year at Georgetown, but didn't like the city much. Then I spent a year at Princeton, bur that was to stuffy. Finally I returned home and got my degree in a school in Mendoza."

" What was your major?"

" Biology. I wanted to be a doctor like my brothers. My father has been less then encouraging. Now I'm not sure if I want to go to medical school."

" I'm sure you'll make a fine doctor."

" Think so?"

" Yes I do."

From behind the girl approach Han and Suzie. The girl turns and sees who had caught his attention. Knight puts his right arm around Han's shoulder and introduces everyone with his free hand."

" Miss Ortiz, this is my business partner and friend Han Li and his fiancee Suzie Ti. Han. Suzie. This is Maria Ortiz, the niece of Ambassador Tomas Javier of Argentina."

Han leans over and whispers in Knights ear.

" Can I talk to you in private."

" Sure. Ladies, if you wouldn't mind, we have a little business to discuss."

It is Miss Ortiz who responds.

" I'm sure we can find something to talk about."

knight and Han walk down the hall as the sound of the orchestra grows fainter with each step. A darkened doorway to the left leads to an unoccupied room where they can talk. After turning on the light, Knight allows Han to enter and closes the door.

" Well, what is so important?"

" I'm sorry to get you away from the party, but this seemed like as good a time as any to bring this up."

" No problem. What's on your mind?"

" Well, you know I'm getting married."

" I'm the best man. Remember?"

" Right. Well, anyhow I've been feeling uneasy about something."

" Getting cold feet?"

" No. It's just that in our relationship, I would like to have total and open honesty."

" And?"

" I want to let Suzie in on what's going on."

" You've got to be kidding!"

" No. really. I wouldn't feel right keeping this from her. We're going to be married."

" So?"

" You told Ana."

" That was my choice."

" And I'd like to tell Suzie."

" Listen, Han, I can sympathize with where you're coming from. But I told you, Bill, Ana, and my mother, may she rest in peace, because I knew I could trust you. These are some very dangerous secrets we're talking about. If you break down and tell Suzie, how do you know she won't go off and tell someone else? Soon we have chaos and panic on our hands. The consequences are unfathomable."

" She wouldn't tell anyone."

" How do you know? How do you know?"

" It's a feeling."

" Maybe she has a close friend, like you an I are, whom she can't keep any secrets from. What happens them?"

" It wouldn't happen."

" Han, I've trusted you with this because I can count on you and your loyalty and friendship run deep. Sure you love Suzie. But does that mean she has to know everything about your past and life. That can be dangerous."

" I believe it's important."

" Have you told her about the women before her?"

" What?"

" You know. The two or three dozen women you had escorted around the globe for one purpose or another. Those women."

" I will tell her."

" Do you think that's wise? Sure, it all happened before you met. But as Ana puts it, you were a real playboy."

" That's all in the past. I can live with it."

" But can she?"

" Yes."

" You're sure?"

" Yes."

" Positive?"

" Yes! Just drop the subject. Okay?"

" Sure. But if you want me to give you the go ahead on revealing what we've done over the years and jeopardize what we have and might accomplish, I'm not going to. I can take measures to stop you, but I certainly do not want to."

" You feel that strongly about this?"

" Absolutely! If you think about it with your head instead of your heart and groin, you'll see the importance of keeping it a secret."

" Well, I've given the matter some thought, but I don't see what the problem is."

" If you seriously think about it I'm certain you'll understand. Would you at least wait until you are actually married? You at least owe me that."

" Okay. I could let it go until then."

" Great! I suppose we better get back to the party or Ana will have security out looking for us."

" Right."

As they leave the room Knight shakes his head. To what extent would he be willing to go to keep Han from revealing their conspiracy? Kill him? Never! Their friendship was too strong for him to resort to that. Although at the moment Han was straining those bonds.

At least he came to him and expressed his feelings before he actually unloaded the dark truths on Suzie. If it came down to choosing between the secret and Han, he would choose Han. Let the secret be known and he would just revise his planning and preparation. Yet he hoped Han makes the correct choice so he would avoid the unnecessary turmoil. Knight touches his stomach and thought it was a small miracle that he didn't have an ulcer.

When they rejoin the party Knight notices that Ana's sister and her boyfriend had arrived. Carmen Ramos was

Ana's youngest sister at nineteen years of age. She lived in nearby in Kansas City, Missouri and was attending Rockhurst University. She had ambitions of following her sister into the business world. Knight didn't like the boy she was with, but Ana said the girl should live her own life.

Kramer O'Connor was a roughneck who dropped out of high school and tended bar in the seedy part of Kansas City. Although on this night Carmen somehow persuaded him to wear a tuxedo and wash his hair, normally when Knight saw him his hair was greased back and his attire consisted of leather and chains. At six-foot-two and one hundred and sixty pounds the boy still show signs that he was once a promising athlete. But at twenty-two his only sports were drinking and fighting. As Knight approaches, the young man puts out his hand.

" Clay! How ya doin'?"

" That's Mr. Knight to you," gruffly states Knight as he grabs the boy's hand and releases it an instant later.

Ana runs interference by walking between the two and points Knight toward a table around which are seated his three GLESA cohorts Mason Rasov, Russell Jackson, and Randy Buck. Rasov and Jackson had their wives at their sides. Buck is single and seemed to be keeping company with an attractive red head. Ana whispers in her husband's ear.

" Why don't you go over and enjoy yourself. I'll entertain Carmen and the boy winder."

Nodding Knight turns and kisses his wife on the cheek and the makes his way toward the table. As he approaches the three men rise, salute, and then break into laughter. The women only smile in confusion as their mates revel in the joke. Closest to Knight is Katrina Rasov who he kisses on the cheek as he passes by while patting her on the shoulder. Then he repeats this with Susan Jackson before approaching the red head. She looks up at him smiling as Buck puts his right arm around her shoulders.

" Randy, I'm afraid I haven't had the pleasure."

" I'm sorry to say neither have I!"

Buck starts to laugh uncontrollably.

" Randy!" shouts the girls as she pokes him in the ribs.

Rasov leans across the table.

" Her name, Randy. Clay wants to know her name."

" It's Frances Rubino. But I call her Frankie. Right, Frankie?"

Knight looks at the other two men.

" How much has he had to drink?"

They both shrug as Buck gets to his feet.

" Not a drop, sir. I'm intoxicated by love."

He bends over laughing and falls backwards into his seat. Knight shakes his head and takes the seat between Miss Rubino and Jackson. He turns so he can be heard above the music.

" Having a good time?"

" Wonderful!" states Mrs. Rasov.

" Good food," offers Rasov.

" Good music," adds Jackson.

" It's probably the best party I've ever been to!" concludes Mrs. Jackson.

" Seriously, how much has he had?"

Jackson leans closer.

" Just three hits. But I think he may have started before he arrived."

" Did he drive?"

" Yes, they came on his motorcycle."

" In that dress?"

The garment in question was quite revealing and it's wearer had much to show.

" Yes. It must have been a sight to see."

" I guess he'll have to stay the night."

" Sounds like a good idea."

" You're all welcome to spend the night. You know we have plenty of room."

" We'll let you know," says Rasov as he rises to his feet. " The night is still young. Katrina, my dear, may I have this dance?"

" Why, of course. Excuse us."

Knight expected the Jackson's to follow but they remain seated.

" Russ? Sue? You're not going to dance?"

" Sue's not feeling well."

" Oh, really? Is there anything I can do?"

" No, Clay. Thanks just the same. Russ is making a big deal out of nothing."

" Nothing? You were vomiting for nearly an hour before we came."

" I'm over it. Honestly, Clay, I'm fine."

" Maybe Dr. Avery should look you over. You seem a little apprehensive about me examining you."

" Maybe you're right. Maybe I should let Dr. Avery look at me. Sorry, Clay. But I would not be too comfortable with you and Russ being friends and all."

" And I'm not a medical doctor."

" Well, technically no."

" It's all right. I understand. I'm sure Dr. Avery would be perfectly willing to look at you. He should be arriving a little later."

" You mean here?"

" No, I don't mean to imply he'll examine you right here. I don't think we're that hard up for entertainment. I'm certain my office upstairs will serve the purpose just fine."

" Okay. Just tell me when he gets here."

An overwhelming hunger entices Knight to call over a waiter and he requests a steak and potato platter with side orders of corn and green beans. To drink he orders a pitcher of milk. As he waits for the meal he talks with the Jackson's while watching the Rasovs and Buck and his companion on the dance floor. The waiter appears with his meal after a few minutes and Knight thanks him heartily.

Just as he is finishing his meal, Knight notices Dr. Avery come through the door. He came alone, which was normal. He thought maybe he would let Ana fix him up with someone, but the doctor refused to allow them to do it. Thus ended their attempt at being matchmakers. The big man grabs a tray of appetizers from one waiter and a pitcher of apple cider from another as he makes his way to Knight's table.

" Why don't you make yourself at home, Bill."

" I'm famished. Been at the office all day going over the data about you-know-who and I lost track of time."

He quickly finishes the tray and notices the plate in front of Knight.

" What did you have to eat?"

" Steak, potatoes, green beans, and corn."

" I'll take a triple order."

" Whatever you say!"

Knight motions the waiter over again.

" Young man, the good doctor insists on three orders of what you brought me earlier."

" Three orders, sir?"

" Yes, or did you want just one pitcher of milk, Bill?"

" Milk? Sure, give me three pitchers."

" Yes, sir."

The waiter walks off toward the kitchen. The Jacksons stare at the doctor in amazement. Knight sees their faces and starts to laugh.

" Where are my manners? Russ. Susan. I believe you have met Dr. Avery before."

Jackson rises to take the big man's hand.

" Yes, we have. Several times in fact. Nice to meet you again. Dr. Avery."

" Why all the formality? If you can call Clay by his first name, you can call me by mine. It's Bill."

Mrs. Jackson looks over at Knight.

" Clay?"

" Oh, yes. Bill, Susan is feeling a bit under the weather and we were hoping you might look at her in my office upstairs. She wanted a real doctor."

Mrs. Jackson fidgets in her chair nervously. She seems embarrassed to be imposing on the doctor. He dark hair seems to have lost it's luster and her brown eyes don't seem to sparkle like they normally do. Knight thought she was much less energetic than a woman of twenty-three should be. Her eyes dart nervously between Knight and Dr. Avery.

" I don't mind. If you can wait, I would like to eat dinner first."

" That's no problem. And thank you."

" Don't worry. Just by looking at you I think I know what it is. But I'll know for sure after examining you upstairs."

" Is it serious?"

" No, no. I'll have to borrow some of Clay's equipment to make sure. But I'm certain it's not serious."

The waiter returns followed by another and they set the platters and pitchers in front of the doctor. He pours a glass of milk and samples it's freshness. After twenty minutes he finishes his feast and asks Mrs. Jackson to follow him upstairs.

Jackson looks over at Knight after they had disappeared through the doorway.

" Do you think it's serious?"

" No. Bill would not have made light of it if it was."

Fifteen minutes later the doctor and Mrs. Jackson return. Mrs. Jackson rushes across the room and sits on her husband's lap and hugs him as she starts to cry. Jackson looks up at the doctor as he approaches the table.

" What is it? What's wrong?"

" Well, first of all, I don't think those are tears of sorrow. They're tears of happiness."

She takes her head off his shoulder and looks into his eyes.

" Russ, we're going to have a baby!"

" Really?"

He lets out a loud cheer of joy. People look over at the couple for a few seconds and then go back to their conversations. Knights picks up another glass of cider and raises it toward the couple.

" May your child inherit the best qualities of each of you. Now I think we have a legitimate cause for celebration."

Chapter fourteen

It had been a week since the party and Knight is readying himself to participate in a game of football. The Earthquake had won the first three games of the season and then had it's win streak snapped at fifty-one games. His team failed to rebound the following week and now had a dismal 3-2 record. Both losses were road games and Knight hoped to turn things around at home.

There had been a rash of injuries due to the increasing number of cheap shots taken against his players. The league commissioner had vowed to crack down on the offenders and promised the rest of the season would be played clean. Knight would see to it that he kept his word.

On this day, Knight would be playing on both sides of the ball because starting center Mike Benden has neck spasms and right outside linebacker Peter Sipple broke his left ankle. Knight kneels in front of his locker and sees to be praying, but he is actually going over the team's plays in his mind. This is his first game of the year and he wanted to make a respectable showing on both sides of the ball. He also tried to figure out how his team had lost two games in a row with the talent that it had.

As with all his sports, he recruited prime athletes and worked them feverishly to hone their skills. While many of them had not been division one All-Americans, they all excelled at their positions. It is a fact that some of the starters had never played a down of football before he drafted them. It was seen as a tremendous risk to draft an athlete from another sport, but it wasn't like he was a pioneer in doing it. Knight figured an exceptional athlete could excel in any sport given the proper training.

The team is deep in talent with the starters being exceptionally gifted athletes. The starting quarterback is John Failla, a second team All-American from Ohio State who is six-foot-four and two hundred and twenty five pounds. His backup is Keith McCoy, a five-foot-eleven and one hundred and ninety pound speedster from Air Force and he is also the shortest player on the team. At running back is Brent Maxwell, a six-foot-three and two hundred and twenty pound bruiser from Pepperdine. His backup is Chris Naylon from UCLA who is six-foot-one and two hundred and fifteen pounds. Starting fullback Pat Thompson is six-foot-two and two hundred and fifty-five pounds and hails from Middle Tennessee State. John Nair does a good job make holes as his replacement because this Elmira College graduate is six-foot-two and two hundred and seventy pounds. Wide receiver Jeff Bogard has excellent hands and makes a good target at six-foot-six and one hundred and ninety-five pounds and was from Ohio

Northern University. Behind him was Bruce Carpenter of Penn State who stands six feet and weighs one hundred and eighty pounds.

The other starting wide receiver is Tom Kratky and he was one of the athletes Knight took a chance on when he converted him from track to football. At six-foot-four and two hundred pounds, Kratky is a physical specimen and he still hasn't lost any of the speed he had as a member of the Texas A&M track team. Relieving Kratky is Kenny Williams of St. Louis University who is six-foot-one and one hundred and eighty-five pounds. John La Fleaur is the starting tight end and is six-foot-five and two hundred and thirty-five pounds and was from Emory University. His backup Larry Ryan, six-foot-four and two hundred and fifty pounds from Madison College, has excellent speed for a big man, but his hands aren't as good as La Fleur.

The linemen for the Earthquake are literally a wall of muscle. Center Mike Benden of Pittsburgh is six-foot-four and two hundred and ninety-five pounds. His backup is Wayne Sheumaker of Midwestern University and is six-foot-three and two hundred and ninety pounds. Starting right guard Sito Tanaka was in training to be a sumo wrestler in Japan when Knight found him. Under the proper training regimen, Tanaka was now a sculpted three hundred and twenty pounds on a six-foot-four frame. His backup is Rob Goodman of Wilburforce University who is six-foot five and two hundred and eighty-five pounds. At six-foot-four and three hundred and fifteen pounds, Yuri Rabinovich is the starting right tackle and he is another converted sports star. Rabinovich won the gold medal in free style wrestling for Latvia at the age of nineteen at the 2044 Olympic games in Stockholm, Sweden. Very little size is lost when Mike Lee of Clemson replaces Rabinovich because Lee is six-foot-five and three hundred and ten pounds. Left guard Bill Cooper of Miami is the largest man on the line at six-foot-eight and three hundred and forty-five pounds. His backup is Tom Perry from North Texas State who is much smaller at six-foot-two and two hundred and seventy-five pounds. Starting at left tackle is one of three first team All-Americans the Earthquake has as starters. Dave Lazzaretti of Nebraska is six-foot-five and two hundred and ninety five pounds and is extremely smart and agile. His backup is Steve Moore of Mankato State and is six-foot-four and three hundred pounds.

The linebacker corps are a very talented bunch and include the Earthquakes other two former All-Americans. Peter Sipple was a two time All-American at Notre Dame who stands six-foot-four and two hundred and seventy-five pounds. Stan Blake of Southern Methodist University backs up Sipple at right outside linebacker and he is six-foot-two and two hundred and fifty pounds. At right inside backer is the always-aggressive Jeff Smith of Oklahoma who is a powerful six-foot-six and two hundred and fifty-five pounds. His backup is Steve Taylor of Michigan who is six-foot-two and two hundred and thirty-five pounds. The left inside linebacker is the final former All-American in the Earthquake lineup and he is John Dunn of Nebraska who is six-foot-three and two hundred and forty pounds. John Meyers of Colorado backs up Dunn and he is six-foot-three and two hundred and fifty pounds. The final starter of the line backing corps is left outside linebacker Rich Bucchino who is surprisingly quick for six-foot-five and two hundred and seventy pounds. Kerry Anderson of Georgia Southern is a competent backup and is six-foot two and two hundred and eighty-five pounds.

The defensive line is very solid for the Earthquake. At right defensive tackle is Kevin Feldhacker of Yankton College who is six-foot-four and three hundred pounds. His backup is Creighton McCaslin of Pittsburgh who is six-foot-four and two hundred and ninety pounds. At nose guard is Daniel Mason who had been a two time gold medal winner in judo at the 2046 and 2047 world games while representing his homeland England. The London native is very cunning and dangerous and feared no one while many feared his powerful fix-foot-three and three hundred and fifteen-pound stature. Behind Mason is Jude Lorenz of Azuza Pacific and he stands six-foot-four and weighs two hundred and eighty-five pounds. Starting left tackle Doug Hall of Tarkio College is six-foot-three and two hundred and ninety-five pounds whole his backup Brian Hall of Tennessee is a similar six-foot-three and two hundred and ninety pounds. Those two are of almost equal skill and evenly divided their playing time.

In the secondary there are many fine athletes that combined to make pass coverage almost child's play. At strong safety is Alvin Miller who spent his college career playing forward for the Kansas State basketball team. While he was a tremendous athlete, his basketball skills were average so Knight convinced the six-foot-six and two hundred and fifteen-pound athlete to give football a try. His backup is Joe Rynes of Navy who is a fierce hitter at six-foot-two and two hundred pounds. At free safety is Todd Bortolottii of Notre Dame who is six-foot-two and one hundred and ninety-five pounds. Following him is Dave Mills of Princeton, a six-foot-two and two hundred and five pound athlete who was a former three time Ivy League athlete of the year. Starting at left defensive back is six-foot-one and one hundred and eighty-five-pound Akira Korin of Japan who Knight convinced to give up track shoe for football cleats. His backup is Gregg Hosking of Army and was the last of the three former military men Knight took a chance on after they completed their service requirements. Hosking is only six-foot and one hundred and seventy-five pounds, but he is a fierce hitter and intelligent in his coverage. At right defensive back is Leon Beck of Colgate university who is six-foot-three and two hundred and five pounds. His backup is Jim Marcuzzo of Temple who is six-foot-one and one hundred and eighty-five pounds.

In the kicking game the Earthquake were almost unmatched. The starting place kicker is Matt Wieler of Angelo State who is six-foot-two and two hundred and ten pounds. His backup is Mark Ewin of Oregon who is six feet and one hundred and ninety-five pounds. The first team punter is Brian Abbott of Michigan State who stands six-foot-one and two hundred and five pounds. Following him is Chris Prom of Louisville who is six-foot two and one hundred and eighty pounds.

The final two players one the Earthquake's fifty man roster are special situation players. The first is Hideki Kagawa of Japan who was a friend of Tanaka's from sumo camp. Kagawa had slimmed down some but was still an enormous six-foot-four and four hundred and forty-five pounds. He is used in short yardage situations on defense, especially at the goal line. The other player is Tito Vasquez, a basketball player from brazil who is seven-foot-seven and two hundred and eighty-five pounds. While he was a good leaper for his size he lacked the mobility to continue playing basketball so Knight enticed him to suit up for the Earthquake to block extra point and field goal attempts. So far he has been fairly successful.

The head coach is Peter Jackson who had been head coach at the University of Virginia for five years. He never won a national championship, but proved to be a winner by leading the Cavaliers to four straight seasons of ten or more wins. At offensive coordinator is Jim Carroll, formally of the Miami Dolphins. As defensive coordinator Knight obtained Brad McNichols, a strategy master who was an assistant at Air Force and a consultant to the Pentagon. Knight felt that the entire staff was top of the line and coaxed the maximum effort out of the players.

While the position coaches stressed the fundamentals and drilled them into their complex game plans, it was up to the strength coaches and trainers to ensure the players were in prime physical condition. Each player is monitored closely and progress is tabulated for the coaches and Knight to see. Players kept fit by training in the complex underground beneath the Blackhole that spanned several acres. It is accessible to the athletes of all his sport teams. The weight and resistance room consists of hundreds of stations with free weights, resistance machines, and bars for chin-ups, pull-ups, and dips. There are also more unconventional methods in use such as canvas bags filled with sand at different weights. An athlete would grasp the bag with one or both hands and perform various exercises. Also available for the athletes are electric stimulus modules, which the trainer would place on the muscle group being worked, and if the athlete has trouble, the module would give a jolt to stimulate the muscle so they could finish the repetition. This led to more repetitions and stronger athletes who were drug free.

There are also running tracks and swimming pools of various sizes for a multitude of purposes. The tracks are cushioned enough as to give somewhat when the athlete runs on them and that resulted in less joint damage and stress fractures. While the athletes mainly worked on speed and endurance on the tracks, speed was also stressed. To work on strength, the athletes wear snug fitting weighted vests when they run. Half their routine would be with the vest and half without. Over time the weight of the jacket would be gradually increased until the point where no progress was being made.

While swimming is an excellent form of exercise, the routines are varied and are taped by surveillance cameras so the strength coaches can observe them and make adjustments in the program if necessary. Athletes also had drills in they water where they would tow floating modules of different weights. They also did work beneath the water at the deep end wearing oxygen tanks while they would work on their running form, agility, and strength.

Knight felt there was no reason that an athlete of any sport or any position should not be in top physical condition. He informed them that he was not only paying them for their performance on the playing field but also for their performance in the training center. To back this up, he offered bonuses for improvement and excellent performance in the training center just as he did if they met their statistical goals in their respective sports.

Knight is looking forward to the game and felt it was a good way to release some of the pent up tension he had inside. There was going to be much contact on both sides of the ball and Knight was known to be one who could dish it out. The opponent that day was to be the Houston Oilers who had maintained a reputation of being a hard hitting team for decades. This year they started 5-0 and news reports quoted it's players as being confident of extending the streak and disrupting the mystic surrounding the Blackhole. It was going to be a classic "smash-mouth" football game and Knight hoped the commissioner's warning insured this would be a clean game.

The Oilers won the toss and elect to receive the ball. The Earthquake choose to protect the north goal and the game is under way. Knight chose not to play on the special teams because he did not want to cut into the playing time of another reserve. The Oiler player takes the ball in the end zone and starts to run out only to be leveled by Hosking at the seven-meter line. Hosking is the captain of the special teams unit and they chose to nickname themselves "The Headhunters."

With the Oilers pinned deep, Knight hoped to keep them there and make them punt after three. Knight watches Smith make a few hand signals and positions himself. The Oiler quarterback Hale Bixby takes the ball from the center and hands off to halfback Kennedy Young who is tossed to the turf by Mason at the eight. Second and nine.

Smith looks over at McNichols and signals that the blitz is on. Bixby takes the ball from center and steps back looking at the fleeing receiver to his left. Knight knocks his blocker into another one who is mixing it up with Feldhacker. Both Oilers go down in a heap as Feldhacker leaps at the quarterback waving his arms wildly. Bixby sees his target and lets the ball go only to have Feldhacker tip it. End over end the ball falls off course and hits the ground incomplete at the fifteen-meter mark. Bixby cusses himself.

Knight readies himself for the center to release the ball again. Seeing the center raise the ball, he takes off and powers his way through the crease where Mason's and Feldhacker's blockers fight. Just as Bixby plants his right foot to throw the ball, Knight dives at the signal caller and secures his right arm around his waist and knocks him to the ground. The Oilers are now on the four and have to punt. The roar of the crowd is deafening.

Kratky takes a booming kick while retreating to the twenty-nine. He circles to the west and starts up the sideline. At the Oiler forty-nine he is upended by two Houston players. The crowd cheers again as the offense takes the field.

At quarterback is Failla, but Naylon and Nair are starting in the backfield due to injuries to the regular starters the previous week. Both teams line up and Knight stands over the ball looking into the eyes of Oiler nose guard Kenny Brown. Brown's eyes squint in anger as Failla call out his count. Knight gives Failla the ball and explodes into Brown knocking him off balance into the on rushing linebackers. Down field Bogard dives for the ball and the

Earthquake have another first down at the twenty-one. it was a bad throw by Failla but Bogard made a great save.

Again the teams line up across from each other. Knight relinquishes the ball and overpowers Brown driving him backwards for five meters. Again the ball is airborne and La Fleur catches it at the seven and is tripped at three. Knight can only see Brown's lips move as the roar of the crowd drowns everything out.

First and goal. Three meters from pay dirt and Knight confers with Failla as they walk up the field. They decide that Nair should get the ball and follow Knight into the end zone. A moment later Carroll signals the same plan, so he might look like a genius if it works. The ball is snapped and Knight strikes Brown hard in the chest with his forearms. As Brown falls over backwards, Nair slips into the end zone while breaking the grasp of a few out reached arms. The extra point is good and two minutes into the game the Earthquake lead seven to nothing.

The rest of the first half follows the same scenario with the Earthquake defense stuffing the Oilers and then moving the ball at will on offense. As the buzzer signals half time the score is fifty-one to zero. It is obvious the Oilers are frustrated. They are in danger of being the third team in history to have one hundred points scored upon them by the Earthquake. Seven touchdowns and a safety accounted for the scoring. The defense had limited the Oilers to two first downs and sixty-eight yards of total offense. Knight is pleased with his performance on defense of nine tackles, eight of which were unassisted, and two quarterback sacks.

At the start of third quarter the reserves are readying themselves to takeover and mop up. Knight knows his team would continue to dominate the Oilers for Coach Jackson was not one to show mercy and expected an all out effort from all his players the entire game. The first teamers had limited time left in the game so they want to make the most of that time.

To start the second half it is Kratky and Carpenter on the goal line awaiting the kickoff. Carpenter takes it two yards deep and brings it out following his blockers. He makes it to the thirty-three before being smothered. This is the worst field position of the day for the Earthquake and Failla knows what he has to do.

On the first play from scrimmage Failla spots Kratky racing up field at a right to left diagonal. The pass is chest high, which Kratky catches at the Oiler thirty-eight and without breaking his stride glides into the end zone untouched as he out-races the pursuing defenders. Twenty-five seconds into the second half and the Earthquake have another touchdown. To rub it in, Jackson calls for a two-point conversion that is successful with a pass from Failla to Bogard. Being down fifty-nine to nothing brings out the tempers of the Oilers and there is some shoving after the conversion which the referees and umpire struggle to break up.

Weiler puts his foot into the ball and it sails past the back of the end zone. Both teams meet at the twenty-meter line. Knight knows that Jackson would be pulling the starters soon so he feels he has to get in a few more hits on defense. On first down Knight meets Oiler running back Tucker Mason in the backfield and levels him at the nineteen. On second down Bixby releases the ball quickly to tight end Jack Palmer who Knight upends at the twenty-three. With an obvious passing situation Knight pumps himself up to attack at full bore. As the ball is snapped Knight rolls over left guard Jon Lubbock and blind sides Bixby as he moves to his right. Somehow the quarterback managed to maintain control of the ball, but he is slow to rise from the seventeen-meter hash mark

Jackson sends Beck out to return the Houston punt. It is a low quick, which he takes at the twenty-five and is quickly met at the thirty-four. The crowd is in a frenzy.

McCoy is in at quarterback as Jackson begins to filter in the second unit. Knight positions himself over the ball as he watches Oiler linebacker Graham Sloan unleash a tirade at his teammates to fire them up. Then ball is in McCoy's hands and then it's Naylon's responsibility. He tries to break through a hole, but is confronted by Sloan who puts him on the turf at the thirty-six. On second down McCoy drops back and connects with La Fleur at the forty-five and he is drags tacklers to the fifty.

Sloan is waving his arms wildly and goes into a tantrum. On first down McCoy keeps the ball and breaks to the right where he is stopped by Sloan at the forty-four. There is some confusion as some players trip and fall near Sloan and McCoy. Then as McCoy is getting up, Knight sees Sloan let a vicious elbow land on the quarterback's right ankle and McCoy tumbles over in pain.

Sloan quickly gets to his feet and walks away as if nothing had happened. Knight rushes over to McCoy as a referee kneels by him. He questions the ref who said he didn't see it. After further questioning it seemed none of the other officials witnessed the assault and the replay cameras discontinued following the play shortly after the tackle.. The other cameras in the complex could not see the infraction because of people in the way. The officials refused to take Knight's word for what he saw and the pain made McCoy semi-coherent and he couldn't answer their questions.

The anger rises in Knight as he takes off his helmet and smashes it to the ground. Then he slips off his shoulder pads and jersey and lets them fall to the turf. He stands there in a gray T-shirt with the team emblem on it as he kicks off his shoes. Then he walks over to the Oiler huddle where Sloan had his back to the officials.

Sloan envisioned himself as a fine martial artist and did hold black belts in three different forms. Knight was about to give him a lesson he would never forget. Two officials try to impede his progress only to be tossed aside. Sloan turns around as his teammates tell him of Knight's approach.

" Got a problem, Knight?"

" It's already taken care of."

" What do you mean by that?"

Knights right foot connects along side Sloan's head sending a cracked helmet back toward his teammates. Sloan falls to his knees as two Oilers rush Knight and are quickly dispatched with a kick and an elbow. Blood is flowing from Sloan's left year that he touches as he looks at Knight as the ire rises within him. He rises to his feet.

" Big mistake, man!"

He rushes at Knight and tries a kick, which Knight prevents by catching Sloan's right ankle with his left hand. He pulls the leg closer and breaks it below the knee with his right elbow. As Sloan lets out a scream another Oiler rushes him only to be sent backward by a kick to the chest while he keeps hold of the broken appendage.

" You know. Sloan, it would be best if you kept your mouth shut for a while."

His right palm smashes into Sloan's chin shattering the jaw. Then he flips him back toward him teammates into a heap with his leg landing in an awkward position. Mason and Feldhacker grab Knight from behind only to be shed like blankets in the early morning. The entire Oiler team is soon surrounding Knight as he prepares himself to take on any on-comers. They start to rush in and fall to the ground as Knight is in a fighting frenzy and the warrior within him made him stand his ground rather than retreat. As they try to attack Knight, he stops their progress with kicks and blows. The rest of the Earthquake team and security manage to intercept some of the Oiler players before they faced the onslaught. As the crowd dispersed, Knight could be seen in a fighter's stance with thirty-one fallen Oiler players at his feet. Then he lifts his head and lets out a savage roar that breaks the silence of the crowd. Then the crowd answers with a roar of their own and cheers in excitement for what they just witnessed.

Security and medical personnel begin removing the fallen Oilers from the field as Knight's conscious level starts to return to normal. Mason and Feldhacker return to his side as Knight shake his head at the damage he had done. Feldhacker held his helmet at his side and Mason removes his and does the same. The smile on Mason's face is broad as Knight looks at him. Then Feldhacker cautiously puts his arm around Knight's shoulder as they walk him back to the locker room. Over the load speaker they could hear an announcement.

" There will be a half hour delay as officials access the situation. Your patience will be greatly appreciated."

Knight looks over at Mason.

" How's McCoy?"

" Fine. He'll be able to play in a couple of weeks. Which I guess is more than I can say for that bastard Sloan. It was quite a sight I must say. It's about time someone did something to make up for incompetent officials."

" Yeah, and the way you took care of those clods from Houston. Me and Danny thought we were going to save you, but you sure didn't need saving. "

" I appreciate that. I really do. But I'm not proud of what I did."

" Doesn't matter," says Mason. " From what I hear the only one you really put the hurt to was Sloan. Most of the others should still be able to play."

" If they don't disqualify the team," responds Knight.

" They wouldn't dare!" roars Feldhacker.

" Clay might be right, Kevin. It's never happened before, though. There's a first time for everything."

Knight is sitting in front of his locker when he learns of the official decision. The game would continue but he was suspended from play. In fact, the commissioner already made the decision to suspend him for the rest of the season and the entire next season. He was also assessed a record fifty million dollar fine for endangering the lives of the other players and for displaying unfit behavior for a team owner. The suspension and fine didn't bother Knight for he was just happy the team wasn't penalized. He could always use the extra time and it seemed a small price to pay to get justice.

Sloan was said to be in serious condition and eight other players had injuries that would keep them out for a few weeks. When the game resumed both teams were lack luster and seemed to just go through the motions to complete the game. Final score was seventy-two to zero. it was possibly the final game in his football career and Knight was happy to have had twelve tackles and three sacks. Now his only immediate goal was to choose a gift for Han and his bride to be.

Chapter fifteen

Knight and Dr. Avery are at work in the basement laboratory of Knight's house. They are going over data compiled over the past several days from tests performed on Ian. Except for his brain, the child is normal. But it is his brain that puzzles them. Apart from the irregular brain wave activity they had been unable to discover what part of the brain the boy had tapped into which enabled him to unleash such great powers. When it came to solving mysteries of the brain Knight was the world's foremost expert. Yet no matter how he approached it, he could gain no insights as to how his son could exploit the powers at will. For all the advanced technology they had at their disposal, the equipment is still too primitive to deal with the given situation. Possibly someone with the wisdom of centuries of research and exploration could help. It seemed a good time to consult Mochar.

Knight sits in front of the screen and taps out the code necessary to contact the moon station. After a few seconds the face of the alien scientist is on the screen.

" Yes, Knight. Is there a problem?"

" Yes, but it does not have anything to do with the impending invasion. It is my youngest boy, Ian. Within the last couple weeks he has gained the powers of the mind which enable him to manipulate matter and the elements at will. It is far beyond any reported cases here on Earth and I was hoping that in your many years, maybe you have some experience with the subject."

" Some, but not enough to consider myself an authority. However, there are two here that would be able to help. Your guests from Yalor could give some valuable input on the subject, but it would be necessary for the boy to come here in person. Will that be a problem?"

" No. We will be there within the next couple of hours. Until then, my friend."

" I will await your arrival. Out."

The screen goes black and Knight turns to the doctor. His features reveal that he is intrigued and deep in thought. Knight rises and starts for the elevator expecting the doctor to follow. He reaches the door only to look back and see his friend stationary, leaning against the counter.

" Bill! Are you coming?"

The doctor seems startled and walks to the elevator.

" I will be granted the opportunity to go along right? I am not mistaken in this, am I?"

" You've never been there? I guess you haven't. Certainly you can accompany us on this short journey. I am sure Mochar will be delighted to meet you. First I have to inform Ian and also contact Ana to let her know of our activities. Then I'll inquire as to whether the prince and his entourage would like to join us. The shuttle should leave within the half hour."

" Isn't Han due to arrive shortly?"

" True. He would also like to meet Mochar. Why don't you contact him and find out his ETA and we can coordinate the take off to coincide with his arrival. Tell him to land his jet near the shuttle bay."

" Will do."

The doors of the hanger open at a moderate pace as Knight checks the controls in the cockpit. All systems read to be operational giving Knight the assurance it is safe to begin the start up procedure. He place his right hand on a sensor plate which scans his vital statistics to establish both is identity and his health to make sure he is capable of space flight. Once that is verified by the shuttle's computer, a metal panel next to the scanner raises to reveal two buttons: one red and one blue. To activate the shuttles engines the proper sequence was to push the blue twice and then the red once.

If for some reason he desire to destroy the shuttle, he would only press the red twice at which time a beep would signal a request for a countdown time. The series blue-red would allow one hour for escape, red-blue allows ten minutes, and red-red again would only allow two minutes. To deactivate the self-destruct series the blue needed to be pressed three times. Any not recognized sequence entered after the self-destruct sequence would automatically detonate the explosives.

To escape the shuttle a person would enter a compartment the size of a small closet. Once the door closes the floor would quickly retract and an air pocket carries the person down the chute. Halfway along the chute the person would slide into a pod. When the sensors indicate that the person is in the pod, it quickly closes and the air current increases velocity. The pod is shot from the shuttle in torpedo fashion with it's guidance system immediately making adjustments to avoid hitting any obstacles. A turbo rocket propels the pod as the on-board computer requests instructions. The occupant has the options of taking manual control of the pod's guidance system, letting the computer determine the course, or stopping the rocket and allowing the pod to drift in space. If the nearest known destination is at a great distance, the occupant may want to instruct the pod's computer to covert the interior of the pod to a suspended animation atmosphere. While the occupant is preserved, the pod would conserve power by only firing the rocket for a few seconds every hour to maintain velocity and course. The shuttle had fifteen such pods and the system reset fast enough to allow them to escape at five-second intervals. The compartment door automatically opens when the system is reset and operational.

A quiet, low-pitched hum indicates that the engines are gaining in power and it would be possible to take off within the next five minutes. Knight retreats from the cockpit to open the passenger loading doors at the rear. The interior of the shuttle is spacious and capable of holding two hundred people comfortably. From front to back the shuttle is three hundred and fifteen feet long and sixty feet wide and twenty-five feet high. A complex six engine system was needed to get the vehicle air borne and an even more complicated panel system underneath the shuttle enabled it to break the gravity field of any planet and enter the weightlessness of space.

Knight opens the doors to see Dr. Avery and Ian on the ground waiting to come on board. A hydraulic stair case lowers and folds out from the side of the shuttle. As each passes through the doorway, a green light flashes indicating they are healthy. If anyone was carrying a harmful bacteria or virus, a red light would flash and a horn would sound. The system would be especially helpful when entering the shuttle after spending time on a strange, unfamiliar planet.

Just as Ian and the doctor make their way to their seats, Han appears at the hanger door and waves. After jogging the short distance and getting the green light, Han is on board and greeted by his fellow passengers. Knight presses a button that simultaneously retracts the stairs and closes the door. He puts his right arm around his friend's shoulder and they advance down the aisle.

" So, where did you fly in from?"

" Tokyo. Making some more arrangements for the wedding. By the way, are you throwing me a stag party?"

Knight takes his arm off Han's shoulder and playfully hits him on the back of the head with an open hand as he brings the arm toward himself.

" Not in front of Ian. We'll talk about it later."

Han nods and smiles as they stop by the seats where Ian and Dr. Avery sit.

" You two look awfully funny sitting all alone in the middle of all these empty seats."

Ian only shrugs his shoulders while the doctor raises his hand for Han to shake.

" Nervous about the wedding?"

Han shake the hand and lets out a sigh.

" Somewhat because it's going to change a lot of things. But there are no regrets."

" Not yet, anyway."

" Thanks, Bill. I thought doctors cured ulcers, not gave them. With any luck we'll do great if things go half as well as it has for Clay and Ana. Maybe someday we'll have a child as sweet as little Ian here."

The boy smiles and looks up at his father who had put his hand on his shoulder. Then Knight looks at his watch and starts for the cockpit. He signals for Han to follow as he turns toward his only two passengers again.

" We better be going if we have any hope of being back by midnight. Ian, you keep the good doctor in line now."

The boy smiles and nods.

" Good. We'll be taking off momentarily. It would be a good idea to fasten yourselves to your seats."

They enter the cockpit and secure themselves into their seats. Han is an experienced pilot and had taught Knight everything he knew about flying. They had designed the shuttle together and there was always a special bond between men and their creations. After all systems are in order, Knight slightly presses the throttle forward and the spacecraft slowly approaches the hanger doors.

Once the shuttle is clear of the hanger, Knight starts to inch the throttle slowly forward. As the speed increases he keeps an eye on the control panel. He presses the throttle all the way forward, slaps a button which fires the turbo rockets, and pulls the control wheel back. The craft is air borne and the two men smile in delight while checking the instrument panel. Higher and higher the shuttle rises until they are several thousand feet above the Earth. Then knight flips a dozen switches up which activates the panels beneath the shuttle.

Besides acting as a heat shield upon reentry to a planet's atmosphere, the panels were also capable of releasing pulses of magnetic waves which were altered to become opposite the polarity of the gravity's pull and this repelling the ship from the planet's grasp. Nearly any gravity field short of a star could be escaped by increasing the frequency of the pulses and altering the polarity.

Breakaway is not violent, but for the few moments before it seems as if the shuttle is sliding against something. Then there is no resistance at all. Knight rechecks the readings and plots a course for the moon development. After a few moments he sets back in his chair much more relaxed.

Han looks over and decides to break the silence.

" Bill mentioned the Ballarians would be going along. Was there a problem?"

" The prince felt that it would be too traumatic for his younger siblings to be reunited with the other members of the escape with the future still holding so much uncertainty. I see no fault in his reasoning."

" Nor do I. And on the topic of reasoning, I've thought long and hard and I've decided not to tell Suzie about our secret activities."

" I'm glad to hear it. May I ask what changed your mind?"

" It was a combination of things. One, I didn't want to put an unnecessary strain on our friendship."

" I would have got over it."

" Maybe. I also didn't want to her to have something like this on her mind to worry about. It might cause her undue stress and keep her up nights worrying about it. She's kind of high strung."

" She is?"

" Oh yeah! This wedding is putting her in a frenzy."

" But that's understandable."

" True. Then I got to thinking that open blanket honesty may not be the best thing. Not only with this. but with my lifestyle before I decided to settle down. She knows how I was, only I don't think it would be a good idea to tell her about each individual girl that I went with."

" If you think so."

" Don't be so condescending. You brought it up in the first place."

" True enough, but I don't want to pressure you into anything. We've been friends a long time and I don't want to have anything put a strain on those bonds."

" Clay, there is nothing that could come between you and me. I can't believe you would think like that."

" Women can have an influence."

" Love and friendship are two different things."

" Right, love is stronger."

" It is?"

" You feel stronger about Suzie than you do about me, right?"

" I've known you longer."

" That doesn't have anything to do with it."

" But I'm closer to you than anyone else."

" That's because in a sense we're brothers. I love you like a brother and you probably feel the same way."

" That's it. You feel like family, but Suzie doesn't."

" So what! You don't want to be marrying your sister. You love her, don't you?"

" Yes."

" Then what's the problem."

" I'm scared."

" You're scared to commit?"

" No, I'm scared to fail."

" Fail? Fail what?"

" I'm afraid I'll do something that would drive her away. Maybe I'm not ready for marriage."

" There's no entrance test that tells if you are or aren't prepared for marriage. You have to feel it in your heart and your gut. If you feel it there, then it's up to your mind to set the time and place. Would you be willing to see Suzie in the arms of another guy?"

" If he's right for her."

" No, no, no. Han, you're the one who is going to marry her. You're the one who's right for her. It should make you cringe at the thought of her with another man. You mean it doesn't?"

" It does. I just want what's best for her."

" That's great. But don't you think you are what's best for her? Or let me put it this way. Do you think she's what's best for you?"

" I don't know."

" Okay. You've played the field for a long time. Has any girl affected you like this?"

" No, but does that mean we should get married?"

" I can't answer that for you, Han. I would think you would know. Maybe you've had too many women and it's clouded your judgment. Heck, I'm the youngest of you, me, and Doc and I'm the only one that's married. Bill's another story that will have to be discussed at another time. Anyhow, when I met Ana I felt that she was the one for me."

" You were just a kid!"

" True. The feelings were there, however, and they were unmistakable. Granted, she was the first and only girl I went with. Yet the chemistry was there and it was as if we were destined for each other. Don't you feel like that for Suzie?"

" Yes. Do you think I could handle marriage?"

" You will be a great husband. Maybe you're just rushing into this. It might be better if you pushed the date back."

" No, if we are to be wed, then things should progress on schedule. I just hope everything works out."

" I'm sure it will."

The shuttle rolls to a stop in the landing bay at the mining facility. Ships three times it's size surround the shuttle. Mining is still very profitable for Knight on the moon although within four months it would be depleted of all worthwhile minerals. At that time he would covert operations so that it would solely process the ore mined on the other planets, their moons, and in the asteroid belt. Knight is also considering expanding operations to some of the planets in solar systems his probes had discovered years earlier.

Knight walks down the stairs with Ian in hand when he spots Mochar and the Vatsali brothers approaching. Han and Dr. Avery follow closely behind and stare in awe at the sight of the three aliens. Mochar grabs Knight with his furry arms and gives him a hug. Then he turns his attention to the boy.

" So this is the subject. Seems to be normal enough, but one can never make an accurate judgment by first appearances alone. We'll need a more controlled environment. Let's adjourn to my office.

As they walk Han and the doctor notice the red-tinted aliens conversing among themselves in sign language. Dr. Avery make an inquiry to Mochar.

" Are all from their race deaf?"

" Dr. Avery, isn't it? "

" Yes."

" Their entire race is indeed lacking in the powers of hearing and speech. They are born without the inner working of the ear entirely and without a voice box. However, these deficiencies are counter-balanced by some rather remarkable abilities."

" Such as?"

" It depends on the individual. Some have the ability to read minds and to project their thoughts into yours. These two do not have that skill. Others are masters of manipulation. Not only being capable of moving objects around, but to actually alter an objects shape and structure. These two are novices at this practice, but they inform me that as they age their power will increase. Within another decade they will progress to the point where they would be equal with any other of their race."

" So their powers increase as they grow older?"

" It is the same as with any species. It takes time for any subject to advance to the status of the adult in that race. These two are actually very young compared to the old age those of their race actually achieve. Even my race has a short life cycle compared to theirs. Droz tells me there were elders on their planet who were twelve to fifteen thousand years old."

" Incredible! How old are these two?"

" Droz is ninety-three and his brother Wir is ninety-one. They are mere toddlers compared to the rest of their race. Although they are intellectually comparable to any other adult, their powers take time to mature. However, it is unknown to them in which order they come or at what interval. Sometimes it is only a matter of a few years. Or quite possibly they could go several centuries before obtaining a new power. It is an inexact science. Even their elders are unable to judge what each individual will do. Some of it may depend on genetics and some may depend on the guidance of some unknown force."

As they reach the door Knight presses a panel and it slides open. Once everyone is in the room. Knight turns his attention to Mochar and the Vatsalis.

" What about Ian? He is gaining such great powers at such a young age and they are coming to him at short intervals."

" Not if you compare the life cycle of your species to that of the Vatsalies. Truthfully, he is at a comparable age to them in relation to their respective life times. Since you live such a short cycle the intervals would seem closer together. But it does puzzle me how one of your species could even obtain powers that are so foreign to your planet. True, there have been isolated cases over the centuries of individuals who possessed limited abilities, but nothing of the advanced nature you have described. For starters, let's examine the physical compositions of the individuals in question."

Mochar signals for Droz to step on a platform and a pulsing ring lowers past his head to the ground and then rises back to the ceiling. Then Wir takes his place on the platform and the ring repeats it's actions. Mochar punches some buttons and a panel retracts to reveal a wall-sized screen. After punching a few more buttons the screen shows two color-patched silhouette images with data continually scrolling to the left of each image. After a few moments Mochar signals to Knight that the boy is to step onto the platform.

" Ian, if you would," states Knight as he directs his son to the platform.

After the ring returns to the ceiling the boy steps down and positions himself next to his father. Mochar again plays at the keyboard a little bit and then the screen is split three ways with the silhouette of Ian on the far right. The scientists study the information and look at each other puzzled. Then Mochar approaches the screen. He picks up a pointer to assist him.

" Their physical make-ups are completely different. Different anatomy. Different chemical balances. At first glance, everything seems different."

Dr. Avery approaches the computer terminal.

" Maybe if we just concentrated on the general area of the brain. It is obvious that is where Ian draws his powers from."

" Well, then bring it up doctor," insists Mochar.

On the screen appear three revolving images of the subjects' brains. Dr. Avery keeps tapping the keyboard to slow and stop the scrolling data every few lines. After stopping the data for the seventeenth time he approaches the screen. He borrows the pointer and indicates some numbers and letters that are similar on all three screens.

" What's this?"

Mochar steps back while Knight and Han walk closer to the screen. Knight holds his head in amazement at the new revelation. His pulse racing, Knight walks over to the computer terminal.

" Those are measurements in parts per billion of unknown trace elements which the computer assigns a random alphabetic tag. Whatever it is, Droz has four hundred and thirty-two parts per billion, Wir has four hundred and thirty-one and Ian has four hundred and twenty-eight."

Dr. Avery walks over to Knight.

" But what is the billion in relation to?"

" Atoms. For every billion atoms, there are four hundred and thirty-two atoms in Droz combined in such a fashion they are recognized as unknown to the scanning system. I think it would be wise for each of us to be scanned to check our measurements of any of these."

Knight, Dr. Avery, Mochar, and Han each take a turn on the platform in that order. After a few minutes screen is split seven ways. To answer their inquiry they discover that Knight has one hundred and thirty parts per billion, Mochar has fifty-nine, and Han and Dr. Avery each only have three parts per billion of the combination in question. They now had an idea from what the individual drew their powers from, but had no way to completely research how the individual tapped into the power, how the chemical was produced, or how much of the chemical had to be present in order for the power to be tapped. After they had studied the information sufficiently, Mochar clears the screen and returns the wall panel to it's original position.

" Maybe a demonstration by each of the subjects would be helpful," suggests Mochar.

Knight agrees but suggests they explore areas that he and the others had not touched on. Mochar sees no problem with that and looks over the data Knight had sent him regarding their research on Ian. He presses a button and moments later three androids appear, each carrying a block of ice. Once the blocks are placed on the ground, Mochar continues in his role as master of ceremonies.

" You have done some research in matter manipulation. As far as I can tell you only dealt with moving objects. This experiment deals with altering the shape of an object. Ice will be used to start because it has a lower density and should be easier to manipulate. Artistic creativity is encouraged, but not required. This will not be a race, so each of you take however much time you need. Begin when you feel ready."

Each individual stands in front of a block and concentrates. A few minutes later the room is filled with the distinct sound of crackling ice. The observers watch in subdued amazement as the three perform their unique style of sculpting. Yet none of the material is actually removed. Rather it is mentally molded into the shapes they desire.

When finished each individual steps back to collect themselves. The product Droz made is a topographical globe of his home planet. Wir made an anatomical model of a hand. Ian had made an architecturally precise model of the capitol building in Washington DC

" Very good," says Mochar. " Now that you are practiced, repeat the process on a more difficult material. Make the same product as on the first trial. This will allow us to monitor the change compared to a common reference."

The androids exit and return carrying blocks of granite. As before the subjects position themselves in front of the blocks. Within seconds each of the blocks seem to pulsate and there is a sharp crackling sound in the air. The elapsed time to finish is less for each of them compared to the ice trial run. With this substance it showed to be no more difficult to alter the shape even though there was a greater density. Also, since they had already constructed their models once, it was easier for them to recreate. A third trial using blocks of vulcanized iron was performed in a time that was very close to that of the second.

Knight and his friends remain in their seats as Mochar supervises the experiments. An android enters the room carrying a crate filled with limestone pellets. Mochar reaches into the crate and removes a handful of pellets. Then he signals for Droz to approach. As Droz positions himself in from to the limestone, Mochar turns to Knight.

" This experiment involves altering the atomic structure of an object. Rather than alter the shape, the purpose will be to alter the composition. Droz will first give a demonstration of this so Ian can observe the process before attempting it himself."

Mochar nods to signal Droz to begin. One at a time the pellets change from white and chalky in nature to a shiny, yellow state. When Droz is finished, Mochar picks up the pellets and places them on a scanner platform. The read-out indicates that there are thirty-one pellets ranging in weight from thirty-four grams to eighty-nine grams. The composition of each pellet is pure gold.

Han and Dr. Avery are obviously impressed, but Knight seems unmoved by the results. A handful of limestone pellets are again placed on the ground and Ian takes his place in front of them. One by one they change and Ian looks at the nuggets with pride when he is done. Scanning shows there are forty-eight pellets and each is pure gold.

Mochar turns to Knight and inquires as to what his appraisal is.

" If I were in a position to be motivated by greed, then I might be tempted to exploit this wonderful gift. There are a multitude of possibilities, however, that may be more beneficial than financial gain. I believe it would be best if you, Mochar and the Vatsali brothers, direct the training and education of Ian in regard to his powers. I'm sure Ana would never go for leaving him here full-time and I wouldn't want to put him in that position either. However, two days a week should be ample time for you to give him guidance and in honing his skills. He will be accompanied by either myself, Han, Bill, or even possibly Ana. Do you approve, Ian?"

" Yes, Papa. But I would like to have some control in which areas I want stressed."

" A well-rounded education is always best."

" I agree, but it would also be wise to improve on the areas that are my strengths and have interest in."

" Very well. Mochar, can you handle the task of educator?"

" Certainly, it will be a most worthwhile experience. Droz and Wir are also most excited about the prospect of enlightening a foreigner as to the ways of their people. And being your son, maybe he will teach us a thing or two about the ways of your people. You're not intimidated by me, are you boy?"

" No, sir. I would, however, like to play with the limestone a little longer if I can."

" Do what you want. I was never one to stifle creativity."

Ian walks over to the crate and scoops out two piles of pellets with his small hands. The boys stares at the pellets and in an instant the entire grouping is transformed into gold. Then he looks at the crate and half the remaining pellets float out of the crate. They remain suspended four feet above the ground and then start to spin. As they are spinning there is a load crackling sound for an instant as he fuses all the pellets together and the color goes from white to yellow. Although it is now revolving at a high rate, it is obvious that it is changing shape. Just over a minute had passed from the moment he started when the boy willed the object to have a soft landing as it's revolutions decreased in speed. The object completes it's last half revolution when it touches the ground and stops motionless with the front facing the group. Before them is a bust of Clayton Knight made of pure gold with an inscription at the base that reads: " Our loving father".

Knight wipes away a tear as Mochar walks over to face him. The Vatsali bothers circle the bust in appreciation for it's craftsmanship and the realization that the boy had a talent for using his powers that was beyond his years.

" I had no idea the boy was so advanced. It would seem that he may be gaining his powers faster than the proportion between the Vatsali's age and his. Maybe it's his metabolism or his intelligence. Whatever it is, I suggest we proceed with caution for it would be unwise to help him release powers if he is not ready."

" That does seem to be the best. Doesn't he seem to use the powers as if they are as natural as breathing? It used to strain him, but now it doesn't seem to. In past studies on people that possessed a small portion of the power he has, there was a fatigue factor or hemorrhaging involved. Now he seems to draw on the power effortlessly."

" As you were a prodigy in science, it seems he is a prodigy at summoning the power. We will try to set a safe pace at which to proceed and one in which he does not feel restricted."

As Knight and Mochar talk, the Vatsali brothers watch as Ian once again approaches the crate. This time he allows the pellets to remain in the crate. Han and Dr. Avery also approach so they can view the inside of the crate. Ian looks at them with a smile and then turns his attention to the contents within the crate. The pellets start to change at a rapid rate, but this time they are not all the same when he is finished. The boy had transformed the limestone into a treasure of gold, silver, diamonds, emeralds, rubies, and sapphires.

Han leans over near Dr. Avery and whispers.

" This is one kid that doesn't have to worry about going broke."

The doctor laughs and the boy looks up and smiles. Ian holds his hands out in front of himself and seems to be staring at the emptiness. Then out of no where, a red rose with a long, green stem appears in his hand. He takes a step forward and stretches out his hand for Han to take the rose.

" For your bride, Uncle Han."

The two men are startled. As Han takes the rose, the doctor summons Knight.

" Clay! Would you please come here."

Knight and Mochar notice the treasure immediately and do not understand their concern. The boy hugs his father's leg and he strokes his son's hair.

" It does seem to be some impressive booty."

" Not that. This!"

Han shows Knight the flower.

" A rose?"

" Ian made it."

" Out of air," Dr. Avery adds.

Mochar quickly snatches the rose and places it under a scanner. Knight looks down in surprise at his son as the boy seems unconcerned with the commotion he has caused.

" It is real. The petals and stem are all living cells. It's almost as if it were just cut."

Han steps forward and retrieves the rose from the platform.

" In a sense, he did just cut it because he just gave it to me to give to Suzie. But to create a living object out of thin air is kind of, well, spooky."

Mochar catches the attention of the Vatsalis and questions them in sign language.

" Droz states that it is not an uncommon skill, but it is normally seen at a much later stage in his people. Neither he nor Wir will be at that stage for at least nine thousand years. They do caution that if the boy already has this ability, he more than likely has several others that he is suppressing or doesn't know about. Wir adds that while it is common for those with the power to produce simpler life forms like bacteria, single celled organisms, and even plants, only a few in the history of his people had advanced to the point of being able to conjure up more complex forms of life."

Knight kneels down to look his son straight in the eyes.

" Ian, are you aware of any other powers you are holding back?"

" No, Papa."

" Did you know you could make the rose before you did?"

" No, Papa. I just felt I could after seeing I did those other things."

" Did you realize you were making a living thing out of nothing but air?"

" I just wanted to give Uncle Han a rose to give to his bride. When I did it, I didn't think of whether or not it was going to be living or not. I wanted a rose and I got a rose. I guess it only makes sense that a rose lives, but I didn't worry about that when I was wishing for it. Sorry I caused so much trouble."

" There's no trouble, Ian. We just want to see what you can do and are curious as to how you do it. And we would also like to know if you are aware of what you are doing when you summon your powers. We only want what is best for you. Okay?"

" Okay. Can I try one more thing before we go home?"

" What do you want to do?"

" When I talked to Droz..."

" Wait a minute," interrupts Mochar as he signs for Droz to come closer. " You talked to Droz?"

" Well, we didn't exactly talk. It was more like an exchange of thoughts."

" the boy had a telepathic exchange with Droz. Since his people are more open to this type of communication they were able to establish a link. Droz claims it was the boy who initiated contact, but all attempts to communicate with Wir have failed. It seems that Droz is a better medium and was able to pick up on his fledgling talent before anyone else. At the rate the boy is advancing, it may only be days before he can establish a link with the rest of us. Although it may also be a matter of months."

Knight lets what Mochar has said sink in and then takes a moment to evaluate the situation. Then he returns his attention to his son.

" You said you wanted to try something. Tell me what you want to do, Ian."

" From Droz I learned that I may be able to levitate. I just want to see if I can."

" I see no problem with that. Do you, Bill?"

" None."

" How about you, Han?"

" I see no reason why not."

" Mochar?"

" There should be no problem and Droz states with the abilities the boy has shown so far, he should be able to master it without harming himself."

" Looks like it's unanimous. Ian, why don't you stand you stand in the center of the room so you have plenty of space to work with. And if by chance something goes wrong, one of us or one of the androids will catch you. Are you ready?"

" Of course, Papa. And nothing will go wrong."

The boy positions himself at the center of the room and closes his eyes to concentrate. A minute passes and he is still stationary. Then he shakes his head twice and nods once. Knight notices that Droz seems engrossed in his thoughts and concludes that Ian is communicating with him. A few moments later the boy starts to rise. The movement is hardly smooth as he starts and stops in the air suddenly and repeats this several times. After a few minutes the boy had risen to the height of twelve feet. He opens his eyes and smiles in appreciation of the new view of the room he has.

" It is wonderful, Papa! Such a feeling of freedom!"

" Good, Ian. That's very good. Are you ready to come down so we can go home?"

" Not yet, Papa. I want to savor this first flight a little longer."

Then the boy slowly starts to move horizontally. First he moves forward, then to the right, then to the left, and finally backwards to his original position. He laughs and starts to wave his arms and legs as if he were treading water. His knees come up to meet his chest and he holds on to his ankles begins to spin head over heels slowly. After his third revolution the speed at which he spins starts to gradually increase. It is on his twenty-first revolution that his father summons him to come down.

" Ian, we really must be leaving. Your mother will be worried if we arrive home at too late an hour."

" Very well, Papa."

His descent is much quicker and more fluid. The boy takes off running toward the door the moment his feet touch the ground. He stops by the door and waves for everyone to follow.

" Hurry up! We don't want to worry mama!"

" We're right behind you son. Dr. Avery will accompany you back to the shuttle...Mochar, I will contact you tomorrow to set up a schedule so that you and the Vatsalis can work with Ian."

" It will be some of my more interesting research, that is for certain. Until then, my friend."

" Until then. We'll see ourselves out."

Chapter sixteen

It is a dark and calm view that Knight views as he stands in front of the window in his GLESA office. A glance at the clock informs him that it is twenty minutes until 6 a.m. He had called an early morning meeting for his fellow task force members. The fact that Mason Rasov is the first to arrive at a quarter until six does not surprise Knight.

" Mason, how are you this morning?"

" Fine. Why did you summon us to such an early meeting? Is something wrong?"

" I would prefer to answer that when everyone is present. However, I will say that we have a long day ahead of us and I called the meeting at this hour so we will have a better portion of the day to work with. You didn't have any trouble with traffic at this hour I would surmise."

" Rarely saw another vehicle."

Russell Jackson enters the room at ten minutes before the hour.

" I'm here. Let's get started."

" Sorry, Russ. But I'm not starting the meeting until everyone is present and Randy has yet to arrive. He still has nine minutes to be on time."

" I'd be surprised if he does. It's kind of difficult to awaken from an alcohol induced coma."

" Was he drinking heavily last night?"

" Don't know. It is how he spends a lot of his free time lately, however."

Rasov shakes his head and Knight slaps the top of his desk.

" How come I wasn't informed sooner?"

Jackson shrugs his shoulders.

" I thought you knew."

" I didn't know it was a chronic problem. The last time I saw him was Ana's party and that was an occasion to justify a drink or two. Mason, were you aware of this?"

" I'm afraid I don't keep tabs on the kid to well. I've been extremely preoccupied by the administrative duties I've been tending to. I really don't have much cause to socialize with him when we're not in the field."

Knight turns to look out the window again. The lack of activity on the street below has a calming effect on him. He talks while still looking into the darkness. Rasov is sitting on the corner of the desk while Jackson begins to pour himself a cup of coffee.

" It seems we have two problems to deal with at the present. Since we do need to rely on each other with a deep trust, it is not viable that we can count on someone who will be incapable of performing the necessary high standards we need in order to survive. The next step is to correct the situation. It would seem that Mr. Buck needs us to intervene in his life to help make him a whole person again."

The clock reads one minute until the hour. Knight turns around and circles the desk until he is facing Rasov.

" It would seem unlikely that Randy is going to be punctual. Mason, if you wouldn't mind. Would you call his residence in an attempt to inquire about his where abouts?"

" Certainly."

" Feel free to use my phone."

Rasov turns the screen around to face him and presses the button with Buck's name next to it. The screen remains black as long as no connection is made. Knight sits on the couch next to Jackson while Rasov informs him of the progress. A counter displays the number of rings in the upper right hand corner of the screen.

" It's on seven rings."

" Let it keep ringing."

" Okay."

" Russ, you keep tabs on the kid more than either of us. Why did you wait and let it progress this far?"

" The kid's an adult. I'm not going to try and run his life for him. He can make his own decisions."

" Can he? Do you honestly believe that someone that ingests as much alcohol as you claim can make a coherent decision?"

" Maybe not."

" I thought you were friends."

" We are! that's why I don't want to interfere!"

" Well, Mason and I aren't as close to him as you are. We're going to step in without worrying how he feels about it. In the end it may be his life we'll be saving."

" I hope you do."

On the fifty-fourth ring the black screen is replaced by the unshaven image of Randy Buck.

" Hello?"

" Randy, it's Mason Rasov. You seem to be late for the meeting."

" What time is it?"

" Six after six."

" Was it for today? Are you sure?"

" Yes, Randy. The meeting was to begin at 6 a.m. Are you feeling all right?"

" Fine, fine. Never better. Is Clay there?"

" Right here, Randy."

" I'm sorry, man. I guess I didn't hear my alarm. Tell you what, I can be there within an hour."

" No need to rush. Get cleaned up and have some breakfast. Be in my office by nine and I'll bring you up to date."

" Will do. I'll see you at nine."

The screen goes black and Rasov stares in disbelief at Knight.

" I can't believe how easy you let him off!"

" He's not getting away with anything. When he shows, we're going to confront him with his problem and force him to go through a detoxification program. It may be best to have two androids from security present to subdue him. Do you object, Russ?"

" No. It's probably for the best. Do I need to be present when you come down on him?"

" Not if you don't want to be. You can get started on the reason I called you here."

" Which is?"

" At eleven thirty-five last night two of our agents turned up missing. Those two agents are Jerry Kliburn and Rex Abbott. We know the exact time they disappeared because that is when they broke contact with the sensors in their uniforms. Some unknown party subdued Kliburn and Abbott before they could notify us of their situation and stripped them naked on the spot before taking them away. The location of the ambush was a warehouse on the north coast of Cuba. It is an isolated location and rarely used.

" It would seem they were following up on a lead on Ruthvan as revealed to them by an informant currently unknown to us. Kliburn and Abbott were continually monitored by satellite, so their exact movements are known to us. Unfortunately, they were only twenty-five minutes from transmitting their next update. At some point between their last report at nine that evening and when they were abducted, they met someone that steered them toward investigating the warehouse. At present there are three teams in Cuba investigating the abduction. Honestly, I don't believe they will find anything concrete. The truth be known, gentlemen, I fear that this is just the beginning to the return of Ruthvan's Satanic followers."

" Do you believe they are as well connected as last time?" asks Rasov.

" It is hard to tell. I am certain that they do have some influential members, however. There are always those who find this type of group appealing and self-serving."

" So what do you want us to do?" inquires Jackson.

" I want you to check the files on all known members of this Satanic organization that we've captured and cross reference by family and known associates. With any luck we may come up with something that will help us out. If not, we will still have a profile on what the typical cult member is like. That too could prove to be useful at some point."

" And you couldn't have a computer do this for you?"

" I could, Russ, but the computer is unable to manually verify the current locations of the people in question. Twenty people from the office staff will be assigned to assist you in making the calls and going into the field. It is 6:22. You had better get started so you can hit the various time zones at hospitable hours."

Jackson exits the room, but Rasov stops in the doorway.

" Do you want me to come back by nine?"

" Yes. It shouldn't take too long to deal with Randy. Try and break away by ten till so you can be here by nine. Let's hope this is a fruitful task. I'll see you later."

It is eleven minutes after nine when Randy Buck casually strolls through the doors of Knight's office. His features show signs of weariness and his uniform is wrinkled and fitting poor. The sight of his wind blown hair indicated that he did not bother to put on his helmet while he rode his motorcycle. Knight is seated behind the desk and Rasov is leaning against the right side of the desk with his hip making contact. Two androids are standing on both sides of the door inside the room and Buck does not notice them as he make his entrance. Knight lets Rasov greet him.

" Do you own a watch, Randy?"

" I know I'm a little late, but I figured since I was late for one meeting, why sweat the next."

" Not very professional. And neither is your appearance. Did you dress yourself or have a blind chimp do it for you?"

" Sorry. I didn't know it was a formal occasion."

Knight rises and pats Rasov on the shoulder as he walks to face Buck.

" To come to the point, Randy. It has come to our attention that you have a drinking problem."

" No way! I have no problem putting down any liquor. Anyhow, I'm just a social drinker."

" Maybe you've been a bit too social."

" What business is it of yours!"

" We care about you, Randy."

" I can handle myself just fine. You have no reason to worry about it."

" Do you believe that you are capable of performing your job? Are you confident that if you had to go out on the streets today, you wouldn't get yourself or someone else killed?"

" I could do just fine."

" I'm afraid we don't see it that way."

" Who the hell is 'we'?"

" Those who are concerned about you."

" Does that include you, Mason? Are you concerned about me? Afraid I'll get you killed out on the street?"

" Listen, Kid, it's for your own good," answers Rasov as he readjusts his stance to a more defensive posture.

" I don't need your help!"

Knight takes a step closer.

" Actually you do, Randy. You're just not in a position to view things clearly or to think all that clearly for that matter. We want what is best for you. That includes myself, Mason, Russ, and everyone who works with you. For your own good, we want you to go through a detoxification program."

" What? Are you crazy? Those are for people with real problems! I can handle my drinking. I won't do it!"

" I'm not asking."

" Think you can order me to do it 'cause I work for ya? Wrong! I quit!"

He turns to walk out the door only to have each android grab an arm. They turn him around to face Knight.

" Let go! Make them let go! You have no control over me. I just quit!"

" It's not that simple. I'm not taking 'no' for an answer. From this moment on you're off the bottle. We have facilities here to help you overcome your addiction. If you still want to quit when you're through, then I'll accept your resignation. Until then, we'll try to keep in mind that it's the booze doing your thinking for you."

" You can't do this to me! I have rights! Mason, tell him he can't do this to me!"

" It's for your own good, Kid."

" Go to hell!"

Knight nods and the androids lift the ranting young man off his feet and start to walk. Buck kicks out at Knight and Rasov as the begin to follow. To counter the kicking one android takes a hold of both arms while the other grabs his legs and they carry him sideways. They people in the halls stop momentarily to observe, but Knight quickly waves them on.

" You can't do this to me! I'll get you for this! I will!"

The elevator door opens and is empty. The androids walk to the back of the compartment as Knight and Rasov stand near the doors and control the buttons. Buck pits and the saliva catches the side of Knight's left knee. As he tries to build up more saliva to spit again, the android holding his torso puts a hand over his mouth. Knight smiles and bends over so that his face is only a foot from Buck's.

" Might as well swallow. That stuffs much better for you than alcohol, anyhow."

The elevator doors open and they enter an isolated corridor. A door is open to the left and the androids stand Buck upright in front of the doorway and push him in. Immediately the door slides shut as Buck can be heard shouting. The androids position themselves on both sides of the door as Knight and Rasov go into the next room.

Within that room are several monitors that show different portions of the building. Four of the monitors are devoted to the room that Buck is in. Each monitor shows a different view from each of the top corners of the room.

The room itself is padded all around from floor to ceiling. Light comes from a single flat panel in the center of the ceiling, which is unbreakable. To the right of the door is a ledge that has half a turntable visible, with the other half obviously in the next room. There is a sliding door between the two halves of the turntable, but it appears seamless on Buck's side. To the left of the door is another ledge that contained the toilet, which is a circle port that retracts by pressing a pressure plate. It also functioned as a bidet, which shot a stream of water up to clean the area in use.

If they saw it necessary, they could keep Buck isolated from all human contact for an indefinite period of time. But he would not be subjected to such isolation. A counselor would visit him daily with the frequency and length of the visits increasing as he becomes more sociable. There is also a doctor available in the building at all times if the need should arise. When Buck progresses to a more satisfactory point, he would be moved to a suite that is more comfortable. Knight is willing to keep him prisoner for whatever time is necessary to overcome the addiction.

The collar seems a little tighter than Knight remembered it being. Either his neck is getting to big or he is somehow wearing someone else's shirt. Dressing formal is one of Knight's least favorite things and he hopes it will be a short ceremony. There are hardly any clouds visible and a slight breeze from the south carries the fragrance of the flowers over the next hill. It seems that the weather is going to cooperate and allow them to have a wedding outdoors.

An ancient Japanese structure stands two hundred yards from where the guests are to be seated. Rows of metal chairs stand in the grass in two sectors divided by an aisle that extends from the alter to a bridge which is built over a narrow stream. As part of the ceremony the bride will cross the bridge from the other side and make her way up the grassy aisle with her father. Two large tents to the north of the alter is where the reception is to be held.

For the fifth time Knight checks his vest pocket for the ring Han had bought for the ceremony. It is adorned with a cluster of multi-carat diamonds on a silver band. Knight feels the smooth surface of the band and removes his hand from the pocket as the clergyman approaches.

Han takes his place on the platform and Knight elbows him lightly which produces a nervous smile from his friend. An eight-piece string ensemble begins to play as Suzie takes her place on the other side of the bridge. Upon hearing the music she starts slowly across the bridge with her father at her side. She is wearing a white, silk gown that is fairly simple except for a few frills and lace. A semi-transparent veil conceals her face as the slight breeze plays with it's light material. Her hands are covered with white gloves that are concealed beneath the flowers she holds in front of herself.

Stepping off the bridge, she stops momentarily to collect herself and then continues up the aisle. The guests are all standing and a few are moving around in an attempt to see the bride better. When she reaches the platform in front of the alter the musicians end their tune and sit down.

" We are all gathered here..." are the only words Knight hears from the holy man before his mind starts to wander. He looks out into the crowd and notices Ana sitting on the edge of the fourth row. On the other end of the row is their governess Jacqueline Davies and his children occupy the seats in between. They are easy to spot among the rows of several Oriental faces. It is amusing to Knight that so many Chinese are on Japanese soil to watch a wedding that should have been in China. Han and Suzie wanted the wedding here, however, because of it's sentimental significance to them and he could not fault them for that.

Han puts his hand in front of Knight alerting him that it is time he relinquish control of the ring. The groom grasps the bride's left hand lightly and gently maneuvers the ring along her slender finger with his right hand. Knight notices than Han already has on his ring as they turn again to face the bishop.

" I pronounce you man and wife. You may kiss the bride."

They engage in a short embrace and then a tender kiss. The crowd is on it's feet as the musicians begin the closing melody. Han shakes hands with the bishop from Tokyo.

Knight also takes time to exchange pleasantries with the holy man before he exits to begin his journey home.

The happy couple remains in front of the platform for several minutes receiving congratulations from the numerous guests. Within minutes the celebration had moved from by the bridge to beneath the tents where more musicians play and a grand feast awaits. When everyone reaches the reception, workers start to remove the chairs and take apart the alter and platform.

At the reception the Knights have their own table with Ana and Miss Davies tending to the children while Knight concentrates on sampling the fine array of food available. At a table across the tent is the Li family with Han's parents, grandparents, brothers, and sister. The table next to them held Suzie's immediate relations, the family Ti. Knight had met many of them the day before and found them to be very pleasant acquaintances.

He has known Han's parents for years and they accept him as one of the family. While Han has three brothers and a sister, they have little in common due to their occupations and age differences. The nearest sibling to Han's age is his brother Chu who is eight years his elder at forty. The eldest brother Mao is forty-seven and is a journalist with a syndicated column that ran in most Chinese papers. His brother Chen is forty-three and is a major in the Chinese national army. At forty-two his sister Kim is the director of the botanical gardens in New Zealand. Chu is a social worker living in Cambodia.

Suzie on the other hand is the middle child of three who are relatively close in age. Her older brother Lin is twenty-seven and is an airline pilot. Mati is her younger sister by one year at age twenty-three and is trying to follow Suzie into the world of fashion modeling.

When Knight had satisfied his appetite, he decides to visit the tables of the families of the bride and groom. Han notices him approaching and rises to welcome him over. His parents are smiling at the sight of the familiar American.

" And here's my best man. You remember my parents, don't you, Clay?"

" For years. And we just saw each other last night. Remember? It's always a pleasure to meet the parents Li. How did you enjoy the ceremony?"

" It was magnificent," says Mrs. Li. " Most beautiful event I think I've ever witnessed. To see the little one finally find someone to care for."

" She couldn't stop crying," adds Mr. Li. " If I didn't know better, I'd say that brook was a creation of her tears!"

" I didn't cry that much!"

" You certainly did! Clay, how long are you able to remain with us?"

" I'm afraid I have to meet a jet in Tokyo in a few hours. Ana and the children are going to stay for a few more days, however, to do some sight seeing."

" Will they come over to the main land?" asks Mrs. Li.

" I'm sure they will. In fact, I'm certain Ana would be thrilled to see your magnificent home once again."

" We would love to have her over. Be sure to tell her she has an open invitation. Whenever she and the children can make it, they are welcome. Our home is your home."

" I will, thank you. It was a pleasure to see you again."

The both smile and nod as Knight turns away followed by Han.

" You really have to leave?"

" I'm afraid so. Too many tasks need to be tended to. Where are you going on the honeymoon?"

" Bermuda."

" Well, stay out of the triangle. I don't have time to hunt for you if you disappear."

" Sure. We're going to be there for two weeks. Think you might need me before then?"

" Not a problem. You just concentrate on enjoying the sights and making little Lis. I'll see that things run smoothly. In fact if they run flawlessly, it may show that you're expendable. Have a nice honeymoon."

" Go on. You have a plane to catch."

" See you when you get back."

They take a step closer and embrace while slapping each other on the back. Then they shake hands and Knight pats Han on the shoulder before turning to leave. As he steps clear of the tent he looks around in all directions and spots an occasional security guard every few hundred yards. As he begins to walk up the hill he presses a button on his belt which alerts his ride. When he reaches the top of the hill a helicopter comes over the horizon and sets down a few yards from him. After getting in he gives the thumbs-up signal and starts the short journey to Tokyo.

Bright lights cause the two men to shut their eyes tight, but the intensity is still great enough to penetrate their lids. They are hanging upside down chained to a wall and have been unable to shave or bath for a week. It was only within the last hour that they had been placed in these awkward positions for the amusement of their captors. They are clothed in makeshift diapers, which someone thought was a funny idea. After what Jerry Kliburn and Rex Abbott had been through the past week, little seemed amusing to them.

From beyond the lights someone is tossing pebbles at the prone GLESA agents. Within the last week the agents had been beaten, sodomized, and subjected to several cruel acts thought up by sick minds. They had been allowed small amounts of food and water, but at random intervals so they could not adjust to a set pattern. Their bodies are covered with cuts, bumps, and bruises. Tolerance to pain has been tested time and again as they often passed out from the results of the cruel experiments. Once in awhile they are allowed to sleep after they pass out, but it is more common for them to be reawakened by an electric shock.

After being pelted by dozens of pebbles, the lights go off. Each man tries to collect himself as the sound of someone with hard-heeled shoes walks toward them on the stone floor. Everything seems distorted as their eyes try to adjust back to the normal lighting. The person stops in front of them. It is someone dressed in black and their head is covered with a large, grotesque mask. Stepping forward the masked fiend grabs each man by the genitals with a gloved hand. Then there is a hollow, distorted laugh as the figure squeezes harder and harder before letting go. Both men cough and wheeze as the figure continues laughing.

" Are you pathetic maggots the best that Clayton Knight could send? If that is so, then is shouldn't be too hard to bring that bastard down to his knees!"

The fiend raises a hand and the lights bright lights go on again. Blinded by the light, they can only hear the sound of the person walking away. Almost simultaneously, they both let out cries of pain. From beyond the lights, someone was now tossing balls of thorns at the helpless two. Some other the balls cut deep into the flesh and continue to hang there. Others cut and tear the flesh as they hit and then fall to the ground. Neither agent has grand visions of escape. At the present their only concern is to stay alive.

Chapter seventeen

Thousands of crickets and frogs sing into the darkness of the Florida swamp they consider home. Earlier that morning Knight was alerted by one of his infiltrators that a large shipment of drugs is to be smuggled into the country by this route. Normally he would have just contacted the Drug Enforcement Agency, but there was too little time to organize a joint venture and the operation would probably run much more smoothly without them there.

Mason Rasov walks briskly to Knight's position, which was chosen for tactical purposes and also for protection from the vicious insects patrolling the surrounding air. Next to Knight is a little black box that emits a high frequency sound that wards off insects and small animals for a radius of fifty yards. Rasov kneels next to Knight behind a fallen tree that is partially submerged in mud. They have a clear view of the waterway that is accessible to the coast. With a force of thirty, ten being androids, Knight feels confident that they can handle any number of drug smugglers that happened to arrive.

At ten after eleven the wildlife goes silent as a medium sized transport ship makes it's way into the inlet. Moments later the deep hum of a large truck can be heard as it advances through the trees to the right. There is a clearing fifty yards from Knight's position with enough room for the truck to turn itself around so the rear could back up to the water. As the ship puts down anchor near the shore, Knight presses the button of the communicator on his wrist that sends a soft beep to notify the agents to move to their new positions.

From his vantage point Knight counts five smugglers that came with the truck and eighteen on the ship that are helping with the unloading. Even with those still unseen on the ship, the agents obviously had the superior force. Only eight of those in sight are carrying visible weapons, but it is a given that they all are likely armed. After two crates had been successfully transported from the ship to the truck, Knight picks up a palm-sized microphone with his right hand and a voice amplifier with his left and turns the amplifier's front toward the smugglers.

" Put down your weapons! You are under arrest! Cease your illegal activity at once!"

As he had foreseen, the smugglers fire their weapons in the direction of the voice. Although is of the smugglers is targeted by an agent, their first response is to fire upon the tires and engine of the truck to render it immobile. Then from out of the darkness behind the protection to the trees shoot two separate laser beams, which are aimed below the water line. They penetrate the hull of the ship and at a slow but noticeable rate the ship begins to sink as the captain attempts to return it to the sea. Again the lasers piece the moving target and the ship starts to sink at an increased rate. Soon the crew are in the water swimming for shore. With their two modes of transportation incapacitated and their assailants still unseen, the smugglers huddle around the truck releasing a nervous volley of gun fire into the darkness at random intervals in a futile show of resistance.

" Lay down your weapons and surrender. It would be most unwise to resist. Each of you is targeted at this very moment and if you do not surrender at the count of ten, I will give permission to open fire."

At times like this Knight wished vehicles still had gas tanks.

" One."

Three smugglers throw their weapons clear of the truck.

" Two."

The three start to walk away from the truck toward the voice as their hands are behind their heads.

" Three."

From behind the truck a gunman fires and kills the three wishing to surrender.

" Four. that was not a wise move."

Rasov moves closer to Knight.

" Five."

" It was a young punk on the trigger."

" Six."

" Want us to take him out now?"

" Seven."

Knight shakes his head.

" Eight. Time's running out."

" Do you want us to kill them?"

Again Knight shakes his head.

" Nine."

At this a young man with a bandanna pulled up over his face rushes from behind the truck with an automatic weapon in each hand while firing in the general direction of the voice. As he reaches his fifth stride, his body twitches and performs unusual contortions as the impact of fourteen weapons being fired from different directions all find their mark.

" Hold your fire! Last chance to surrender. Otherwise, savor your last few heart beats."

A shower of weapons hit the ground on both sides of the truck. One by one the smugglers walk away from the truck with their hands behind their heads and they fall to their knees once in the clearing. The ten android agents emerge from the darkness and place the thirty-four living smugglers in restraints. After scanning the area for possible hidden explosives, Knight emerges from the shadows with Rasov. Long prison terms would be awaiting each of the smugglers, but they are all luckier than the shrapnel ridden corpse near the truck.

Knight stands next to the body holding a light as Rasov kneels down to remove the bandanna. Expecting to see an anonymous face, it is a total shock when a familiar face is exposed. It is Kramer O'Connor, the boyfriend of his sister-in-law. Although he has no remorse for ridding the planet of such an undesirable parasite, he did sympathize with the position Carmen is now in. It would be best if he tells her himself. He would make the trip to Kansas City in the morning after touching home base.

A chill is in the air as Knight steps outdoors. He blows on his hands and shakes his head in disbelief at what the weather reports had stated. It was supposed to be an unseasonably warm day. There was a message from Ana on the recorder that stated they would return in a couple of days. That night they were to visit Han's parents and would likely be persuaded to stay there for those two days. Now he is on his way to break the bad news to her sister.

The time on the dash reads 7:32. He contemplates keeping the vehicle in drive mode so he could enjoy a leisurely three-hour trip down. Yet since he had so much to do, he decides it would be best if he reached the city limits within forty minutes by flying. As the wedge-shaped vehicle rolls down the road, Knight plays with the proper buttons until the craft is airborne. Once he reaches the city limits he will set it down and drive to her condo.

As Knight approaches Kansas City from the North, a car originally from Houston advances from the south with the destination also being the condo of Miss Carmen Ramos. The occupants of the car are acquaintances of Kramer O'Connor and they are upset about not receiving a scheduled telephone call at 1 a.m. The driver is Alex Loudman, a former small college quarterback and current drug dealer. Riding shotgun is his younger brother Quincy, who at twenty-four appeared to be thirty due to his heavy drinking. In the back seat are Richie Nash and Calvin King. Nash might have been a talented heavy weight boxer if he hadn't lost his left eye in a bar room brawl. King is a young black man who knew O'Connor best because they played football together in high school before O'Connor was kicked off the team. The group has a prosperous drug empire that covers nine counties in South Texas.

The shipment O'Connor was in Florida to receive consisted of twenty cases of cocoa and opium crystals. Each crystal is the size of a thumbnail and is a highly concentrated form of a drug. Through processing, a single crystal could be diluted to make twelve high-grade grams of cocaine or twenty quality grams of heroin. O'Connor was only the driver on the trip, but his superiors agreed to pay him by giving him one of the crates. He had notified the four from Houston and they all dwelled on dreams of great riches. But they never received the call from O'Connor on where they were to meet and now they feared a double cross.

King knew that O'Connor had a girl friend and they figured he would either be there or she would tell them where he was. After driving most of the night, they are in a collective foul mood and each had different views on what should be done with O'Connor if had actually betrayed them. It is five after eight when they reach her condo.

As they make their way up the front stairs, Knight starts to pull up the street. Loudman had taken the last parking space on the block so Knight has to drive further down the street to find an available spot. He does notice that the four are at the Ramos residence and is curious as to who they are. Although he is tempted to double park, he feels it is best not to block traffic because he did not know exactly how long he would be. Six blocks from her condo he finally finds a space. It did not seem to be the start of a very good day.

Miss Ramos opens the door to see four unexpected visitors. Three are strangers but she had seen O'Connor talking with King occasionally when they went to Greystone's Pool Hall. A crisp breeze rolls past her toward the warmer interior of her abode.

" Yes? What do you want?"

" We want to talk to Kramer," answers the elder Loudman.

" He isn't here. I haven't seen or talked to him since yesterday morning."

" Why don't we check ourselves!" blurted the habitually intoxicated Quincy Loudman as he pushes past Miss Ramos and immediately starts to check the rooms.

" Hey, come back here," says a flustered Carmen Ramos. " He can't do this!"

" It will only take a minute. We just want to see if Kramer is here. Richie, you and Calvin help him. Why don't you step away from the door. You might catch a chill."

Loudman shoves the young lady against her right shoulder, which sends her stumbling backward, and she falls on the oval rug in the entryway. He closes the door and starts toward her. Although it is a cool morning, she had dressed with the warmer weather reports as a guide. She has on a knee length denim skirt, white blouse, denim vest, and a pair of casual brown leather shoes.

She rises and glares in anger.

" You can't treat me like this. I know some very important people."

" Don't we all, honey."

" Come on, guys. I have a class at ten and I really have to be going."

" Here that boys? We have us a college girl. Maybe she can teach us a thing or two."

He grabs her by the arm and marches her into the living room and tosses her on the davenport. Her head bounces off the wall and her long, black hair cascades down in disarray and covers her face. She brushes the hair away with her hand and touches the back of her head that is beginning to pulsate with pain.

" You bastard!"

" Now, now, missy. That's no way to talk to your playmates. If you're good enough for Kramer, you're good enough for us."

The other three enter the living room.

" He's not here," informs Nash.

" Well, then it would seem that it's up to this pretty young thing to see to it that it's not a wasted trip. Party time!"

He falls to his knees in front of the woman and forces up her skirt to expose her white under pants. She tries to push the skirt back down as to Louderman's surprise King grabs him by the shoulder and pulls him back. Miss Ramos attempts to get up and start for the door, but Nash slaps her down with the back of his hand and then pins her arms to the couch while his right knee rest on her abdomen to restrict her movements. The elder Louderman rises to confront king as his brother stands behind the would-be hero to prevent a retreat.

" What the hell do you think you're doing?"

" Hey, man, we just came for Kramer. This is not the kind of trouble we need to be getting into."

" Then you can stay out of it!"

As he shouts, Louderman punches King below the left eye with his right hand. His brother grabs the reeling victim and keeps him on his feet as Louderman lands five more punches to the face and two to the ribs. After the beaten man falls to the floor, both Loudermans add a kick to the ribs. Then they return their attention to the young woman. She lets out a high, pitched scream as they approach before she is muffled by Nash's right hand.

Knight had just started up the stairs when he heard the scream. He is quickly at the top step and tears the door off the hinges with a solid kick. Within moments he is in the doorway of the living room and sees three startled men standing over his sister-in-law whose blouse had just been ripped. They obviously had little respect for the lawman's uniform he is wearing for they unwisely stand their ground.

" Clay!" she shouts and starts to rise only to have the elder Louderman grab her by the hair and pull he back.

Without saying a word Knight walks toward the girl. Nash moves into front of him as Quincy Louderman charges from the side. The punch Nash throws never connects as Knight grabs the incoming arm by the wrist and forces the big man into the oncoming foe while keeping a tight grip on the arm. Young Louderman is knocked off balance and flies shoulder first into the wall. The former boxer's arm is now being twisted and he kneels in an attempt to relieve the pressure. A loud snap echoes into the hallway followed by a low-pitched yell. An elbow to the back of the head knocks the enforcer of the group unconscious.

Young Louderman just gets to his feet as Knight catches him with his left foot to the side of the head. Blood and teeth flow from his mouth as he falls to the carpet. His arms land in front of him with the palms down on the carpet as the drunken thug begins a pain induced sleep. The right hand lies in Knight's path as he starts toward Ana's sister. With the heel of his right boot he stomps and then raises his toe so only the edge of his heel makes contact and grinds the hand into the carpet as it crackles with the sound of tiny bones being broken and rubbed against each other again and again.

The elder Louderman still has Carmen by the hair and had now produced a knife, which he has pressed against her throat under the chin. He looks in disbelief as the lawman finishes grinding his brother's hand into useless pulp.

" You're sick man!"

" And you're under arrest. Put down the knife."

" Like hell! That is my brother."

" You mean, Lefty? He got off lucky. You're not."

" From the look in his eyes, Knight knows the assailant is willing to commit murder. Then as Louderman slightly raises his elbow to bet more leverage to cut, Knight raises his right arm and slaps it with his left. Before the blade can penetrate the skin, a laser severs the man's arm just below the elbow. It takes him a second to realize he is no longer cutting. By that time, Knight is upon them and pulls Carmen and the separated limb forward simultaneously.

Louderman looks at his stub in shock. There is no blood because the laser catheterized the area as it cut. He looks at his left arm, and then his shortened right arm. His face is contorted as he looks at Knight.

" Look what you did to me!"

" I didn't think you'd want your brother to be too self-conscious."

" I'll kill you!"

Louderman takes two steps forward before Knight nails him between the eyes with three shots from his firearm. As he hits the ground lifeless, Knight tosses the limb on the body.

Carmen looks around her living room and breaks into tears. Holding her sobbing face against his chest, he tries to comfort her as he strokes her hair. Then he guides her into the hallway and they sit down on the stairs that lead to the upper level. She dries her eyes and tries to smile at Knight.

" Why did you come? And I'm thankful you did."

" Kramer O'Connor was killed this morning in a confrontation with the legal authorities."

She turns her head away and bites on a knuckle. A few more tears roll down her cheeks before she looks at Knight again.

" They came to see Kramer. Then when he wasn't her they.. they... I'm so glad you showed up."

He sits on the step next to her and she leans over and gives him a long embrace.

" Do you want to come back home with me? Ana will be coming home soon and I'm sure you would be better off with family right now."

" I'm sure you're right. But I think I want to go home to Brazil and see my parents. I'll call Ana from there."

" If you need any help catching up in your classes don't hesitate to call."

" I think I'll come back by next Monday, so I shouldn't miss too much."

" Why don't you go upstairs while I have the appropriate authorities come and take care of the mess in there. I'll see to it that the carpet gets cleaned and the door's fixed, too."

" Thanks. I don't think I'll be able to stay here, however. When I get back I'm going to look for a new place."

" That would probably be best. Go get some rest and I'll take care of things down here. Then I'll take you to the airport."

She nods and ascends the stairs. Reentering the living room knight notices the fourth man on the floor on the far side of the room. He shrugs it off and taps the buttons on his wrist communicator. The story on the fourth man could wait until later.

Chapter eighteen

It was a quarter after noon when Knight started back to Omaha. A private jet was charted to take Miss Ramos home to Brazil. he had already lost much of the time he normally spent going over the reports on GLESA's activities and had yet to make an appearance at the headquarters for Knight Enterprises to make sure everything is running smoothly in Ana's absence.

When he is only fifteen minutes from Omaha's city limits a red warning light starts to flash which is accompanied by a soft, buzzing sound. Immediately Knight assumes it is a malfunction with the vehicle, but the on board computer quickly alerts him to the real problem.

" Danger. Severe weather system is forming three miles ahead on current course setting. An alternate route to the east is advised."

As Knight alters the course of the vehicle, he can see the dark clouds to the north. He curses himself as he flies toward another bank of dark clouds that seems to be circling from the east. for all the advances in science he and man had achieved, predicting the weather still is an inexact procedure.

A break between the two storm systems is to the northeast and Knight maneuvers the craft toward it. To his dismay the gap disappears as both dark masses quickly merge to become one fearsome adversary. Knight knows that he had better land or risk being caught in the storm. Thunder shakes his craft as he makes his descent at a forty-degree angle. It is darker than a moon-less night, but Knight is aware of the terrain below due to the vehicle's sensors.

Suddenly the craft is rising and Knight's pulse quickens as he attempts to maintain control. It is a tornado that has him and he is calling on all his flying skills while attempting to keep the craft upright. The craft has the horsepower to combat the fierce winds, but the experience is a severe test of nerve. Knight pulls back on the throttle and takes the craft straight up. He feels the winds try and pull him back down as the craft spins through a dozen revolutions. Only he refuses to submit and the upward the craft goes. He believes that he has maneuvered the vehicle out of the grasp of the winds and is starting to level off when a bolt of lightning strikes the ship. It entered through the front of the craft and overloaded the power systems.

He starts to plummet while being encased in what is now a collection of useless metal. All of the craft's systems are dead and he is receiving minimal response from the flaps and rudder as he tries to gain manual control. If given the chance he might be able to glide it to a safe landing although he is now flying blind. That chance soon disappears as a second tornado takes it's turn playing in the sky.

The craft rolls and flips as Knight frantically tries to maintain control. He winces in pain as he touches his abdomen. His left hand tries to steady the wheel while his right probes the soreness. When the lightning went through the ship he happened to be in it's path. Although his force field was operational and able to deflect the majority of the surge, there was some penetration and his abdomen and right hip are severely burned. The power in his belt is starting to wane as a result of the power surge and Knight hopes to crash soon so that there might be a minimal power level strong enough to protect him upon impact.

The tornado releases the craft into the control of some weaker cross winds and a violent jolt signals the transition. The flaps respond to his commands and the winds start to aid him be guiding the craft toward the ground. There are a couple of up drafts which delay his descent momentarily, but for the most part the brisk winds are willing to cooperate in sending the craft downward toward destruction. Knight shakes his head in disgust when he thinks it would have been much easier to land when he had full power. Yet no one wants to crash and fighting a tornado is not the best situation taking the time to plan strategy. Only a few hundred yards separate the craft and the ground when Knight is finally able to make visual contact. That distance is subtracted in a few seconds as the craft makes it's impact.

To Knight's surprise the craft is under water when he looks through the windshield. The craft is on it's side and one third submerged in the mud at the bottom of a river, lake, or pond. He really didn't care where he is for he is alive. The power pack on his force field is now dead and he discards the extra weight as he plans to swim to the surface. His communicator is also not functioning properly. There is the possibility that someone would be there to rescue him, but he might run out of air before they arrive. Another factor to influence him is the small tear in the side in the vehicle that is allowing water to drip in. He would rather drown trying to reach the surface than while just sitting in a box.

The laser cuts a large hole quickly as Knight holds the metal circle in place with his left hand. After taking a deep breath he allows the water to force the disk inward and he pushes it aside as a steady stream of water showers him. He pulls himself through and glides through the water with powerful motions.

As he nears the surface the water is very turbulent. Like a dolphin he bursts past the watery barrier and gasps for air as he arcs backward toward the water. While he tries to keep his head above the short waves the pull of the current moves him rapidly as the rain pelts him from above. At this time he realizes he is in the Missouri River. The danger of drowning is still quite real and may become a reality if he is unable to escape the current. His eyes strain to spot a bend in the river and the inviting shore. Yet the current is reluctant to release it's captive as it takes Knight on a course away from the shore and toward the river's center.

Fear touches Knight's mind only to be replaced by anger as he violently shakes his head. With a powerful thrust Knight propels himself upward and he is only in the water from his knees down. He throws his self forward and with his last remaining energy battles the storm produced waves patrolling along the shore. Finally he can feel solid matter beneath him and he walks along the muddy river floor until he reaches the shore. Mud and grass serve as a resting-place as knight collapses and lies on his back allowing the rain to massage his tired muscles. The soothing melody of the rain on the water lulls his weary body to sleep.

When he awakens the setting has changed for now he is obviously in the sterile environment of a hospital room. As he turns his sore neck he sees Ana sitting in a chair along the wall to the right. She is working on her portable computer and seems to be tired herself. Dr. Avery enters the room and alerts Ana that Knight is conscious. Placing the computer on the nightstand, she quickly advances toward Knight and sits on the edge of his bed. Tenderly she caresses his right cheek and jaw with the back of her right hand.

" Ana."

" Quiet now. You've had quite an experience."

" No kidding. What's the date?"

" October fifteenth."

" I've been out for two days?"

" Yes. We're just happy you're still in one piece."

" Anything major, Doc?"

" First degree burns to the abdomen, right hip, and right buttock. Your right shoulder was dislocated and you separated some rib cartilage."

" Then it's nothing major. Where are my clothes? I have to get to headquarters."

" I would advise against it. As much as you try to test the point, you're not immortal. Give your body a chance to mend and rest."

" Normally I might consider it, Bill. But I have too much to do. I've already had two days of rest and I'm sure I can heal just fine at my office and at home. I'll be sure not to do anything too strenuous."

Dr. Avery shrugs his shoulders and leaves the room. Knight grasps Ana's hands between his and tries to smile through his bruised lips.

" Believe me, Ana. I'm fine."

" I may not be a doctor, but even I can see you're in no condition to rush back to work."

" I know my limits."

" And you're always testing them. Is it really necessary for you to do anything immediately? Can't Mason handle it? At least for a couple of days."

" It might be able to wait. Only I can't take the chance, Please get off the bed so I can get up."

" Why not just roll off the other side?"

" Fine. Be that way."

His muscles, stiff with pain and lack of use, hesitate to allow him to leave the comfort of the current resting-place. Ana rise and circles the bed to help steady him as he places his feet on the floor and stands upright. He gives his wife a hug and then slowly starts for the closet while Ana follows close behind.

" How long before they found me?"

" Bill said it was only a half hour from when you crashed. The security systems at GLESA and Knight Enterprises supposedly went to red alert as the computer subtlety informed everyone that you were in danger."

" Just one of the advantages of designing the system myself and placing my condition as one of the computer's highest priorities. Luckily I went to see your sister in uniform and not casual."

" I've talked with her a couple of times. She is upset that you went down after visiting her, although she is very happy that you did go there. Poor kid. What an experience. I'm glad that you happened along the scene too."

" Me too. When did you get back?"

" We were in flight over Colorado when Bill contacted me and informed me of what happened to you. My heart was turned inside out from that moment until I saw you in that bed."

" And you still haven't slept since, have you?"

" No."

" I love you."

He kisses her on the forehead and continues dressing.

" Your message said you weren't due back until today. Why did you cut the trip short?"

" A combination of things. The kids were getting tired, we were drained by keeping track of the kids, and I wanted to get back to work."

" That's what you were doing on the computer?"

" Yes. Like you, I have a hard time staying away from my work."

" Seems we were made for each other."

" Sure, by a demented craftsman."

" You better get to sleep. Lack of it makes you mean."

" Not until I stop by the office."

" Okay. Then you can drop me of at GLESA on the way."

Two days have passed since Knight discharged himself from the hospital. His wounds are healing satisfactorily due to the medication and oxygen treatments. Knight is sitting as he watches the monitors focused on Randy Buck's quarters.

That morning they had moved Buck from his cell to a luxury suite because he is no longer a threat to others or himself. Two counselors visit with him regularly through out the day. Russell Jackson is currently in the suite talking with his friend for the first time in two weeks. Knight decided he would not approach Buck until his treatment is over. He hopes that time and counseling will mend any ill feelings Buck may have toward him. Yet he will honor the young agent's wishes if he no longer wants to work for him.

As Knight leaves the observation room, a young, female agent hands him a sheet of paper. After reading the contents he hands it back.

" Thank you, Cindy. Have them brought to my office. Also alert the laboratory to stand by."

" Yes, sir."

She hurries down the hall as Knight waits for the elevator. The doors open and he enters the empty compartment. Pressing the desired floor number, he cringes in anticipation of what will be waiting for him in his office.

Two small packages had arrived with the postmarks from rural New Mexico. Preliminary scanning showed nothing harmful, but there are human DNA present. With two agents missing at the present time, Knight fears this will be some indication as to their fate.

A single agent, Gretl Harting, is in the office holding the two packages. Knight shakes his head and points to the desk where she places them. Adjusting the setting on his laser, he proceeds to quickly cut off the top of each package. After a moment of hesitation, he simultaneously removes the tops of each package. Miss Hartung gasps and then averts her eyes.

In each box is a human head wrapped in transparent plastic. Their eyes had been gouged out, their teeth are missing, and there are multiple lacerations on each face. Although they had been disfigured, Knight can tell that they are Jerry Kliburn and Rex Abbott.

Knight places the lids on each box and turns his attention to the agent present. He puts his arm over her shoulder and guides her to the door.

" I'm sorry you had to see that, Gretl."

" I understand."

" It gives you an understanding of the type of minds we are dealing with."

" They were such good men, Clay. So..."

" I know. We'll see that those responsible answer to the appropriate justice."

" I would like to be involved in this investigation."

" I'll inform Mason. He will bring you up to date."

" Thank you, Clay."

" Let's just catch these bastards."

She nods and heads down the hall. Knight reenters his office and speaks into his wrist communicator.

" Dr. Tannum, send someone up to bring these packages in my office to you. I want your report before the day is out."

Chapter nineteen

A single candle poorly lights the enormous cavern in which the dark figure is standing. Thoughts of action are being contemplated and the serenity of this place make the task easier. From the rear of the cavern someone can be heard approaching. Without vocalizing, the figure raises a gloved hand and the on-comer stops four yards behind the person in black.

The young man is dressed in a black robe and his hood is up to conceal his features. He falls to his knees and bows his head. Minutes pass before the figure waves a hand to signal for the follower to speak.

" The task is done. Do I get my reward?"

The figure nods and motions for the man to follow. A closed door at the side of the cavern marks the entrance to their destination. Lights flood the cavern as the figure opens the door, allows the man to enter, and follows him in while closing the door.

They are in a well-lit room that is obviously used for living quarters. Along the south wall are bookshelves and electronic entertainment paraphernalia. To the right is a kitchen and dining table. On the left is a large bed covered with a bearskin and the ceiling and walls in the sleeping area are adorned with mirrors. At the edge of the mirrors is a stone fireplace that already has flames dancing in celebration.

The man remains motionless in the center of the room as his leader walks over to the table. On the table is a platter on which there is a human heart. The figure raises the platter to eye level and the man approaches the table. Repositioning the platter on the table, the figure pulls off the gloves and places them on the corner of the table. Then the man helps remove a large mask, which they set down next to the gloves. Bowing the man returns to the opposite side of the table where he can see the light catch the smiling face of Maria Ortiz.

She licks her lips as she eyes the young man. Then she grasps the heart in both hands and takes a large bite. Happily the young man accepts the heart into his hands as she chews. He greedily devours the entire portion while his supervisor observes. When he is finished, she walks into the kitchen area and removes two crystal goblets from their stand and chooses a bottle of wine from the rack. Her long black hair bounces as she returns to the table. With a nod she indicates he may sit down and he pulls a chair closer to the table.

" You did very well, Pablo. We have cause for celebration. Let us toast the downfall of Clayton Knight! May he join Sebastian Ruthvan in Hell!"

Their glasses chime as they touch. Each drains their respective glass and Miss Ortiz readily refills them.

" What I would give to have seen Knight's face when he opened the boxes."

" It would have been a sight, Señorita."

" I'll give him credit for one thing, though. He certainly has some tasty agents!"

They break into laughter. His is induced by alcohol while hers by insanity.

Pablo Garcia was from a family of farmers and always wanted to escape that restrictive life style. Less than a year previous a friend invited him to attend a social function. There he met Miss Ortiz and quickly fell into her favor. Being close to her meant wealth and power and he is willing to do anything to remain on her good side. That even included killing his friend who had brought him into the cult when he expressed wishes to leave.

When they have finished the bottle, she walks around the table and takes him by the hand. Without hesitation he accompanies her over to the bed. Like a wild animal she tears at the clothing he wears and in a moment has him out of his robe, shirt, and trousers. Standing in the nude, the mirrors capture his image from every angle. She falls back on the bed and raise the robe to reveal she wears nothing underneath. After shedding the dark fabric, she laughs and beckons him to approach.

The mirrors hide nothing as the light from the fireplace casts a golden glow on their passionate bodies. Fueled by youth and lust they continue well into the early morning hours as the flames grow tired with them.

Checking her schedule, Ana Knight confirms the time of her lunch with prospective clients. She is pursuing a fashion agency to show off her new cosmetic line, which is her new pet project. The Dious Agency of Italy is the front runner and she is to meet with their president Charles Lorenzo and Warren Huxley, the company lawyer. Accompanying her will be Martin Fraser, Knight Enterprises Senior Vice-President of marketing.

After her secretary reconfirms their reservation at Meade's, one of Omaha's few high society restaurants, she walks down the hall to Fraser's office. The door is open and the slender built man in his late forties smiles. He finishes the conversation on the phone and focuses his attention to Mrs. Knight.

" Ana, this is going to be great, The word is that Mr. Lorenzo has severed ties with Senor Jarvis of Barcelona. That would indicate he feels we have a better product to compliment his fashions. This lunch should run so smooth that I might even have an appetite to actually eat."

" Let's hope so. Are you ready to go?"

" Sure. Is the limo out front?"

" Martin! It's only two blocks. We can walk and not have to worry about noon traffic."

" Whatever you say. Just let me grab my coat. It looks windy out there."

" Forget the coat. Reports are that it's unseasonably warm."

" Are you sure you don't want the limo? The wind might mess up your hair."

" No, I'll just wear a hat. Give me a minute and I'll meet you in the lobby."

" Sure thing."

Martin Fraser checks his watch as the elevator doors open. Ana Knight emerges in a gray hat that matches the gray dress suit she is wearing. The ensemble is completed by matching midnight blue scarf, belt, handbag, and shoes. She removes another scarf from her pocket and uses it to secure the hat to her head. Then she puts on a pair of dark sunglasses as she reaches the door.

" How do I look?"

" Corporately divine."

" Then we better get a move on."

As they exit the building Fraser checks his watch again. The briefcase in his left hand almost slips from his grasp due to suddenly sweaty palms. They cross the street and Fraser stops and sets his briefcase down as he steps onto the curb. Ana takes three steps before noticing he is no longer at her side. She looks back and sees him bent over as if trying to catch his breath.

" Are you all right, Martin?"

" I'll be fine. A moment is all I need."

" Do you have a medical condition?"

" Not that I know of."

Suddenly a limousine with smoked windows pulls along side the curb and four gunmen emerge and are quickly upon them. Mrs. Knight Walks closer to Fraser in an attempt to protect her ailing friend. The driver positions the vehicle so that an open door is in parallel with Mrs. Knight.

" Get in the car, lady!" one of the gunmen shouts as the others close in.

" Run, Martin!" she shouts as she kicks the gun out of the hand of the nearest gun man.

Fraser grabs her arm and starts to pull her when a bullet to the throat fells him. She throws herself on top of the limousine and rolls off the other side. One of the gunmen runs around the back of the vehicle and confronts her as her feet touch the ground. He fires a shot and is dumbfounded when she is unfazed. She kicks him in the ribs and elbows him in the chin as she spins close to his body.

Taking the gun from his limp fingers she runs across the street toward Knight Enterprises. Shots ring out and two innocent by-standers fall on the sidewalk ahead of her. She wheels around and fires the gun. As she catches all three of the gunmen between the eyes, the tires of the limousine squeal because those in the limousine decide to make a retreat and leave their comrades behind.

Within seconds there are sirens cutting through the air as law enforcement vehicles approach from all directions. A GLESA security officer emerges from the front doors of Knight Enterprises. She turns to face him as he approaches.

" Frank, could you contact Clay. Be sure that he knows I'm all right, but I want him here as soon as he can."

" Yes. Ma'am."

He runs back into the building as she walks back across the street as law officials start to cordon off the area to hold back curious spectators. At first count she sees twelve Omaha police department vehicles, three from GLESA, and one from the Douglas county sheriff's department. A GLESA agent approaches her as she stands over Fraser's lifeless body.

" I'll take that, Mrs. Knight."

She hands him the gun.

" What happened?"

" Attempted kidnapping, I guess. Poor Martin."

" Those three weren't so lucky either. Some fairly deadly shooting."

" Clay insists that I practice and says shoot to kill. I wouldn't have fired at all, but innocent people were getting hurt."

" They should be fine. One gentleman took a bullet in the thigh an unfortunate young woman took one in the shoulder."

Two agents pick up the lone surviving assailant and place him in a security ambulance. They say that she broke his jaw. When they close the rear door, Knight's automobile pulls up. He and Mason Rasov emerge and cross over to where she is being kept company by the agent.

She embraces her husband as he strokes her hair. When she pulls away she sees that officials from the coroner's office are about to begin collecting the corpses.

" What happened, Ana?"

" Someone tried to kidnap me. There were the four gunmen and at least two others inside the limousine. There was a driver and someone who held the back door open, but if there were others I couldn't tell. I couldn't see the faces of those in the limo. It seems like the one in the back seat was wearing dark clothing and I could almost swear that he had a hood pulled up over his head."

Knight sees Rasov flinch at her final description.

" Why were you here to begin with?"

" I had a meeting. Damn! I have to call the restaurant. Well, that can wait. Martin and I were walking over to Meade's for lunch with possible clientele. When we reached this side of the street Martin seemed to have a spell of some sort. I stopped to help him..."

" You say Martin Fraser had a spell?" interrupts Knight.

" Yes. Maybe he had a medical condition I was unaware of."

" Fraser was a prime physical subject. He had no record of any ailments. But Ill check the autopsy. Please continue."

" Well, I started back toward Martin when the limousine pulled up and the gun men surrounded us."

" Did you get the license number?" asks Rasov.

" Unfortunately not. Let's see. As they approached me, probably intent on forcibly putting me in the car, I told Martin to make a run for it. He was in no condition, though. Poor man. I knocked the gun out of one man's hand when Martin grabbed my arm and was making an attempt to pull me to safety when one of them shot him."

" I doubt that," disagrees Knight.

" They're putting him in a bag right now! How else did he die?"

" Not that. One of them did kill him with a bullet that tore through his throat and shattered a neck vertebra. It was Fraser's intent that I question."

" What..What do you mean?"

" On the way over the security computer alerted me to the fact that Fraser placed a call to a public phone booth just before you probably left."

" What? A phone booth?"

" More than likely he was alerting your attackers that it was a good time to strike."

" Why?"

" Money, most likely."

" Money? Hell, we paid him better than anyone else with a similar position."

" Maybe he was greedy. Or maybe they enticed him with something else. One thing is for certain: he was not totally innocent."

" Then why did they shoot him?"

" Maybe the gun man missed. Might have been trying to shoot you and hit him. Or they were double-crossing Fraser so they would not have to pay him. Or they killed him to cover up the trail to them I don't know, which was the reason, if any. I'll have to check the surveillance tapes of the security system from our building over there and see if they shed any light. Please continue with what happened, Ana."

" This is nuts! Okay, okay. After Martin went down I tried to escape over the top of the limo and one of the gunmen was there to meet me when I made it to the other side. I disarmed him after he shot me. By the way, I love this little belt you made. And I love you."

" I love you, too."

" Okay, I knocked the gun man out and started to run across the street to escape not wanting any more to do with the situation. But the bastards were shooting at me and hit some innocent people. in order to protect the other people, I returned fire and killed the armed punks."

" Nice bit of marksmanship, I must add," offers Knight.

" Practice made perfect and you're a good teacher. Well, finally the law arrived on the scene and I recrossed the street. I met this nice, young agent of yours who relieved me of the weapon."

" Thank you, Tony. Did you get all of that on your recorder?"

" Yes, Sir."

The young agent leaves as Knight and his wife once again embrace. When they finish she whispers to him.

" Clay, if you don't need me for anything else, I need to make a few calls."

" Fine. I know where you live."

" See you later."

She hurries across the street as Rasov walks closer to Knight while turning off his recorder. He puts a hand on his friend's shoulder.

" Quite a woman you have there."

" No argument here."

" She held up pretty well."

" Seemed to. But inside I know she's all torn up. It seems to me, Mason, that this was the work of the late Ruthvan's followers."

" I have that impression also."

" They are trying to get personal. Please see to it that security is increased on my family and close friends."

" Consider it done."

" Why don't you finish up things here and I'm going inside to obtain the security tapes."

" Sure, Clay. I think this is just the beginning."

" Oh, it already started days ago. Now I fear they are getting bolder and more organized. I'll be out in a little while to go back to headquarters."

A day has passed since the kidnapping attempt and Knight sits in his office reviewing the security tapes from Knight Enterprises. The system did record the entire incident from two different views. The moment Ana was approached by the gunmen, the system sent out a warning to alert building security and it notified the legal authorities. Since it happened so quickly, the first to arrive actually got there after the danger had passed. He felt that he would have to improve the automated portion of the security system because the human response factor would likely remain the same. Admittedly, the human response time was exceptional, but it was still too late.

At the moment he is having a laser and sonic sound system installed to the exterior of Knight Enterprises and GLESA headquarters. The laser mechanism would be attached to the cameras and would pan with the movement of the camera. Special speakers are also being installed at street level which are capable of releasing sonic pulses of sound at a frequency that would be determined by the computer depending on the danger.

In slow motion Knight watches the events unfold as his wife handled the situation heroically. He stops the tape, rewinds it slightly, and watches the scene again. By pressing a button, the tape becomes even slower until the movements of the players are minimal. Punching a few more keys, the computer superimposes the potential trajectory of each of the gunmen's weapons. Knight intently studies the actions of one gun man in particular. For the first few moments, the trajectory is obviously focused on Ana's torso. Then it blatantly switches over to Fraser. The gun man had originally intended on putting the bullet in the area of Fraser's heart, but as he started to pull on Ana's arm his body lowered to the right and the bullet hit him in the throat instead. This shows that they were intent on executing Fraser rather than it being a misguided bullet he caught.

Knight allows the pace of the tape to quicken and then slows it down when Ana was facing the attacker on the other side of the limousine. The trajectory of the bullet showed he was only intent on wounding her. The fired shot would have hit her in the left shoulder had it not been for her protective shield. He has to smile at the skill in which she disarmed the gunman.

Again the action quickens as Knight watches the final sequence at it's normal progression. Then he rewinds it and again has the computer plot the potential and actual trajectories of each of the weapons. Although they did have trouble with a moving target, five of the sixteen shots they fired would have hit her. One bullet would have entered the back of her head, two to the spine, and one to the back of her left knee. The final bullet would have connected with her pelvic region after she turned around. Had it not been for the force field, she would be dead. It was obvious that they were ordered to kill her if she escaped their kidnapping attempt.

The trajectories of her weapon were all on target as she hit each of her assailants between the eyes in less than a second. He watches her fire at normal speed and then slows the tape to minimal movement. In a fluid motion she proceeded from target to target, firing the instant the trajectory was on it's mark and immediately moving on to the next target. It was obvious that she was extremely confident in her marksmanship and Knight is happy he had encouraged her to practice.

The progression of events showed Ana had acted in the best manner under the circumstances. Her assailants were obviously intent on killing her and she only returned fire when it was clear that others around her were in danger. This should clear her of any controversy that might arise out of the situation.

Reviewing the tapes Knight notices the license plate of the limousine. However, is would later be disappointed but not surprised to learn the vehicle had been stolen in Colorado two days earlier. It was later found abandoned in Arizona that same day with the interior burned out. A team of forensic specialists were dispatched to examine it just in case the occupants had been careless.

With the contents of the tapes copied onto his computer, he places the tapes in their respective cases. They would be returned to Knight Enterprises and placed in a vault for the security system's backup storage tapes. As he puts the tapes on the corner of his desk, the image of his secretary, Michael Penn, appears on the screen of his terminal.

" Excuse me, Clay."

" Yes, Michael."

" Would you be willing to see agent Buck at this time?"

" Of course. Send him in."

That morning Buck had successfully completed the treatment program and Knight requested to see him. It would be the first time they will have spoken to each other since Knight forced Buck into treatment and Knight feels awkward about it. A series of four knocks strike the closed door.

" Come in."

The young agent enters in uniform clearly refreshed and sober. Knight points to the couch and Buck takes a seat. Knight rises and slowly walks around the desk and sits on the corner closest to the couch.

" How are you feeling, Randy?"

" Better. A lot better."

" I see you are in uniform."

" Yes."

" Does that mean you are staying?"

" If you'll have me."

" But of course."

" I realize you probably don't want me on your team anymore.."

" Nonsense! If you can put up with me, I'd be happy to work side by side with you again."

" Thanks, Clay. I mean for everything. Maybe I should be angry, but hell it was the best thing that could have happened to me. I'm clear headed, my nerves are steady, and I feel fit."

" I'm glad to hear it. Has Russ informed you of the current situation?"

" No, we didn't talk shop. What's up?"

" It seems there is a resurgence of the Ruthvan movement."

" The devil cult?"

" If you want to call it that. Two agents, Jerry Kliburn and Rex Abbott, were abducted and executed. Did you know them well?"

" I'm afraid I never buddied up to the former Bureau guys. I think we did meet on one occasion, however. How were they killed?"

" The precise cause of death is unknown. The fiends only sent us their heads."

" What? That's sick!"

" We're dealing with a lower class of human here, Randy. Yesterday they attempted to abduct Ana, but she escaped."

" Is she all right?"

" Physically, yes. I'm not sure about otherwise."

" Where was she?"

" Across the street from Knight Enterprises."

" Bold sons of bitches, aren't they?"

" I'm afraid so. New security measures are being implemented to the corporate building and here at headquarters. "

" Who's running the case?"

" Mason and myself. You can report to Mason and he can brief you on everything you need to know."

" Sure thing. And thanks again, Clay."

" Just make me proud."

" Will do."

He rises and leaves the room closing the door behind himself.

Knight ponders a point that the agent had made. The actions of the cult were getting bold, but how bold were they willing to be. Under Ruthvan their actions were fearsome although their numbers were likely greater then. It is the leadership that determines the actions, however, not the size of the force. Judging by recent events he fears that the cult's new leader is just as dangerous as Ruthvan. Only time could put in perspective which leader would be the one to have a more terrifying reign of terror. The current leader seemed to have a personal grudge against Knight himself and he shudders at the thought.

Maria Ortiz stands in front of eight men who are in her quarters. Two are kneeling on the stone floor while the others stand three feet behind them. She does not wear her mask for this is her sanctuary and it is not a ceremony.

" How can you return empty handed?" she wails. " Where is the Knight bitch?"

" She got away," one of the kneeling men offers.

" She got away! She got away! How could she get away? There were six men. Seven counting Fraser. How could seven men not handle one woman?"

" She was quick and a fighter," meekly states the man who had been the driver.

" Fools!"

She steps forward and hits each man in the face with the leather gloves she holds loosely in her hand.

" If she escaped, then why is she not dead? All reports explain she is fine. Just a smug bitch sitting in her tower and down playing what happened to her. Can you explain this? Can you?"

There is silence for a moment and then the driver speaks softly.

" She got a gun from one of them and killed the others. They fired at her but kept missing. There wasn't anything we could do."

She walks over to the table while putting on her gloves and picks up two daggers. The men remain kneeling with their heads lowered and their hands at their sides. She laughs as she approaches the two who failed in their mission.

" These things happen, I guess. It would have been nice to get the upper hand on Clayton Knight. Maybe we'll get another chance. Who knows?"

She stops behind the two men and then steps between their kneeling bodies.

" This could be a situation we can over look. Something to be forgiven. Do you agree?"

Both men nod and relax their tense muscles.

" Only I don't forgive!"

As she shouts she bends down and each arm goes around a man. Her right arm goes over the right shoulder of the driver kneeling at her right. Her left arm goes over the left shoulder of the other man. The sharp blades touch their throats simultaneously as she violently pulls the weapons across their exposed flesh. They struggle momentarily, but the blades penetrate quickly as she draws tremendous strength from her insanity. Blood drenches her gloves as she repeatedly tears each blade back and forth until she touches bone. As she rises, their lifeless bodies fall forward into the pools of their mingling blood.

" Failure will not be tolerated!" she rants as the six remaining men look on in terror. " Either die at the task or die at my hand!"

She walks over to the sink and runs water over the daggers and gloves in an attempt to rinse off the blood.

Once them appear clean, she place the daggers on the counter and peels off the gloves and tosses them by the fireplace. Washing her bare hands is soothing and calms her. Turning to the motionless men she appears more relaxed.

" Johnson, get those two out of here and clean up the mess. Gentlemen, it is time to proceed. One setback will not stop us and it will even be eventually righted. We have business to attend to, for we have an empire to topple."

Chapter twenty

The calendar reads October 23 and Knight studies the reports in front of him. It would seem that the forces of evil had been extremely busy the last couple of days. Five prominent members of the international business community and thirty-nine religious figures of various faiths had been assassinated within the last forty-eight hours. Seven office buildings and fourteen places of worship had been destroyed by explosions that killed another one thousand three hundred and eight. In addition, twelve explosive devices had been used to destroy bridges carrying heavy traffic at various locations across the globe. Another three hundred and eleven fatalities resulted from those rush hour catastrophes. The only common factor between all of the incidents is a factor that would not be immediately noticed by most people.

None of the individuals involved or any of the structures had any connection to GLESA or Knight Enterprises. Not a single individual or any of the structures destroyed were under the protection of Knight security. Granted, it is unlikely that an individual of lower standing in a particular religious organization would seek his protection. The higher members of the hierarchy usually seek that. Yet it is something all the individuals shared. In the same vein, Knight Enterprises constructed none of the bridges.

It is easy for Knight to see that the terrorists are not only going after him personally, but also intended on damaging his public image. He knows the attacks on people and structures with religious connections are more for pleasure to the cult, while the others are more motive oriented. The public would not make the connection as quickly as he did, but someone would likely make the connection. He would have to head off this public relations sabotage by being fairly open with the public about how he will combat the situation. He will try and keep everything as positive as possible because he knows eventually someone will accuse him as being behind the terrorism. To make him falter in the public eye would surely give the cult great satisfaction and he would do his best to counter it.

His best recourse for dealing with the situation is to bring down the cult. This, however, was proving difficult since he had been attempting to make headway in that area for nearly a month and had made little progress. Until that time he knows his public image will suffer to an extent, as would those of GLESA and Knight Enterprises.

In an attempt to have one day of relaxation before things turn really ugly, Knight decides to attend the first game of the World Series. The first game is scheduled for October 25 in Omaha and is pitting his National League winning Thunder against the New York Yankees. For the year the Thunder finish the regular season with a record of 138-62 and won the playoffs four games to one over the Cincinnati Reds. The Yankees finished the regular season with a 104-96 record and escaped the American League playoffs four games to three over the Seattle Mariners. Knight really didn't care what the outcome is this night, as long as it is a good game.

Ana decided to join him in the owner's box after he informed he of the battle they would be facing. A night of enjoying the spectacle of sport would be refreshing and she decided to make a small party out of it. As a surprise for Knight, she invited Dr. Avery, Han and Suzie Li, Mason Rasov, Russell Jackson, Randy Buck, and all their respective wives and girlfriend. All informed her they would be delighted to attend.

As Knight enters the owner's box a broad smile lights up his face as he sees all his friends already there. He kisses his wife on the cheek and enters with her arms intertwined.

" I hoped you wouldn't mind," she whispers.

" Not in the least. It will be good for everyone."

Han stands as Knight approaches and the two shake hands. Suzie smiles and raises her glass at Knight. then his friend steers him from the crowd.

" I understand we are heading for some choppy waters, Clay."

" Only some public relations trouble."

" Which leads to financial trouble."

" We'll get it cleared up before too long."

" Are you sure of that?"

" Actually, no."

" Then it's a major problem."

" We're working on it. Nothing has happened yet to hurt the business and there isn't anything you can do about it. Now let's enjoy the game tonight and start on our ulcers tomorrow."

" If you say so."

" Everything will fall in place. You'll see."

Knight watches as his friend walks back to his wife and reflects on the situation. He didn't want to panic his friend, but events were turning worse. Within the last two days five more businessmen and twenty-one religious figures had been killed. Two more office buildings, seven traffic bridges, and four religious structures were also destroyed killing another two hundred and forty. None of the people or structures involved had connections to GLESA or Knight Enterprises. He knows it is only a matter of time before someone starts preaching about guilt by non-association. While he thinks that is somewhat off the wall, he realizes it takes little to sway the mood of the misguided public.

After the national anthem, Dr. Avery leans forward and talks toward Knight.

" Hey, Clay! How come you're not in uniform tonight? I'd like to see a few home runs."

" I'm not on the roster for the series. Anyhow, my heart wouldn't be in it. With any lick, Royov or Wise might be able to satisfy your hunger for the long ball."

" Maybe they will. And how come Villa is starting ahead of Cortez? Or in front of anyone else for that matter?"

" Although it's true that Cortez went 38-6 during the regular season, Tomas Villa also had an impressive 34-10 season. The coaches feel that Tomas is readier than Pablo. Pablo will start tomorrow night if you want to see him pitch."

" Think your team is going to do it for the fourth year in a row? they seem to have lost that over powering edge."

" I hope they do. Sure, they haven't won as many as the two previous years and kind of slumped toward the end of the season, but they have the experience and talent. I don't believe there is a team that can overcome them any time soon."

" We'll see if you're right."

The Yankees are starting the ace of their staff, a right hander from Cedar Rapids, Iowa named Galen Stanek. He was 28-5 during the regular season and picked up three victories in the playoffs. It may have been better if he had more rest and pitched the second or third game, but their coaches feel he has the best chance of beating the Thunder and he agreed to forgo the extra rest.

The game is a scoreless pitcher's duel through the first four innings. Villa has a no-hitter going and keeps the Yankees hitless in the fifth. Going into the bottom of the fifth, center fielder Sean O'Casey has the only Thunder hit. He is due up again this inning after Ortega.

Right fielder Juan Ortega works the count to full and then fouls off six straight pitches. A roar comes from the subdued crowd as ball four is outside and high. On the first pitch to O'Casey, Ortega races toward second base and beats the catcher's throw.

To the Yankee's surprise, O'Casey lays down a bunt toward the third baseman. The third baseman has a late break on it and the pitcher stays out of the way. Ortega advanced to third as O'Casey is safe by two strides ahead of the throw by Yankee third baseman Zeke Kozol.

Shortstop Victor Wise waits patiently as Stanek throws two ball outside the strike zone. As the third pitch approaches his eyes widen because the ball seems so large. The bat comes around quickly as the right handed batter droves the ball down the left field line. The ball never descends for the Yankee players and carries over the fence to the right of the foul pole. The stadium erupts as the home run puts the Thunder on top three to nothing.

The only other scoring in the game comes in the seventh inning and is done by the Yankees. Villa walks the first batter and then loses his no-hit bid as catcher Kerrey Strauss loops a hit over jumping second baseman Kim Hamako while the runner on first advanced to third. The next batter grounds into a double play as Hamako fields the ball, shovels it to Wise, and Wise fires a strike to Royov at first base. However, that only made two outs and the original batter took the opportunity to score. Villa gives up a single to right field to the next batter, but cools the Yankee hopes by striking out Zeke Kozol on three pitches.

Jose Verde closes the ninth by striking out the first two Yankee batters. On the first pitch, the next batter lifts the ball into the air behind home plate. Catcher Anthony Vega discards his face protector and watches the ball fall down into his waiting glove. Cheers fill the stadium as Vega tosses the ball to Umpire John Adams.

A three to one score is fine with Knight since his team had the three. His friends pat him on the back and shake his hand. Glasses clink as Knight watches his players head for the clubhouse. One victory is a nice foundation as the team tries for another championship.

Distant stars decorate the South American sky as they flicker in random sequence. The air is thick with humidity as tireless insects navigate intricate patterns near the isolated light on the mountain. It is a faint light not visible from the meadow below, but it is becoming increasingly popular with the winged pests. Then the light becomes brighter, inviting the invaders to come closer. A smile catches the moonlight as the distinct crackling sound signifies the deaths of many little life forms.

Maria Ortiz sits on the balcony with her feet up on the guardrail as she cradles a glass of bourbon in her lap. She feels at home in the darkness for it provides a natural barrier that ensures privacy. The glass touches her lips as she reflects on triumphs of recent days. Her long black hair flows over the back of the chair as she tilts her head backwards and closes her eyes.

In the two weeks since her organization began it's activities, they had assassinated twenty-two important business figures and one hundred and twenty-nine religious figures. The property they destroyed was valued at just over eight billion dollars while they killed another six thousand four hundred and fifty-three innocents in doing so. Everything is going according to plan for it is simple to pick on targets not under the protective blanket of GLESA or Clayton Knight. She is proud of the chaos she caused and is intent on continuing the mayhem.

Darkness is momentarily interrupted by the out-reaching light from the interior of the mountain as the sliding door opens and then closes. Pablo Garcia walks forward carrying a glass and a full bottle of bourbon. Miss Ortiz empties the last of her bottle and throws the empty container over the side of the balcony. Breaking glass can be heard as it meets the rocky terrain below.

" Would you like some company?"

" Since you're the one with the full bottle, sure. Take a seat and put that bottle where I can reach it."

" So are we drinking to celebrate? Or drinking to be drinking? "

" Choose whatever reason lets the juices flow easier for you. I don't care."

" What do you think of on nights like this?"

" Many things. My childhood for one. The night I lost my virginity, for another."

" What a lucky man he must have been!"

" I was the lucky one. It was our late mentor, Sebastian Ruthvan, who parted me and introduced a shy school girl to the ways of the flesh."

" How did you meet? Were you already in the sect?"

" No, it was when I first entered over seven years ago at the tender age of seventeen. A friend, his name escapes me at the moment, informed me of a weekend party haven hidden away in the jungle. Some of my girlfriends and myself had nothing to do that weekend, so we decided to check it out. The five of us must have gotten lost a dozen times before we eventually found the place.

" We arrived a little after one in the morning and the party still seemed to be going strong. After we entered, the place was wall to wall with people. Hours passed as we danced to our hearts' content and fewer and fewer people remained. The sun had risen and I was still full of life and energy as my friends sat at a table sitting, drinking, and sleeping. There were few people left with me on the dance floor and I was basically dancing by myself. Then I saw him.

" His skin was darkened by the sun and his hair grayed by the years. Yet I could tell he was an American. He sat alone in a booth at the back of the room. But I noticed him watching me. I tried to ignore the stranger, but something inside me drew me toward him.

" It was Ruthvan and he seemed so elegant that I fell for him the moment I saw him in decent lighting. We talked for a few minutes and he noticed my friends were preparing to leave. He asked me to return the following week and I agreed. I rejoined my friends and we started our journey home with me thinking of Ruthvan the entire way.

" That was the summer after I finished secondary school and was very pre-occupied with the details of preparing to attend Georgetown University in the United States. With so much to do I had little time to think of my meeting with the stranger. When the day came, I was very nervous and was considering not going. Then I thought I owed myself one last night of fun before I went off to college in a strange land.

" The establishment was again wall to wall with people and I circled the building time and again searching for the stranger. Disappointed, I started for the door intent on going home. Before I reached the doorway, he was there blocking the exit. I was angry that he had kept me waiting and tried to push past him.

" He prevented me from exiting and pleaded with me to stay and apologized for his tardiness stating he was detained by unavoidable circumstances. Finally, I relented and allowed him to escort me back inside. An employee of the establishment stood by a table, which was reserved for us until we arrived. At that moment I realized the man owned the establishment. I questioned him to see if my hunch was true.

" He stated that he did indeed own the place, but it was in the name of a friend. I thought that was strange and he assured me it was done for legal reasons. Later I found out he did it so there would be no direct ties to him because of his fugitive status.

" We talked and drank into the early morning hours. He asked me if I shocked easily. I said no. First he told me that he knew who I was, but that didn't bother him because he had strong feelings for me. He said he was willing to risk going with someone from a high exposure family. It was then he told me he had to maintain a low profile because he had some trouble with the law.

" My brain told me I should have left then, only I was attracted to the older man. He said that he was currently involved in a large-scale drug operation Then he held my hand and looked into my eyes as he asked if I could fall for a man such as he. I said yes.

" Then we left and went to his residence. It was actually a very simple abode, isolated in the forest, just as the club had been. Since no one knew where I was, it scared me to an extent to be alone with him. His charm and grace calmed me greatly, however, and it soon seemed natural to be in his presence.

" We talked for a while and then he led me to the bedroom. Naturally, I was hesitant being a virgin and all, but he patiently coaxed me out of my clothes. Looking back on it, knowing Ruthvan for who he was, it was all a game with him. If I had not submitted under my own free will, I am certain he would have raped me. Yet as it was, I was a willing partner and he was the teacher for a type of education I had never had before.

" Afterwards we talked and I was hesitant to leave my newfound over and go off to a strange foreign land. But he convinced me it would be good for me to see the country he came from. Every time I returned home I would relate my sights and experiences to him. He felt he would never see his homeland again and eventually he was right. He said my telling of my experiences were a good substitute for him.

" While we were lovers for nearly two years, it was not until I returned to finish my schooling closer to home that I was introduced to the ways of the sect. I amazed me the first time he took me to a ceremony and I found it compelling. At the third or fourth ceremony I attended there was a sacrifice. It was some farm girl they had captured. As Sebastian raped her on the alter I was extremely jealous. When he later lowered the dagger into her chest I felt vindicated. To me the killing seemed justified and after that I basically accepted all the other sacrifices without giving it a second thought. I was a member and proud of it.

" There was something that was always eating at Sebastian, though. That was the fact that Knight had beaten him and had driven him from his nation of birth. Sebastian deeply missed it and vowed to regroup his empire of terror and make Knight rue the day he thwarted him. Unfortunately, he did not live to see his dream come true. However, now his wish is being granted and his memory will always serve as a driving force for me."

" So you're dedicated the downfall of Knight to the memory of Ruthvan?"

" Something like that."

" Think we can do it?"

" You don't have faith in me?"

" It's not that. No, no. It's just that he is so powerful. You know."

" We'll do enough to see him suffer and then I want him dead."

" It will be hard to get at him."

" No one is unreachable. No one. He's a public private person or a private public person. Whatever. Eventually he'll slip up and I'll make a special trip to spit on his grave."

" May I refill your glass, Ma'am?"

" Certainly. I've got a thirst I can't quench."

She sips a little of the liquor and the taps her fingers against the glass as it presses against her chin. Gazing upon the stars she wonders how long before the death blow is struck and she can revel in the ultimate victory. While she is young and has time, patience is not one of her strong points. if it came to it, she would go after Knight personally. She didn't think it would come to that. Chaos will reign and she will be the driving force.

Walking along the marble floor Knight glances at the portraits of previous Presidents as he heads for the Oval Office. Two days previous, on November 4, a presidential aide personally delivered a request for him to meet with the President at ten this morning. The topic of the meeting was not revealed to Knight, although he has strong suspicions as to what it will be.

Peter Heathcote is a competent leader for Knight's native country and he likes the man, but he does not feel bound to hold allegiance to no single country. Yet he loves and protects his homeland to the best of his ability. However, it is the well being of the world as a whole that he always kept in mind and his actions support that philosophy. To the fanatic patriot fringe he might be seen as a traitor, although Knight never had nor would ever do anything to harm the people of the United States.

He stands outside the closed oak doors for a few minutes before the secretary signals he can go in. The President is seated while looking over several documents scattered on the desk in front of himself. He raises his head and smiles at Knight as he reaches for a large, unopened envelope. With his free hand he points at a chair opposite his desk.

" Please take a seat, Clay."

" Thank you, Sir."

The gray haired gentleman picks up a pearl handled letter opener and breaks the seal on the envelope. He looks over the enclosed papers as he continues talking with Knight.

" So, Clay, how was your trip?"

" Uneventful."

" Well, I guess that's good then. I heard of the encounter with some bad weather you had a few weeks ago. Are you recovered yet?"

" I'm still under-going treatment for the burns, but other than that I've recovered satisfactorily."

" Very good."

The President puts the papers on the desk with the others. He looks into Knight's eyes as he learns forward and rests his chest against his folded arms at the edge of the desk. The smile disappears as he searches for the right words.

" Clay, I have a favor to ask of you. Would you be able to oblige me?"

" Depends on the favor."

" Fair enough. As we both are aware, there is a terrorist group causing havoc for the fair citizens of our country and others."

" It's common knowledge now."

" There are some reports circulating that you may be responsible for these actions."

" In an indirect way, but I am not in control of the force behind the terror."

" I realize this, as do my political brethren, but the public perception..."

" I am well aware of the public perception, Mister President. I was aware of the public's possible reaction from the first day the terrorists struck. I am fully aware of all aspects of the situation. I will not, however, alter my position in the community or discontinue my association with GLESA again."

" Why would you?"

" I thought that was the reason you called me here. It isn't?"

" Goodness, no! While some of the public may be soured on you the other world leaders and myself want you to know that we are behind you one hundred percent."

" Really?"

" Certainly. It would be extreme stupidity to denounce the only person capable of dealing with the current situation effectively. You did it once and we have faith that you will be able to do it again. We recently recognized the strategy the terrorists are using and saw through their ploy. It seems only natural they'd want revenge against the one who caused their last downfall. In your endeavor to do it again, we are behind you one hundred percent."

" Thank you. Actually, I'm quite stunned. Then what was the favor you spoke of?"

" The favor. Okay... In frankness, Clay, your organization GLESA is far superior to any in the world. For reasons we have been unable to understand, you have surpassed the FBI, CIA, Interpol, and categorically every other law enforcement organization in the world in what has been a relative short period. Some of this may be due to the personnel you were able to entice in joining you. Some may be due to your gift for creating new technologies. For whatever reason, your organization has been able to infiltrate areas others are unable to. With that capability, I'm certain that your people will be able to get a line on the terrorists before anyone else."

" We're working on it, believe me."

" The favor actually has two parts. The first is when you actually get a line on the terrorists, alert us so we can assist you."

" Actually it would be more efficient if we handled it ourselves. Yet an alliance with a multi-national joint effort would greatly improve the public image that has been attacked recently. While GLESA is multi-national itself, it would be good to have individual countries offer small task forces. Okay, I'll agree on the condition that all those coming fall under my command."

" It would be highly irregular for a civilian to lead military personnel, but considering your record I'm certain I can convince everyone to agree."

" And the second part of the favor?"

" What I'm telling you must never leave this room. Do you comply?"

" Believe me, Mister President, I can keep a secret."

" Good. Now judging by the past history of this particular terrorist organization..."

" Which is a devil worshipping cult."

" Right."

" And is very dangerous to society as a whole."

" Right."

" And of which one of their primary founding members was a former employee of your government."

" Now we had no knowledge of that! Ruthvan was a product of a previous administration..."

" Drop the politics, Sir. I know the type of people I'm up against and what they're capable of. What is the rest of the favor?"

" I was getting to that. Now due to the threat that these people pose to the rest of society, when they are caught, it is the consensus that they should be.. should be..."

" Exterminated?"

" Putting it bluntly, yes. Now I know you think of yourself as a lawman, but in the past you have to admit you have been heavy handed when it comes to such matters."

" No, no, I agree. Under the circumstances I think that would be the best course of action. But tell me, Mister President, how far would you be willing to carry this out?"

" What do you mean?"

" Basically, once my people have infiltrated the cult, it will be possible to obtain knowledge of who their members are worldwide. Would you condone a silent witch hunt to assure that the world is purged of these vermin once and for all."

" A good point. Was it your intention to do this anyway before I made this request of you?"

" Honestly? Yes."

" Then it doesn't matter that I or any other world leader condones your actions when they are separate from our alliance."

" Nice dodge, Sir."

" Tell me, Clay. Do you have the capabilities at your disposal to carry out such a venture."

" Yes."

" Interesting. Would you be willing to disclose the extent of your capabilities?"

" No."

" Fair enough. Thank you for taking the time from your busy schedule to see me. I will relay to the others your willingness to allow us to join in the crucial offensive."

" I hope it's soon."

" Don't we all! And I appreciate the courtesy you have shown toward this frail old man before you."

" Old? You're only sixty-six."

" True, but just the same I'm older than you. I could see the slight strain in your face and hear it in your voice each time you said 'Mister President'. I appreciate you're being so courteous, but I know of your reputation for preferring to be on a first name basis with all those around you as time permits. On that note, it would honor me greatly if you just called me 'Pete'."

Knight laughs and rises from his chair.

" The honor is mine, Sir. To be on a first name basis with the President is a rare privilege. Thank you, Pete."

" It is only a small gesture. I trust you will keep me apprised of the situation."

" Of course. And I'm sure we'll have another meeting like this in the future."

" Really? What will we talk about?"

" That will be revealed by the stars. Until that time may your days be productive. I truly enjoyed the chance to talk with you, Pete."

The President rises and walks around the desk while looking up at the larger man. He extends his hand, which Knight shakes gently.

" You're a good man, Clayton Knight! I'll always remember this meeting with fondness despite the circumstances."

" I'll see myself out, Pete."

" Okay. You have a good day."

" You, too."

" Actually, once you reach my age, any day you wake up is a good day."

Both men laugh while Knight opens the door and closes it upon exiting. He smiles at the two Marines outside the door, but they do not respond. They stand there basically out of tradition because the two GLESA androids standing at the opposite side of the office are much more capable of protecting the President. Given current events, however, they may be no such thing as too much protection. He ponders the President's words as he once again walks down the hallway adorned with the political paintings.

Chapter twenty-one

Nervously Knight paces in the hospital waiting room as his children run around him. It is February 15, 2050 and Ana is about to give birth to their nineteenth child. A nurse is supposed to come and inform him when Dr. Avery and Ana go to the delivery room. It has been a half hour since they admitted her as Knight's watch reads 2:31 p.m. Dr. Avery immediately took his wife while Knight helped Miss Davies escort the children to the waiting room.

" Mr. Knight?"

" Yes!"

" Dr. Avery and your wife just went to delivery room four."

" Thank you. I know where it is."

His pace is brisk as he goes down the hall. Although they have many children, he is just as nervous as when she had the original quintuplets. A nurse is waiting for him in front of the delivery room doors.

He quickly steps through the scanner and it reveals no dangerous microorganisms. Then he places both arms inside a machine and removes them with both arms sealed in pliable plastic up to the elbow. Then he steps into a chamber where a transparent orb lowers to encase his head. Lightweight apparatus is also attached to his torso and then to the orb that allows oxygen to be filtered directly from the atmosphere and helps maintain a comfortable temperature while the wearer is in the sterile environment of the delivery room.

Once he is properly attired he enters the delivery room. He is full aware that many children come into the world under much less sanitary conditions, but he is not going to take any chances where his children are concerned. Quickly he approaches Dr. Avery, his wife, and the two android assistants.

Ana is on a cushion bed that contours to support the body. Every square centimeter of the bed is monitored and controlled by computer. The surface can become hard if necessary or very pliable to give the sensation of floating on water. It also can gently grasp the person as it raises them forward or as the bed tilts to an angle.

An electric shock gently numbs Ana's skull as a ball lowers from the ceiling as it pulsates with energy. Then a slender needle extends from the ball as it nears her head. The needle penetrates the skull and releases a chemical into the pain center of the brain. The entire process is closely monitored as scanners help produce an image of what is taking place on a screen behind the bed.

A monitor on the wall gives a continual readout of the mother's and baby's life signs. Heartbeat, brain wave activity, oxygen flow, and numerous other measurements appear on the monitor as the scanners continually pick up new readings. At the moment all readings appear normal as the mother and baby are healthy.

At the time of delivery the bed tilts up while it suctions onto Ana's legs, rear, and lower back. Knight looks at the wall-sized monitor that shows the baby inside the mother's womb getting ready to exit. He holds Ana's hand as she concentrates and he watches the monitor. The head becomes visible as Knight looks and offers encouragement to his wife. With a few more seconds of effort the baby is clear of it's mother. The monitor states the infant is twenty inches in length and weighs eight pounds and four ounces.

The bed returns to a horizontal position as the two androids begin cleaning the area. Dr. Avery holds the baby and touches it's rear with a device that emits a mild spark. A healthy cry escapes the young lungs and the doctor cleans the infant gently. He then wraps the infant in a blanket and offers him to the proud parents.

Knight helps Ana sit up as Dr. Avery brings the baby over. Since it is a boy. the name they decided on is Lancelot Arthur Knight. Official time of birth was 3:24 p.m. and the Knights happily welcome the newest member of the family to the world.

" This is the last one," whispers Ana.

" No argument here," Knight whispers back.

He holds his wife with one arm and helps support the baby with the other. Tears of joy roll down his cheeks and streak the lower portion of the orb. Ana sees this and puts a kiss on her fingers and then places them on the orb where his mouth is. Both cherish the tender moment as Knight ponders that if life was a card game it would have to be black jack. Now his family has twenty-one.

Two weeks pass before Ana decides to start back to work with four-hour days at the office. All remaining business would be conducted from her office at home. When she is home, the baby is with her at all times whether it be in the office, dining room, or bedroom. When she is at the office, Knight rearranged his schedule so he could be with the baby.

Knight sits in his office at home while little Lancelot rests peacefully in a crib by the desk. Ana would be home in about an hour and his journey toward Omaha would normally begin shortly after that. On this day, however, he would try to deal with everything from his home office because guests are arriving that afternoon.

At around 3 p.m. Han and Suzie are due to stop by for a visit of two or three days. That meant Ana would have about three hours to rest after she returned home. It also meant that he has nearly four hours to complete the tasks he would take an entire day to do. The clock on the wall keeps him apprised of the countdown.

It had been nearly four months since his meeting with the President and GLESA had not made any significant progress in finding the terrorists. He wasn't having any luck with his thousands of infiltrators either. On a brighter side, law enforcement officials had been able to thwart a dozen assassination attempts while killing forty-four cult members in doing so. The legal authorities either killed the cult members or they killed themselves rather than being captured. Further assassinations may have been averted because many people enlisted the security services of GLESA. Under the circumstances, he offered the services at a reduced rate to all customers until the crisis passed.

As Knight interacts with the computer, he hears a soft rapping on the door.

" Come in," Knight tells the knocker.

The door opens and his son Ian enters. He walks up to the desk and stops between it and the crib. Knight finishes his train of thought and then gives his attention to his son.

" Can I help you with something, Ian?"

" How come I have a new brother?"

" It's the miracle of life. Your mother and I decided it was a good idea."

" Did I do something wrong?"

" Of course not. Why do you ask?"

" I was the youngest and then you got him. You must not have been happy with how I was doing."

" Is that what you believe?"

" Yes."

Knight shakes his head and looks toward the heavens. He looks at Ian and waves for him to approach.

" Please come here, son."

The boy walks around the desk and gets up on his father's left knee.

" Ian, you should be happy to have a new brother."

" Well, I'm not."

" Are you jealous?"

" Yes!"

" Why?"

" Because you'll love him more than you love me!"

Knight smiles and hugs his son.

" Ian, your mother and I love you all very much. The amount we love each of you is the same. And that amount of love is very large. In fact, it is the same love that we give to each of you. With love you can use it over and over and it never wears out. And you can keep giving and giving and it never runs out. So you see Ian, we love you all a great deal and we love you all the same amount. Do you understand?"

" I guess so."

" Do you feel any better?"

" A little."

" I know what will make you feel better."

Knight stands up and carries his son over to the crib. He sets Ian down and picks up Lancelot. He cradles the baby in his arms and walks over to the couch and sits down. He pats his knee and Ian runs over and climbs onto the couch and sits on his knee.

" Ian, this is your brother Lancelot. But we'll call him 'Lance'. Say hello to your brother Lance, Ian."

" Hi, Lance."

The boy rubs gently against the baby's garment.

" Now you two are brothers, so that means you have a special bond. Part of that bond is love. You love your other brothers, don't you?"

" Yes."

" And your sisters?"

" Yes."

" Then that leaves poor, lonely Lance. You have so much to give, Ian. Could you see it in your heart to love your only younger brother?"

" Okay."

" Okay what?"

" I love him, too."

" Tell him. I'm sure he'd like to hear you say it."

" I love you, Lance."

" And he loves you, too."

" How can you tell?"

" By the way he looks at you."

" Really?"

" Yes, I think he already knows you're his older brother and he already looks up to you. Just the way you did when he brought you home. You looked at Frank, Jake, Vince, Hank, Chris, Rich, Alex, Doug, Manny, Kenny, and Curt the same way."

" I was just a baby! They probably all looked the same to me."

" That may be true, but I'm sure you loved them all the same. Believe me Ian, this little kid here looks up to you."

" And will he look up to the others, too?"

" I'm certain of it. This little bundle is just full of love. Right now he needs to be receiving a lot of it so that when the time comes, he knows how to give it out himself."

" I love you, Lance."

" Very good, Ian. Do you feel better?"

" Yes."

" How much better?"

" A whole lot better."

" Very good. Tell you what, why don't you watch Lance in his crib while I try to finish some work. Okay?"

" Okay."

" Then when your mother gets home you can help her watch Lance."

" Sounds good."

" Great."

Ian jumps onto the floor and Knight stands to return the infant to the crib. Ian sits on the floor looking through the wooden bars of the crib as the baby falls asleep almost immediately. As Knight sits behind his desk, he decides to ask Ian about his sessions on the moon.

" Did you have a good session yesterday, Ian?"

" Yes, Papa. Mochar and Droz and Wir are good teachers."

" Did you learn anything new?"

" Not really. They said I should really get good at stuff I already know before I learn something new. Mochar did say it would not be long before I do learn something new. That must mean I am getting really good at the stuff I already know."

" That's what it sounds like to me. How does Dr. Avery like the trips to the moon?"

" I don't think he likes them a whole lot. He doesn't really talk to me while we are in flight. He likes to talk to me when we are landed, however."

" I always thought Bill had a fear of flying."

" He fears flying?"

" Actually, it's the crashing he probably fears."

" Big Dr. Avery is afraid?"

" I think so. Many people have fears of things they can't control. Many times it is what is called a phobia. People can be helped to over come these fears. I should talk to Bill about getting help."

" Maybe I can help him."

" How?"

" Tell him how free it feels when I'm flying."

" That might ease him a little, but as I said I think it's the crashing that worries him."

" Then I'll tell him I won't let it crash."

" You know, that just might cheer him up. Why don't you tell him that when he gets back from his trip."

" Okay."

" Now if you would, I need to finish some of this work and I need silence. Can you be a good boy and sit there silently while I work?"

" Yes, Papa."

" Good. When your mother gets home I'll be certain to inform her of what a fine little gentleman you are."

Knight continues to interact with the computer. Although he has had great advances in voice interaction with computers, he still enjoys a hands-on approach. He reads report after report to keep abreast of the on going operations of GLESA. Then he starts planning an immediate course of action for each agent should take on their respective cases and forwards an electronic memo stating his thoughts to each agent. The minutes race by as he completes a major portion of the desired tasks by the time Ana arrives home.

His wife enters the office wearing a predominately peach colored outfit consisting of slacks, blouse, and scarf. She waves at her preoccupied husband while smiling at the sight of her two youngest children. Kneeling, she gives Ian a hug and then removes the sleeping infant from the crib. With Ian at her side, she walks over to the side of Knight's desk to observe what he is working on.

" Are you going to be finished by the time Han and Suzie arrive?"

" More than likely. Anything I don't get done can wait until this evening. I'm expecting Mason to send an update on developments on the Ruthvan case. It's supposed to be in the system between five and six this afternoon. I'll probably print it off and read it downstairs after everyone has gone to bed. Prolonged contact with the computer has become very tiresome lately."

" Tell me about it. I'm taking Lance to see if he has an appetite for Mama's milk."

" Sounds tempting."

" Clay! Not in front of young ears."

" Oh, yes. Ian wants to be your little helper in watching after Lance."

" He does? You do, Ian?"

" Yes, Mama. I love Lance and want to protect him."

" Very well, then come along, Ian. We'll watch over your brother elsewhere while your father gets back to work. I'll see you when they arrive, Clay."

" Maybe before then. It depends."

He watches the three exit and then submerges himself into the stream of continuously flowing information. His focus constantly switches as he checks the data bank of his super computer after completing each task. Absorbing the material, his brain sorts and stores it for future reference in the structured vault of his memory. After a few hours he glances at the clock and decides her should greet his guests. With a sigh of relief he presses the terminal's off switch.

Chapter twenty-two

Ana is standing in the doorway as a vehicle stops by the front steps. Han and Suzie emerge from the rear doors as the driver and an android begin unloading their luggage. The vehicle had brought them from the airstrip where their plane is being placed in a hanger.

Knight appears in the doorway behind Ana as the Lis make their way up the steps. Suzie takes a moment to check the luggage before turning to her hosts with a broad smile. Han gives Ana a quick kiss on the cheek and shakes Knight's hand vigorously.

" Man you look beat, Clay," observes Han.

" Curse of the working man. So how was your flight."

" Smooth. I know better than to fly through storm clouds."

" Excuse me," interrupts Suzie. " Where should we put our baggage?"

" I have the room already picked out," instructs Ana. "Follow me and I'll show it to you. The help already knows where to take it, so they'll go on ahead."

" Sounds good. Does that mean we'll be in a different room than last time."

" Yes, unless you want to be in the same room again."

" No, a new room is fine. In fact, I prefer life to be a bit unpredictable."

" Well, good. Let me show you the room."

They walk down the hall and disappear around the corner. Knight and Han look at each other and laugh. After he closes the door, Knight puts his arm over his friend's shoulder."

" So how was you honeymoon? I've never really had an opportunity to ask."

" Let's just say the majority of the scenery on the trip consisted of the hotel room."

" I see. Then you picked yourself a passion flower."

" Clay, I have a bouquet."

" So...are you ready to start a new project?"

" A new project? Do you think that would be wise considering the public climate?"

" I believe it is an excellent time. We've seen the worst as far as negative public relations are concerned. In fact, I am positive that in the not too distant future it will begin to rise back toward it's previous status."

" You sound pretty confident. You're nearing a solution to the terrorist problem?"

" Nothing concrete but I've decided on my next course of action."

" And that is?"

" I am going to launch a major offensive against the international drug industry. While it is something that should be done anyway, I suspect that drugs are a major source of finances for the cult. Sure, they may still have a few wealthy benefactors, but the scale at which they are operating would require a substantial cash flow. More than likely drugs are the main source of their revenues."

" I think you may be on to something. And even if you're wrong, you would be tackling an important problem. It's a no loss situation."

" Yes and no. If this doesn't have an impact on the cult, then I don't have any other ideas at the moment on how to get at them. "

" What is the project you want to start?"

" First, let's go into the living room where we can be more comfortable."

" Okay."

They walk down the hall and emerge through a wide doorway into the living room. Knight walks over to the bar and pours himself apple cider into a chilled glass mug.

" Can I get you anything, Han?"

" A little red wine, if you wouldn't mind."

" No problem. Ana seems to like this label, so you can tell me if she has any taste or not."

Han takes a sip and takes a few seconds to savor the distinctive flavor.

" Excellent! She most certainly has good taste. May I see the bottle?"

" Of course."

" I will make a point to pick a case the next time I'm able."

" Now about the project."

" Okay, what do you have in mind?"

" For some time I've been curious about the characteristics of radiation. I believe under the correct conditions it would be possible to break down radioactive materials, rather than letting them break down naturally over many years. This could basically eliminate the problem of toxic waste. It may also turn out to provide a new source of energy because I believe that the process of breaking the radioactive material down into inert matter would release large quantities of energy."

" Intriguing. And dangerous. Very dangerous."

" It does have it's drawbacks. I admit. But do you think you would be up to tackling such a project? Or are you priming yourself for a more active administrative role?"

" And what's wrong with that?"

" Nothing. You and Ana seem to like that sort of thing much more than I do. Personally, I like to stay active and keep my hands just as busy as my mind."

" So I've noticed. Does Ana support this project?"

" She sees it's merits. However, she thinks I should tackle this project myself."

" Why don't you?"

" When? You know I'd like to pursue this myself as I have with so many of my other pet projects. But I don't have the time at the present and won't on the foreseeable future. Since I have turned other projects over to you and Bill in the past, I thought I would do it again. Let's just say I'm practicing my administrative delegation skills."

" Do you have any ground work laid for this project?"

" I've put some thoughts to paper. Basically I have an outline you could follow to get the project off the ground. It will more than likely take you through the first three months. After that it will depend on your findings as to what you do."

" Okay, I'm hooked. What about my team?"

" Pick anyone you want from research and development. When you're ready, inform Ana and she'll give you the green light to allocate any materials and personnel you may need. And if you need any input, don't hesitate to contact me."

" You better believe I'm going to be contacting you. With your unique insight to the ways of the universe, you can bet that I'm going to be picking your brain quite often. I'm going to take this baby slow and cautious."

" Fine by me. Set the pace at whatever you are comfortable with. With that out of the way, let's try and make your stay here enjoyable. Are you rested from your trip?"

" Yes, why?"

" I just didn't want any excuses after I've beaten you at billiards."

" As I recall, you are a very poor billiards player. Have you been practicing?"

" No."

" Then let's play. I'd like to do some gloating over dinner."

" We should be able to get in five to seven games in before then."

They just finish the seventh game when Ana informs them over the intercom that dinner is ready. Han places his cue in the rack and rubs his hands with glee. Knight shrugs his shoulders as he allows Han to celebrate winning five games to two.

" Sure, live it up. I know you've played the felt in every hall from Bangkok to Singapore."

" So I've been around. We all have our hobbies. Don't take it too hard, you won two games."

" Only because you scratched on the eight ball."

" So this isn't your game. We all have limitations."

" Maybe I should get some pointers from the children. They seem to shoot about as well as you do."

" Don't be such a sore loser. It will make your food taste funny. By the way, what's for dinner?"

" Shark!"

" Did you arrange the menu?"

" I only make suggestions."

" Yea, right. And I breath through my belly button."

" So that's how all that hot air escapes."

" Okay, okay. I promise not to brag over dinner if you keep that sharp tongue in check."

" Deal."

" Are we really having shark for dinner?"

" Among other things."

" Good. I'd hate to be an ungrateful guest, but I don't really care for sea food."

" I know."

" Wait a minute. Is the entire course sea food?"

" Now, would I do that to you?"

" Yes."

" Well, I didn't. There is also roast beef and chicken."

" Great. Sorry for accusing you."

" Don't be sorry. Ana wouldn't let me."

" And I'm scheduled to spend another day in your company?"

" Isn't it great?"

" I'll let you know."

The four sit at the table enjoying the feast and the conversation. Knight takes a sampling of everything while everyone else restricts their choices to fewer and smaller portions. A refreshing glass of cold milk compliments

Knight's dinner while the other three-drink wine. He turns toward Han as his friend talks.

" Bill couldn't join us?"

" I'm afraid not. His mother had a birthday yesterday and he's staying a few days."

" That's nice."

" Oh, Clay!" interrupts Suzie. " I wanted to say congratulations about the World Series and I'm sorry about the Super Bowl."

" Thank you. The trophy case is upstairs if you'd be interested in seeing it. While the trophies are nice, what makes it all worthwhile is the unrelenting joy expressed by the players after winning. The football team , on the other hand, took it pretty well and should rebound strong next year."

" I think I will look at that trophy case later. Do you know where it is, Han?"

" Yes, I'll show you after dinner."

Knight's baseball team won the World Series in the seventh game by beating the Yankees seven to five. The Earthquake fell short in the Super Bowl by losing to the Miami Dolphins seventeen to sixteen in one of the great defensive battles of all time. Both teams made Knight proud of their efforts and he rewarded the players with extra bonuses win or lose.

" That was a wonderful meal, Ana. Please give my compliments to the cook."

" I'll be sure to tell him."

" If you don't mind, I think I'll retire after Han shows me the trophies. The trip seems to have taken more out of me than I thought."

" No, go right ahead. Have a pleasant sleep."

" Are you feeling all right?" asks Knight.

" I'm fine. I haven't had much sleep lately. Everything will be fine once my head hits the pillow."

" Good night then."

Han escorts his wife out of the dining room as the servants remove their plates. Ana lays her head on Knight's shoulder as he looks at his watch. It reads 6:06.

" It's still early. I wonder if Han will be back."

" I don't know, Clay. Do you think anything is wrong with Suzie?"

" She seemed fine except for the obvious fatigue. Her sleeplessness would contribute to that. Maybe she has something on her mind."

" Like maybe she's pregnant?"

" I didn't say that."

" But she could be."

" Did she say something to you?"

" No."

" She could be a lot of things. Just don't go jumping to conclusions."

" Do you think Han would be a good father?"

" Sure but give it a rest, Honey. I didn't say that she was and I don't know if she is. But just to make you happy, I will secretly scan her tomorrow so you can have peace of mind."

" Thank you. I'm going to check on Lance. Want me to come back later?"

" Thanks, but I have some more reading to catch up on. Have any suggestions on a comfortable chair?"

" Sorry, you're on your own. I'll see you when you come to bed."

" Okay, but that might not be until late."

They kiss and Ana pushes her chair back and stands up. As she leaves the room Knight reaches for another piece of chicken and then pours himself another glass of milk. After satisfying his appetite he starts for his office to retrieve the desired material."

It is after midnight before Knight reaches the living room because he had become engrossed in the reports on the data bank sent by the infiltrators and he had lost track of time. The time was 11:40 before he glanced at the clock and he cursed himself for getting side tracked. Since it is late, he took the opportunity to change into his sleeping attire, which consists of a navy blue sweatshirt and gray sweat pants. He also wears a navy blue, knee length robe and leather slippers with camel hair interiors.

The report Rasov had sent is one hundred and forty-five pages long and mainly consists of the testimony collected over the past week from people acquainted with known cult members. He picks a chair near the fire place so that he will have extra lighting and so he can bask in it's warmth. An end table serves as a resting-place for his glass of apple cider as he props his feet upon a foot stool.

His eyelids grow heavy as he reads the report in such a comfortable environment. For a moment his eyes close and then are wide open as he shakes his head and then rubs his neck. After a sip of cider he feels ready to finish the reading. As he reads he fails to notice the person in the doorway.

The individual is dressed in black and is covered from head to toe. A silver wire is wrapped around the two hands with a razor-sharp strand extended between. Silently and slowly the assassin approaches Knight from behind. When the person is within a four feet the pace quickens as the urgency of the deadly task requires surprise.

As the wire comes down over his head toward his throat, Knight instinctively raises his hands up for protection. The papers scatter as the wire cuts both hands to the bone while the assassin tries to pull the instrument of death through his jugular. The pain causes Knight to scream out as he twists and falls over the side of the chair pulling his assailant with him.

When he hits the floor, he pushes the wire away from his face with his mangled hands and rolls over to bring himself to his knees. His hands are still tangled in the wire, which the assassin tries to regain control of. He winces as his hands are a bloody mess as he tries to free himself. The assassin kicks him in the ribs, but he ignores the blow as his right hand gets free. He brings his left hand closer with a powerful tug that pulls his attacker closer to him. Fully aware of Knight's skill as a fighter, the assassin releases the wire as the gloves slide off the hands. Quickly the assassin retreats backwards before Knight is able to inflict any harm.

Knight untangles his left hand as a continuous cascade of blood flows onto the floor. He staggers a couple of steps to the right because the sudden lose of blood makes him lose his balance. Fighting to regain composure, he notices the assassin retrieve two daggers from the belt around the waist. Again the assassin charges wielding a blade in each hand. Knight is able to deflect the first thrust with his right forearm, but the other blade penetrates deeply into his left shoulder.

He violently pulls away causing the assassin to release the grip on the dagger which remains buried in Knight's flesh. As the other blade tries to find it's mark, Knight kicks the assassin in the knife wielding right shoulder which knocks the attacker over backwards. Collapsing from the spent energy and loss of blood, Knight watches the killer scramble to retrieve the dagger that landed on the opposite side of the room. Just as the assassin recovers the weapon and starts back toward Knight Han appears in the doorway.

The assassin charges as Han quickly races across the room and dives at the attacker. His momentum carries both of them over the top of Knight and they land on the coffee table, which they transform, into kindling. The assassin rises first and still possesses the dagger, which is waved dangerously close to Han's face. With his right hand Han grabs the assassin by the knife hand wrist and tosses the assailant over his shoulder. He keeps a firm grip on the wrist and forces the dagger out of the resisting hand.

Knight crawls over to the assassin who lays stunned on the floor and removes the mask. To his surprise and Han's horror it is Suzie. Han recoils in disbelief as Knight pulls himself into a sitting position. As he slowly pulls the dagger out of his shoulder Ana appears and rushes to his side. She is also shocked to see Suzie all dressed in black on the floor less than a yard from Knight.

" Clay!" Ana shouts. " How bad are you hurt?"

" It's not fatal if I can stop the bleeding. Help me get to the lab."

He points to the daggers and wire which Ana pick up. She then helps support her husband as he staggers to his feet. He holds his bleeding hands close to his body and Ana puts her arms around his waist as he tries to walk. Before they exit he turns to Han.

" Han..Han!"

" What?" answers his dazed friend.

" Please keep an eye on her. We'll call security and they should be here soon."

They exit leaving a trail of blood. Han sits on the edge of the couch looking at his wife like she is a total stranger. She finally regains her senses and pulls herself into a sitting position.

" Why?" he shouts.

She smiles and slides closer to him.

" What's the matter lover? Is his loss going to bring sorrow into your heart?"

" He's not going to die. The wounds aren't fatal."

" Damn!..Well, it doesn't matter. Someone else will succeed where I have failed."

" Why? What did he do to you?"

" You have to ask? Are you blind, Fool? He must be stopped. Stopped and destroyed for what he did to the master."

" You use me to get to him!"

" Now you're catching on. But you have to admit the sex was great. You sure could fill me up."

" Shut up!"

" We could still have a life together. Help me escape before they get here and I promise you endless nights of ecstasy."

" Not after I've seen what you're capable of."

" What do you see in him? You idolize him, don't you? Too bad. You'll have to be destroyed along with him."

" You're crazy! You have to be sick in the head to actually think the way you do!"

" That might be, but I'm not going to let that bastard pick my brains and torture me into betraying my friends. It was nice while it lasted."

She pulls a chain from under her collar and bites down on the capsule encased in plastic at the end. The poison acts quickly and she falls backwards as foam and blood drips from the side of her mouth. Han falls to his knees and crawls over to her lifeless form. He places her head in his lap.

" You stupid bitch! Why?"

Tears roll down his cheeks as he lets her head hit against the floor. He stands and starts for the doorway only stop and return in anger to the motionless body. He vents his frustration by kicking the corpse in the side over and over.

As he turns to finally exit, he looks back for one final glimpse of his former wife. Five security guards rush into the room just as he reaches the hall.

" She's dead. Ingested some sort of poison. Have someone clean up in here while I go check on Clay."

He approaches the elevator completely drained of all emotion. A numbness dominates his body and mind as he slowly steps on to the platform. Although he can see his hand press the button for the proper floor, he feels nothing as he staggers backwards only to be stopped by the rear wall of the compartment. At the moment he thinks he is lost inside his physical shell and struggles to gain control. The doors open and he stumbles into the corridor. An android standing there prevents him from falling. Patting the android on the back, he rights himself and walks over to the table Knight is laid out on.

A tube runs from his right forearm to a machine that holds two liters of blood, which had been cloned, from a sample given by Knight in the past. It slowly pumps the blood into his body until sensors indicate his body is back to normal levels.

Another tube carried oxygen that is released through the small plugs in each nostril. With the input of fresh blood and oxygen, Knight can feel his strength starting to return. Although his wounds are very sore, they are no longer bleeding as he examines the bandaged areas.

A team of androids had stopped the bleeding and closed the wounds with lasers. They had swabbed out the damaged areas with antiseptic and proceeded to reconstruct the separated muscle, nerves and flesh with microsurgery. The wounds were again washed with antiseptic and bandaged to protect the tender areas. The whole procedure only took a matter of minutes.

As Han approaches knight turns his head and Ana looks up from the stool she is sitting on while caressing Knight's hair.

" Did the security arrive? " asks Knight wearily.

" They did, but it didn't matter. She is dead."

" How? What happened?"

" She had a poison capsule and took it. Killed her almost instantly."

" We're sorry, Han" responds Ana.

" Thank you but I was only a used as a pawn by her until she had the opportunity to get at Clay. I'm sorry I didn't sense something. At some point during our months together one would think that I would have picked up on something. I guess I never actually knew who that person was."

" Who could have known?" offers Knight. " While it may be safer to be paranoid about letting people into our lives, that isn't a healthy outlook. I guess I shouldn't be too surprised with the extent that I have infiltrated other organizations, others could be expected to do the same to ours. But I am both angry and regretful that they were able to hit so close to our hearts."

" I'll get over it. I'm just happy you survived."

" So am I. And I'm grateful that they did not have the foresight to coat the weapons with poison. Otherwise, I would be a goner for certain."

" She threatened that there would be other attacks. And she indicated that they would come after me now."

" We'll just have to increase security. Damn! I thought I was always safe in my own house. Ana and I decided that internal security within the living area wasn't warranted and Ana wanted a degree of privacy. Now, I don't know. That bastard Ruthvan must be laughing at us as he looks up from Hell."

" And now she's laughing there with him It was lucky I came along when I did."

" Did you notice she wasn't in bed?"

" For all I knew she was asleep. After she went to bed I came down here to the lab to look over equipment and some data. Luckily I got hungry and went up to raid the kitchen when I heard you scream."

" Did I scream?"

" Yes and I had to look in a few rooms before I found where you were."

" I'm glad you did because I could not have fought for much longer. I'm also glad I put up my hands when I saw that cable or it would have sliced through my neck like a hot poker through virgin snow."

" If you two don't mind, I'm going to retire. I'm also going to sleep in a different room."

" That's fine and we understand."

" Do you want me to help you make it up?" asks Ana.

" No, I'll be able to handle it myself. Thanks anyway."

" Good night, my friend. I'll see you in the morning."

" Good night, Clay. Ana."

" Good night, Han."

They watch him enter the elevator and the door closes. Knight closes his eyes while Ana leans over and kisses his cheek as a tear drops on his forehead. He opens his eyes and manages a smile.

" Do you weep for me or Han?"

" Both of you."

" I'm going to remain here for a couple more hours. Are you going to remain?"

" Of course."

" Good. Tell me, did you hear me scream too?"

" I don't know. I might have because something startled me out of my sleep. When I saw you were not in bed yet, I went to check on you. And then to see you like that.."

" I'll be fine, don't worry. I'm afraid I'll probably come out of this better than Han."

" Yes, I think you may be correct. Although he was never one to show his emotions, he is visibly shaken and understandably so."

" And physical scars heal a lot more quickly than emotional ones. If he is willing, I'm going to ask if he wants to stay the week."

She nods and leans over to kiss him on the forehead. He closes his eyes and is lulled to sleep by the hum of the electronic equipment near him. Ana remains sitting next to him, holding his bandaged right hand while wiping away the occasional tear.

Knight stands outside the door to Han's room collecting his thoughts before he knocks. His shoulder and hands are still bandaged and stiff with soreness. With the back of his right hand he raps on the door. A moment later he hears Han calling for him to enter.

Han is seated at the desk near the window and has several papers scattered on the surface before him. Knight sits on the edge of the bed.

" You didn't come down for breakfast."

" I'm not hungry."

" It's not healthy to stop eating even if you are in mourning."

" I'm not in mourning."

" You're not?"

" I don't know! How am I supposed to handle this thing? I was married to her. I loved her. I can't deny that. But what she did... what she did...I thought I knew her and it turns out I didn't. Almost a year of my life wasted so I could be a pawn. I tell you, Clay, I'm hurting. My hear and brain are sending mixed messages and at the moment I have no idea which way is up. Man, if she had actually killed you..."

" But she didn't."

" I know. Yet I would never forgive myself if she had."

" I'm fine. Just a few more scars for humility. But this was not something that could have been foreseen. You know I am about as paranoid as they come when it comes to taking precautions for protecting my family, friends, and myself. And believe me, I did a background check on her and she came up clean.

" These are people who operate in the shadows away from prying eyes and reveal themselves only when it suits their purpose. This is twice in recent months that they have gotten much too close to me for comfort. I increase the security and still they find a way to reach me. The moment I let my guard down and think I'm safe they attack. You may have been a pawn, but I'm the one they're trying to checkmate out of existence."

" Yet they wouldn't have had the opportunity if I hadn't brought her into your home."

" Han, we're going in circles here. She was your wife. Of course I welcomed both of you here with open arms. You made the choice to settle down and get married and she seemed to be perfect. Unfortunately, we were unable to see beneath the surface. We'll get through this together, but only if you stop beating yourself."

" I'll get over her, but I never will let anyone get that close to me again."

" You don't know that."

" Yes, I do. Never again will I open myself up and expose myself to another person only to be betrayed."

" That's not a healthy attitude."

" It's a damn sight safer."

" So is locking yourself away and becoming a recluse. Don't turn bitter by closing your heart or I will feel guilty for as long as you stay like that."

" Why would you feel guilt?"

" Because...Because I reassured you to go through with the marriage when you were having doubts."

" That doesn't apply here."

" Doesn't apply? If I hadn't talked you into a warm glow to thaw those cold feet, you never would have taken the vows of matrimony."

" Maybe. You were just trying to be a good friend."

" And that's what I'm trying right now. Please don't close yourself off from future opportunities. If you do that, then those devil worshipping bastards will have claimed a victory of the grandest magnitude."

" We'll see."

" Okay, just give it time. Eventually things will right themselves and you can reenter to flow of things. Give it time and you will get over it. Go ahead and keep your guard up, for we all will have to do that. only don't put up any barriers that will be impossible to get down."

Han shrugs his shoulders and then draws a deep breath. Knight rises and pats Han on the shoulder before leaving the room. As he closes the door behind himself Knight wonders if his words penetrated the layer of confusion Han is cloaked under. It pains him that his friend suddenly has so much turmoil in his life. This gives him more motivation to deal with those who created the situation.

Chapter twenty-three

In order to deal with a problem that had long been a source of international misery Knight set out on finding a solution. The problem was drugs and even though Knight had already taken measures on this issue, he feels it is time to escalate the effort. A major factor in his new assault is a fleet of satellites he launches to monitor the flow of air and sea travel.

Any air or sea vessel that is not authorized to be where they are would be searched. Efforts are also increased to scan the cargo of all planes, trains, sea vessels, and buses for traces of chemicals associated with drugs. All packages to be delivered by courier agencies would also be scanned.

Law authorities began driving through neighborhoods scanning for illegal chemicals. While they occasionally find a place where the drugs are being processed, most of the arrests involve people buying and selling drugs. Planes equipped with the scanners search even rural areas.

By the first week of April, 2050, the flow of drugs is drastically decreased while Knight and GLESA receive most of the credit. When it is a big raid, Knight often participated to capitalize on the positive press.

It becomes obvious that there is a direct correlation between the drugs and the terrorist activity. As the drug flow decreased the terrorist activity also decreased. Knight had surmised that drugs were a major source of the terrorist financing and is relieved to be proven correct. As long as he kept up the pressure, the terrorists would be forced to minimize their activity. Although such an effort called for the utilization of several personnel and finances that might have been devoted to other activities, Knight knows the efforts are worth it. At some point he feels the terrorists will strike out in desperation and such an attack will likely be directed at him.

As each day passes the probability that the terrorists will strike at him increases. Security is increased to the maximum level and all agents are on alert. The waiting creates great tension, which Knight attempts to lessen by playing soothing music over the intercoms at both GLESA and Knight Enterprises.

With the defenses primed for a major assault, Knight begins to hone his strategy. He would basically be aware of their approach long before they arrive because he has sentries monitoring all directions. Even if they are intent on guerrilla tactics, he is confident they will be dealt with because of the precautions taken far beyond the perimeters of each building. Androids walk the streets in civilian clothing while scanning for weapons and explosives on the people and vehicles. Several agents are also on the rooftops with rocket launchers in case there is an air assault. Since he would be aware of their approach, he decided he would allow them to advance so that his forces could surround and slaughter them.

A large crate sits in the corner of Maria Ortiz's quarters. The lid is off and the contents are revealed to be thousands of concentrated drug tablets. With the crate filled to the top edge, Miss Ortiz kneels and runs her fingers through the tablets. She laughs and picks up a handful and lets the drugs fall between her fingers. A young black man stands twelve feet away watching the scene nervously.

" Do you know what these are, Eddie"

" Yes, Ma'am."

" There are millions of dollars worth here and I can't do a damn thing with them. We were lucky to get these out before the plant was raided. But here it is and no where to go. Because of that bastard Knight I can't transport these to get in the market.

" I had counted on him being out of the picture by now, only I am surrounded by inept fools who are unable to accomplish the tasks I assign them. Well, it's time to eliminate him once and for all so we can open the market up again. Take whoever you need and bring his precious building down around his ears. And I want his head. Bring me that souvenir and I will shower you with riches."

" It will be done."

" Then go. Bring me his head so I can mount it above my fireplace. It is supposed to be there already and I am annoyed by the vacant space. Go!"

The man scurries from the room as she continues to finger the tablets. Her laughter fills the room and filters into the outside cavern. Madness dances in her eyes like the flames in the fireplace. Driven by obsession, she is determined to see either Knight or his wife dead within the next twenty-four hours.

Knight had arrived at GLESA headquarters before dawn to meet with his department leaders about their responsibilities when under siege. The meeting, which lasted an hour, was concluded with Knight giving a motivational speech. When everyone had exited the conference room, he laid his head on the table to rest his eyes because he knows it will be another long day.

He had persuaded Ana to conduct her business this week from the security of their home. Since she is still only putting in half days, the journey to and from work would be increasingly perilous as long as the danger remained. She also agreed because it would allow her to spend more time with her new child.

At a quarter after ten a buzzer alerts Knight that someone was approaching the outer perimeter. After checking the computer he learns that a van with armed men passed one of the surveillance teams ten miles from headquarters. Within the next five minutes another twelve vehicles had passed the preliminary surveillance line. They all stopped and gathered at three locations within a block of Knight's position. The total count is one hundred and twenty-eight terrorists. By some standards that would be a large force, but Knight is prepared for a much larger invasion. He also keeps in mind that this may only be the first wave.

The terrorists remain at their three gathering points while Knight receives word that there is indeed another wave of vehicles approaching. Yet this group of eight vehicles stop at four locations one to three blocks from Knight Enterprises. The count is fifty-seven terrorists that would be attacking the corporate building. Each group has gathered in parking garages or parking lots where they can mingle without being too obvious.

At 10:30 each group starts to advance and Knight signals his snipers and other agents to pick their targets. When they are in sight of the building Knight gives the order for the snipers to open fire as he activates the security system manually which fires lasers and unleashes a bombardment of sonic blasts. As the terrorists realize they had walked into an ambush they attempt to retreat only to be confronted by GLESA agents approaching from the flank. In the crossfire the entire hostile force is either killed or seriously wounded. After the last shot is fired the agents quickly step among the fallen terrorists to secure the few that still lived. Of the total invasion force of one hundred and eight-five, only fourteen are still alive.

Knight starts to breath a sigh of relief when the radar picks up five approaching air craft that are not in authorized flight patterns. Three are on course for GLESA headquarters while the other two are headed for Knight Enterprises. He alerts the agents on the rooftops to be ready and orders ten agents to take to the air in their combat vehicles. Just as the ten approach the altitude of the attack planes radar picks up another twelve planes using unauthorized air space.

Knight orders the ten airborne agents to intercepts the planes on the outer perimeter while leaving the others to the agents on the rooftops. The two heading for Knight Enterprises reach their target first and fire missiles. Each missile is harmlessly detonated by the building's security lasers long before they reach the target. As the terrorist planes circle to make another pass the GLESA agents let loose with a volley of small missiles and lasers of their own. Both planes explode and small debris showers the rooftops and the streets below.

Knight orders the agents near GLESA headquarters to fire on the incoming planes before they unleash their missiles. Moments later he hears three loud explosions and goes to the window to observe the shower of terrorist particles. Although the explosives the missiles used by the GLESA agents were extremely volatile and were effective in breaking what they came in contact with into small fragments, the building security lasers blast the fragments into even smaller pieces before they hit the ground.

Looking at the street below he sees several bodies sprawled on the concrete. As soon as the metallic shower ends officials from the coroners office come out from under cover and continue to collect the dead. Knight is happy that the general population of the city had the good sense to stay out of the way although he is certain there would be a few civilian casualties. The result would be lawsuits from the families, but he will gladly pay out of court and consider it a necessary expense for dealing with the terrorists.

His airborne squadron quickly dispatched of the other twelve terrorist planes outside the city limits and are returning when their scanners pick up two vehicles on the interstate that are full of explosives. Knight surmises that this is the last desperate attempt at striking at him. The drivers of the vehicles are more than likely on kame-kazi missions and have little regard for their own lives which is typical of a cult member. Rather than allow them to enter the city Knight orders the agents to destroy them right there on the interstate. The resulting explosions damage a large portion of the driving surface, but that will be much easier to repair than buildings.

To play it safe Knight instructs the agents to remain airborne for two more hours while they scan the routes of travel surrounding the city. When they finally return everything in the city has been cleaned up with the exception of minor repairs needed by some buildings and vehicles, which Knight would gladly pick up the expense for. All agents remain on alert for the rest of the day just in case they plan a final assault in hopes of catching them off their guard. Fortunately that final assault never comes which indicates to Knight that the terrorists had nearly exhausted their resources.

The final tally of the dead is one hundred and ninety-six terrorists and two civilians. Of the eight terrorists that initially survived five died before they could receive medical attention. The other three were interrogated and then executed. Nothing was learned from the three because they were only hired labor for the cult. Seven civilians were wounded during the assault and Knight assured them he would pay for their medical care. Five GLESA agents had sustained injuries during the attack, but nothing was serious.

It did turn out to be a major assault and Knight is thankful that their leadership was not more organized. Although they really had no chance against the resources Knight had available. they could have been more challenging if they had used everything in one massive maneuver. Yet Knight is happy they did not because civilian casualties would have been much higher and there would have been more extensive property damage. He is just happy it is over so he can begin planning his next move.

Chapter twenty-four

On April 15 Knight receives an extremely lucky break. Due to the waning membership the cult has been trying to recruit new people and one of those invited into the fold was an infiltrator. For hours at a time Knight remains by the monitor reading the information the infiltrator is sending. His heart races with each moment his secret agent is in the company of the cult members gaining their trust.

On the seventeenth the infiltrator is ordered to kill a member who had betrayed his brethren. Since the man was of the criminal element, it is within the infiltrator's programming to carry out the task. Once the deed is done, all the cult members warm up to the new member and invite him to take a trip to the international sanctuary of the order. Knight is beside himself while enjoying his good fortune.

None of the three terrorists he took brain readings from had ever been there. Two had heard of the place but did not know the location. All had been content to participate in the activities of their local chapters and never had ambitions of moving up in the cult's hierarchy. When the call came for each of them to participate in the attack on Knight, each was honored and agreed to follow blindly like the worker drones they were. All had been flunkies of the organization and each was proud of their respective positions.

In the early morning hours of April 19, the infiltrator traveled through the forests of Peru until they reached the Andes Mountains. After navigating the rocky terrain they reached their destination at four after nine. Immediately Knight summons all his agents to begin their journey to the location of the infiltrator.

Keeping with an earlier promise, Knight contacts the President who in turn alerts the other world leaders. An elite force of twenty members from varied branches of service represent the United States. England, France, Israel, and the Ukraine also send forces ranging from fifteen to thirty members. With the two hundred agents Knight has nearing the scene, the total would be three hundred and five of the world's best which he would lead against the forces of hell.

Everyone is present outside the fortress by six-thirty that evening. They determine that the fortress has four entrances including the balcony high above the surface. To make things simple he breaks the force into three groups of one hundred that would strike at the three lower entrances while five android GLESA agents and Knight would gain access to the balcony using jetpacks. The assault is to begin at seven sharp.

Since he has been granted complete control, he delegated that authority to his three-team members Rasov, Jackson, and Buck who would lead each of the three groups. Rasov is to lead the group of the thirty Ukraines and seventy GLESA agents against the north entrance. Jackson has a group of twenty Israelis, twenty French, and sixty GLESA agents, which he is to lead through a pass that approaches the west entrance. Buck has the twenty American soldiers, along with the fifteen British, and sixty-five GLESA agents, which are to attempt to access the south entrance. Another factor in their favor is that the infiltrator is inside and would start killing cult members when it is aware the attack is in progress.

The top of the hour arrives and everyone approach their assigned targets. The five androids float up the side of the mountain and set down on the balcony. Rasov signals him that his force blew the door off the hinges but they encountered a defense system of lasers and force fields. Buck reports the same while Jackson informs him that his force is pinned down by snipers with conventional weapons and lasers hidden above the pass. Knight hears an explosion and a beep signals him the androids had gained access to the balcony entrance. As Knight prepares to rise to the balcony, Jackson reports that the snipers have been eliminated but they have encountered the same security system.

Knight knows that the system more than likely was the design of his old foe Ruthvan and the three groups would have difficulty getting past the entrances. That means he will have to disable the system so the operation can run as smoothly as intended. That leaves the problem of finding the control room. he hopes that the infiltrator or one of the androids finds it before he does.

In an instant he is on the balcony where only one android remains because the others had gone into the fortress. He discards his jetpack and asks the android to make contact with the infiltrator. After doing so the android makes a sketch of the interior with the quickest path from the balcony to the control room. Then Knight thinks it would be easier to have the infiltrator disable the system and asks the android to make contact again. After repeated attempts the android is unable to make contact and Knight is both worried and confused.

He and the android enter the corridor and he signals his agent to approach the bend in the corridor and report if anyone is in sight. Knight tries to use his scanners but they seem to be malfunctioning as is his communicator. As he starts to examine the surface of the walls the android turns to approach him. Before the android can complete it's first step an intense energy blast comes from around the bend and it envelopes the android. In a steaming heap the remains of the android fall as Knight braces himself against the wall.

He quickly glances at the sketch the android made and starts running down the opposite corridor. He turns a corner with his weapons now in both hands. No one is in sight and he stops to listen. It doesn't sound as if he is being followed and he starts running again. The pounding of his heart fills his ears as he realizes he is all alone in the realm of the unknown.

What was that which destroyed the android? The energy level had to be extremely high to melt one of his androids like that. It also seemed to be very well concentrated because it seemed to have centered on the android and never touched any of the other walls. All he knows at the present is that he has no way to defend against such a weapon and it is best that he stays out of it's line of fire for he is certain his force field could not hold off such a blast more than once.

He stops and looks at the sketch again. The control room should be around the next corner, down the corridor, and to the left. After examining the sketch closer he notices that the desired destination is a section of the corridor he just ran from to avoid. It is obvious that he needs reinforcements to deal with this high powered force so his only choice is to approach the corridor and hope he doesn't encounter the weapon.

After turning the corner he stops because four men in robes confront him. For a moment he considers running but notices they only have conventional weapons. He runs up and gets airborne so he can kick the two closest one in the head with the heels of his boots. They fire but he feels nothing. Before he hits the ground he returns the fire on the other two and tears them apart with the assault of gunfire. He stops and listens while straining to see the end of the passageway. No one is coming so he advances cautiously.

He reaches the end of the passageway and stops before he turns the corner. His back is against the wall and he can see part way down the corridor in the opposite direction he needs to go. Holding his weapons against his chest he slowly slides along the wall toward the corner. Upon hearing the sound of several boots making contact with the stone floor he stops and takes a deep breath. After looking down the passageway from which he came he sees no one trying to out flank him. As the footfalls get closer he considers retreating only to dismiss the thought by jumping into the center of the corridor and lets loose an intense volley of gunfire. There had been fourteen, only now there are none to oppose him because his barrage had ripped through them like rain through the air.

As he steps over their lifeless forms he notices that they represent several different nationalities and one was a woman. All had been armed, but none of the weaponry seemed unusual. Once he has stepped clear of the bodies he checks the sketch again. The control room is supposed to be in this corridor somewhere ahead. Slowly he walks down the corridor as he looks ahead and behind. Somewhere in this corridor the person with the devastating weapon had been and he hopes they are not in the control room. After several minutes he finally reaches the doorway which leads to the equipment he wishes to destroy.

The door is partially open and he takes a quick look through the crack before bracing against the wall. There are three men near the control panels and two more standing near them with weapons. There may be others out of his line of vision so he will have to act fast to determine the positions of the others and be ready to retreat if necessary. He kicks the door wide open and starts firing before it even hits the wall. Immediately he takes out the two-armed men before him and then blasts the three sitting personnel out of their seats. Out of the corner of his right eye he notices someone standing along the far wall and he fires as that person also raises their weapon. Ducking into the hallway he notices the person had only fired bullets and he returns to the control room to find his shots had found their mark because the man sits with his back to the wall with the top part of his skull missing.

He takes a moment to look into the corridor and once he realizes no one is approaching he turns his attention to the security system controls. After he sets his laser, he quickly cuts the machinery into an inoperable mess of metal, wires, and circuit boards. With the system disabled he knows the three bands would soon be within the mountain. He knows they will fare much better against the human resistance.

yet there still remained that very powerful weapon. It disturbs him that somewhere in these winding corridors is someone with a very sophisticated tool of destruction. With any luck he might be able to get the jump on them before they see him.

He starts into the hallway and sees several men running toward him from both directions. With a weapon in each hand he repeatedly fires in the opposite directions cutting down the attackers as if they were wheat being felled by a sickle. They had obviously come to investigate why the security system had failed and he sent them to the next world with the answer.

The majority of the remaining cult members would be more than likely be offering resistance to his forces, so he knows he will encounter very few people. Yet he proceeds with caution for there is still a very dangerous enemy somewhere in the mountain.

He reaches a three-way intersection that allows him to remain on the level he is on or to go up or down by taking one of two ramps. He chooses to descend to the next level by taking the ramp strait ahead. Upon reaching that level he is faced with the same choice and he decides to investigate the present level. By estimating the height of the mountain and taking into account the height of the ceilings of the two levels he has been on, Knight figures there are possibly five hundred separate levels within the mountain. With the caution that is warranted he knows it will take considerable time to search all the passageways.

Upon finding the level he is on deserted, he decides to proceed upwards. He returns to the previous level and then takes the ramp up to the next one. There is not another ramp leading upward so he revises his estimate to a possible three hundred levels inside the mountain. He walks down the passageway and enters an enormous cavern.

Looking at the top of the cavern he notices a panel that can be lowered to allow sunlight or moonlight to enter. On the opposite end of the cavern he sees the alter with something on it, but he chooses to explore the immediate area before investigating that side of the cavern. He comes across a hand panel, which he presses, and a rockslides to the side to reveal an elevator. He glances inside the compartment and sees it has only one button that indicates that it is most likely a link between the ground floor and the ceremonial chamber.

He closes the elevator and proceeds toward the alter. Before he is half way there a door opens behind the alter and out steps Maria Ortiz. Knight holds his fire because he is stunned to see a familiar face at the present time. She is dressed in her robes of the high priestess. A smile comes to her lips as she notices the expression on his face.

" Welcome, Mr. Knight. I'm glad you could take the opportunity to join us."

He steps closer.

" It took a while to find you or I would have crashed your party long before."

" Yes, I'm sure you would have. Very clever of you to allow your friend here to gain access to my fortress."

Upon closer examination Knight sees that the disfigured pile on the alter had once been his infiltrator.

" Did you do this?"

" I'm sorry did I break your toy? It doesn't matter because it served it's purpose. Didn't it?"

" Yes."

" As long as you're here, there's someone who wants to meet you."

She turns away for a moment as Knight raises his weapons. When she turns to face him her features have changed into something rather demonic. A booming voice has replaced her female tones.

" It's been a long time Knight!"

" Ruthvan?"

A chill goes through Knight as he takes two steps backward. The demon smiles and pushes the remains of the infiltrator off the alter.

" You were always a smart one, Knight. You have so much going for you. I know young Maria did her best to try and take some of that away from you. Yet where she failed I shall succeed for I would like nothing better than to watch your face as I tear that blessed heart of yours from that massive chest. Unless...Unless you would be willing to join forces with me and my kind."

" Join forces with you? Never!"

" It's just as well. We wouldn't want a hypocrite in our midst anyhow. I knew you wouldn't deprive me of the pleasure of killing you."

The demon laughs as he looks upon the weapons Knight is holding.

" You wouldn't shoot a woman, would you Knight?"

" You're no woman."

" Then what do you call these?"

The demon tears the cloth covering the torso revealing an ample pair of female breasts. Allowing the cloth to rest against the side of each breast the demon takes one in each hand and gently shakes them. An evil laugh fills the cavern as the disfigured hands position the torn cloth to cover up the exposed area.

" Your host gave up her identity the moment she freely allowed you access to her body. As far as I'm concerned, she no longer existed."

" You know, I'm really going to enjoy killing you."

Knight fires as the demon floats up over the alter and sets down in front of him. The bullets seem to have no effect as the demon continues to advance. While he retreats to the center of the cavern, Knight places the weapons in their holders and sets his laser. Again and again he attempts to stop his foe by making several deadly cuts but the body of the demon appears unscathed. Wither the demon protects his host from all harm or he is creating the illusion that the body is not affected by the wrath Knight is attempting to unleash.

Once again the demon is airborne and Knight wildly waves the laser with a deadly arc which does not affect the evil being but it does cut through some rock of the cavern ceiling. Several large portions of stone fall crashing to the floor and catch Knight's attacker in the shower. A large pile of rock sits across from Knight and he takes the few moments to rest. Then the rocks start to fall away and the demonic presence of Sebastian Ruthvan emerges from the rubble.

" You are really beginning to annoy me, Knight!"

With minimal effort Ruthvan lifts a large boulder and hurls it at Knight. As Knight has his attention on the on coming stone which he side steps, the demon charges and lunges at Knight. Catching Knight around the waist, both tumble backwards as Knight loses his balance.

The demon loses his grasp and Knight rolls free and rises to his feet immediately. Ruthvan is quickly upon him throwing blows which Knight skillfully block. When a blow finally does connect Knight is unfazed and the demon steps back.

" That is very unfair of you, Knight. Hiding under the protection of that force field you must feel pretty smug. I think it's time I relieved you of your security blanket."

Raising his hands above his head, Ruthvan creates a little ball of fire, which he balances between the heels of each hand. Realizing that this is the tremendous weapon he had been trying to avoid Knight attempts to retreat. After taking a few steps Knight notices the fire glow much brighter and then shoot from Ruthvan's hands. He attempts to dive out of it's path, but it alters course and envelopes him. After a moment it fades away and Knight notices that his force field is no longer operational.

" I should finish you off this instant, But I think I will give you the beating of your life before I do. No matter what you say, it is the body of a little girl that will be the instrument of your destruction."

The demon laughs and then charges. Rather than retreat Knight stands his ground as the fires of battle begin to boil his blood. Ruthvan throws a disfigured hand at hand at Knight, which he catches as he swings the demon over his shoulder onto the stone floor. The clawed hand pulls free from Knight, scratching his palm as it does. Knight winces as he steps back to prepare for the next attack.

They circle each other and Knight decides to go on the offensive. He steps in close and delivers a kick to the ribs with his right instep. Then he knocks the demon off balance with a kick to the sternum with his left heel. While the demon is reeling he charges and catches his enemy with the side of his right foot with a blow that would have broken a human foe's neck.

Seeing his efforts as futile Knight steps back to reconsider his strategy. He watches as the demon floats up and hovers over him. A horrendous scream emanates from the being as Knight covers his ears.

" I'm tires of your games. Your time has come, Knight!"

Quickly the demon drops on Knight and is scratching with it's claws and trying to bite Knight's throat with dripping fanged teeth. Fighting with a desperate urgency Knight repeatedly punches at the beast, which grows more, disfigured by the moment. A fang pierces his neck as Knight lodges two fingers into the demon's eyes and pushes the head to an arm's length away. The claws continue to tear the cloth of his uniform and rip into his flesh. With a new energy drawn from the pain, Knight pushes the demon to his left as he rolls to the right. He rises to his feet and discards the tattered fabric of the uniform that leaves him bare from the waist up. Blood rolls from his neck, chest, and abdomen as numerous fang and claw wounds cover his upper body. Some of the gashes are deep and he knows he will need medical attention if he happens to survive the present encounter.

Slowly the demon rises to his feet. The longer it remains in the host body the more it metamorphosed. It discards all the clothing and there are no signs of whether it is a male of female. Again the demon lets loose an ear-shattering scream. Then it laughs. Then it laughs and points at Knight.

" It would seem," states the demon as it notices the scars on Knight's torso, " this is not the first battle you have been in. Let me remind you of past anguish before I hand you the ultimate defeat."

As the demon raises his hand Knight notices the pain return to his palms and shoulder from the recent assassination attempt. Then his burns begin to throb and sear with pain. Finally the scars from the failed attempt on his life from years earlier begin to bleed. He falls to his knees and then over onto his left side. He moans as a pool of blood forms beneath him.

" If only I could make that pain eternal! But I can not. As much as I enjoy watching you in pain, I believe this is a good time to end your life."

A new fireball is formed and starts to grow bright. Just as it leaves the demon's hands it toward Knight it is extinguished. Knight is barely conscious but can see that the demon is as confused as Knight as to what happened. Then a voice bellows through the cavern.

" Enough!"

" Who dares to interrupt my execution?"

The demon stomps around in anger then looks up to see a portion of the top of the cavern disappear to reveal the evening sky with the moon and stars. Down through the opening a being that has the appearance of a human floats. The gender appears to be male and he is dressed completely in white with a shirt jacket, pants and shoes. Again the being speaks.

" It is not his time. His work here on this world is not finished. You have no claim on him."

" I have every right to claim him. Out of my way!"

" You have over stayed your visit demon. Be gone!"

As the being waves his hand the demon disappears in a cloud of smoke. When the smoke clears the mangled remains of Maria Ortiz lay in a pile. Shaking his head the being raises his hand again and the body disappears.

Then the being turns it's attention to the gravely wounded Knight. He walks over and kneels next to the fallen warrior. Placing both hands on Knight's shoulders a golden glow is produced which blankets the entire body of the large man. Knight fades in and out of consciousness before he starts to feel his strength returning. As their eyes meet, the being gives Knight a reassuring smile. After a few minutes the being steps back as Knight sits up.

Upon self-examination Knight is totally amazed at what he sees. All of his wounds had not only stopped bleeding, but had completely healed and there is no sign they had ever been present. Even the flesh that had been previously scarred is now clear. He looks up at the smiling being.

" Are you...are you, God?"

" No, Clayton, I am not God. You might classify me as your guardian angel."

" Then why did you wait so long to interfere?"

" Unfortunately I am restricted to only step in when it is absolutely certain that life is about to be lost. Everything that happens to you before that point is of your own doing. Lucky for you, your services here on Earth are still demanded. However, when your time does come, it will be my honor to accompany you to the great beyond."

" Why did you heal my old scars?"

" You kept them as a physical reminder of your mortality. Due to your struggle here today, that mortality was challenged in the strictest sense. By all rights you should have died here today, but since Ruthvan left his domain for a purpose not allowed by the powers that be, his efforts have been nullified. So now you have a second chance at life and the slate is wiped clean, in a figurative and literal sense."

" So I take it those like Ruthvan are not allowed to return for the purposes of revenge."

" Correct."

" But do they ever succeed?"

" Every once in a long while. Something goes wrong and an guardian is unable to step in before they are killed. Once they actually fall into death we are forbidden to revive them."

" That doesn't seem right."

" No it's not. But it involves a pact made eons ago between the powers that be. If evil is ever able to gain a triumph, then that victory shall stand. We work very hard to make sure those are few and very far between. But believe it or not, even an immortal has an off day."

" Then I am very grateful that you were at your peak today. Thank you. Thank you very much."

" There is no need to thank me. Just continue in your pursuit to help your fellow man."

" I will. Only..."

" Yes?"

" Will I have to change my ways and possibly pursue a more peaceful approach to life?"

" That is a choice you will have to make on your own. It is likely the circumstances of the day will dictate what actions you should take."

" I thank you again. And please don't take this the wrong way, but I hope I don't see you again anytime soon."

" I understand. Now you take care of yourself, Clayton Knight, for I am also none too anxious for our next encounter."

They shake hands and Knight rises to his feet. The angel floats upward and disappears into the darkness above the cavern. He takes a moment to collect himself before he walks over to the elevator. After he steps into the elevator he presses the button and notices that the platform is descending rapidly. As it nears the bottom the pace lessens and it sets gently down on the ground.

As the doors open Knight sees Rasov and Buck. When he steps off the elevator they notice him and rush over to greet their friend. They are also obviously perplexed as to why he is bare-chested.

" Did you lose something, Clay?" asks Rasov.

" Maybe there was a wild orgy up there," inserts Buck.

" It's a long story and I'll save it for another day. So you're mopping up. Any idea on the total number of casualties? And were you able to capture any of them alive?"

Buck shrugs and Rasov steps forward to bring Knight up to date.

" Our forces lost a total of eleven: two GLESA agents, three Russians, three Americans, and three Israelis. We also sustained about thirty-five wounded. As for the opposition, the count so far is five hundred and forty-six dead and we have been successful in capturing nine alive."

" Only nine?"

" You know they prefer death to capture," answers Buck.

" They must realize they would be eventually executed so rather than submit to interrogation they kill themselves or allow themselves to be killed. The fanatic is always hard to deal with. Buck, why don't you go square away everything with the forces that helped us.

" Sure thing."

After he leaves Rasov leans closer to Knight.

" What happened up there?"

" I'll tell you later."

" And what happened to your scars?"

" I'll can't wait to hear this one."

A sunrise greets Knight and his men as they finally begin to evacuate the mountain. Hours had been spent searching the many levels of the fortress for terrorists and informational materials. With the documents that were found, Knight would be able to implement a hunt for cult members worldwide. He knows they will not get all of them. but he will be content to reduce their numbers to a very small percentage. With the majority of the membership eliminated, the remaining few would hopefully fade from existence. Knight only hopes they will not regroup and start over, growing in the darkness.

Chapter twenty-five

Knight sits behind the desk at his home office while he struggles with a personal morals issue. Although he basically decided to continue living his life the way he had been, he is hesitant to act on some of the thoughts he once had. To fulfill his obligation regarding the terrorist issue he already has infiltrators acting on his command to exterminate all known cult members. However, he had once intended to use the extermination process to eliminate another faction of evil as well.

Originally he had planned to order the assassinations of all the crime leaders of the world. His infiltrators are in positions that would make this possible within a short span of time. To justify his actions he would claim that the crime leaders were in league with the terrorists. While it is true that some actually were and would be dealt with, Knight had intended to eliminate all the crime lords along with those closest to them in the hierarchy. Worldwide that would involve the elimination of over three hundred and eight thousand individuals.

Such an action would put the crime world in chaos and the recovery time would likely be extremely long. He could monitor the progress that they make in filling the power vacuum and that way keep them in check. Yet he is already capable of doing that without eliminating their hierarchy. It seems that his actions may not be necessary due to his current capability of watching over them.

What right does he have to eliminate them? Just because he is capable of doing it doesn't mean that it should be done. What would the result of the chaos be? There is the possibility his upsetting the balance of power may entice small time criminals with ambitions of greatness to resort to drastic measures to claim territories of their own. It may create a situation like Chicago in the early twentieth century but on a worldwide scale. That would mean that in order for him to deal with the chaos he would have to eliminate those trying to rise to power. That means he would have to order more killings. At some point the troublemakers would all be eliminated. But what will the next generation bring? Will the cycle of killing have to start again? When would the killing stop? Or did it have to begin?

Another consideration is the state of the world on a whole. There is the possibility such chaos would transform the planet into an apocalyptic wasteland. For years he has helped push the standard of living upward due to his advances. There is the possibility that all he has worked for would be for nothing if everyone is reduced to the level of thinking only of survival.

He knows he is considering a worst case scenario, but it is a chance he is not willing to take. The world has to be strong, not vulnerable, if it is to survive the impending invasion. So he decides not to order the assassinations. It would have to be enough to rely on the infiltrators and GLESA to keep the crime powers in check.

With the issue resolved Knight decides to turn in for the night. Before going to bed he makes a stop in the chapel for his experience the previous day did give him a new appreciation for religion. A few minutes pass as Knight kneels in mediation. He then rises to head for bed so he can rest up for another day.

The next morning Knight is in the basement of his home working in the laboratory. Han had arrived a few hours earlier after spending a week soul searching in his native China. As Knight checks the data bank, Han prepares the groundwork for his research on radiation. A loud buzzer startles them both as Knight receives word from an android that there is a communiqué from Mochar. He rushes over to the monitor and can see that the alien is not happy. Han positions himself behind Knight as the two begin to talk.

" What's wrong, Mochar?"

" Dire news, I'm afraid. As you will be shortly aware, the probe above Terial has been destroyed. So has the one in the adjoining Meric Erita solar system."

" This doesn't sound good. Not much chance this was some horrible coincidence, I suppose."

" Very unlikely. Either a Terialian has betrayed his beliefs or someone else made them aware of our presence. Did you see that? The probe in the Io Sagi system just went off the screen."

" Okay, so they're aware of us. How long until we can expect the war party?"

" Not much time I'm afraid. Could be a day. Maybe a week if we're lucky. The last transmission from the Terialian probe showed they were testing the war crafts. You can be certain when they are through testing, they will be on their way."

" So you're saying he's going to send the entire armada after us?"

" Judging by past conflicts, yes. If he were facing a weaker force he would only send the minimal number of ships necessary to complete the task. But since he is aware we have been spying on him, he will assume we are a worthy adversary. He will come at us with everything he has."

" Then the time has come. I'm afraid we may have just lost our edge. Let's hope our preparations will enable us to give him a welcome he will never forget."

www.ingramcontent.com/pod-product-compliance
Lightning Source LLC
Chambersburg PA
CBHW031150020726
47499CB00002B/311